TANGI & WHANAU

To Dain

Thank you

for everyone

Love

2x

Also by Witi Ihimaera:

Pounamu Pounamu (1972)
The New Net Goes Fishing (1977)
Into the World of Light (ed. with D.S. Long) (1982)
The Matriarch (1986)
The Whale Rider (1987)
Dear Miss Mansfield (1989)
Te Ao Marama (ed.) (5 volumes, 1992 –)

WITI IHIMAERA

TANGI
&
WHANAU

Two classic Maori novels

SECKER & WARBURG
New Zealand

Tangi first published 1973.
Whanau first published 1974.
This combined edition first published 1994 by Secker and Warburg, an imprint of Reed Publishing (NZ) Ltd, 39 Rawene Road, Birkenhead, Auckland 10. Associated companies, branches and representatives throughout the world.

Tangi copyright © Witi Ihimaera 1973
Whanau copyright © Witi Ihimaera 1974
This combined edition copyright © Witi Ihimaera 1994

Reprinted 1996.

ISBN 0 7900 0353 8

The author wishes to express his gratitude to Rarawa Kerehoma for the use of excerpts from *Waiata Tangi*, translated by Barry Mitcalfe, in *Tangi*.

Printed in Australia

TO MY FATHER

One

This is where it ends and begins. Here on the railway station, Gisborne, waiting for the train to Wellington. Here begins the first step into the future, the first step from the past. I am alone now. So long reliant on father, so long my hand in his; now myself, my own keeper, for his hand has slipped away.

The platform is crowded with people. They stand in small groups talking to one another. A well-dressed woman smooths her dress and pats at her hair. A young boy kisses his mother, then looks around hoping nobody has seen. A little girl holds tightly to her father's hand. A group of teenagers laugh and joke with a friend who is travelling from Gisborne this day.

Rows of cars line the barrier to the station. A green station wagon pulls to a halt, and a schoolboy opens the back to get his father's suitcase. Together they rush to the booking office, disappearing among the crowd.

At the platform, the train for Wellington is standing. People cluster along the carriages, milling thickly round the steps to each carriage. Railway porters are loading suitcases into the luggage compartment. Already, passengers are stepping onto the train. A woman is winding down a window so that she can talk to her friends on the platform.

A little boy sits on his small suitcase, reading a child's book. He traces the lines with a finger, and silently mouths the words.

Soon, I too will board the train. I will sit at the window, looking out upon the platform. It will be crowded with people

I

shouting farewell. The train whistle will blow. The bell on the platform will ring. The train will move away, along the railway tracks as they cross the road leading into Gisborne from Waikanae. Red lights will flicker on and off at the crossing. The traffic will stop, letting the train pass. I will journey away from Gisborne.

But I will leave my heart here, to be reclaimed when I return. This is where my heart belongs; this is where my life begins.

This day, too, is beginning. The morning is brisk with the wind. The sky is crystal clear. The air is crisp with frost and far away, the morning mist still clings to the hills. There, rising above the city, is Kaiti Hill.

Today, Kaiti Hill incises a sharp edge into the sky. It sparkles with a serenity not yet destroyed by the brooding city below. The noise and haze of the city lie close to the ground. The soft singing of the sea still rises above the city's gathering whisper. But Gisborne is slowly awakening. Already, traffic bumps across the railway lines at the crossing, rushing toward the city. A cyclist weaves amid the speeding cars. Along the pavement, office girls hasten to work. For them, today is like any other day. Nothing will upset the tempo of their hours. But for me, this day is the first. This day to be lived alone and in sadness, and followed by other days to be lived alone. Thousands of days to be touched, claimed and finally lived; and this day, beginning on a railway platform is the first of them.

Eyes, close out the world. Let darkness come apace. I wish to wander there and be alone. In that darkness, I may weep without the world's knowing. There I may remember another world filled with forever sun. I may look back to that happy time when a boy laughed with his father; in that forever world, before the darkness came.

Two

———————————————

Wellington.

I am at work. It is Tuesday, the second day of the week, and still morning. A day like any other day. The telephone rings, clamouring for my attention.

— Mr Mahana? Waituhi calling, Mrs Kingi on the line.

A warm stream flows in my body. Waituhi, my whanau, my home so far from Wellington; Ripeka, my sister.

— Tama?

My sister's voice fills me with a flood of happiness and brings joy to the day.

— Hello, Ripeka.

The flood rises, and memories of my whanau and my sister softly eddy in my mind.

— Hey, it's good to hear from you, Ripeka. How are things at home? All right? Oh, it's good . . .

But she does not answer. The 'phone is silent. A cold stream begins to seep into the warm flood.

— Oh, Tama . . .

My sister's voice breaks and driftwood splinters float in small eddies. Then softly she begins to weep, scattering the stream with a rain of tears.

— What's wrong, Ripeka? Ripeka, something's wrong.

The soft sound of her weeping echoes to me from home. From Waituhi, where there is no sadness. A cold wind suddenly swirls across the waves.

3

— Oh, Tama . . .

— Ripeka, what's wrong?

But she still weeps, the wind rising, the waves rippling colder
and colder, the driftwood splinters scattering upon the warm
stream.

— Turi turi, Ripeka, I call. Hush now. That's it. Now tell me.
Quickly now.

My sister is silent for a while. Then her voice lifts from the
silence, calm and soft. She speaks with measured dignity as if
speaking lines from a play.

— Dad . . . he's dead, Tama.

Her voice is clear; her words are clear. But my body, it feels
so numb, so numb. The current has changed, grown suddenly cold.

And the world is dimming, the light darkening in the office. The
rain is sweeping across the sea.

— He's dead, Tama. Dad . . .

Why is it so dark? It is only morning. And look: there is a small
canoe adrift on the waves, the cascading sea, amid the falling rain.

— Dead, Tama. Dad's dead.

— No . . . No . . .

— You'll have to come home.

My sister begins to weep again. The sound of thunder is in
her voice, gathering across the greying, tossing waves.

— Oh, Tama. He's dead.

I call to her. My voice is filled with disbelief. It does not belong
to me. It is somebody else's voice, somebody else's father.

— Dad, dead?

No. Not my father. Not Dad.

— Come home, Tama.

— No . . . Not Dad.

— He's dead, Tama.

The wind blasts open my mind. The current changes, wave
upon wave of coldness, reaching up to drench the sky then
plunging down upon a small canoe adrift.

— You'll have to come home.

And I drift away amid the swirling, freezing tide, upon that
endless sea.

— Oh, oh Ripeka . . .

4

Three

The forever world is ended. The tangi is over. Father has been laid to earth in the graveyard near Rongopai. The world runs calm again.

Here I stand waiting for a train. I'm going back to Wellington. My mother waits with me. She weeps because I am going away. Ripeka and Mere, two of my sisters, are also at my side. Ripeka is weeping. Hone and Marama, the youngest in our family, cling tightly to Mum, afraid that she may be going away too. I open my arms, reaching out to enclose them.

— Don't cry, I say. I'll be back. Don't cry, don't cry.

Mum puts her head on my shoulder.

— How long will you be away? she asks.

— About a week, e ma.

— Too long, too long, she whispers.

— I'll be back, Mum, I answer. I might only have to stay a few days. A week at the most.

Marama tugs my hand.

— Tama? she asks in her small voice. Why do you have to go?

I look down at her. Her eyes shine with sadness.

— I've got to tell my boss I won't be working in Wellington any more. I've got to tell everybody that I'm coming back home, back here. All my clothes and things they're all in Wellington and I'm going to get them. I got no clothes here, Marama. All my friends, they'll want to say goodbye to me too.

— Oh, she says uncertainly.

5

— But he's coming back, Hone tells her. Aren't you, Tama? You're not going to stay in Wellington all the time are you? You're coming home to look after us, ay.

— That's right, Hone. I'm coming back.

He nudges Marama.

— See, Marama! he says. I told you!

Marama pushes him away.

— Hone, he thinks he's the boss, she tells me.

I let go of Mum and kneel down to them. I gather them in my arms.

— Both of you, I begin, looking first at Hone and then at Marama, are the bosses while I'm away. I don't want you two to fight. You got to be good kids. You've got to help Mum. That means you must be very strong and always do what she says. If she wants you to chop some wood, Hone, you'll have to try very hard to do it for her. Daddy's not here any more. And Marama, if Mum's sad, you cheer her up ay? You sing her a little song and make her happy.

— I know lots of songs, Marama says. I know Jack and Jill and Ba Ba Black Sheep and . . .

— I know those songs too, Hone cuts in. Ba ba black sheep have you any wool, Yes sir, yes sir, three bags full. One for the master and one for the . . .

— I'm sick of those songs, Mum grumbles.

I wink at Hone and Marama.

— Don't you listen to your Mum. She's a real moaner, ay.

They nod their heads together.

— If you see her getting sad, I continue, you just tell her not to be hoha. Then, you sing her a little song. And don't forget, you got to help Mum while I'm away. Okay?

They turn to each other with grave looks on their faces. They nod again.

— Give me a kiss then, I say. Marama first. Mmm. Now you, Hone. Mmm. And don't forget what I said.

— No, we won't forget, they tell me.

— Cross your hearts?

Solemnly they trace their fingers over their jerseys.

I stand up. I hear Hone whispering. He thinks I can't hear him.

— I'm the boss, he tells Marama. Tama said so.

6

— Me too! Marama answers. Eee, Hone! You always think you're the boss. Tama said I was the boss too, same as you are. So there!

I smile to myself. These children and my family, they are my world. When they are sad, I am sad. When they are happy, I am happy. These other people waiting on the railway platform, they belong to another world. It is strange that this other world can surround you with voices and yet you can exist apart from them, not hearing nor caring to hear. These people too have their own lives. They and I are strangers to each other, holding only one bond in common: that we travel together. For each of us, the rest of life and other people are a kind of dream, a blurred remoteness.

Among this remoteness I must drift the coming days, reaching out for happy sounds and joys to replace my sorrow. I must restrain my emptiness from the overwhelming and terrifying despair of knowing that father is not now with me. For me the world has gone awry, swinging crazily from its axis around the sun. It collides with moons and stars and rips the wispy threads of nebulae apart.

My father. He's dead.

Four

— We're truly sorry, Tama.

My friends at work cluster at my desk. I look at them, dazed. The world is so dim and they are shadows without faces. Why are they sorry, why sad? Does the world end for them too?

— His father's dead, Tama's father, they whisper to each other behind their cupped hands. Tama's father.

Why do they whisper so? Are they laughing at me? A moment ago, only a telephone call away, they were all working at their desks. Now, they know.

— He'll be going home now, someone whispers.

— Where does he come from?

— Gisborne somewhere. A Maori place just out of the town.

— Oh.

— Who's dead?

— His father. Tama's father.

Why do they whisper, why are they afraid? Oh, my friends . . . Yes, you must only speak in whispers. Don't shout. If you shout, Death may come for you, angry that you speak of Him without reverence. He may think you mock Him. So speak in whispers, only in whispers so that He does not hear. He is everywhere like God. Better not to say His name at all. Then He will pass you by and lift the shadow of His cloak over someone else.

— Aue, e pa . . .

Dead, father? Dead?

8

I close my eyes, tightly, tightly closed.

Dad, when I was home last, you wanted me to stay. You asked me not to go back to Wellington.

I need you here, you said. I need you to help out on the farm. I'm getting old.

I laughed, Dad, because to me you were never old.

You don't need me, Dad, I answered. You've got more kaha in you than I have. You're still a young man.

But you shook your head.

No, you said. I'm getting on, my blood is old. I need you; you're my eldest. You're my son. You stay home with me, ay?

But I didn't stay. I came back to Wellington.

Dad, I should have known . . . . It's just that I didn't understand. Now I remember that you were old. Your hair was greying, your face was tired, your body heavy and stooped with years. And your eyes, Dad, they were like candles curling a feeble flame. Why didn't I see it then, e pa? That you had suddenly become an old man? Why did you get old?

I suppose I should have realised, that last morning before I came away. You were sick. I heard you coughing and I saw your shadow lifting out of bed to come to me.

Wake up, Son, you whispered. Come and have some kai, and then I'll take you to the airport.

We ate in silence. Afterwards I went with you to feed the dogs. The morning was cold with frost. You were still coughing, and now and then you had to rest.

Are you all right, Dad? I asked.

You nodded.

Ae, Son. Don't you worry about your father. He's all right. You just have a good time in Wellington.

Why didn't you tell me then, Dad? Why didn't you tell me?

At the airport, your eyes glistened. I didn't know they were tears.

Haere ra, Tama, you whispered.

E noho ra, e pa.

We shook hands. Then you embraced me tightly, tightly.

Haere ra, Son.

We pressed noses. You kissed me. I came away.

9

Dad, why didn't you ask me to stay then? Why did you let me go? If I'd known, Dad, I would have stayed. Oh, e pa . . .

— Are you all right, Tama?

I open my eyes. Ray stands near me. He puts a hand on my shoulder.

— Just leave me alone awhile, Ray, I ask. Just let me be a minute.

He presses my arm, understanding. He whispers to my friends, and quietly they disperse, going back to their desks.

E pa, e pa . . .

Now dead, e pa?

Look, friends: Death's lips are sweet with funeral incense and the dank moistness of His breath is beautiful. But His sweetness is also poison and flowers wilt at His passing.

And father will lie amid such white, blossoming flowers.

Five

The flower wreaths have wilted above the soft earth; the petals scatter in the wind, like a host of butterflies fluttering across the graveyard on a hill at Waituhi.

A small girl chases white wings as they flit and circle upon the railway platform.

Elsewhere, an old woman cradles a child on her lap, singing the child to sleep. Two lovers hold hands against any invasion of their world.

— If you loved me, you wouldn't go away from me, the boy whispers.

His girlfriend looks up into his face.

— But I do love you, Rob. I do love you so.

— Then why are you going?

— Please, Rob, we've been over it before. Don't make it harder for me. I'm going because I've been transferred down to Wellington. You know that.

— You could have said: No.

— Oh, Rob ... We'll see each other. You can come down to Wellington sometime; or else I'll come back here one weekend.

— Sometimes I wonder whether you really loved me at all, Anne.

— Rob, don't hurt me.

Above the railway platform a large ornate clock snaps the time forward. Five minutes to eight. Five minutes before the train is due to leave. Five, ive, ve, e.

E pa, if I could I would grasp those ticking hands and force them back through all those yesterdays gone, just to be with you again. We had such good times together. It was good to feel your hand in mine.

Do you remember, e pa, that time when you took me into town one crowded night so many years ago? I was only a little boy then, about five, I suppose.

You wait here, you said. Then you disappeared with the crowd and left me waiting for you on the pavement.

E pa, I waited and waited. But you didn't come back. Where did you go to? I tried not to cry because you'd said that only babies cry.

Are you lost, little boy? a lady asked me.

No, I told her. My Daddy, he's just gone away for a while. He's coming back to get me, though. He told me to wait here.

So the lady left me. I wanted to shout: Come back! But she was gone.

I waited and waited, e pa. I was frightened. All those people, they jostled and pushed against me. They couldn't see me; I was so small. I felt as if I was in a land full of giants.

In the end I cried, Dad. I couldn't help it. And some of the passers-by, they asked me if I was lost, just like that lady asked. But I pushed them away and decided I would find you.

I wandered along the streets and everybody was laughing and having a good time. Where were you, Dad? I brushed my tears away and looked carefully at everybody but I couldn't find you. I pulled at a man's coat to make him turn around. But he wasn't you, either. I went into the shops, pushing between people's legs; I tried to look in all the dark places, but I wouldn't go there because I was scared.

I went into a hotel and I said to the man: Have you seen my father?

Go away, kid, he growled. You're not allowed in here.

So I ran out.

I saw Auntie Ruihi among the crowd. I ran to her but by the time I got to the place where she'd been standing, she had gone too. I was all alone. Why was everybody happy when I was sad?

I sat down on the curb. I looked at everybody passing but I

couldn't see you. I tried to be brave. But my tears, they wouldn't stop.

Then I saw you. You were looking for me just as I was looking for you. And I shouted:

Dad! Dad!

And you lifted me up and hugged me.

Turi turi, Son. I'm here.

I hit you hard.

Don't leave me again, Dad. Don't you leave me again.

You promised you wouldn't.

The clock ticks, the clock ticks. Here I am on the railway platform, waiting for a train. I cannot stop the clock. You have left me, father. I will never see you again.

Six

—————————————

— No . . .

A telephone call from home, and two words have destroyed the
calm of my world: Dad's dead.

— Oh, Ripeka.

The tide of grief overwhelms me. Seaweed drifts upon the
summer. The wind sighs. It is sprinkled with the soft sounds of
my sister weeping.

— Mum rang me about five this morning. You know how early
she gets up. Hata answered the 'phone. I was still asleep. He woke
me and said: Your Mum, she wants to talk to you. Then she told
me. I couldn't believe it, Tama. Not Dad . . .

The sea is thundering. The small canoe has dipped beneath
the cascading waves.

— Me and Hata went straight out to her, to Waituhi. I'm
ringing from there. Mum was still lying beside Dad in their big
double bed. She wasn't even crying, Tama. She was just lying
there as if she was waiting for him to wake up. Oh, Tama. You
know what Mum was doing? She was talking to him, softly, and
while she spoke to him, she was knitting a jersey. For him, for Dad.

The sea is pounding louder and louder. It seems as if I am
standing on a towering cliff watching the whirling currents seething
among the rocks, the deep flow of grey water and the ebb and flow
of the ragged kelp.

— She looked up when we came in. We embraced. Then she
smiled at me. Her tears began to fall but she kept smiling. She

brushed Dad's forehead and kissed him. Then she said to me,
To papa, to papa . . . kua mate to papa. Your father, your father,
he's dead. And all the while she spoke to him, her tears still falling.

My sister's voice breaks. And in my mind a window glimmers.
The curtains billow from it that I may look in. I see my parents'
bedroom, soft and dim with morning light. Mum and Dad
are lying together in the big bed which all of their children would
crawl into when winter was cold. Mum, Dad and their children,
all huddled beneath the patchwork blankets. The children are
curled between their parents. The younger ones are still asleep.
Mum is propped up among the pillows, knitting a jersey. She
nudges Dad.
— Time to get up, she says. Rongo! Get up!
He moans and pulls the blankets around him. One of the
children pulls them back. Mum sighs. She pokes Dad with a
knitting needle.
— Aue! What do you want to do that for? he moans.
— E koe, you mangere thing! Mum laughs. Now get up!
Dad puts his feet onto the floor.
— Brrr! Makariri!
He tries to get back into bed but Mum pushes him away with
her feet. He grumbles.
— Now you're up, Mum says. Light the stove ay? Put the
kettle on. I'll make the kai soon.
— Why don't you do it? he moans.
Mum laughs again.
— This bed, it's warm. You're up, you do it.
He grins ruefully at her. Then he kisses her.
— None of that, Rongo, Mum whispers. The kids, they might
see.
He kisses her again.

Now, father is dead. The place where he used to lie is empty.
Only my mother is there, calmly knitting, behind the billowing
curtains.
— But how, Ripeka?
— I don't know, Tama. He was old. He's been sick for a long
time. He just died in his sleep, while Mum was sleeping. She

15

didn't even know he was dead. She woke up this morning and shook him and told him to get up. But he was cold. Then she knew.

E pa ... You should have asked me once more to stay. Why didn't you, e pa? Why did you let me go away?

Seven

So many people are here this bright morning. A whole world here with me, waiting to travel away on a train to Wellington. A thousand lives revolving, a thousand destinies evolving. Chapters begun, chapters ending, chapters continuing.

— Thanks for having me, Uncle.

— That's okay, Kim. Come again soon.

— You will look after yourself, won't you dear.

— Yes, Mum.

— You'll write?

— Of course, Mum. Don't worry.

— If you loved me, you wouldn't be going away.

— Oh, Rob . . .

I am one of these people. Tama Mahana, twenty-two years old. My father is dead. This is my life beginning.

I look at Mum. Her lips begin to quiver.

— Don't cry, e ma, I whisper.

— Who says I'm crying? she asks. What do I want to cry for?

— I know you, Mum. What a tangiweto you are.

She fumbles for a hanky but decides to use her sleeve. She tries to be calm.

I put my arms around her.

— Kia kaha, e ma, I whisper. Kia kaha.

— I'll be lonely without you, she says.

— No you won't, Mum, I answer. Ripeka and Mere will stay

17

with you. And you'll have their kids crawling around home to keep you happy.

— Those hoha kids! Mum cries.

— But just think, Mum. All those nappies for you to wash. That'll keep you busy.

She giggles.

— I'm not washing any kids' nappies, she sniffs. Those days are over for me. No more wiping dirty bums either.

She wipes at her tears.

— Boy, by the time you get back, she says to me, you'll be lucky if the house is still standing. Those kids'll wreck the place.

— Eee! Mum! Ripeka says. Don't you talk about my kid that way. She's a lady.

— Anyway, Mere continues, your house is falling down enough already.

Mum just sniffs again.

— Look, she says, I know what your kids are like. You kids were wreckers yourselves. Before I had you everybody used to admire our house. Now look at it. And your kids will be just the same as you fullas were. Real haddit.

We all laugh. For a moment the world is happy.

With love, I look upon my family. Here stands my mother, two of my sisters, and the two youngest. Ripeka and Mere have a baby each and it looks like Mere is hapu with her second. Wiki, my other sister, returned to Auckland last week with her husband. I am the eldest. And Dad is . . .

My heart begins to ache. I try to contain my sadness. I look away from my family. Waiting on the platform are Hata and Koro my brothers-in-law, Uncle Pita, Auntie Ruihi, Nanny Paora and Auntie Arihia. They have come to see me off too. They stand together, watching. Auntie Ruihi dabs at her eyes. I see them, and cannot stop the sadness.

Eight

Aue, e pa . . .

The darkness and the storm abate. I am alone upon the towering cliff. Even the wind has gone, sweeping away from this place to look upon my father.

— Poor Tama, my friends whisper.

— His father is dead.

— Poor Tama.

I look at them but they turn away from my gaze. Is Death so shameful, friends? We are all lepers in this world and our aging is our leprosy blossoming. Why are you afraid?

There is no time for tears. I must go home. I must tell Mr Ralston, my boss, that I have to go home. But he already knows. He shows me into his office. I sit down.

— Are you all right, Tama? he asks.

I nod my head.

— I have to go home, Mr Ralston.

As I say the words, my head whirls. My body, it seems to fall from the cliff, down, down toward the beach.

— Tama! Are you okay?

— Yes . . . Yes, Mr Ralston. I'm just a little dizzy.

— Don't you worry, Tama, he says.

He picks up the 'phone. It clicks as he dials. Then there is the quiet staccato buzzing of the call.

E pa, why didn't you tell me to stay, why didn't you make me stay that last time I was home?

19

You wanted to go back to Wellington, Son. I didn't want to stop you having a good time.

But Dad, now you've gone, and I didn't even say haere ra.

Never mind, Tama. You're coming home now and that's all that matters. You come home quickly, ay?

Ae, e pa.

— Hello? Booking office? I want to book a flight to Gisborne today. Yes, as soon as you can. You can do it? Good. This afternoon, Flight ... Yes, I got that. It's for Mahana. M-a-h-a-n-a. That's it. He'll pick the ticket up at the airport. Thanks.

Mr Ralston puts the 'phone down.

— Bear up, Tama.

His voice is comforting, yet helpless to soothe my grief. It is a flame blazing in the darkness. Only I can make the journey to snuff it out. My friend, the Piwakawaka, flits ahead of me and chirrups his cheeky bird call.

Come Tama! Come Tama! he calls.

His fanned tail bobs and flashes ribbons of fire.

Come Tama! Quickly Tama!

This is my journey into the Underworld. Far ahead I can see the points of flame glittering.

— Thanks, Mr Ralston, I whisper.

— What now? he asks.

— I suppose I'd better go to the flat and pack a suitcase.

— I'll take you, Tama.

— It'll be okay.

— No. I'll just get the keys to the car and then we'll be off. After you've packed I'll take you to the airport.

— Thanks ...

— Have you got enough money?

— I'll manage.

— All right. I've got some if you want it. No? Well, you just wait here. I'll get my coat. Won't be long.

He closes the door after him. I am alone. My tears begin to fall. Once started, they will not end. But no tempest rises. No agony, no grief. Simply tears trickling down a calm horizon across a peaceful twilight. And silhouetted there, a sudden memory of myself and father walking home and whistling after a day's work done.

Mum had told me to find Dad.

— Your father, she'd said, he's still out there, and it's getting dark. That Rongo, he doesn't know where his home is. You find him and tell him to come home before he gets a good hiding.

So I'd walked the darkening hills, calling out to him.

— Dad! Dad! Where are you!

I'd found him fencing in a far paddock.

— Dad! You got to come home. Mum says . . .

— In a minute, Son.

— Now, Dad! Mum said you have to come home right now.

— Boy! That mother of yours, he'd grumbled.

He'd packed up his things and then we'd walked home. We came to a ridgeline. Dad stopped. He motioned me toward him. Down in the valley the house was shining with lights. Everything was quiet and drowsy. We were silent for a while. Then he spoke to me.

— That's our home, he began. This is our farm. Whenever you go away and you are sad, you just remember that this is where you belong. When you grow up, don't you forget.

— No, Dad.

— You're the eldest, Tama. If anything happens to me, you come home straight away. The eldest always looks after the younger ones of the family. I was taught that as a child; I teach you the same thing now. If I should die, you come home to your mother and your younger brothers and sisters.

— Don't talk like that, e pa.

— I got to die sometime, Son. Everybody dies.

— Don't be hoha, Dad.

— You just remember, that's all.

— All right.

He'd pressed my shoulders, gently. Then we'd walked down the ridge following the path home. And as we'd walked down from the hills, Mum had come to the doorway and yelled out:

— Rongo! Rongo Mahana! Come home! Come home!

The hills had echoed her call.

Dad had smiled at me.

— You just remember, Tama. You're the eldest. Look after your mother and the family. Okay?
— Okay, Dad.
— Good. Good boy, Son.
We'd walked toward the house.

Now father is dead.
I'm coming home, e pa. I remember.
The door opens. Mr Ralston comes in. He puts on his hat.
— Right, Tama. You ready?
— Yes, thanks.
I hide my tears from him. He must not see me crying. Together we walk through the office, out into the corridor, and down the steps to the car.

E pa, I remember.
Mum has called to me.
— Tama! Tama Mahana! Come home! Come home!
Kua mate to papa . . . To papa . . . kua mate . . .
Your father, he is dead.
Come home.

Nine

— Eee! Mum says. Now look who's the tangiweto.

She nudges me playfully.

— I'm not crying, I tell her.

— What's those, then? she asks, brushing at my face. Maybe it's the rain, ay.

— Get away, Mum.

She grins at me. Then she turns to Marama and Hone.

— Look at your big brother, she says. He's worse than you kids. A real tangiweto. You kids were good compared to him.

The kids laugh and yell.

— Tama's a tangiweto, Tama's a tangiweto!

— You just watch it, you two, I say to them. I won't bring you back any presents if you're funny to me.

Quickly they look up.

— Are you going to buy us something, Tama? What you going to buy us in Wellington?

— That's a secret.

They giggle with excitement.

— You got to be good kids, I tell them.

— We'll be good.

They whisper to one another and giggle again. And Marama tells me what Hone said to her.

— He said you're still a tangiweto!

— I did not! Hone says.

— You did so.

23

— Don't you listen to her, Tama. She's telling lies.
— Not.
— You are, too.
— I'm not! You said, Hone! I heard you.
— I did not.
— You did so.
And Marama runs away, while Hone runs after her.
— Just wait till I get you, Marama. Just wait!
Ripeka and Mere laugh. Mum does too.
— Don't you worry about me, she says. I'll be all right. You just remember to come back to me. You tell those neat Pakeha girls you already got a girlfriend.
— You?
— I'm better looking than some of those girls you drag home.
— You? Dad must have met you in the dark.
Mum hits me over the head.
— Ana! Take that!
We laugh again.
Then Mere touches me.
— You better get on the train, she says. I think it's going soon.
I look at the clock. One minute to eight.
— Ae, I better go.
I link hands with Mum. We walk across the platform toward my relatives and join them. We talk. But my thoughts are only with my mother. She is my world now.
I look at her, with aroha. The railway platform becomes blurred with shadows. My mother's face gleams alone like a glowing star.

It is a handsome face, framed with a long, black scarf. The features are sculpted of earth and sky; the chiselled planes softened by wind, rain and sun. It is a face that has seen the passing of the seasons and understands that all things decay and fall of their own accord. A calm face, which accepts the inevitable rhythms of life: that the sun rises and sets, night follows day, and that winter always comes. Yet, she has always been a stubborn woman.

Once, she looked out the window and saw the hills streaming with rain. Her husband was still out there somewhere. And there were more battens to be taken across the river.

She put on her gumboots and a raincoat. Then she went down

to the shearing shed where the battens were stacked. She loaded the packhorse with the battens, saddled a horse, then rode down the track toward the river, in a torrent of rain. Her husband saw her coming.

— Go back, Huia! Go back!

But she would not listen.

The river was swollen and thick with silt. It roared with the voice of thunder. Every now and then an uprooted tree would leap past upon the heaving water.

— Go back, Huia!

He watched her coming. I watched too. And he rushed down to the river waving her back. She took no notice.

Her horse whinnied and backed away from the rushing water. She screamed at it and there was fury in her voice. She whipped at it, urging it into the river. And she pulled the packhorse after her.

Her husband and her son watched as the horse battled against the current. She held on tightly while the yellow water pounded down upon her. The horse wanted to turn back. But she pulled its head round again, toward the bank where we waited.

— Hang on, Huia! Hang on! Dad cried.

Still she came. Her face was calm. And her husband waded toward her to help her. She reached the bank and he lifted her from the horse. He embraced her in the rain. And above the roar of the storm I heard him whispering to her.

— Oh, Huia . . . Huia . . .

She had always been like that. If it was dark and her husband wasn't home, she'd sometimes saddle her horse and go looking for him. She'd take a lamp and it would glow in the darkness. The hills would echo her shouts to him.

— Rongo! Rongo! Where are you? Come home!

Her name was Huia and she was my mother. She was only a small woman but so defiant. She'd married my father, worked with him to get enough money to buy their own farm and then set about carving out a life for her children. Even when she was sick she wouldn't give in.

There was a time when her husband was away shearing. Only she and her children were left on the farm. While he was away they were stricken with fever. But this woman, she refused to

25

accept it. The crops had to be planted. It was time. She would do it.

She fought the sickness. Every morning she tended her children. Then she moved from the house, coughing and retching, out to the fields to bend her labours to the green maize shoots. I would follow after her and say:

— E ma, you're sick. Come back.

— No, I'm not sick, she would answer.

— Then I'm not sick either, e ma. I'll come with you.

Together we would work in the fields. I would try to joke with her.

— I'm going to tell on you when Dad gets back.

She would try to laugh, and then whisper in a hoarse voice.

— Don't you dare! Or else I'll give you a good hiding!

— I'm not frightened of you, e ma.

— Don't you tell him. Don't . . .

This was the woman my father loved. This is why I loved her, fiercely proud that she was my mother.

My mother was the Earth.

My father was the Sky.

They were Rangitane and Papatuanuku, the first parents, who clasped each other so tightly that there was no day. Their children were born into darkness. They lived among the shadows of their mother's breasts and thighs and groped in blindness among the long black strands of her hair.

Until the time of separation and the dawning of the first day.

Ten

— How's Mum, Ripeka?

— All right, Tama. She's so calm, I'm afraid for her.

A telephone call from home. Aue, e pa . . .

— Tama, it's been horrible. A nightmare. Hata and I have been with Mum all morning. Uncle Pita was here when we arrived. He's been arranging the tangi. Dad's old friends have been dropping in to see him. He was supposed to pick up the shearing gang this morning for Maera Station. The 'phone's been going all the time for Dad. Where's Rongo? people ask. They don't believe he's dead.

Clouds scud slowly across the landscape of my mind. There is a pall over my sun.

— He's in the front room at the moment. Until the marae is ready at Rongopai. Uncle Pita took his boys down there to open the meeting house and set up a marquee next to it. The fire has been lit in the cookhouse to feed all the people who will come. I can see the smoke from the window, curling across the hills. Everybody knows that someone is dead. They know it's Dad.

Below the growing pall a carved house shimmers. The meeting house of my ancestors, of my people, holding up the sky.

— Ripeka, how are the kids? Are they all right, Ripeka?

— They don't understand, Tama. They wanted Dad so Mum took them into him and told him he was gone. Hone asked: Really gone, Mum? And Mum said: Yes, Dad's gone now, and you've got no Daddy anymore. They cried, Marama and Hone,

27

because they didn't want Dad to go away. And Marama started shaking Dad and crying: Wake up, Daddy, wake up.

The desolation of the world is immeasurable, the pall over the sun complete. Rongopai is covered with shadow.

— Are the kids all right now?

— Yes, Tama. Auntie Arihia took them around to her place to play with Maka and Erua. Tama . . . You must come home.

My sister begins to sob. She shatters my world with her grief.

— Some of the women are here with Mum. They just sit with her, wailing softly. But she's so calm, Tama. So calm.

— Let me speak to her, Ripeka.

The phone falls silent.

E pa, e pa . . . Dead, e pa?

There are obsidian splinters at my heart, tearing at the green-stone landscape of my mind.

— Tama?

— Oh, Mum . . .

The painted panels of Rongopai crumble, the beams of that ancient roof fall.

— Hello, Son.

My mother's voice is soft and subdued. For a moment I cannot answer. My words are crippled, without wings or speech.

— Are you all right, Mum?

— Ae, I'm all right. Don't you worry about me.

— I'm coming home, Mum.

— Yes, you come home soon, ay? You come home to me. He was a good husband, your father.

— Don't cry, e ma.

— He was a good man.

My mother weeps. I hear her and sadness consumes me.

— Now that he's gone, I'm so lonely, Son. I want him to come back. Come back Rongo. Rongo, Rongo, Rongo . . .

My mother whispers her grief, my father's name over and over again. The wind begins to mourn within Rongopai. Then Mum is calm again.

— Tama, you come home soon, ay? You come home today.

— Ae, e ma.

— Your father, he waits . . .

28

Her voice whispers away. The 'phone falls silent.
— E ma . . .

Tama, you must look after your mother and sisters and brother if I should die. That's the Maori way.
Dad, don't talk like that.
I was taught that as a child. I teach you the same thing now. Never forget.

— Tama?
— Where's Mum, Ripeka?
— She's weeping, Tama. The kuias, they're comforting her.
— I'm coming home, Ripeka.
— She keeps saying Dad's name over and over again.
— Coming home . . .

E pa, you were a giant Kauri giving shelter to your family. One day, I too will be a Kauri. My mother and sisters and brother are my roots. I will spread my shadow over them, protecting them as you have done.
One day.

Eleven

The train whistle shrieks. The people on the railway platform put their hands over their ears, waiting for it to end. Then the whistle fades away.

— Time for me to go, e ma.

My mother looks like a little girl, all alone.

— Ae. You go now.

My mother, my sisters, my relatives, they crowd around me.

— Haere ra, Tama, Ripeka whispers.

— E noho ra, Sister.

It is sweet sadness to press noses in the hongi. It is sweet sadness to mingle my tears with the tears of my people, my family. I am more than my father's son. For these people I am son, friend, father too. They are to me in turn, my sons, daughters, fathers and mothers. That is the Maori way: not to talk of one family for we belong to each other, not only family living but family dead.

— E noho ra, Mere. Look after Mum while I'm away.

— Ae, Tama.

The tears fall, among us mingling. The deep sighs of sadness are the winds gathering from Waituhi our home. The winds gather, the winds join; from the desolate emptiness of Rongopai they come.

— E noho ra, Hata. Koro, don't forget those cattle got to be moved from the far paddock. Uncle Pita, e noho ra. Don't weep, Auntie Arihia, you'll spoil that neat black stuff on your eyelashes. Nanny Paora, goodbye Nanny. Auntie Ruihi, e noho ra.

The winds bring memories of the tangi. They whisper to me of a graveyard where the earth still lies warm above my father. I stand in his place now and I must be a giant Kauri.

— Come to me, Marama. You too, Hone.

The children embrace me.

— Give me another kiss. Mmm. Mmm. No not on the cheek, Hone, that's not a proper kiss.

— I don't want a kiss, he sniffs.

— Come on! Mmm. That's better. Don't forget what I told you kids. You're the bosses while I'm away.

The farewells are ended. My mother waits, alone. Silently we embrace each other.

— Haere ra, Son.

— E noho ra, e ma.

My mother, don't weep. I'm only going away for a short while. I'm coming back.

— What a tangiweto you are, Mum.

— What's those then, ay? Mum says, pointing at my own tears. I suppose you call that rain.

— Hone, Marama, look at Mum. She's the crybaby, not me. She . . .

I look at my mother. One last embrace. Our love is expressed in the soft, moist pressing of our noses together.

— Tama, you come back soon.

— Ae, e ma. E noho ra.

The train whistle blows a final blast. The porter hastens along the platform.

— All aboard. Move away from the train, please.

I step onto the train. All around me, other goodbyes are being said.

— Give our love to Jim.

— Thanks for having me, Uncle.

— Bye bye Susan.

— Don't forget to write, dear.

— Goodbye.

— Goodbye. Goodbye.

I look toward the hills. The mist is lifting, the sun flooding the sky. Nestling among the hills is Waituhi, my home, my whanau.

All along the train, windows are wound down and hands flutter from them. My family and relatives crowd round the steps of the carriage. My mother's hand tightens on mine.

— Haere ra, Tama . . .

— Mum, don't weep.

Steam hisses from beneath the train. The couplings grow taut, strain, then jerk tight. The train begins to move.

My mother's eyes glisten. Once, Dad was her guiding star. But he has drifted beneath the reddening horizon. Now, she gleams her own light.

— You come back soon, ay? she cries.

Her grip tightens. She won't let go. The train moves down the platform and still our hands are linked.

— E ma . . .

The train moves faster, forcing our fingers apart. Slowly they untwine, drifting, drifting away; and the separation is agony. Yet, Mum still follows along the platform. She pushes through the other people, her face distraught.

— Tama . . .

She begins to run. Her long scarf falls from her hair. People watch her, curious.

The train draws away. Mum stops and covers her face with her hands. Mere and Ripeka try to comfort her. Hone and Marama cling tightly to her skirt.

The train gathers speed. I lean further from the steps to keep my mother in sight. The rest of the station is a colourful blur receding.

— E ma, I'll be back soon, I yell.

The wind snatches the words and flings them into the sky. I lift my arms to wave. My mother waves back, and the children wave too.

— E ma . . .

My mother's face gleams like a star reflected in the sea. The sea is calm with night. As the train moves away from the station the star slowly submerges, slowly drowns beneath the waves.

— E noho ra, e ma.

The star sinking, slowly disappearing, until there is only a small pinpoint of light, shimmering beneath the emerald cascading waves.

Twelve

The houses are little flags fluttering past. Some are drab, others gaily painted; a jumbled mass of roofs extending across the plain to the mountains. Now and then is a glimpse of a road streaming with morning traffic, of a green field or a clump of trees.

Before Dad bought the farm at Waituhi we lived in a small wooden house on the other side of this town. It was old even before we moved in; but to my small boy's eyes it was a palace. The memories before we began to live there are blurred with a succession of draughty shearing whares, shepherds' quarters and one-room scrubcutters' shacks; of hazy glimpses of Mum struggling to cook kai at an open fire; of long nights filled with the small, flickering light of a solitary candle; and of huddling with my brothers and sisters in a wooden bunk on a straw mattress.

Mum always tried to make each whare beautiful. After Dad had finished a contract job at one farm, we would pack our belongings and move to the next job. It seemed that we always arrived at a new place at night, and it also seemed that each new whare was dirty, its walls smeared with black smoke, the table and cupboards still strewn with the mess left by the previous hands, and the floor littered with broken crockery or broken chairs. Sometimes a window would be broken or a door just managing to stay closed on its one, rusty hinge. We would stand in the doorway, surveying each whare in silence, until the light cast by a match burnt out. Always at night, it seemed, we arrived.

34

For all of us, it was as if we were back at the beginning again. There were so many desolate beginnings, and whenever we finished at one place and were on our way to another, I would close my eyes and cross my fingers and pray: Let the next place be a nice place, please let it be a nice place. But it never was.

Even now, sitting in this train travelling to Wellington, I look down and see my fingers crossed in that same childish way. Yet I am twenty-two years old; no longer a child. I suppose it's an impulse felt because Dad is dead. This journey is like one of those many journeys I remember when I was a child. I have the same feeling as I had then after we'd arrived at a new home; that I am back at the beginning, starting all over again.

— You kids, go and help your Dad bring our things from the truck, Mum would say.

We would nod. At the time there were seven of us: Mum and Dad, Rawiri, Ripeka, Mere, Wiki and myself. I was the eldest. Although Rawiri my brother had died when he was a baby, he was still counted as one of the family. Marama and Hone hadn't been thought of then. In those days, Mere and Wiki were the babies. They would stay with Mum while Ripeka and I ran back to the truck. Sometimes it meant going for miles because some of the places we went to were a long way from the road or nearest track. There were even times when Dad had to leave the truck on the other side of a river and we'd have to wade through the water to get to our new home.

In those days Ripeka and I were never scared of the dark because we were often left alone when Mum and Dad were working late. Dad would still be shepherding or scrubcutting or maybe he was bringing the sheep in for the next day's shearing. Often Mum would go out and help him. So no matter how dark it was or how far we had to go to reach the truck, we were never afraid. All we had to do was keep our eyes fixed on the headlights shining far away. Anyway Dad was with us so nothing could happen to us and not even kehuas could frighten us.

— What shall I take, Dad? Ripeka would ask him.

— What shall I carry? I would ask too.

He'd be standing in the light of the truck and he'd look at us and think for a moment.

35

— Ripeka, you take those blankets. You, Tama, you take that big box. I'll bring this suitcase and this other box. Okay?

— Okay, Dad.

— You fullas feeling strong? he'd ask. We'll have to come back for this other stuff.

— We're very strong, Dad.

He'd laugh.

— Show me your muscles then! Your muscles first, Tama. Aeee! Big ay. Now yours, Ripeka. Only pipis so far, Ripeka.

— Not! Ripeka would say. My muscles, they're just as big as Tama's. You feel again, Dad, you just feel.

And Dad would have to say that she was as strong as I was, even if she wasn't. Then we'd set off together, pushing through the scrub toward the whare. Sometimes we'd have to rest.

— You kids feeling tired, ay, Dad would say.

— Not! We're just stopping so you can rest, Dad.

We'd set off again. After we'd dropped off the load at the whare we'd return to the truck to get the next few pieces of our belongings. We never had much then. Some crockery, blankets, two dogs, a few pots, a saddle, a big suitcase of clothes, lots of nappies, perhaps some leftover kai, a bottle of tomato sauce, a rooster and some hens, and a couple of dreams. We would have had a horse except that our truck was too small.

The memory eddies softly like a warm wind. I look out the carriage window and see Gisborne gradually receding. The houses stand isolated now, not grouped together. The countryside is opening up. On one side of the train is the sea. On the other are the hills which enclose Poverty Bay. Ahead rise the Wharerata Ranges. The main highway out of Gisborne winds its way upward across the Ranges. When I was a boy I used to marvel that our truck could make that climb. The road wasn't sealed then and our truck, it was so old. Although we didn't have that many belongings, it would groan and shudder so much we'd have to get out and push.

Wherever we went, we took our household with us. Mum and Dad sat in the front of the truck with the babies sleeping between them. Ripeka and I sat in the back with the dogs and the hens and the rooster, and sometimes with the chickens if there were any. Ripeka, she hated Roos because he used to chase her round the paddocks. Sometimes Mum would find her crying in the small fenced coop with the rest of the fowls. Even when she got older Roos always thought she was a fowl. And every time Christmas came around, Ripeka always asked Mum if we'd have Roos for dinner. But when Dad finally killed him because he was getting old and he was put on the table, Ripeka burst into tears and wouldn't eat him.

— Huh? Dad asked her. I thought you didn't like Roos.

— He was a good Roos! she screamed. And you killed him, Daddy!

We also had a pig, but he came much later. He was a good pig except that he had piglets, which astonished us. We didn't have to carry him from the truck to our new whare in those days when we had no home because he would follow us quite tamely.

Back and forth we'd go from the truck to the whare then back to the truck again, our pig trotting after us. Every time we got to the whare, Mum would have cleaned it up a little more.

— No time to sit down, she would say to us. When you've finished, then you can rest.

Sometimes Dad wouldn't listen to her. So she'd get her temper and hit him with her broom.

— Hurry up, Rongo! Plenty of time for sitting down later.

When Mum had her wild up, Dad always did as she said.

We left the hens and rooster until last. Dad would put Roos under one arm and one of the Mrs Roos under the other. I would take two of the other hens and Ripeka would carry the pullet. Our hens were very tame like our pig, unless they were clucky. Then they were just like Mum when she was hapu, and pecked at us all the time. If there were any chickens, we'd carry them in our jerseys and pockets. When we were travelling from one place to the next on our truck, those chickens slept with us in our blankets.

On the first night at a new home, the fowls and chickens and Roos would sleep by the fire. Kuri and Tim, our two dogs, would sleep outside with our pig. Mere and Wiki slept with Mum and Dad, and Ripeka and I slept together. If the whare was big enough, I'd have my own bed. But there was so much to do before we went to bed. We'd all have a cup of tea. Dad would try to sneak off.

— No you don't, Rongo! Mum would say. We got a lot of scrubbing to do yet.

And she would thrust a scrubbing brush into his hands before he could get away.

— I got to feed my dogs, Dad would grumble. I got to fix my saddle, put up a fence for these fowls. If you think I'm going to sleep in the same room as fowls you got another think coming, woman.

But Mum wouldn't listen.

— Plenty of time for that tomorrow. Now start scrubbing!

Then Dad would sigh, bend on his knees and get busy. Ripeka and I would slosh the water on the floor, then follow Mum and Dad with mops. Every now and then we'd have to stop the fowls from running over the wet floor. Sometimes Mere would try to splash the water in the bucket. She loved water.

Scrub, scrub, scrub, until it was finished.

Scrub, scrub, scrub. The sound of the train clacking along the rails toward the Ranges echoes the sound of Mum and Dad as they scrubbed every whare. The floors, the walls, even the tables and chairs until they gleamed so much you didn't like to touch them.

Most times Ripeka and I were very glad if our new place had dirt for a floor instead. Even then, Mum made us sweep it and sweep it until she was satisfied it was clean.

— Now you can go to bed, Mum would say.

So Ripeka and I would get our pyjamas and warm them by the fire before putting them on. Dad would sigh and start pulling off his boots.

— Not you, Rongo, Mum would tell him. Still plenty for you to do.

— Have a heart, Huia, Dad would moan. Leave it for tomorrow.

— No. I know you Rongo. If you leave it till tomorrow, nothing will get done.

And Dad, he'd have to do what he was told: fix that chair, move the table, chop some wood for tomorrow, unpack the bags, put a board across that broken window, bring the pots over to this corner and kill that spider! Mum, she was hard on Dad sometimes.

But after everything was completed for the night she used to melt like butter. Then it would be:

— I'm sorry I'm so hoha, Rongo.

— No, you're good to me, Huia. What do you want me to do next?

— It's all right, Rongo. Go on, go to bed.

— You come too. Come on.

— Oh, Rongo! I'm so awful to you and you're so good to me.

— Don't cry, Huia. You'll wake the kids.

— I'm so porangi, Rongo. I'm sorry.

— Don't, Huia. You're a good wife . . . . Dad would lead Mum to bed and comfort her, and she would make warm noises as soft as those of a sucking dove. But it never lasted. The next morning, it would be: Get up, Rongo! Rongo? Did you hear me? Come on, move yourself man! And Dad would moan and I'd hear him walking about the whare and lighting the fire.

— What a woman, he would say. What a hoha woman.

— What did you say, Rongo? Mum would ask.

— Nothing, dear, nothing, he would answer.

Mum and Dad, they were always like that: growling each other one minute then the next minute loving each other. It often puzzled me, and once I asked Dad about it. He just shrugged his shoulders.

— That's love, he said. One day you'll understand. Even the last time I saw Dad, he and Mum hadn't changed. I'd laughed at him.

— That's love?

— Ae, Son, he'd sighed. Ae . . .

That last time, I should have stayed home and not gone back to Wellington. E pa, he's dead. Mum is alone with nobody to growl. She will be waiting for me. I won't be gone long, e ma. I won't be long in Wellington. I'll be back soon. Together we'll build a new life, a new home, and you can growl me all you like. Don't weep.

The first few days at a new home were always the busiest. Dad often had to start his job straight away. If it was scrubcutting he'd sharpen his machetes, cut some parao rewana for lunch, kiss Mum and us too, and then be off. If he was a farmhand or a

39

shepherd, he'd go to see his boss. Sometimes we'd have to go with him.

— This is my wife, Huia, Dad would say.

Mum would shake hands with his boss and the boss's wife if she was there.

— Pleased to meet you, she would say.

Mum, she knew lots of manners, because before she'd married Dad she'd been a servant for some people in Gisborne.

— These are my children, Dad would continue, introducing us. Then it was our turn to shake hands. We were sometimes very embarrassed because we didn't like shaking hands. Dad, he told us that we got our shyness from Mum because she was shy with strangers too. Sometimes we'd be asked in for a cup of tea.

— No, thank you, Mum would answer. Perhaps another time.

The lady of the house would agree.

— Yes, perhaps another time. You must have a lot of settling in to do.

Then the questions would be asked. Is the whare all right? Are you comfortable? It's in a bit of a mess, isn't it. Ah well, if you ever need anything, just sing out and we'll see what we can do.

— No, we'll be fine, Mum would answer. Don't you worry about us.

Mum, she always said that even if things were really bad. She didn't like being a nuisance. She was forever telling us not to be nuisances either. We were there to work, not to bother the people we were working for.

— We'll go now, Mum would say when she thought we'd stayed long enough. We'd shake hands again and walk back to the whare. When we thought we were far enough away, Ripeka and I sometimes whispered to each other.

— What a neat house.

— All those flowers.

— And Ripeka, did you see that beaut car?

— Yeah! . . . And what about those nice chairs and that stove and carpet and . . .

— How do you know about those chairs and things?

— I saw behind the lady.

— Boy, I wish we had a house like that . . .

— And the lady, Tama! She was all dressed up, too.
— Wish we had a house like theirs . . .
We used to gabble on like that all the way back. We never thought we might be hurting Mum. But once, she whispered at us to stop it. We looked at her and there were tears in her eyes.
— What's wrong, Mum?
She hugged us both.
— One day we'll have a house like that. You kids will have the best of everything. But we got to have money, kids. That's why your Dad works so hard; that's why we move around. We won't always be working for other people. We won't always be poor. You wait and see, Tama. You just watch, Ripeka. One day.
Mum and Dad, they kept their promise to us in the end. We grew up, as Mum had said we would, with the best of everything. After all those years of our wandering, Dad was able to buy a farm and give us what he and Mum had worked for. The farm was only small, even smaller than the one that rushes past the train. But it was a start. And although Dad is dead, there is still much to do to the farm and for the kids. His eldest children have grown and made their own lives, but there are still the younger ones, Marama and Hone. For them too, Dad promised the best of everything. That is what I will give them, like Dad.

It took a long time for Mum and Dad to make enough money to buy the farm. There were the wandering years, and then the years in Gisborne to be lived through. The wandering years however will always seem a long time in my memory. Or perhaps it only seems to have been a long time because of the loneliness and hard work of those days. Dad would wake early each morning and somewhere in my drifting dreams I'd hear the soft stamping of his feet and the clink and rustle of strange sounds. I'd hear him and Mum whispering to each other and then the rustle of her dressing gown as she moved round getting him some kai. A match would flare, casting a sudden light in the morning darkness. Then the light would begin to flicker from a candle or lamp in the room. Dad would light the fire and Mum would hang a billy of water on one of the wire hooks above the burning wood. Smoke would billow into the room when the wind gusted down the sheet-iron chimney. Mum would cough. Then there'd be more soft sounds

41

as Dad had his kai and then the soft scraping of his chair when he'd finished. Perhaps Wiki would cry from her cradle. Dad would whisper to her for a moment. Then softly he would kiss her, Mere, Ripeka and me.

— Goodbye, Daddy, Ripeka would say sleepily.

— Goodbye, Daddy, I would say too.

I'd feel the touch of his lips.

— Look after Mum, Tama.

— Okay Dad.

The door would creak. Mum would curl her arms round Dad's neck. For a moment there'd be silence. Then the door would shut and far away in my dreams I'd hear Kuri and Tim barking as Dad untied them. When I awoke Dad would be gone. Throughout the day I would sometimes find myself looking out the window or across the hills, waiting for him to come back again.

I look out the window of the train upon the rushing landscape. The plain rolls away toward the Whareratas. A farm passes by. Then a small ribbon of houses along the main highway. For a moment the train blurs past a small railway siding. Bartlett's township. The Wharerata Ranges begin to crowd the sky with rugged peaks.

All my days I will look out for Dad. He will not come back again. He is dead. One day I will stop looking for him. Yet he still whispers to me, for this is another morning beginning.

— Look after Mum, Tama.

Ae, e pa . . .

Thirteen

I'm coming home, Dad. Wait for me, e pa.

I look out the window of the car. The street is a strip of steel sloping across a crowded suburb in Wellington. Every now and then it intersects another which arrows through the suburban sprawl. Traffic glides up the street, draws abreast, then rushes past in a sudden blast of noise receding. The car dips down between two crowded ridges and the sky constricts, becomes a smaller patch of blue as the houses rise up to spike the skyline.

— Left here, Tama?

— Yes, at Baldwin Street, Mr Ralston.

I am going home to Waituhi. First I must pack my bags, then catch the plane for home. Home . . . kua mate taku papa.

The car slows down. A red light flickers on the dashboard, on, off, on, off, then ceases as the car turns into Baldwin Street. Ahead, the street winds up a steep hill cut off by the sky. Telephone poles bend past. A sparrow flits between the taut wires. A dog whines at a closed gate. There, a young girl is walking down to the bus stop.

— It's number forty-one, Mr Ralston. The house with the flight of steps.

The steps ascend between a thin stand of trees, disappear into the shadow of a small alleyway, then reappear, leading up to an old house, crushed with other houses on the side of the hill. So many old houses in this part of Wellington. In this city my life has been measured out by moving from one flat to another, from

43

one old house to the next, just like our family did in that long, grey afternoon before we bought the farm. My flatmates will be at work. I must leave them a note telling them that . . .

The car draws to a stop.
— Do you want to come up, Mr Ralston?
— No. I'll wait here.
— I won't be long.

The door of the car slams shut behind me. The sound echoes along the street. A slight wind blows, rippling the branches of the trees. They shiver and whisper to one another, and their shadows reach across the pavement to clutch at me with flickering fingers. Between the shadows the steps rise up into the deep darkness of the alleyway.

The first step. And many more to follow. Suddenly, I hear a car turning in the street. I look back. And it seems as if Dad is there, standing at the bottom of the steps, looking up at me.
— Dad!

I call but he does not answer. My tears begin to fall.

E pa, why are you leaving me? Don't go away . . .

Still he does not answer. His face is wan with sorrow and love. We meant so much to each other. Perhaps he understands that although I am a man now, I am still very much a child. He has come to comfort me.

I look upon him with aroha. His face, so calm. But old, so old, e pa. My eyes, they have always seen a young man. You never seemed to age, e pa. But now, so suddenly, I notice the grey streaks in your hair and the light dimming in your eyes. Why haven't I seen these things before? Why?

The moment grows long between us; then closes as he lifts his hand to wave to me.

Haere ra, Son.

I too feel my hand lifting to farewell him.

E pa, haere ra.

I turn away and continue up the steps. Behind me I hear Mr Ralston turning the car to point back down the street. The engine stops and there is silence. I look upward, toward the house.

I am alone. Time has caught me unaware and taken my father

44

away. Strange really ... that time should seem to pass only where you are. Everywhere else it is suspended and people there are suspended too, still young, still the way you left them. Even when you're with them again your eyes are blinded and you see them the way they've always been. Then your eyes are opened. You discover that time has leapt ahead even there. You are left wandering dazed among a wake of remembered moments. And the sound of a clock ticking away the minutes penetrates your world with an insistent clamour.

I run up the steps into the shadow of the alleyway. The darkness closes; only dull light shining between the pickets of the tall, wooden fence between the flat and the house next to it.

And in that darkness a child cries, confused because the Nanny he has loved has died and now lies beneath the earth where there is no light. Surely she must be lonely in the dark. His fear mounts and he screams for it is not his Nanny but himself who is under the earth. The darkness is perfumed with the sweet smell of funeral ointments. Moist wads of cotton wool are in his ears and mouth. He spits them out, sobbing. There is a rising terror in his voice, a small boy's terror of the dark, when the door has finally closed and the steps of his father have long clicked away down the corridor. His dreams are ugly and deformed by his fear. He wakes and he cries out:

— Dad!

And he thrusts his arms upward and outward, searching for quilted walls which are not there.

Again and again, he cries for his father. But the darkness taunts him with silence. Then out of the silence come the serpents and demons of his dreams ...

— Dad!

And suddenly, a light. Finally, a light. It is like a star twinkling far away. As the star burns brighter, swings closer, the demons disappear and the serpents slither away. Until there is only the star, bursting through his glistening tears. Then not a star, but a lamp. And at last, father has come. At last father is there.

— Don't be afraid, Tama.

— Dad ...

— Hush, Son. I'm here.

45

The alleyway opens into the backyard of the flat. It is cluttered with wood, tin, bottles and other debris, all lit with the sun. The windows are shut and the blinds are drawn. The key, hidden under a brick. With a scratch and a grating sound, the door to the house is unlocked.

The house is dark, the passageway silent and dark. Open the windows and part the curtains, for darkness is fearsome and other dreams may come. Let the light fill every corner of this room and chase the darkness away.

Wellington. Grey and windy. The harbour is choppy and the waves are flecked with foam. The roofs of the houses fall away from the side of the hill, tiers of multicoloured tin tumbling down to the sea. Cars glide along the Esplanade. A liner is entering the harbour. Its bow thrusts through the waves and its hooter blows a mournful cry. Beyond the harbour, the hills are dark and bleak. Above them, a brown haze seeps into the sky.

Below in the street, a man waits in his car. No time to cry. There's a plane to catch at the airport. No time for remembering. Get the suitcase. Open it. Now pack.

What to take . . . The black suit. Better take the grey one too. Might need it. Two white shirts. Underwear. Pair of shoes. Toilet gear. Electric shaver: a birthday present from Dad . . . No, don't remember. Just keep doing something. Anything. Suitcase doesn't seem very full. Must be something else. No. Everything needed is there. Must ring Sandra at the airport. Tell her to let Ian and Allan know I won't be back for a while. Tell her that . . .

No time to remember. Shut the suitcase.

The silence enfolds me. The light shines dully in the room. It is a small room, furnished with a single bed and a chest of drawers. In one corner is a large wardrobe, inset with a long, glistening mirror. On one wall is a painting given me by Sandra. Mum made the quilt on this bed. There, on the bedside table, is a photograph of myself with Dad. I was a young boy then. Dad, he looks young too.

Dad, I didn't understand.

Never mind, Son.

I should have known, Dad. I never thought of you as old. I never thought you would die, e pa. Never . . .

46

Hush, Tama.

Dad, it's too late now. Too late . . .

Tears spill from my eyes. The pain in my heart rises as if it wants to shatter my body. The world streams with tears.

I think of Dad, lying asleep. My mother sleeps beside him, her body curved closely into his. A shadow crosses the moon. A candle flickers in a sudden eddy of wind. Father moves slightly.

In her sleep my mother frowns. A sudden feeling of cold, a chill. She huddles closer to father and brushes his face with her lips.

The shadow passes. The candle flares high and becomes the dawn arising. My mother calls to Dad.

— Rongo. Time to get up. Rongo? Get up, Rongo . . .

And the Piwakawaka sings disconsolately at the window.

E pa, if I could I would find a lamp and burn the darkness forever away. But this is not a child's nightmare, e pa; this is not a dream. I cannot come to you. Kua mate taku papa.

I hide my face in my hands. The silence closes so that the rest of the world cannot hear my sorrow. There is all the time in the world to remember Dad now. All the time in the world. A world flickering memories of him like flames flaring suddenly in the darkness. The flames light up brief glimpses of him and I remember him.

Father in all seasons and moods. So completely the sculptor of my life.

Fourteen

———

The train thunders toward the Wharerata Ranges. As I look out the window, I recall a phrase Dad always used to say to me.

— To manawa, e taku manawa.

He would point at his heart and then mine. I too, would place my small palm upon his chest and then on my own. As long as I felt his heart beating beneath my palm I was not afraid.

— Your heart is my heart.

And I remember one magical afternoon when we were walking along Wainui Beach. We came across a fisherman putting out white-winged floats to take his fishing hooks out to sea. Dad knelt beside me, pointed toward the floats, and whispered a dream to me.

— Look, Tama! See the Fleet coming? See? Across the great ocean of Kiwa they come: from Hawaiki nui, Hawaiki roa, Hawaiki pamamao. See how they ride the waves to this shore! The Tainui, Te Arawa, Mataatua, Kurahaupo, Tokomaru, Aotea ... And there, Tama, there comes the Takitimu! Look how they come!

I followed his gaze and the floats indeed became the seven legendary canoes which brought the Maori to Aotearoa. Even now, looking at the sea curving into the hills, it seems that white sails are coming. They recede as the train strikes inland.

In a later year, confused, I asked father:

— E pa, what is a Maori?

He said to me with fierce pride:

48

— Takitimu, Tainui, Te Arawa, Mataatua, Kurahaupo, Tokomaru, Aotea ... They are the Maori, Tama. As long as you remember them you are a Maori. Then, again, he pressed his palm against my heart.

— To manawa, a ratou manawa.

Your heart is also their heart.

And if ever I was confused again all I needed to do was to recite the legendary names to calm my heart.

But only seven canoes, e pa? E pa, there is a legend which tells of an eighth canoe. Its name was Karamurauriki and it brought Aitua to Aotearoa. The bow piece and stern piece were fastened and decked with streamers of white albatross feathers. The bailer was Tataeore. Karamurauriki: the canoe of Death. It has taken you away from me, e pa. Now the world is a place of whirlwinds. The calm point is gone.

I close my eyes. The sound of the train rumbling begins to fade and there is only the calm swaying of the carriages, the gentle swaying.

Father was always calm. He quietly rode the ebb and flow of the world. As long as he was there, I was not afraid. Nothing could harm me. Even when I grew older and went away from home I did not fear storms, for I would only have to call and he would answer.

— To manawa, e taku manawa.

His calmness was his strength and he wove it so well that my days as a child seem fused together; a separate world from that I know now. He was the axis of my universe; my world took motion from him. He could have spun the world if he wanted to.

E pa ... Sometimes, he would take me out working with him.

— Your Mum can look after herself today, he would say. You want to come with me?

I would nod eagerly. I remember myself as a small boy, about four years old, being bundled into a blanket one early morning and then sitting on a fence watching Dad catch a horse for us.

— Up you come, Son!

And Dad would hoist me onto the horse, with him. We'd ride out into the hills. Sometimes Dad would sing a song or tell

49

me a story. Sometimes he'd even let me take the reins and let me be the driver.

— Giddy-up, horse! I would yell, making clicking noises with my tongue. Dad used to laugh at me. It seems, looking back, that it was always a long way from the whare to where Dad was working. Maybe he was putting up a new fence for a farmer or cutting scrub. Perhaps it only seems to have been a long way because I was so small and the world was so big. But I recall most of all the calm of being with Dad and the way his laughter echoed across the hills. Then there were the silences too and the sunlight rippling across the paddocks. While Dad worked, I'd sit under a tree or small bush and watch those sunlit patterns softly whispering away, away, away. Dad would wave to me. I would wave back.

I look out the window again. The sunlight falls across the country, lighting up the greenstone years of a boy with his father.

Sometimes I'd help Dad by piling the scrub for burning or dragging battens down to the fenceline he was working on.

— Good boy, Tama, Dad would say. I would grin at him. If he wanted a drink of cordial, I would run to the saddle pack and get the large flagon of lime cordial for him. If he was resting for a while, I'd try to dig a few spadefuls of dirt so that he wouldn't have so much to do. I used to get tired because that spade was heavy and I was too small. So Dad would take over and I'd watch him and hope that someday I'd be just as strong.

Sometimes, Dad would tell me to go and find some watercress or mushrooms.

— Your Mum wants some, he would say. Find a lot so that we have a good kai tonight.

He would rub his puku and make big eyes to show just how much he loved watercress. I'd wave to him, get the flax kit and wander away.

I was never afraid of being alone even if the day was clouded with rain. I'd wander through the scrub or along a small stream or among the shadowed ravines. Dad was there, I had no need to fear.

But once I wandered too far and couldn't find my way back. I wanted to cry. Night was coming. But boys aren't supposed to cry. So I waited and watched the stars springing into the sky. Then I heard Dad calling.

— Tama! Tama!

I yelled back. Dad rushed down to me and crushed me in his arms. Afterward he growled me for wandering too far away. I didn't care even though a grave tear trickled down my face. Dad was there. I knew that I could never be lost because father would always be there to find me.

Sometimes I'd have to stay at the whare. Those were lonely times because I liked being with Dad.

— Look after Mum today, ay Tama? he would say to me. I would watch him going away. My heart would try to fly with him. Long after he had disappeared I'd still be waving haere ra. Then Mum would call me into the whare.

— Your Dad, he'll be back, she would say. Don't you worry.

I'd brush at my eyes and nod. But always I would watch from the window and see the lowering clouds, and a voice in my mind would cry out.

— Dad . . .

Dad . . .

The sound of the train echoes my boyhood cries to him. But no answer. Only silence.

I grew accustomed to silence and loneliness. Nevertheless my days were measured with father's going away and returning. Even when I grew older and was going to school, my first thoughts were for him. We owned our own farm then and I would get home from school and ask Mum:

— Where'd Dad go today, Mum?

— I don't know. I never know where he goes these days. Out there, somewhere.

If it was late I used to be afraid for him. I'd go looking for him just as Mum had done when her children were young.

— Dad! Where are you? I would yell.

The hills would echo my call to him. And from somewhere he'd whistle back. Then the panic in my heart would recede and my laughter would soar in the air. The world would be calm again.

— Dad! What you doing? Come home!

If there was something he wanted to finish before going home I'd help him do it. Then we would go home together. If we were too late returning, the hills would echo Mum calling:

— Rongo! Rongo Mahana! Come home! Come home . . .

His calm was his greatest possession. He moulded my life and tried to make me understand that you could not always escape the whims of the world. He tried to show me how to accept them. His was the quiet dignity of a man who lived close to the earth. With such calm he could shrug off setbacks. Nothing could disturb the tempo of his days: not storms, not drought, sickness or fever. He made his world my world.

Tona manawa, e taku manawa.

I lived in that world without comprehending his calm and without understanding that father, even father, could decay and fall. He grew older without my realising it. Now my world has collapsed because he is dead. It brings the sound of thunder to my ears. I mourn not only my father's death; my world, it is dying too.

The hills rear up; the train curves into shadow. The sky is a cleft disappearing between upthrusting peaks.

My father was the Sky. He held dominion over night and day. He was both sun and moon, keeping constant watch over his children. Every day he arose to keep Papatuanuku warm. Every night he cast his wistful light upon her. Sometimes he wept and the dew of his tears fell softly upon her. She, to console him, grew beautiful with crops and fruit and flowers. And often she would rise with the mist from the hills and reach out to brush his sorrow away.

Now the Sky has fallen. His first children hold sway over the earth. Rongomatane, who first tried to separate Rangi from Papa. Tangaroa, Haumiatiketike and Tumatauenga, who also tried without success. Tawhirimatea, the wind, who blasts his brothers with anger for the separation. And Tanemahuta, god of trees and birds, who raised his arms and pushed Sky and Earth apart so that there was light.

Yet they bring darkness to my world. Tempests, storms, and fierce winds. The long Po has begun for me. Some day, the light will return again: Te Aomarama.

Tona manawa, e taku manawa.

His heart, is my heart.

And now that his heart lies still, so also does my world.

Fifteen

Dad ... He was always calm. He drew his strength from his understanding of Papa tuanuku, the Earth Mother. She was his life and his was the patience of a man who loved her, despite her whims. No matter if she was wilful; he would be forgiving.

So calm; and I must be calm too. No more weeping. I am a man now. There is a plane to catch. Brush my tears away. Smooth my clothes. Close the windows. Along the hallway.

Lock the door.

Now down the steps, beneath the whispering trees, to the car and Mr Ralston waiting.

— Everything all right, Tama?

— Yes, Mr Ralston. Thanks.

— Put the suitcase in the back. Sure you haven't forgotten anything? No? Let's go then.

He starts the car and it moves silently down the street. I look up. The sky seems far away and dark with thunder.

To manawa, e taku manawa ...

E pa, you gave light to my universe, the sun to my day. Although you are dead, the sun still shines to light my way. Yet even this sun is dimming, e pa. The dark clouds mass beneath it and the wind is rising. Someday there will be a new sun; the sun of my own day. But always, the Sky will remain. For you were the Sky ...

E pa, I shall greet you every morning. Every day I shall wake with my mother the Earth, arising from the strands of her hair

53

to spread wide my arms with aroha for you. When snow falls, I shall catch the flakes and press them to my cheeks. When it rains I shall let your tears fall upon my lips. I will not fear your thunder for I know you love me. But, e pa, bring the light soon. Let me laugh . . .

And my mother Earth, do not weep, for I shall comfort you. I am your son, the son of Earth and Sky. Although the sky has been wrenched from you, I shall make you happy. I will give you grandchildren and they will sing and thread flowers in your hair.

E pa, you only clasped the earth so tightly to protect your children. You tried to give your calm to me, your son. I shall try to be calm.

See, e pa? These are not tears; they are only drops of rain falling. My heart throbs not with grief, but with aroha. And my arms reach up with love, not pain, for you. See? I smile now.

I am calm, e pa.

Sixteen

The train breaks across the highway between the clanging bells of a railway crossing, and thunders slowly through the Whareratas. At the crossing an old truck waits for the train to pass. There, on the back, two children stand and wave. I lift my hand to wave back to them. But they are suddenly gone. Two children . . .

When Ripeka and I were children and our family roamed from one whare to another, we were sometimes lonely because we met few other people. When I grew older Mum used to be surprised that I even remembered them.

— Ae, Mum, I remember Bulla. He was a rabbiter Dad met when he was out fencing. Bulla had kai with us. We had some mussels, and there was a small crab in one. Bulla, he said: Mmm, good! and he swallowed it whole! Yes, I recall the Heperis too. Mr Heperi was a roadman and he and Mrs Heperi used to come and play cards when we were staying at Mr Jobson's farm. And Mum, you and Dad used to gamble, and don't say I'm telling lies, because I saw you gambling! Georgina? She had a big puku because she was having a baby. We met her in Gisborne one night and you and she had a good cry because she didn't have a husband. You told her to come out shearing with us and she did. No, I don't remember what shed it was but I remember Georgina though. She was good to me and she played marbles with me sometimes. I remember all those people, Mum. Yes, even Boy Boy and Miriama and Sambo and . . .

We never did get to know them for long. The day would come when we had to move again. But I've always remembered them with aroha: like Mrs Karaka and all her kids who walked for miles just to say goodbye because we were moving on. The truck had been loaded with our belongings and we were ready to go. Then we heard Mrs Karaka yelling out to us.

— Hey! Rongo! Huia!

There she was, wading across the river, holding the smaller kids above the water. Behind her came the other kids: Ani, George, Danny, Ron and Roimata. Ron was giving Ani a piggy-back. Roimata was almost drowning because she was carrying a big sack above her head so it wouldn't get wet. Their dog, he came too.

We rushed down to the river and helped them up the bank. We all had to help Mrs Karaka up because she was very fat. Dad grabbed one hand, Mum grabbed the other, and Ripeka and I pulled at her puku. Her kids pushed her up from the back.

— One, two, three and heave! Dad yelled.

And she burst out of the water like a big whale and sat gasping on the grass.

— We come to say goodbye, she said.

She opened up the sack which Roimata had been carrying.

—This is for you, she said.

Inside was some Maori bread and scones, still warm from the oven.

— You shouldn't have, Teria, Mum said. You shouldn't have. To come all this way . . .

Mrs Karaka laughed and poked Mum with a finger.

— Takes more than a river to keep me away, Huia, she sniffed. Anyway, about time these kids had a bath. Get rid of all their kutus.

— Eee, Mum! the kids yelled. No kutus on us. It's the dog, he got all the kutus!

Their dog, he just whined and cocked his head as if he was offended.

We all sat down on the grass. Mum spread the kai. She opened her arms.

— We share your kai. Come.

We sat in silence, miserably munching at the scones. Mum

57

began weeping and so did Mrs Karaka. Soon all us kids were weeping too.

— Have another piece of bread, Teria, Mum would sniff.

— Ae. And you too, Huia, Mrs Karaka would weep.

We didn't want to leave each other. We shook hands with all the kids and kissed Mrs Karaka. Dad started the truck.

— Come back and see us sometime, ay? Mrs Karaka said.

— Ae, Teria, Mum answered. Soon.

Then we left. But I never saw Mrs Karaka again. I suppose I would never have recognised the kids if I passed them in the street.

And I crossed my fingers and whispered:

— Let the next place be a nice place. Please . . .

Always that same phrase, as we moved from one place to the next. Until one day, there was no need for it to be said. We came down from the hills and made a home in the city.

The train curves outward, following the railway track as it loops along the perimeter of the Ranges. It passes through a deep ravine, along a steep embankment, and through a series of tunnels. Then the hills unfold, rugged and rising up to the sun. An almost limitless vista stretching into a distant sky.

In the same way it seemed that life too, was opening out to us when our family made that last journey. Mum and Dad must have known that night when we were packing our belongings onto the truck, that it was the end of all the wandering. But they didn't tell Ripeka and me because they wanted it to be a surprise. Yet we caught some of their excitement. Mum had that sparkling look which meant something was up.

— Where we going, Mum? Ripeka asked.

— Ask your father, she said.

— Dad, where we off to this time? we asked him.

— Ask your mother, he answered.

We felt cheated. It wasn't fair. Dad grinned at Mum and she grinned back. They whispered to one another behind cupped hands.

— What you saying! What you saying! we yelled.

— Don't be nosey, Dad laughed.

They were mean!

— Just hurry up, you kids, Mum said. Take the blankets up to the truck. Then the clothes and the hens and the chickens. Otherwise we'll never get there.

— Where! we yelled.

Mum grinned.

— Ask no questions and you get no lies.

— Eee! Mum! You're awful to us, we moaned.

We hurried up the packing, hoping that if we were very good they would tell us their secret. But they didn't, no matter how hard we tried to wheedle it out of them. I worked on Dad; Ripeka worked on Mum.

— Mum said you can tell us now, Dad, I said.

— Dad said you can say where we going, Ripeka said to Mum.

But they were too clever for us. They didn't fall for that trick.

— You'll see, they told us.

And they nodded their heads in a secretive manner. It was very strange. So we tried opening our ears as wide as possible just in case they dropped a hint. Mum and Dad must have seen our ears flapping because they began to talk in Maori. That wasn't fair either.

— Tell us! we moaned.

But they weren't budging. They started making fun of us, eyeing us and giggling like two kids. We sighed then, Ripeka and I. We'd just have to wait. But as we sat at the back of the truck and rode through the night, we couldn't help wondering what the great secret was.

— Where do you think we're off to? Ripeka asked me.

— I dunno. Somewhere good I reckon, I answered.

We'd peer in through the back window and see Mum and Dad having a cuddle while Dad was driving. We didn't care about what they were doing. We looked further, to where the headlights of the truck were shining on the road. Somewhere out there in the night, was something nice. Somewhere nice. Ripeka, she crept under the blankets and whispered to the chickens about a dream place. They folded her whispers under their wings while they slept. We slept too, until Dad woke us.

— We're here, he said.

— Where? we asked, sleepily.

— Come and see.

We jumped down from the truck. Dad was carrying Mere, Mum had Wiki in her arms.

— What we doing in town? I asked.

Dad didn't answer. He walked up a small path toward the door of an old house. He fumbled in his pockets and brought out a key.

— I'm cold, Dad, Ripeka said.

Dad, he bent down to her.

— You won't be, any more, Ripeka, he answered quietly.

The door opened. We all went inside. It was dark. Then Mum put the baby down. Mere started to cry. Dad lit a match. The flame flared and lit up an empty room. It had a wooden floor and smelled very old. But there was no wind, no smoke, and only one broken window. Mum's eyes glistened.

— Where are we, Dad? I asked again.

He lit another match.

— No more gypsy life, Son. This is our home.

We were back to the beginning. But this was a different beginning. I wouldn't have to cross my fingers and make fierce wishes anymore. This was our own place. At last our life was really beginning.

The train suddenly shudders. Another bend. But it does not shake away the memory of that first home. It was old but it was ours. We still had a long way to go, more money to earn and the farm to buy. But it was home, our first real home.

The train jerks again, up an incline. Suddenly the window is drenched with blue, the colour of dreams, the colour of the sea. Below the train, the cliff face falls away onto a long winding beach. A promontory juts into the sea. Dark clouds of gannets wheel above it. White foam curls among the rocks below. Slowly the sea unfolds until there seems no land. Only sea merging into sky. And this train seems to be swaying along the very edge of space . . . and Time.

Time has taken my father away. And this too is my life beginning again.

Seventeen

Time . . . suddenly so important. A 'phone call from home, just a few hours ago and here I am bringing the last moments of a boy with his father to a close. Tomorrow, the world is changed. Father is dead. E pa, if I could I would force those ticking hands back from the top of the clock, back to the faraway side of the hour. But I cannot. The clock still ticks.

— You got the time, Tama?

— Almost five to four, Mr Ralston.

— Good. You don't have to check into the airport until ten past. Plenty of time.

Time to catch the plane. Before me, the road unwinds, curving along the Parade. The wind has risen and the sea slaps angrily against the sea wall. Kelp writhes beneath the surface of the water. Sand churns muddy patterns among the waves as they break on the shore.

A young boy plays with his small terrier on a stretch of sand. He throws a stick for his dog to fetch and shouts soundless commands to the wind. Further along, a man leans into the wind as he walks along the pavement. He grips his coat tightly and holds firmly to his hat. And there, in a calm patch of sea, a covey of seagulls calmly waits out the rough weather.

— Was he an old man, Tama?

— Dad? No, about fifty-six I suppose, Mr Ralston.

He nods. Silence falls again.

Strange: I've never thought of Dad as old . . .

61

— And your mother, Tama? She taking it well?

— Yes. Ripeka and Mere, two of my sisters, are with her.

— How many in the family?

— Nine. Mum and Dad, Ripeka, Mere, Wiki, Marama and Hone, Rawiri and myself. Marama and Hone are the youngest. I'm the eldest, Mr Ralston.

— A big family! he laughs.

— Not really. Rawiri died when he was a baby, so that makes eight actually. No. Seven, now that Dad is . . .

I look away. Sadness consumes me again.

— Tama . . .

Mr Ralston presses my arm, reassuring and comforting me.

— I'm okay, Mr Ralston. It's a bit of a shock, you see. I've never thought that Dad would . . . He's been sick for a long time. I thought he'd come all right. I'm okay now. Okay.

The car turns into Evans Bay and for a moment is buffeted by the wind. Small boats bob and sway in the marina.

— Bit of a wind! Mr Ralston smiles.

I try to smile back. My lips curl only with sorrow. There is no joy in the world now that Dad is dead.

— Soon be there, Tama.

Soon be there. At home. Waituhi. The homestead. Mere will meet me at Gisborne airport. It will be dark, almost night. We will drive through Gisborne where people are laughing and happy. Even before we reach Waituhi, I will hear the women wailing from Rongopai, our meeting house.

Haere mai ki o tatou mate e . . .

Come to our dead, come.

Dad will be lying there, under the eaves of the porch. Waiting for me. The women will be sitting round the casket. Already, some flower wreaths will be placed there. His photographs too, showing how he was when he was younger. A feather cloak will cover his body. And it will unfold from him like the wings of a giant, gleaming moth.

Haere mai ki o tatou mate e . . .

I look upward, at the sky. It races with dark clouds. But above them, the sun still shines . . .

Sun, move quickly now. Let the three days of the tangi, the

62

mourning time, pass by like a dream. Once, you moved quickly over the sky and men were angry because you brought night too soon. You rose, raced fiercely across smaller hours, then plunged quickly into the sea. Then Maui came. He waited for you to rise and ensnared you with a magic net. You battled against him and scattered the sky with flaming sparks. It was a long battle. Maui would not give in. Finally, you surrendered and promised him you would move more slowly and make the days longer. Only then did Maui release you.

Ae, Sun: I see the white whorls of light, the remnants of those taut thongs. I see your anguished form, still bent from that battle. But listen: your agony is my agony. Do not prolong it with such slow procession. Move quickly. Quickly now. Let my grief pass soon away, Sun. More minutes bring more tears.

— Almost there, Tama.

I look ahead. The road curves round the bay. The car turns onto the highway leading to the airport. Far in the distance I see the runway. A plane is about to take off. It gathers speed, then lifts into the grey sky. There is a thunderous rumble as it passes overhead. As it disappears across the hills it leaves a thin, wispy vapour trail.

Almost there . . .

I watch the plane disappearing until it becomes a red light, winking on and off, in the sky.

Almost there, e pa.

I shall wait, son. I know you come. My heart is still, but I wait for you. Don't weep.

The car joins the stream of traffic moving toward Rongotai Airport.

Rongotai . . .

Rongopai . . .

Rongotai the airport; Rongopai, my meeting house. And I am going home.

My tears fall. Through them I see the terminal building, the parking lot, the blurred colours of cars and people milling around the entrance. My heart, it weeps too. And I reach out a hand to my father.

Aue, e pa.

Eighteen

The train curves back through the hills. At one section of the line, men are working. The train slows down as it passes them. A man leans on his shovel, wiping the sun's heat from his brow. Another lights a cigarette. Then they are gone.

We lived six years in the city. At first, for both Ripeka and myself, it was a frightening time. We'd been accustomed to being alone; now we found ourselves in a long street surrounded by other houses.

That first day we just sat on the fence watching the people and traffic stream past. As she walked past a lady said: Hello! We were too confused and shy to answer her. We watched some schoolchildren run down the road and heard the school bell clanging in the distance. We were both afraid and excited because we were going to start school ourselves the next day. Most of all we were afraid, because going to school meant going away from Mum and Dad.

That next day, we walked to school in our new shoes and jerseys, clutching each other tightly. I was six and Ripeka was five. I'd been to a school before but this was Ripeka's first day at any school. Mere tried to come with us too. She followed us down the street and she was crying.

— Go home, Mere! I called.

But she just kept following and in the end she sat down in the middle of the road, rubbing at her eyes.

64

— Tama! Tama!

We had to take her home then. That made us late for school. Mum hadn't come with us. She'd said I was old enough to take care of myself and Ripeka. So we sat down on a bench in a big hall and waited. Ripeka whispered to me:

— We go home, Tama. I don't like it here.

Her voice echoed loudly and it frightened her. So we stayed. Along the hallway we could hear murmuring noises from classes. Ripeka started to cry.

— We go home, ay?

— No, I answered.

I had to be brave. I patted my sister on the shoulder.

— We'll be all right.

She sniffed and brushed at her tears.

We sat there for a long time. We'd been forgotten. Then a lady passed us.

— Goodness! she said. You children should be in class.

Ripeka started to cry again.

— We're new, I explained.

The lady smiled and calmed Ripeka.

— Nothing to cry about, she said brightly. She had a nice voice. Come on, she continued. You take my hand and we'll see about getting you two enrolled. School is fun!

We weren't so sure about that. I turned to Ripeka.

— Come on, Ripeka. It's all right.

She clung tightly to me.

—No, I won't leave you, I told her. We go now.

Somehow we made friends. After a while our loneliness left us. I wasn't as easy-going as my sister and she made more friends than I did. But every now and then she would come looking for me. Once she'd found me she'd smile, then go back to her playing.

We'd go home together with our friends. Mere would be waiting at the gate. When she saw us coming she'd toddle down the road to meet us. Ripeka would let her carry her satchel, and even give Mere a sandwich left over from lunch, if there was one. As time passed and Mere became accustomed to the city, she used to accompany us all the way to school. She'd insist on carrying Ripeka's satchel. She even carried mine sometimes.

— They're not heavy! she would yell.

And so there were three of us, joining others on the way to school.

— You have to go home now, Mere, we would tell her when we had reached school.

— Can't I come to school too? she used to ask.

— Next year, Mere, I would answer.

Then we would say goodbye and she would wave her hand until we went inside. Sometimes when school had ended, she'd be waiting for us at the gate and demand to carry the satchels home.

— They're not heavy!

Eventually, she too started school. She was very happy. And I had two sisters then, who would come to see where I was, smile, and then go back to playing.

The sun slants brightly through the window of the train. The calm swaying of the train as it traverses the mountains brings back the memories, like photographs thumbed through quickly. Happy friends, happy events. Ripeka's seventh birthday, when all our relatives and friends crowded into our small house and Ripeka said she wanted me to blow out the candles with her because I'd never had a birthday. Going to the two o'clock pictures at the Majestic, or to the Macrae Baths with friends. Shopping with Mum and Dad on Friday nights. The Agricultural Shows, where Dad used to compete in the sheep shearing events. And always, our lives opening, opening outward. Even the difficulties and disappointments and hard times have not the power to overshadow the happiness of those years.

But there were occasional shadows. Our Nanny Puti died when I was eight years old. For a long time after she was buried I had to have the light on in my room during the night. Even then, I used to wake up, screaming, and thrust my arms into the air searching for quilted walls . . .

Often Dad couldn't find work in the city. So he'd go away shearing or scrubcutting or on long shepherding trips. Then Mum would be left alone with us. Sometimes she'd be lonely and we would all sleep in her big bed to keep her company. And I was going to have another brother. But Mum was working at a factory and something happened and she lost him. So I didn't have a brother and I was very sad. For a long time afterward Mum was dazed and Ripeka and I had to make the kai for Mere and Wiki, clean the house and take turns at staying home and looking after Mum. The schoolteacher didn't understand. He growled Dad and so Auntie Ruihi came to stay for a while. I was nine years old. Then it seemed as if Mum woke up from a long moe. She was herself again.

— Don't be sad, Mum, I told her. I can wait.

But it wasn't until I was about sixteen that Mum gave me Hone, the brother I'd always wanted. I remember that Ripeka was very embarrassed because she thought Mum was too old for that sort of thing.

— Oh, Mum! she'd wailed. What will the kids at High School say?

And it was the last straw as far as she was concerned, when Mum produced Marama the next year. Mum had just laughed at her and said:

— Don't growl me! You go and tell your father off, he did this to me!

And Ripeka did just that.

— Boy, you're just like your mother, he answered.

Mum heard what he said and poor Dad, he had both of them growling him.

It didn't take Ripeka long to love Marama. She used to sneak into Mum and Dad's room and take the baby to sleep with her. Sometimes, Mum and Dad locked the door so she couldn't get in. Then, she'd get all the blankets off her bed and sit down outside the door and wait.

— Go to bed, Ripeka! Dad would yell.

— I'm not budging, she'd answer. I'm going to sleep here all night if I have to. You just open this door.

— This door's not opening for you, Ripeka Mahana.

— I don't care. You got to come out sometime. I can wait.

So in the end, Dad would open the door. Ripeka used to be in tears.

— You're awful to me, she'd tell Mum and Dad.

Then she'd get Marama and take her to her room.

All that happened during and after the time we left our city home. While we were there in the city, we were always conscious of Mum and Dad's dream. We all tried to help toward it because it became our dream too.

When Wiki started school, Mum went out to work in a number of factories, or out picking tomatoes, fruit and maize. During the holidays Dad took us all out shearing with him. Sometimes, we went to Hawke's Bay for the fruit-picking season. Once, we even went to the South Island for the shearing. That's where the big money was, so Dad said. I got a job delivering newspapers after school. Ripeka worked a few hours each weekend at Jobson's kennels. Mere used to help too by looking after Wiki.

It was a hard life; but it was a happy one, too. I drew my strength from my father. With aroha, he constructed and set my world firm.

Now that world has fallen. E pa, he is dead.

The hills fall away. The train speeds from the shadows of the Whareratas and clacks along the widening river valley. A highway follows the river out of the hills and runs parallel with the railway. The valley widens, and with splayed fingers, takes on final grasp of the earth. The train roars past the fingertips into Nuhaka and steams slowly toward the station.

— Can we get off here, Guard? a man asks.

— Sorry, he answers. We'll only be here a couple of minutes. We'll be stopping at Wairoa for refreshments.

A brief stop. For a moment, the world stops too. A young schoolboy gets on the train. He lifts his suitcase onto a luggage rack, then smiles excitedly through the window at his parents. The train begins to move again. Life begins again. And for this young boy, perhaps it is his destiny beginning . . .

Out of Nuhaka, the train speeds. Past green paddocks and small wooden farms. A milk truck trundles along the highway and the driver looks disinterestedly at the thundering train. Then, there is the sea, sparkling with the bright sun. It is a long blue ribbon, tying the land to the sky. Sand dunes reach up, cutting the ribbon, until there is only earth and sky.

Father too, has been severed from me. His life was my life. And this life without my father is another life beginning. Even though the tangi has long been ended, I still mourn.

Nineteen

Rongotai Airport. The car glides up to the entrance of the terminal building and stops. The engine idles quietly.

— Well, Tama, here we are.

I nod. Mr Ralston begins to say something, then hesitates. He gets my suitcase from the back.

— Thanks, Mr Ralston.

For a moment we are silent. Solemnly, we shake hands.

— Tama, I . . . he begins again. Then he makes a gesture of helplessness and smiles ruefully. Let us know when you'll be back, he says. Good luck.

Then he is gone. The car speeds away from the airport and joins the stream of traffic travelling back toward Wellington.

I am alone now. I turn and enter the terminal building. The entrance door opens and closes behind me. And I am amid the echoing sounds of people sitting and conversing with one another, and the sharp clicking of people hurrying across the gleaming floor. A man brushes past me, through the doors, to hail a taxi. The wind disturbs a small shrub near the entrance. A woman laughs as she talks with her companion. A small boy clutches his toy truck and eyes me curiously. An air hostess flashes a quick smile from behind a counter. A thousand destinies in motion. Mine is one of them.

And suddenly, I am a child lost in a crowd. The heat and suffocation fill me with terror as I wander through a crush of people looking for my father.

E pa, where are you?

Here, Son. Here.

Hold my hand, e pa. Don't let go, don't go away. Don't . . .

The desk clerk looks up.

— Yes?

— My name's Mahana. You're holding a ticket for me. For the flight to Gisborne this afternoon.

— What name did you say?

— Mahana.

He turns away and flicks a button on an intercom system. He confirms the booking, writes out a ticket, and checks my luggage in.

— Your flight departure time will be announced soon, he says.

— Thanks.

But he does not answer. No matter: his silence separates us both, as great as the distance I must travel this day, as great as my loneliness.

World, surround me with a rush of silence. Let no sounds of joy or happiness come to me. There should be no world now that Dad is dead, nor any joy . . .

I wander aimlessly through the crowd, the blurred faceless people. I must be calm. These people must not see my sorrow. Where are you, Dad? Hold my hand.

— Tama!

A voice splits the silence.

— Hey! Tama!

Through a gap in the crowd a figure emerges, running toward me and laughing. Kopua. A cousin. From home, from Waituhi.

— Gidday, cousin! he yells. Long time no see, ay? Where you off to? I've just got in from Christchurch. From one big smoke to the other! Hey! What you been doing lately, been home? Man, Christchurch, what a place!

He keeps talking, on and on, and spills his laughter through my silence. As I watch him, I am filled with both happiness and sadness.

— Boy, you can talk, Kopua, I whisper. Once you get started, you never . . . stop . . .

My voice breaks, and I sway, suddenly dizzy.

— Hey! What's wrong, Tama!

I try to smile.

— It's good to see you, Kopua.

He steadies me.

— Hey . . .

— I'm okay now, Kopua. I'm going home. You see, Dad, he's dead. Kopua, it's good to see somebody from home.

Kopua holds me tight. We sorrow together. Then he leads me to a seat and sits beside me.

— The old man, dead? he asks.

— Last night.

— Your old man?

— Ae. Ripeka rang me this morning. I'm catching the plane home.

He swears and the sound is explosive. He gets out a cigarette and lights it.

— How long before you catch your plane?

— I don't know. Sometime soon.

— I'll stay with you. Your old man, old Rongo . . .

We sit in silence. Kopua is tense, tightening his hands on the armrests.

— He was good to me, your old man, he says. Now gone? Jeez, just last year, he was still playing football. And I stood on the sideline yelling out to him: Get off the field, old man! You'll get hurt! But he wouldn't listen, ay. Hard as nails. The old man . . . And that time when Mum kicked me out of the house? Your Dad, he took me in. He was good to me.

He shakes his head.

— They'll be having the tangi at Rongopai, ay.

— Ae, at Rongopai, I answer.

His voice is suddenly fierce.

— You tell your Mum I'm coming back home for it. Tomorrow.

— What about your work?

— Bloody Hell! he cries. The old man's dead! I'll be back. Nothing'll stop me.

Two women glance disapprovingly in our direction and whisper to each other behind cupped hands. Kopua makes a sign with his fingers. They gasp, pretending they haven't seen.

— How'd it happen? he resumes.

— Dad, he's been sick for a while. But you know Dad. He wouldn't let on. Didn't want to worry anybody.

Kopua nods. He understands how my father was.

— You remember, he begins, that time when we wanted to go to a dance at the Ritz? So we asked him for the truck, and he said we could have it.

— Ae, and we saw him, Dad, walking into town. We stopped to pick him up, but he said: Not to worry, I gave the truck for you to have a good time. He would have walked all the way if we hadn't seen him.

— Now, dead? Kopua shakes his head, stunned. I don't know what to say . . .

I try to joke.

— That's a change. You were always the one for the talk. And Dad, he used to tell you: Kopua! No wonder your Mum kicked you out of the house!

— Yeah, Kopua grins. Me and my big waho. I almost talked myself into getting married a while ago.

— That girl's lucky, all right. Aue! You and your talk. The pain of it.

We laugh, but I am still sad.

— Kia kaha, cousin, Kopua says.

— Ae, I answer. Kia kaha. But you know, I'm going to miss Dad. I don't know what I'll do about the farm. I wasn't any good at farming.

— You were okay.

— Oh, yeah? What about that time when Dad tried to teach me to shear? But I was left-handed, ay, and I almost strangled myself with the handpiece.

— Boy, that was hardcase, Kopua says.

— All right for you to laugh. It was easy for you.

— I was born to that game, he boasts.

Then his voice grows soft.

— Hey, if you need a hand, cousin, you give me a yell. Don't forget, ay? Don't . . .

And his eyes suddenly glisten.

— The old man. Jeez . . .

The loudspeaker crackles into life. A voice announces that the plane for Gisborne is about to depart.

Kopua becomes calm. He stands up.

— I'll come to the gate, he says.

We go down the walkway following the other Gisborne passengers. We stand at the gate, watching them leaning into the wind, walking quickly across the tarmac to the plane.

— Well, e noho ra, cousin, I say.

We shake hands.

— I'll come up home as soon as I can, Kopua tells me. Probably tomorrow. Haere ra, Tama.

— I walk away.

— Hey! he yells.

He runs up to me and digs into his pockets.

— You got enough money?

— Enough.

— Here. You have this.

— No, Kopua, you might need it. Keep your money.

— No, you take it. Nothing wrong with it. I give it to you. It's yours . . . For the old man . . .

He thrusts the money into my hand and breaks away.

— Hey, Kopua!

But he is gone.

My eyes prick with tears. And suddenly, the world is aglow with the sunset. The clouds seep with flame. There is a lull in the wind. The flames spread higher through the clouds as if they were the branches of a burning tree.

At Te Reinga, at the northernmost point of Aotearoa, there is a Pohutukawa tree which grows on a promontory jutting into the sea. The promontory is called Rerengawairua. Dad, he will be there soon, for all Maori dead make their last journey to that place and wait for the sun to set. He will descend Akakitereinga, the Root to the Underworld, to a rocky platform on the edge of the sea.

And suddenly, a deep hole will appear, fringed with floating seaweed. The way across the sea. A shadow will leap . . . The waves will flow in. The seaweed will sweep over the hole. The platform where he was standing will be empty . . .

Perhaps Dad is already there. The tree already drips gold from the sun and the blossoms catch fire. The sea burns . . . And Dad is looking back for me, from a high summit at Te Reinga.

73

E pa, wait for me. Wait. Do not farewell earth nor leap seaward yet. Let the sea turn crimson and the Pohutukawa tree blossom with flame, but do not go.

Even now, through my tears, I see him. He is a shadow moving into the sunset and waving in farewell.

— Haere ra, Tama.

Haere ra . . .

I can only watch, helpless, as he walks slowly away.

— E pa. No.

The sky aflame and father gradually disappearing. Suddenly the flames enfold him, like the petals of a crimson flower closing.

Twenty

The train clatters, the train sways and clatters. Across the land of Maui it rushes, along a jagged fin of Te Ika a Maui. In the sky the sun leaps toward midday.

People are dozing in the heat. A child cries because he is thirsty. His mother strokes him tenderly, looking with glazed eyes out upon the passing country. And the schoolboy takes off his cap to brush at his forehead.

It wasn't so long ago that I was a schoolboy going to school in the city. Some of the memories are vague; others are knife-sharp. Of teachers who drifted in and out of my life, forming parts of it, destroying parts of it. Of friends: some have remained friends, others now pass by with a brief nod of acknowledgement. It was a time of joy and puzzlement, and sometimes much confusion; of growing older and realising that the world extended far beyond my family. It was a world filled with new things to understand or to comprehend; and with pushing out, or being pushed out, bewildered, into that world. Of questioning, searching; sometimes finding answers, sometimes not. And sometimes, of not understanding at all.

There was that little girl who lived in a street close to ours. Every day, she'd be sitting on her fence, waiting for me to pass on my way to or from school. Every time she saw me coming, she'd scream and yell:

— Maori boy! Maori boy!

There was such spite in her voice that I'd feel ashamed and puzzled. Because, you see, she was Maori just like me.

There were other bitter times too.

I made friends with a boy who'd come from England and he asked me to come to his tenth birthday. Then his mother rang up and said he was sick so I couldn't come. I'd already bought him a present.

— You take it round to his place, Mum said. You take some books for him too.

So I went to see him. I knocked on the door. His mother answered it. Behind her, I could see my friend and other kids, dressed in party hats and playing. He saw me and was embarrassed.

— Hullo, he said.

— Hullo.

— Do you want to come in? his mother asked me hesitantly.

— No thank you, I answered, trying to be brave.

I gave my friend his present.

— It's not much, I told him. I just came round to give it to you. These books, too. You can have them.

— Thanks . . .

— I better go now, I said.

All this time, I could hear those other children laughing.

— Happy birthday . . .

Then I went away, and I couldn't help it, the tears just came.

I couldn't understand. Something inside me always shrivelled up whenever somebody started saying scornful things about Maori people. And when Wiki started school, she made Mum give her a new handkerchief every day, clean her fingernails, brush her hair with a kutu comb, because her teacher used to inspect all the children every morning.

When I was older, a teacher gave us a lesson on the Maori wars. I walked out of his class.

These were isolated incidents and the pain has now been dulled by the years. They were a part of growing up. The world not only opened up to excitements and new interests but to bewilderment and groping also. Even Dad hadn't the power to shield us from all disappointments.

The train clatters over a railway bridge. A startled kingfisher

77

skims the water and casts the shadow of its outstretched wings across my mind.

I suppose my other Maori mates at school didn't really care; or perhaps they kept so closely together that nothing destroyed their calm. That was the way that Mere chose. She was at High School then, in a top form. Maata, another girl from Waituhi, was in the same class. Then Maata left. Mere was alone. Without telling Mum and Dad she changed to a lower class. Mum and Dad found out and growled her. Mere, she came to me.

— They don't understand, Tama, she said. There's no other Maoris in that class. I didn't want to stay. No others . . .

During my own time at school I could have made the same decision as Mere many times. I didn't, and school became more lonely as I progressed upward from one form to the next. My Maori mates dropped out earlier and went out working. I stayed on because that was what Dad wanted. By then, it seemed as if the world had indeed changed. Or perhaps it's only as a child or young boy that you are hurt. I was never hurt again because I took a firm step forward into the Pakeha world. Firmly, I retained it.

Somehow, I managed to stride both worlds. With some amusement, I recall it was difficult at first.

When Mum and Dad spoke to me in Maori, I'd cock my head to one side and look puzzled.

— Ay? What you say? Speak English!

That used to make Mum angry.

— What a hoha kid! she used to moan.

When I was with my Pakeha friends, I would also cock my head.

— Ay? What's that word: Mowry? And what's all this py korry business?

And if anybody started speaking pidgin English, I'd calmly wait until they'd finish. Then, I'd speak in my very best English accent.

But because the world I was growing up in was a Pakeha one, it was difficult to retain my Maoritanga. Even when I was trying to be humorous about it, there'd still be an ache in my heart. Sometimes, I even forgot my Maoritanga and its values. I remember how shattering it was, when I realised it.

I went to stay at Uncle Pita's place. He showed me where I was to sleep — in a huge double bed, all to myself. During the night I got up. I wanted a drink of water. I walked toward the kitchen and in the sitting room, I found Uncle and Auntie sleeping. On a mattress on the floor. Then I knew. I woke them up.

— Uncle, Auntie, I asked. Have I changed that much?

They wouldn't answer.

— Look at me, I whispered. It's me, still me. Tama, your mokopuna.

We embraced each other.

It was more difficult to live in two worlds as I grew older. The Maori part was so easy to forget. Not being Maori, but what being Maori meant; the customs, the traditions, Maori aroha. After a while I discovered that all I needed to do was remember Dad and my whanau, my big Maori family, and my world would right itself.

Hone has started school now. Ahead of him lies the same confusion which I went through. Like me, he has asked the same question I asked of Dad those many years ago:

— What's a Maori, Dad?

— Why, Son?

— A boy told me I was a Maori, Dad.

— Yes you're a Maori, Son. That boy, he's only jealous.

— Oh. But what's a Maori, Dad?

— Takitimu, Kurahaupo, Tainui, Te Arawa . . . Remember the names, Tama? Remember?

Now, e pa is dead. I am left to answer Hone's questions as best I can. To make him happy; to be a Kauri. Maybe I won't be able to teach him much Maoritanga for even when I was a boy, that was dying. But Maori aroha, that will never disappear. I will help Hone and Marama with their schoolwork just as Ripeka, Mere, Wiki and I tried to help each other on those long nights when we were struggling with it. Dad and Mum couldn't help us because they knew little of such things. That didn't seem to matter to us; their knowledge was of the earth and of loving the earth and that seemed more important.

Most of all, I will teach Hone and Marama of Maori aroha, the love we hold for one another, so that they will never be alone if some day they leave Waituhi and go to the city. I will teach them open heart and open life, as Dad would have done, and the

79

humour to laugh if the values of the Pakeha are too strong for them. Maori aroha . . .

The door to the carriage opens. The guard enters. He passes down the aisle.
— Wairoa in two minutes. Time for refreshments, he announces.
The passengers stir and begin to chatter amiably.

— Dad, why do I have to learn? I ask.
I am a young boy, confused.
— Tama, he answers, you remember when we used to travel all over the place working? It was hard, ay.
I nod, remembering.
— That's why you got to learn, Dad says.
— Oh, I answer, not understanding.
Dad curls his hands around my head.
— Your father, he's dumb. He can only work with his hands. See them? Hard and rough. Me and your Mum, we been working all our lives for you kids. We don't want you to have hard lives like we had. Sometime, you may have to look after your Mum and brother and sisters. That's why you learn, Tama. That's why, Son. You understand now?
I feel his lips upon my head, and the rough clasp of his embrace.

I look out the window.
Ae, e pa. I understand.
You do it for me, ay? he says. For me.
All for you, e pa . . .
The train roars into Wairoa.

Twenty-one

I sit alone at the window. Outside the train, people mill about the railway cafeteria, shoving forward to the counter for pies, soft drinks, cigarettes and perhaps packets of lollies. Others stand beside the train, conversing and laughing. A young man puffs at his cigarette and watches the girls pass by.

Wairoa. A small town.

Gisborne, although larger than Wairoa, is also very much a small town. But when I was a small boy it seemed very large. Its long main street intersected other streets which splayed out toward the sea and hills like long thin fingers. As I grew older however, Gisborne seemed to get smaller as if the fingers were curling slowly into the palm of the city.

Our family lived in Kaiti, a suburb shadowed by Kaiti Hill, near Poho-o-Rawiri, a large meeting house. That was where we played, my sisters, friends and myself: hide and seek around the meeting house or war games beneath the rusting cannon which points across the harbour just below the crest of Kaiti Hill. Sometimes we'd pick the toetoe for spears and chase each other through the flax and bush on the Hill. Other times, we'd get our bikes and race each other down the road which winds from the lookout point. If ever we were brave enough, we'd sneak into the meeting house to look at the carvings. The meeting house must have been very angry with us sometimes because we liked sliding along the floor, it was so good for sliding on.

And always, when it was getting dark, Mum would call out for us.

— Tama! Ripeka! Mere! Wiki! Come home!

We would hurry home as quickly as we could because Mum would keep on calling, and she had the loudest voice in the neighbourhood. She didn't care about the neighbours. When we eventually left the city, they told me laughingly, that they missed the sound of Mum calling us.

— Where you fullas been! Mum would growl.

— Playing, we'd answer.

We never told Mum about our going into Poho-o-Rawiri because if she found out she'd give us a good clip over the ears. That meeting house was sacred.

— Well, she would say, you've had your play. Now it's work. Get to it!

And I'd have to help Ripeka peel the potatoes or make the kai.

— This is the women's work, Mum, I'd moan.

— All right, then! she'd answer. You go and chop some wood or weed the garden.

She was cunning. I used to get annoyed and would mumble to myself.

— What you saying, Tama Mahana?

— Nothing, Mum, nothing, I'd answer hastily.

Mum, she had a powerful hand. Even Dad said so.

E pa . . . He towered over my life like Kaiti Hill. The Hill in all seasons, mirrored his moods. In summer it was diamond sharp, cutting a clean edge into the sky. In winter, it brooded with low lying clouds. Autumn brought flame to the willows and burnished reds to the fir and pine trees. And in spring, the Hill was bright with the sun.

I liked walking alone up to the lookout point. From there, I could look out across Gisborne, curving around the Bay. On a clear day, there seemed so much sky, so much sea. And once, almost on the edge of space, I saw the tall spume rising from a whale's deep plunging. But as time passed during those summer years, I found less time to visit the lookout. And it seemed only natural that my sisters and I should begin to separate, find new friends and make other lives. There were occasions when we didn't do things together, when we quarrelled and hurt each other.

But despite our quarrels, most of all there was the calm of those years.

Dad too, he became interested in strange things. On Saturday mornings, he would disappear to some mysterious place called the TAB. Sometimes, he'd take us with him. We'd have to wait for him in the truck because children weren't allowed into the TAB. So we didn't go after a while. It wasn't much fun. But once he won some money from that place and bought us some roller skates. We were happy then. And afterward, Dad even took us all to the pictures, even Mum. And at night time too!

During those years we also began meeting some of our relatives. We hadn't had much time to see them before and we were overwhelmed at our big family. We'd be walking along the street with Mum or Dad and meet one of them and have to press noses or shake hands.

— Who was that lady? Ripeka would ask.

— That's your Auntie Arihia.

— But wasn't that Auntie Arihia we met last week? I'd ask.

— Oh, that was a different Auntie Arihia! Mum would reply.

It seemed to us that we were related to every Maori in Gisborne and the East Coast. No wonder we were confused sometimes: there were so many names to remember and some of them were even stranger than ours.

Gradually, we got to know them. Nanny Katarina, she was the one with the moko. Uncle Pita, he had a big puku. Cousin Anaru, he was the cheeky one. Nanny Whiti, he always had a tokotoko, a walking stick. And Auntie Bubbie, she was different from our other Auntie Bubbie because she had no teeth. So many of them, and all our relatives!

— Your Auntie Maka, Dad would tell us, she was married to my brother Tamihana. And she's really his cousin down the line because her father was your Nanny's uncle. His name was Hepa and he was married to Mereira on your mother's side. And . . .

We tended to get confused when Dad was explaining how we were related. Even Nanny Maaka, who could recite all the whakapapa or genealogy of our family off by heart couldn't make us understand.

— We wait till you fullas are older, he said finally. Then you won't be such dumb mokopunas.

With Dad and Mum's immediate family, it was easier. Especially with Dad's family who just about all lived at Waituhi where we visited sometimes, and where we finally lived. With Mum's family it was different because we hardly ever went to Opotiki where she came from.

Hardly ever. Hardly ever. And on the platform at Wairoa a group of children play.

My favourite cousins were George and Miriama. During winter they came into Gisborne every Saturday because the Waituhi men's and women's hockey teams would play at the Reserve. Their mother was my Nanny Miro, and she became my favourite Nanny after my Nanny Puti died.

It was fun being with my cousins. Sometimes we'd find some spare hockey sticks and play on the fields.

— Get off, you kids! someone would yell.

Miriama, she would poke out her tongue; she wasn't scared of anybody. If the women's team was short, Nanny Miro would tell Miriama she had to play. Miriama was a good hockey player.

Sometimes the old people would give us some money to go to the pictures at the Majestic. We'd buy some fish and chips first and go down to the river bank, next to the Wi Pere Memorial. We always liked it there because Wi Pere was our great-great-grandfather and that memorial seemed to be not only for him but for all the Waituhi people too. That's where he came from, and he had been a Member of Parliament which meant he was very important.

We liked to play around the Memorial and we fed the seagulls with spare chips if there were any. Then we'd go to the pictures and really loved it if it was a Western with Indians and cowboys. Afterward, we'd return to the hockey field and say haere ra until the next Saturday. We'd wave at the bus until it disappeared, wishing we could go with them to Waituhi. Waituhi was home . . . It was Dad's home, and he was always talking about it. Even though we lived in Gisborne, it wasn't really our home. Home was Waituhi. It was all the family living together around Rongopai, the family meeting house. It was living with our family present and our family dead who slept on the hill near Rongopai.

— That's your home, Dad would say when we visited Waituhi

or when he was talking about it. One day, kids, that's where we're going. Back home. Back to Waituhi.

Before we even lived there, we knew Waituhi was indeed home. And Mum and Dad, they saved and worked together to return there.

E pa ... I look out the window, with loneliness. It is difficult to feel happy away from Waituhi.

— What's mine is yours, Nanny Miro used to say.

— My house is your house, Uncle Pita also used to tell me.

We lived belonging to each other, not apart from each other. That's the way Mum and Dad loved each other too. That's the way they taught us to love.

Sometimes, Dad was away working for a long time while we were in the city. Often we never saw him until the weekends. Those nights without Dad were very lonely.

— You kids come and sleep with Mum tonight, ay? Mum would say. We make each other happy.

We used to be glad, especially if it was winter, because Mum was always warm.

— Come on Wiki, Mum would say. Come right next to me, because you're the smallest. Now you, Mere. Ripeka, come, haere mai. And Tama, you stay on the outside. Your feet are too cold.

— My feet aren't cold, Mum.

— They are too! Mere would yell.

And Mum, she would laugh.

We often played games in bed, Mum and all us kids. All sorts of games like Snap! and Chinese Checkers and even Snakes and Ladders. Ripeka was good at games and she mostly won. Other times, Mum would tell us about her courting days. About how Dad fell in love with her at first sight and used to come on his horse across a river just to see her. She'd get out the photograph album and show us how pretty she was and how ugly Dad was, but we knew she was only joking because Dad was very handsome. She used to regale us with story after story and always warned us: Don't you tell Dad what I told you! Because most of her stories, so Dad told us, were all lies.

— It was your mother, he would say, she was the one who came across the river on her horse.

85

Sometimes, the best times, we'd just lie in bed with Mum while she sang us songs.

> *Tahi nei taru kino, mahi whaia-ipo*
> *Ke te wehenga, aroha kau ana,*
> *Haere mai ra, ki ahau nei ra,*
> *He aroha tino nui, haere mai . . .*

And some nights, while we were asleep, Dad would come home. I'd feel him lifting my sisters back to their own beds.

— You home now, Daddy? Mere would ask sleepily.

— Ae, Mere. Home.

Ripeka, she would put her hands round Dad.

— Goodnight, Daddy, we would say.

Then he would be gone. Far away, in my dreams, I'd hear Mum weeping, happy that he was home.

— Turi turi, Huia, he would whisper.

With his whisper came such calm that there were no storms nor any loneliness.

> *Oh, how it grieves me, to look within your heart,*
> *And think of parting, which brings such sorrow . . .*

A song that Mum used to sing. As I remember it, I see a young girl standing with her grandmother, an old kuia, on the platform.

> *There'll be a welcome, when you come back,*
> *You know my heart is yours, come back to me.*

The girl boards the train and finds her seat in the carriage. She winds down the window and whispers affectionately to her Nanny.

— E ma, kauai koe e tangi e ma.

— E tangi ana ahau mo taku mokopuna.

— E ma, ahakoa e haere tawhiti ana ahau, to manawa, e taku manawa, mo ake, mo ake.

— Nanny, don't you cry, Nanny.

— I'm crying for you, my mokopuna.

— Nanny, although I'm going away, a long way, your heart is my heart, for always, for ever . . .

I listen; I sorrow. For this girl has said: to manawa, e taku manawa, and that's what Dad used to say to me. It wasn't so long ago that I left home, like this girl, to go to Wellington. While I was there, e pa, he left me.

The old kuia, her lips quiver, and she brushes her tears with the edge of her scarf. She presses her face against the window and reaches up to caress her mokopuna. I look away. There is such sorrow in parting. Perhaps, this girl will never see her Nanny again. Perhaps . . .

A bell on the platform rings. Passengers rush back to the train, shoving past the kuia. She looks around her, bewildered. Then she looks at her mokopuna again.

— Haere ra, Arihia. Haere ka hoki mai ano.

— Mea kau ake, e ma.

— Goodbye, Arihia. Come back to me soon.

— Soon, Nanny.

The train moves away from the platform. The girl waves at her Nanny disappearing.

— E ma, she whispers. E ma . . .

Twenty-two

The clouds catch fire from the sun. Below, the land is streaked with long shadows cast from the hills and Wellington already glows with evening light. Above the clouds, it is still day. And the sun is a glowing orb upon a sea of clouds.

Everything is at peace here, away from the world storms. This quiet time is the sunset of my world. Soon, the dawning of my own day will burst with the wailing and grief of the tangi. Yet be still my heart; be calm, for these hours are calm.

I feel a soft arm touching me. I smile, for the woman who sits next to me is afraid. This is her first flight on a plane.

— Are you sure we'll be all right? she asks again.

— Quite sure, I answer. Don't you be afraid.

— Oh, dear . . . she says, biting her lips. She leans across me to look out the window.

— It feels so strange, she begins, to be so far off the ground.

I smile again. I try to change the conversation.

— Do you come from Gisborne, too?

— Oh, dear no! I'm a grandmother!

— Pardon?

— Well, she laughs, my daughter got married a while ago to a doctor. He practises in Gisborne. They've just had a baby. It's my first grandchild. It's such a special occasion, that's why I'm flying there . . .

She pauses.

— And you? she asks. Do you come from Gisborne?

— Gisborne's my home, I answer. I'm going home to see . . .
to see my father.

My voice breaks. I look away, out the window.

Going home . . . and perhaps others of Dad's family are journeying
home this coming night, to Waituhi. Perhaps Dad has sent his
wairua to them. They see him in the twilight, waving from a
Pohutukawa tree ablaze.

— Haere ra, haere ra, he whispers.

The spirit, my people say, always visits members of his whanau.
Once he has visited them, they will travel the long journey home.
Dad has gone to them in the traditional manner and said his
farewells and they will come to mourn him.

— But how do you know he is dead? people may ask.

His kin will look to a weeping sky or a moth flitting against a
window and say:

— We know. He has come to us.

They will journey then. Through calm or storm they will
travel. In their minds they will already see Rongopai and the hill
where the whanau dead are buried. Toward the hill they will
journey like fireflies attracted to the light of the marae.

People will already be at Rongopai. The whanau will be
preparing throughout the night for the tangi. The women will be
sitting beneath the eaves of Rongopai where father is laid so that
he will not want for company, so that he won't be lonely.

The voice of the tangi has curled across the land. A member of
the whanau has gone, and the breaking apart is so profound that
the sudden emptiness is felt in every heart.

— Haere mai ki o tatou mate e . . . Haere mai, haere mai . . .

Come to our dead. Come, welcome.

The tangi . . . the mourning for the dead. For three days, Dad
will lie on the marae at Rongopai. My mother Earth will keep
him warm, my whanau will weep for him. The stars and moon will
circle once, twice . . . The sun will rise and set once, twice . . .
then the third night will be my life beginning, without father. For
on the afternoon of the third day Dad will be buried close to
Papatuanuku the Earth.

— Are you all right, dear?

The woman's face is concerned.

— Yes . . .

— You looked a little strange. Is anything wrong?

— No, nothing. I'm okay.

She settles back into her seat.

— It'll be such a relief when we get back on the ground!

She prattles on but I do not hear her.

E pa, do you remember when Nanny Puti died? It was a sunny day, but while we were standing on the hill it began to rain.

Ae, Son, I remember.

I asked you: Why is it raining, Dad?

Yes, you were a little boy then. You didn't understand the tangi. You held my hand, afraid because of the grief. It was sad for you to see your Nanny going away. Ae, it rained.

And e pa, when I asked you, you answered: It always rains when a Maori dies. No matter if the day is sunny. It always rains because the wailing makes the sky sad.

It was a sad time, Son.

E pa . . . Will it rain for you?

Tama, it always rains when a Maori dies. As you weep, it will rain.

E pa . . .

— . . . so when my daughter, Sarah's her name, told me she was expecting, I just couldn't believe it. Me, a grandmother? No!

The woman laughs.

— You don't look old enough to be a grandmother, I answer.

— Thank you! she says. It's a boy, you know, the baby. Andrew they've called him. After my husband. I'm a widow.

— Oh, I'm sorry.

— That's all right. It happened a long time ago. You get over it after a while. At first it's such a shock but . . .

Will I get over you, e pa?

Some day, Tama. Sometime.

But don't you remember, e pa, what I was like when Nanny Puti died? Ripeka, Mere and I were at school and you came to get us. We didn't know what death was. It was just a reason to go away from school for a while and we were happy.

90

Don't be ashamed, Tama. You were just a boy.

We had to pick up Uncle Arapera first. He'd come all the way from Auckland by bus. He was waiting for us at the bus station and he looked lost. When he saw you, Dad, he cried because you were the eldest and he was the youngest and he had only you to look after him now.

The eldest always looks after the youngest, Tama.

Ae, e pa. All the way to Waituhi we children sat at the back. You and Mum were in front and Uncle had his head on your shoulder. You and Mum spoke to him in Maori so we couldn't understand. And Uncle was so sad that he made us sad too. Mere started to cry. But you were so calm, e pa.

Your Nanny, my mother, she was old, Tama.

But I couldn't understand why she had to die, Dad.

You were too young.

She was just lying there, Dad. In her bed, as if she was just asleep. And all those old ladies, they were weeping and sobbing. When we came into the room, they started to wail. I was scared, Dad. And Uncle, he flung himself across Nanny, holding her and yelling her name. But you were so calm. I held you tightly and whispered: Don't you die, Dad. Don't you leave me. And all the time, e pa, the wailing . . .

Don't remember, Tama. Be calm, as I was calm.

Ae, e pa. I shall try. But my Nanny she was such a good woman. Even after all these years I still remember her. And my heart, it aches. I shall try to be calm, e pa. Like you were. I am the eldest. But e pa, you were so much my world, I shall never forget you.

I look round the plane. These people must not see my grief. Their world is happy. How can that be so? My father is dead, yet they laugh and chatter. Why?

A few seats ahead, the air hostess sits playing with a child. Two businessmen talk. A girl leafs through a fashion magazine. A man sits idly smoking. The cigarette smoke curls softly overhead.

Aue, e ma.

The dirt falls quickly upon my Nanny disappearing. Around the graveside, the people are stricken with grief.

Aue. Aue.

And my Nanny, she is going away from me, never to return. Her casket lies in the earth. Her suitcases and photographs are thrown in. A feather cloak falls to keep her warm. I weep, partly because I am afraid, partly because my Nanny she was good to me. Sometimes I was a mean mokopuna to her. She was a good Nanny.

The wailing soars, and lifts across the hill. I clutch Dad tightly. In his face is such calm, yet such agony.

E pa, she was a good Nanny, wasn't she?

He smiles. And although it is a sunny day, the rain softly begins to fall, mingling with the tears of the mourners. The sky weeps too.

Once again it will rain. It always rains when a Maori dies.

My father, he is dead.

— Oh, look!

The woman next to me points toward the sun. I look, and the sun blazes in my eyes. It is moving below the clouds, like a golden meniscus glowing. Behind it, the stars are springing upward. The night is coming like the black winged feathers of a bird spreading across the sky.

— Isn't it beautiful? she asks.

I nod. And as I watch the sun disappearing, the sunlit shafts are like paths gradually receding across the clouds. Walking into the sun is a shadow.

— Haere ra, Tama. Be calm.

Look after the family.

Then night leaps up. The sun disappears.

— Ae, e pa . . .

The night comes, drenching the sky with darkness. And with the night comes Hine-nui-te-Po, whom all men must follow into Rarohenga, the world after death. She was the first child of the world and her father was Tane, who mated with the woman he had fashioned from red earth. Hine was born, and Tane took her also to wife. Her name was then Hinetitama, the Dawn Maid. She was very beautiful.

Then she discovered her husband was also her father. Overwhelmed with shame, she left Te Ao, the world of light, and fled to Rarohenga. She reached the guardhouse of Poutererangi and sought entry from Te Kuwatawata, the guardian of the gateway.

But before entering, she looked back and saw her husband following, weeping as he came. She called to him:

— Haere atu, Tane. Hapai a tatou tamariki i te Ao.

Goodbye, Tane. Raise our children in the light. I shall stay here, to gather them to me in death.

Then she entered Rarohenga, and became Hine-nui-te-Po . . . Now she has taken father from me.

I look toward the sun dying and the night advancing. The plane hums softly through the night.

E Hine, you wait for father. He comes to you. Once you were beautiful. As Hinetitama, you were the dawn. Now your mouth is that of a barracouta, your eyes flecked with greenstone. Your hair is sea-kelp still moist with the sea. You wait for all men, and they fear you now. But I shall come to you, and not be afraid. Across these dark clouds, these dark strands of your hair I shall walk. And I will plead with you to give my father back.

E Hine, I shall come. Toward Rarohenga, unafraid. From Te Kuwatawata, I will gain entrance through the gateway. And I will come to your house, Wharaurangi. In the courthouse before your house, I will plead with you.

I plead now, Hine. Give my father back to the light. And me, your child, take me instead. Me, e Hine. Take me.

Twenty-three

The girl still weeps, her face reflected in the window of the train. Over and over again, she calls softly to her Nanny.

— E ma . . . E ma . . .

Perhaps this girl will never see her Nanny again. She will go to the city and enjoy life, forgetting about her Nanny. Then maybe the telephone will ring or a telegram will come . . . Then she will know where her heart lies as I know where my heart will always be. At Waituhi, my whanau.

I look away. The train speeds across the countryside, scattered with small farms. For a moment it stops at Raupunga. Then onward, along a ridge, then clattering across the Mohaka viaduct. Far below the bridge, a road winds down the side of the valley, to twist and turn its way upward from the other side of the river. The river from this height is like a small stream trickling amid the dense bush. The water is white with foam, deep with dark green and the wind scatters the surface with a sudden shimmering of stars.

Such a river as this ran near Waituhi. Often, Dad would take us out there, and we would stand beside the river, watching it swirling past.

— Soon, he would say, this river will be our river.

He would spread his arms, encompassing the land which lay on either side of it.

— This too, will be ours.

94

And we would look at the land with excitement. This was Dad's dream, and soon it would be our dream too.

— When, Dad, when? Ripeka would ask.

— How soon! I would ask as well.

He would smile and hug Mum. She would wink at him.

— Just wait your hurry! she would tell us.

— Maybe in another few years, Dad would say.

Then we'd walk back to the truck, waiting at the roadside, and travel back to Gisborne.

The viaduct falls behind. The train curves round the side of the valley through the hills. The sky is wide and bright with the sun, the hills are like jagged fins thrusting proudly into the horizon. And I remember how our life in Gisborne continued to broaden and open out to us as we grew older. It was a time when we all searched in that world and ourselves, and what we found made us what we became. For Ripeka and Mere it was easy because they were easy-going. They were able to take life as it came. But living so long with the loneliness of those first years of my life when we moved from one small whare to another had made me hesitant and draw back from the world. However, I did make friends. Even then, I preferred the company of my father and he became my best companion as well as my father. We went to football matches together on Saturdays or to hockey. Dad would watch me play in the mornings; I would stand on the sideline watching him race down the field in the afternoons.

— Go, Rongo, go! the crowd would yell.

My heart would race just watching him pounding toward the goal. Sometimes he made it and there'd be a big cheer. Sometimes he didn't and the crowd would groan.

— What's wrong with you, man!

Dad, he would grin. And his favourite answer was either: Maybe next time, or: Sometimes you win, sometimes you don't.

Even when he grew older and we were living on our farm in Waituhi, Dad would still go down to the football or hockey field. He was still game at fifty. If a team was short, he'd trot onto the field as if he was a young man.

— Show these young fullas how to play a real game of football! the men of his own generation would say.

— Get off the field, old man! the young would yell.

But they would cheer when he got the ball, and boo a young man if he tackled Dad.

— Hey! Leave that old man alone!

And Mum would be there too, looking very worried.

— Rongo! Rongo Mahana! You just come off that field!

Dad would just grin at her.

— I still feel young, he'd yell.

Mum would just smile to herself and fold her arms.

— We'll see . . . We'll see . . . she used to say to herself.

And she had no pity for him the next day when he moaned and groaned in bed with an aching back.

— Still feeling young, ay Rongo?

— Aue, my back, my feet, my arms . . .

Mum would pull him out of bed.

— If you're young enough to play football, you're young enough to fix the fence. Now up you get. Ana! That'll teach you!

Mum, she had no mercy sometimes. She would follow him down to the shed, just to make sure he saddled his horse and didn't sneak off anywhere to lie down.

— Don't you love me, Huia? Dad would moan. I stay home today, ay? And you love me better, ay?

But no. Dad couldn't get round Mum like that.

— You better finish that fence by tonight, Rongo Mahana! she'd yell after him. And if it isn't, you just stay out there and don't you come home!

She'd come back to the farmhouse and laugh. But during the afternoon, she'd get worried, and always, when it was growing dark, she'd stand on the verandah and yell:

— Rongo! Rongo Mahana! Come home!

And she'd give Dad a clip over the ears for staying out too late. Either way, Dad never won.

A sudden shaft of sunlight dazzles my eyes a moment. Then the train moves into the shadow of a ridge. The land continues to unfold toward the sky.

Strange: even as I grew older in Gisborne, my father never seemed to age. He seemed always the same as if life had just streamed round him and left him unchanged. I suppose when you are young you don't recognise the signs. Anyway, I was more interested in going with Dad wherever he went. Out fencing, mustering or shearing. If ever I heard the truck starting up, I'd run outside.

— Can I come with you today, Dad?

Sometimes, he'd let me. Or else, he'd shake his head and tell me that school was more important.

— You stay home and look after your mother and sisters, ay? And you do all your homework and be very clever. Not like your dumb father.

His children's schooling meant a lot to my father. He hadn't stayed at school for very long; he'd been brought up by his grandparents who were very old. But his wisdom in the ways of the land was immense and he understood its whims with the deep patience of a man who had lived all his life close to the earth. If the land was wilful and did not grow his crops or if a storm laid the maize low, it did not matter. He would be patient. Some time, the calm would come again. He loved the earth as if she was his wife.

My mother too, hadn't had much education. She often told Ripeka and me of days when she had to walk to school, a long way. Her father had no money to afford such things as we were accustomed to like shoes and nice clothes. In winter, she and her sisters used to bind their feet up with sacking so that they wouldn't get cold. She'd told us how she was so ashamed at school because she looked so much like a rag doll. Like Dad, Mum was also brought up by her grandfather, and it was when she was seven that her mother had first gone to bring her home. But her grandfather wouldn't let her go because he needed her to milk the cows and do his housework. He wouldn't let her have boyfriends when she grew older.

— All the same, I had plenty before your Dad came along, Mum used to tell us.

In the end, she ran away from her grandfather and pleaded with her mother to let her stay with her.

Both Mum and Dad had left school early to work. Dad had gone out shearing and scrub-cutting with his father. Mum had taken jobs as a cook and a servant. They'd both had a hard life and they didn't want us to have the kind of life they'd had, they kept telling us.

— You fullas stay at school as long as you can, they would say. You do that for us, ay? For us . . .

Because that was what they wanted, we tried our best at school. Ripeka seemed able to catch on quickly and she did very well. Mere too, had a quick mind, and her special brand of cheekiness endeared her to her teachers. She was always asking questions, and her favourite one was: Why? If a statement was made, Mere would always ask: Why? and in one school report she received, the teacher had written that Mere kept her on her toes.

At school, I was just a slogger, just like my father. Mine was not a quick mind and I found the complexity of education difficult to absorb.

— Never mind, Son, Dad would tell me. Some people run a fast race, some people run a slow race. In the end you'll get there.

The train crawls up an incline. The sky opens slowly like a window upon those years at Gisborne. The girl has stopped weeping now. She gets up from her seat and walks past me toward the back of the train. Our eyes meet; she quickly turns away. And ahead, the sky opens . . .

I was thirteen when we left our home in Gisborne. I was almost a man, yet still very much a child. Growing up was a bewildering time, both exciting and sad. Exciting because of the new perspectives, that life brought me; sad, because even though the family was still the centre of my life, life seemed to be leading me away from it. I was walking into a strange new world. One that could be filled with love, and then at a turn, with anger. But always there was father, unchanging, to stabilise my world. As long as he was there, I had no need to fear.

However, as I grew older, I also seemed to be walking away from him too. That was the saddest thing of all. Dad seemed to grow smaller as I grew taller. Sometimes I would discover faults in him. We argued and there were bitter words. But he was patient with me as he was with the earth. And then there was his calm and his aroha. With such calm and aroha, he bound our family closely together. If there were arguments they were soon healed. If there were momentary hurts, he salved them. It was all part of growing up that we should sometimes quarrel. But Dad was always forgiving.

98

— The hurt, it is in here, he would say, pointing at his heart. It is very deep. But deeper, is my love for you. I give you my love; you do with it what you want. You walk away from me, that is all right. But don't you walk away from your family. You're Maori. Never walk away from that either. I don't mind how far away you go. Just remember you're the eldest. The eldest always looks after the younger children. If I should die, you remember that.

Dad, he sometimes made me feel ashamed. He gave everything he had to his children. He expected nothing in return.

— To manawa, e taku manawa, he would tell me. Your heart is my heart. Wherever you go, I go with you. If ever you need me, I will come to you. You will never be alone, for I will always be with you. To manawa, e taku manawa.

I look out the window. The world rushes past. In the sky, a bird flies softly and calmly like a white feather drifting. Higher above it, another bird flies, a sparrow hawk. The hawk glides upon the streams of air. Its wings hardly move and with outstretched pinions it follows the whim of the wind. It surveys the land through the slits of its eyes and sees a white feather flickering over green fields. The wings fold back. The hawk plummets down. A scattered turbulence. Then the hawk rises triumphant. Within its claws is a small white bird. I watch the hawk slowly ascending. Then it is gone, like a dream. Only clear sky remains. The girl comes back to her seat. She is calm now. She sits, her head erect, looking out at the passing land.

To manawa, e taku manawa, Tama.

No, e pa. My heart, it was your heart. And now that you have gone, my heart dies too.

In the sky, the sun falls into the afternoon.

Twenty-four

The air hostess walks down the aisle, pausing to bend and talk with passengers.

— Are you all right, Sir? Would you like a magazine, Madam? We have Time, Newsweek, Australian Post, Pix . . .

The woman next to me watches admiringly. Then she nudges me.

— She's very efficient, isn't she?

I smile.

— Just imagine! the woman continues. That girl spends every day flying on a plane, and here I am, wanting to get my feet back on the ground.

She giggles and while she is giggling, the plane dips in an air pocket. The stars wheel and fall from the night sky.

— Oh dear! the woman gasps. She clutches tightly to the arm rest. Did you feel that? Oh . . .

The plane rocks again. The air hostess comes aside the woman.

— Just a bit of turbulence, Madam, she says reassuringly. Nothing to worry about.

— Are you sure? the woman asks.

— Quite sure. The weather over Gisborne isn't the best at the moment. It's raining on the ground you know.

— Really? It's not raining up here, though.

— We're above the clouds, Madam. We'll be beginning our descent soon.

The woman sighs.

— I suppose I'm just not meant for flying!

— Is this your first time? the air hostess asks.

— Yes. I'm going to see my grandchild. My daughter told me flying is the only way to travel, so here I am!

They laugh together and talk with one another. I turn away. Outside, the night is dark. Above, the sky is sprinkled with stars. The moon is wan and softly glowing. Nothing else but sky, stars and moon, so calm and peaceful. Magical.

Like other magical nights, when the sky was so clear that it seemed you could see to the end of forever. They were the calm summer nights of those forever years when father was always with me.

And there was one night in particular when I went eeling with you, e pa. I was very young, about nine I suppose, and we travelled a long way from Gisborne to a river in the middle of nowhere. We had oil lamps and wandered along the banks of the river. We came to a place where willows drifted their branches in the dark water.

This is a good place, you said.

You placed a lamp over the edge and I could see the flame reflected in the water. The eels came, attracted to the flame, to twist and slide steely shapes beneath the river.

Now! you said.

And we thrust with spears at the eels. I never got any but you did, e pa. You lifted one from the river and it flashed the moonlight from its wriggling back. It was beautiful to see the eels you caught rippling with silver, but it was sad too. You understood my sadness.

Don't be sad, Son, you said. Such a strange one, is my Tama! This is the earth that brings the eels to us. She is kind this night. She brings us kai to eat.

We stayed beside the river for a long time, e pa. Then the lamps burnt out and there was no more oil. But the night was still bright with stars, like these stars shining, and there was a haze around the moon as there is around this moon glowing.

We go now, you said.

And we wandered through the bush, back to the road and along the road to the truck. I placed my hand in your hand and there was such calm just being with you. But still I was sad.

Sometimes, life is sad, you told me. Sometimes it is happy. But the world isn't happy all the time. You're still a child and I try to protect you from sadness. One day, you'll be a man. I cannot help you then. You're lucky, Son. If you have nightmares, you need only to wake up and they are gone. When you're a man, sometimes life has its nightmares. And you cannot awaken from life. You remember that. Life is sometimes sad. But it is happy too. If sad things happen, you be calm. Be patient. The happiness will come again.

A star falls from the sky, blazing a brief trail of light across the night. The plane dips and sways again, buffeted by the night wind.

A star fell too, that night, e pa. While we were walking back to the truck, I saw it pencilling a long white arc across the sky.

Look! I said.

But you were too late. You saw a long road of stars, but not that one star falling.

I crossed my fingers, and wished. You laughed, amused.

My strange Tama! you grinned. Tell me . . .

You're not allowed to tell what you wished, I told you. If you do, they don't come true.

Still a child, still a child, you whispered.

E pa, I am alone now and still a child. I will be patient and calm, as you were calm. Let the nightmare of your tangi be over quickly, e pa. Life, bring me happiness again. Let the laughter come again soon.

The wings of the plane dip. The engine hums more softly. The air hostess breaks her conversation with the woman next to me.

— We're beginning our descent to Gisborne airport now, she says. We'll just check that your safety belt is fastened, shall we?

— Oh, yes please! the woman says.

— Yes, that's all right, the air hostess says. And you, Sir? Fine! She smiles and begins to walk along the aisle, checking the other passengers.

— Could you put your cigarette out now, Sir? Thank you. Yes, Madam, we'll be at Gisborne soon.

The plane begins to descend toward the dark clouds. Far ahead, the clouds are hazy with the lights of Gisborne.

And suddenly it is that night again, and I am walking with father along a silver road.

— I'll race you, Tama!

— Okay! But you better give me a head start, Dad.

He nods. I run down the road a way.

— Ready? he calls. Here I come!

I begin to run. There is a slight breeze. It cools my face. I can hear Dad laughing behind me.

— Here I come!

I try harder, forcing my legs to run quicker. But father passes me. He rushes down the road, between the rustling shadows of a cluster of willows.

— Come on, Son! Catch me!

He fills the air with his breathless laughter. I try to catch up to him. But he begins to disappear into the distance.

— Dad, wait for me! I laugh.

He is a shadow on a shadowed road.

— Dad, wait!

— Come on, Son!

I begin to panic. The stars crackle and whirl in the sky. Dad is too far away to hear me, running on into the darkness, his footsteps sounding like a clock ticking away, away, away . . .

I close my eyes, trying to forget.

E pa, I was frightened when you ran from me. My heart raced with fear, because I was alone. The darkness closed with clouds, and I ran and ran, but couldn't catch you. Where were you, e pa? Where?

You caught up to me in the end, Son. I was waiting for you at the truck.

I know, e pa. I wasn't frightened anymore, because you were there. E pa, this is a different road now. I am a night traveller and this is my journey beginning. I am not a child but a man. Yet I am still afraid. And the road unwinds its shadows before me . . . Don't go away, e pa.

The plane rocks more violently.

— Oh, dear! the woman gasps, clutching me. I feel so strange! She giggles again.

— I'm awfully sorry! she says.

103

— That's okay, I answer.

E pa, wait for me . . .

The plane descends and suddenly we are through the clouds. The window streaks with raindrops flicking away into the night. Far below is the sea, like a sheet of tin made silver by the moon, rippling with silver. And nestling in the bay is Gisborne, dripping with gleaming lights.

Almost there, e pa. Soon, e pa.

My heart sorrows again. My body is numb with its aching.

— Oh, isn't it beautiful!

The woman cranes her head toward the window.

— Yes, I answer.

— So beautiful.

The city is like a shimmering necklace curving around the bay. The streets are beaded with yellow lights. The centre of the city is a cluster of gems, spilling outward toward the hills. And as the plane circles toward Gisborne, the lights leap up as if this is the entrance to Rarohenga . . .

There, father is waiting for me. At the gateway, looking back.

E pa, I come. I come to farewell you and then to return to the road unending. If I could, I would be Maui who tried to bring immortality for all men. Accompanied by the Piwakawaka and other birds, he passed through the gateway into Rarohenga. He sought out Hine-nui-te-Po, where she slept in her meeting house, Wharaurangi. There, he planned to enter her body as she slept, and cut her heart out. But the Piwakawaka laughed and Hine-nui-te-Po awoke and crushed Maui.

> *I mate mai te rangi*
> *Ia Maui i komia*
> *e Hine-nui-te-Po,*
> *Waiho ki te ao, na i —*

> *Death came to the mighty*
> *When Maui was strangled*
> *by Hine-nui-te-Po,*
> *And so it remained in the world —*

E pa, I am not Maui. I cannot bring immortality to you. I

will weep as I turn away from the gateway. I will shed tears as I walk away. I will try to be calm. I will look after the family as you have taught me.

The hum of the plane whines lower and the earth rises. Ahead, the airport twinkles in the dark. Lining both sides of the runway are glowing lights. They are points of flame flickering.

— Is anybody meeting you? the woman asks.

— My sister, Mere.

Mere, I am coming. You see the plane lowering quickly from the sky and you are hiding your tears in the night. Don't weep, my sister. I'll soon be with you to look after you. I come to say: haere ra, e pa. After that, all my life I will look after you. My family, I am coming. Mum, I'll soon be with you. E pa, wait for me.

The plane glides lower. The wheels unfold beneath the wings. The landing lights flash on and off, on and off. And suddenly the runway leaps up and the shadow of the plane soars down to the tarmac. A sharp shriek of tyres, a jolt, and the plane rolls quickly between the flickering lights.

And tears spring suddenly to my eyes.

The plane taxies toward the air terminal. The passengers peer out into the cold night at the people huddled in the blazing light, waiting. Where are you, Mere?

— Well, we're here, the woman says with a sigh. On the ground. Goodbye.

— Goodbye, I answer.

The passengers begin to file out of the plane. I watch them as they step quickly across the tarmac toward the lights of the terminal building. They are shadows, moving into the light of another world. I unbuckle my seat belt and stand. My head whirls.

The air hostess smiles.

— Goodbye, Sir.

Almost there. Almost there. No time for tears. Father waits.

Mere, where are you?

The wind is cold. My body is numb. My feet click slowly across the tarmac into the arc of lights. People are milling at the gateway, greeting, laughing, and embracing one another.

Where are you, Mere?

One step. And one step further now.

Then I see her, coming out of the darkness.

Oh, Mere . . .

She walks toward me, through the milling people, through the laughing crowd, toward the gate.

Mere, don't weep. Almost with you now.

We see only each other. All these other people embracing and meeting one another are only shadows existing on the edge of our universe. I stumble through them. I walk along the barrier toward my sister. Her face is wet with tears.

— Aue, Tama . . .

She rushes into my arms. Our tears mingle with the falling rain.

Twenty-five

The sea is a strand of blue sparkling with the sun. The rays fall brilliantly upon the land, ropes of the net cast across the sun by Maui. On the other side of the train, a cliff face gleams.

Once, not long ago, the sea rushed over this land the train traverses. That cliff face felt the sting of the sea's spray. Then Ruaumoko awoke from the breast of Papatuanuku, and split the earth with his awakening yawn. With his fiery hands, he pushed up the land and toppled the city which has been rebuilt there.

Napier. With a hiss of steam, the train halts at the platform. Passengers alight, passengers depart. People rushing on the platform. Bags unloaded, luggage loaded. Passengers boarding the train. In the background, the city is strong with life.

Some day, my life too, will be rebuilt again.

A whistle blast. A voice over the loudspeaker announces the departure of the train. It is a long journey, this train journey to Wellington. It is just past midday; the train will not arrive there until late at night. Across this land of Te Ika a Maui it will roar, through Waipukurau, Palmerston North and small towns of this country. A long journey. But there is a longer journey ahead for me. A long road which I must travel alone.

The train thunders through the city. Houses have been built where the sea once was. A road runs where there was once no road. Farmland has been developed on the old sea bed. Passengers look out the windows upon the passing houses. The carriage is filled with their chatter and laughter. The houses form small clusters along the railway track. Then the clusters enlarge, thicken and expand around Hastings.

The train comes to another stop. The cycle of people departing and boarding the train begins again. A thousand destinies evolving like a wheel forever turning. Each destiny is separate and at different places of the wheel. Some rising; some falling. Mine is one of them.

The minutes pass, the clock shunts each destiny forward. More minutes gather on the faraway side of the hour.

Then away from Hastings the train rumbles. Past houses, parks, humanity blurring past. The passengers settle themselves for the long journey. The carriage hums with their quiet conversations. A chance meeting, perhaps. Introductions exchanged. A life enriched with a new friend. Laughter. Sadness. Life too, is people on a train . . .

The city recedes. The train travels through the greenstone country, taking me further away from the greenstone years of a boy with his father.

This sun, it is also the sun shining above Waituhi. The shadows will be falling there too, casting from the hills and slanting with the slow spinning downwards of the spokes of the sun.

The greenstone years. The greenstone country. Waituhi. On the outskirts of the whanau, there was a farm which finally became our own. And one night, while we were having kai in our home at Gisborne, Dad said to us:

— Kids, that farm we've been going to look at. It's ours now, ours.

The long heartbreaking life was over. No more gypsy life. No more moving from place to place and the endless packing and unpacking and the endless road to travel. Just once more, with happiness. This was our beginning again, different from all those other beginnings because we were going home. To a farm at Waituhi, our home. Still a lot of work to do and long days of hard work ahead. But home.

And there was that never to be forgotten first night when we stood in the doorway of the farmhouse. It was very old and dark. No windows were broken, there was a cooking range instead of an open fire, a floor with linoleum and carpet and not just one room but many rooms.

Dad lit the wick of an oil lamp and the kitchen glowed with soft light. Mum whispered:

— Oh, Rongo.

And she wandered slowly through each room, touching light to the lamps until the house glowed, room after room.

— Turi turi, Huia, Dad said to her.

— Oh, Rongo.

We followed Mum and Dad, and my sisters were very excited. They rushed from one room to another, bouncing on the beds, opening cupboards and wardrobes and yelling each new discovery to each other.

— Look, Ripeka! See what I've found!

— Mere, you come and try this bed. It's soft!

— Come on Tama! Come on Wiki!

After a while, Mum got tired of our shouting.

— Turi turi, you kids! she grumbled.

Then she told Dad to get some wood for the kitchen range and that she would make some kai because we hadn't had any tea. I went with him to the woodshed and held a lamp while he chopped the wood. When he'd chopped enough wood we went back inside. And there was Mum, scrubbing the kitchen floor.

— Oh, no! Huia! Dad moaned. Not tonight!

— Oh, yes, Rongo! Mum answered. You just get to scrubbing while I make the tea. And you kids start bringing in the blankets and pots from the truck. Plenty of work to do. We scrub the floors tonight and then tomorrow we see about getting some wallpaper, and we clean this house good and proper.

It was just like the old times, as if we'd arrived at another whare. But this time it was different, joyful and not heart-breaking. This was our home. And even though Mum made us stay up very late with the scrubbing, it was worth it just to see how the floor shone. Wiki went to bed early because she was too young to stay up. But she couldn't go to sleep. Every now and then, she'd peep through the door at us.

— I want to help, too, she'd wail.

— No, you go to sleep, Mum told her. Tomorrow, then you can help. Tomorrow.

— What about leaving the scrubbing for tomorrow? Dad grumbled.

Mum stood over him with her mop in hand.

— What did you say, Rongo Mahana? Ay?

And she squeezed the water over his head and laughed.

— Take that! Now get to it, man!

It was fun that night. Mum gave the orders and we obeyed them. She showed us our rooms: one for Ripeka and Mere, and my own for me. Wiki would sleep in Mum and Dad's room until she was older.

— Can't I have my own room too? Ripeka asked. The one at the end of the house?

— Later, Mum answered, unless you want to sleep with the spiders. Big hairy ones in that room.

Ripeka went quiet.

— All right, she said. Me and Mere, we sleep in that other room. No spiders in there, ay.

Ripeka, she didn't know that Mum was only kidding. Every now and then, she'd whisper to Mum.

— If there's spiders in that other room, are you sure there's none in mine and Mere's room, Mum?

— None there, Mum would answer.

— Are you sure?

— I'm sure.

— Really sure, Mum?

And in the end Dad had to go and make sure. Ripeka made him look everywhere: under the bed, behind the drawer, in all the corners. Only when she was satisfied that there were no spiders, did she let him go.

— I knew there weren't any, she said.

All this time Mum was shouting and giving orders: make the beds, get the pots, wipe the ledges, bring in the bags, hang your fullas' clothes up, sweep your floors, come and help lift this table . . . until it was finished. At least for that night anyway.

— Now, Mum pronounced, we go to bed.

We warmed our pyjamas by the kitchen range and had baths. Then we kissed Mum and Dad goodnight. Quite suddenly, I was very tired. But I couldn't go to sleep because I was so happy. I lay in bed, watching the warm glow of the lamp flickering across the ceiling. In the kitchen, I could hear Mum and Dad talking about tomorrow.

— Some material for curtains, Rongo. Some paint, a new carpet.

— Ae, Huia. All those things. And tomorrow, I'll take a look round the farm. The fences. The shearing shed. Later, we buy some sheep. Cattle sale soon, too.

— A pig, maybe some hens . . . You'll have to make a fowlhouse, Rongo.

— You and your fowls!

I heard them laughing and grumbling at each other and Mum started to weep.

— Rongo . . .

— What a tangiweto you are, Huia.

— Our own place.

Our own place. Not belonging to somebody else but to us. Tomorrow I would wake up early and go with Dad and feel the earth, our land, beneath my feet. I would see the sun soaring over our hills and feel the wind blowing across fields we would plough and grow with wheat. I would throw a stone over the river and let the water ripple over my hands. And I would help Dad make this land live. Maybe our relatives would help us too. This was our home, our family. Still a lot of work to do, as Dad said. The mortgage to be paid off. Many years of hard work ahead. Some of the trees round the house would have to be chopped down to let in the light. A fowlhouse to build. A new roof put on the shearing shed. Sheep and cattle to be bought. Seed to be planted. So many things to be done. Yes, my uncles, my family would help. This was Waituhi, our whanau, our family. And we had come home.

I lay there for a long time, looking at the lamplight flickering through the room. A moth came through the window, flitting from one patch of light to another, follow.ng the brightness as it flickered on the walls and ceiling. There, on one wall, I would start measuring how tall I was growing. The pencil marks would still be there in later years for me to see. On another wall, I would scrawl both sad and happy memories so that I'd always remember this beginning and this life. On a desk in the corner, I would pile my schoolbooks and it would become a bigger pile over the years. In the wardrobe I would hang my clothes and see them changing from schoolboy shorts to a young man's trousers. In this bed, my body would change, through adolescence to manhood. In the same way, my sisters would grow from young girls into women boys fought over. Ripeka would marry at twenty; Mere would forsake the chickens she used to bring in front of the kitchen range during winter when it was cold, for Koro her husband. Little Wiki, she would leave school early to go nursing in Auckland and there meet Matiu and marry him. And I would go to their weddings, just knowing that everybody would ask: E hara! Here's your young sisters getting married and what's wrong with you! You having too much of a good time in Wellington, ay?

All this would happen and much more. The roof would leak the first time it rained and we would place pots, pans and even cups under each leak while Mum growled Dad for not fixing the roof earlier. Bees would build a nest in the roof and we'd be stung every summer. Storms would come and after the storms, the heart-breaking work of setting the land right again. Mustering for the shearing. Shearing during the summer. Hard days of sweat and the drone of the handpieces in the shed. Helping Dad as I grew older. Ploughing the land. Going down to the river to fill tanks with water for the fields during droughts. Mum weeping over dying plants and the maize taking the moisture from her tears to grow again. Quarrelling with my sisters and even Mum and Dad. Going to school each day and then returning home to work late into the night, helping the farm grow.

Long years ahead, filled with aroha and momentary pain. Hone and Marama would be born and I would have the brother I always wanted. Sickness would come to my mother and leave her helpless in bed. Dad would be thrown from his horse and I would search through the rain for him, and see him crawling toward me, his leg broken. Ripeka would run away from home for a while and then a bus would come, and she would be home again.

This would be my life. Some pain, mostly happiness. But always, there would be Dad, at the centre of my world. He would be like the lamplight in this room and surround me with his calm. Sometimes, I would hurt him as I reached further toward my own life and into that other world outside the family. In the end, I would leave home for Wellington and stay there for a long time. And every visit home, he would have grown older without my realising it.

— You come home, ay? he would ask. You come home to your father. He needs you. He's getting old now.

He would ask; I would not listen. I'd return to Wellington. While I was away, he would die.

I look out the window of the train and it is a window upon that first night.

I lay awake and I was very happy, those many years ago. I heard Mum and Dad talking and laughing with one another and then the soft sounds of their readying for bed.

— Go to sleep, Tama! Dad growled. Lot to do tomorrow.

I couldn't sleep, not yet. The moth kept me company. Then it started to whir against the glass of the lamp. I turned it down and slowly the darkness fell. The oil burnt low, but the light still flickered with life. Not as harshly as the sun does this day. As I finally drifted off to sleep, my happiness curled round that flame and with a small whisper, snuffed it out.

E pa . . . You have gone from me and I am sad. If I could, I would turn back the clock. Back to those days so calm that the quarrels we did have seem never to have happened. If I could, e pa, if only I could. And we could walk together through the greenstone years again, along the road which runs through Waituhi our home. I see it now, e pa, as it was then and as it always will be.

Waituhi . . . It is the place of the heart. A Maori village a few miles from Gisborne. There are no shops, no reason at all for Waituhi to be here except that this is the hearth of the Whanau A Kai. This is their home and here they live.

A road runs through the whanau and the houses are strung like beads along the road. Some of the houses are very old, with paint peeling from the boards and rusting corrugated roofs. Others are State houses, shining and new. Some are just tin shacks, with newspaper and pictures from magazines as wallpaper. Dirt tracks lead from the road and along them live others of my family. Small wooden houses dot the fields. Some are hidden in tall waving maize. Others are clustered about with fruit trees and willows. On one side of Waituhi are the hills, pushing small spurs down toward the village. Upon them graze cattle and sheep. On the other side, the flat land rolls away to the river. The river has changed its course across this country many times. During the winter, it becomes swollen with silted water. But it does not overflow across the land as it once used to because not long ago, men came to control the river and created a new course for the ravaging water. From the road, you can still see the loops and bends of the old river bed, now green with pasture. This river, for me, is like that river which once flowed through Eden. And this place, Waituhi, is my Eden.

Just as there was a gateway to Eden, so also is there a gate to Waituhi. The road curves round a small hill where an old colonial home now stands. Once, there used to be a Maori stockade upon that hill. You can still see the terraces where the tall wooden fences used to be. Every day, returning from school in Gisborne, the bus passed by the hill. Eagerly, I would peer forward. The hill would slide past. The road would curve round it. There, in front, would be Waituhi. A small place.

At one bend, houses cluster near an old church. Dad and I would often walk along the road, past these houses. If we met anybody we would stop and talk. Sometimes, somebody would wave to us and we'd wave back. If it was twilight, always somewhere we'd hear a guitar being strummed. This was the Whanau A Kai. This was home.

On another bend in the road, is the meeting house, the house of the whanau. Rongopai. It is set near the side of a hill. Beside the meeting house is a tin cookhouse. Behind, there are fields, some covered with gorse. Rongopai. The meeting house of the Whanau A Kai.

People often pass by in their cars and never see Rongopai. For them perhaps, it is just another meeting house, decaying in the wind. But for me, Rongopai is like my father. Home. The place of the heart. The centre of my universe. And Dad would often take me there. He would unlatch the gate and we would stand before it, silent a moment. I would see the roof, sloping upward to the painted koruru at the apex and it would look as if it was holding up the sky. I would see the paint peeling from the panels of the maihi, the boards extending like arms from the koruru, to welcome me. Inside the porch, I would glimpse swirling kowhaiwhai designs and other painted decorations. This was the meeting house of my tupuna. And it was my meeting house too.

It was built for Te Kooti, Dad told me. That was long ago, even before Dad's time. The work was carried out by the young men, who painted it with bright swirling colours. It was one of the very few painted meeting houses remaining and still beautiful to look upon, despite the decay brought by wind, rain and sun. But when it was finished, the elders came and were shocked at what they saw. The young men, in decorating the house, had departed from the traditional designs. The old reverence and dignity had gone. In its place, the young men had blended both Maori and Pakeha art and scenes of life together. For the elders, this was not right. But you told me, Dad, that perhaps even then, the young men had seen that the old life was ending. And this meeting house for you, was a symbol of the twilight years of the Maori. As it had been foretold, so it had come to pass ... the shadow behind the tattooed face had come to claim the world.

> *Kei muri i te awe kapara he tangata ke,*
> *mana te ao, he ma.*
> *Shadowed behind the tattooed face*
> *a stranger stands, he who owns the earth,*
> *and he is white ...*

You said this with sadness, e pa, the very first time we visited Rongopai. With resignation, you told me that everything in this world decays and falls. I did not understand. Then you stepped onto the porch, unlocked the door and beckoned me inside. As I followed you, it seemed as if I was entering another world. There was no other light except that which streamed through the open door.

I gasped, e pa, at the sight of the house. I was filled with wonder. The panels were like tall trees, elaborately decorated, extending along both walls like a pathway into a forest. Some of the panels were painted with Maori designs and some with sinuous twining plants, like vines curling upward to the roof. Fantastic birds flew through that timeless forest and fruits and flowers seemed to open crimson petals to the light. People climbed among the branches and glittering creatures of another world soared upward to the rafters.

As I followed you into Rongopai, that world reached outward to enclose me. The floor was dirt and it seemed as if the panels were living trees, taking root there. Here was where my tupuna, my ancestors lived. You pointed them out to me, e pa, and showed me how the young men had changed tradition. On one panel, was an ancestor who wore in his hair not the royal huia feather but a Scotch thistle. On another, a young woman stood, timeless in a Pakeha gown, holding a rose to her lips. Strange animals appeared from amid the painted foliage. At a third panel, I knelt down to take a closer look at two men sparring in a boxing match. And there, on a fourth, horses gleamed as they lifted their hooves in a never-ending race. Right at the end of the building, figures reached out of the darkness to brandish taiaha and mere at me.

I held you tightly then, e pa. You laughed and told me not to be afraid. These were my people and this was my meeting house. This house and these people were glad that I had come, you said. I listened and it seemed as if I heard laughter, glittering like a waterfall in my ears . . . and I was not afraid.

And I looked up at the roof, my eyes following the glistening creatures as they slithered amid the stars of that woven sky.

We stayed there for a long time, e pa. I felt the heart beating in that house. You spread your arms and told me that all this was why the elders had prophesied that Te Kooti would never enter Rongopai. They made it tapu. Te Kooti never did visit Waituhi.

Then we left Rongopai. I watched as you closed the door. The light narrowed within the house and the forest plunged into darkness.

We turned and walked away. I looked back.

E pa, Rongopai, it was holding up the sky.

I walked that road many times during the greenstone years. The hill where there was the Maori stockade at the first bend. Rongopai at the second. At the third bend the tall ridge rising into the sky. Near the bottom, a monument and Takitimu Hall.

Here, on an occasional Saturday night, a dance was held or a wedding or a haka night. All Waituhi came, attracted by the sound and the lights blazing in the hall.

But my eyes look up to the top of the ridge . . . Here, near to the sky, the whanau dead are buried. This is the graveyard of all people in Waituhi. All my family . . . And when I was a boy, my sisters and I would run up the ridge and into the graveyard, to play with Rawiri, my brother who died when he was a baby. Mere would pick flowers for him. I would dig the weeds away from his grave. Ripeka would help me, and hold Wiki tightly in case she was afraid.

When I was older and working on the farm with Dad, we would sometimes go to the graveyard to cut the gorse away and mend the fence surrounding our family.

You could see all Waituhi from that hill. The road curving away and the houses of the whanau. And far away on the outskirts, was our farm and the farmhouse. Even from the hill, you could make out the gabled eaves and the verandah. Often I would go to the hill, just to sit and be content. This was my world, and the surrounding hills defined its limits. In winter, the mist cascaded down the hills or sleets of rain covered Waituhi with a gray haze. In summer, it seemed that my world extended as the hills receded into the sky. Spring brought green fields and crops of maize and the orchards grew ripe with fruit. Autumn was the season of falling leaves. But no matter what season, it seemed to me that Waituhi remained unchanged. Sometimes, when the sun was going down, the hills would be set alight with a coronet of fire. At such times, I would look at the lights of Waituhi and be calm. Far away, I would see the lamplight gleaming from our own house, and know I was not alone. And always, during the closing night, as I walked from the hill back home, there would be the sound of a guitar and a voice to sing my loneliness away.

> *Me, he manurere, aue,*
> *Kua rere tito, moenga,*
> *Ki te awhi toti, nana,*
> *Aue, aue, e te tota huri mai . . .*

The carriage fills with the strains of the girl as she strums idly on her guitar and sings quietly to herself. The train rocks and sways, as if to the rhythm of her song. This girl, she is recalling her own life with her Nanny. Her song also fills me with more memories, taunting and playful, of Waituhi my home. Some of the images are wistful and magical and as fleeting as the wind.

Of a gathering of Dad's family at the old homestead where his parents lived. All my aunties, uncles, cousins and friends were there. The men were preparing the hangi. The children yelled and played games among the flax bushes. My mother laughed with the women as they prepared the kai. My Nanny Puti had been brought onto the verandah into the sunlight. Perhaps she knew that this would be the last family gathering she would ever see for although she was smiling, her eyes were glistening.

A Maori hockey tournament at Waituhi. The teams coming from all over Poverty Bay, parading with self-conscious pride around the muddy field. Pennants fluttering in the wind. Auntie Ruihi hopping onto the field in her gumboots, her dress tucked into her pants, because the home team was short. Fierce games and humorous arguments. Roars of pleasure and displeasure from the side-line players. Goals scored and recounted with pride afterward. Myself playing against my father and his whispered words to me: You let your father get a goal, ay? He's old. You be a good son! And the laughter when Dad did get a goal: Hey, Tama! Don't let your old man beat you!

The close kinship of the shearing gang. Five o'clock starts, day after day through summer. The drone of handpieces. The bustle of women on the board. The cry of Sheepo! Hot dust. Somewhere, the clanking of the press. And listening to my cousin, Kopua, bragging as he sheared: I was born to this game!

Maori action songs at Takitimu Hall. The thunderous applause and yells for a number well sung. The swishing and crackling of the piupius. The quivering of hands moving in unison. Then the stamping feet of the men as they moved through the ranks, chanting the haka:

> Ko Ruaumoko e ngunguru nei!
> Au! Au! Aue ha!

And standing beside father, grinning at him: Come on, old man! Lift those feet! Not enough kaha!

A dance at Patutahi. Myself and Kopua standing near the door, eyeing the girls as they walked past. Which one do you want, coz? he says. That one there, in the red dress, I answer. Eee, that hakuri thing! he laughs. Then, when we'd picked the girls we'd wanted, joining the other Waituhi crowd, embarrassed because we didn't know how to dance . . .

A party at Nanny Whiti's home. The beery songs echoing through the darkness. People going, people coming, people passing out. Nanny Whiti saying to me: Come on, nephew, have a glass, I won't tell your father. Come on, it'll make you a man! And

arriving home after the party, drunk. And Mum waiting for me:
You just go and sleep with the dogs, tonight, Tama Mahana!
I'm not having a drunk in this house. And afterwards, being sick:
Good ay, Tama! Have some more of the pirau! And next day,
hearing Nanny Whiti say to me: Boy! How does your old man put
up with your mother! She really gave it to me because I made you
drunk last night!

Waituhi ... It was the close kinship the whanau shared with
one another so that we never lived apart from each other. And
Ripeka used to moan that everybody knew each other's business,
even before they did themselves. It was big family with big heart,
laughing and squabbling, then laughing again. It was helping
each other with money or in the fields. It was growing up with
uncles, aunties and cousins as one family.

It was keeping open house, too. If anybody didn't have a home,
you invited them in. Kopua came to stay with us for a month
because his mother had kicked him out of her house. I went to
stay at Uncle Pita's after a party one night, scared that Mum
would smell the beer on me. The next day I sneaked home but
Mum was waiting for me: Boy, you're just like your father, don't
know where your home is.

I got a big wallop from her. She still had a big hand and Dad
shrugged his shoulders and said: That's love, Tama. That's love.

Waituhi, the place of the heart. When you went out getting
kina and paua at Makarori Beach, you stopped off at other houses
to ask if anybody else wanted to come with you. When you returned
home, you told everybody to come to your place and have a good
kai. If somebody got married, you didn't wait for an invitation,
you just went to the wedding, because you were a member of the
family. And if there was a tangi, you stopped whatever you were
doing, no matter if you were working in some flash factory or at
some flash job, and you went home to help out. One of the family
had died and the tangi, it was the homecalling.

Waituhi is family. The whanau is my home. The love and affection
they hold for each other are the ridgepoles of my heart. The sharing
and enjoying of each other are the rafters. And within those walls
and roof, my heart is shared with my whanau, so closely inter-
twined, that even now, I pine for home.

Taku manawa, a ratou manawa.

My heart is their heart. And their heart is mine. I am their father, son and friend. They too, are my mothers, fathers, sons and friends. Away from them. I feel lost. Away from the heart I am lonely. But soon I will return. This train takes me further away from Waituhi. I will walk the streets of Wellington and I will be sad. Then I will return home, still lonely, because Dad has gone from me. Mere will be waiting for me as she was the night I returned home to farewell my father.

Kua mate taku papa.

Twenty-six

— Kia kaha, Mere.

I clasp my sister tightly, as I must clasp all my family now.
Together we must build a new world. Around us, the passengers
from the plane laugh and talk with the friends who have come to
meet them. They mill round the doorway to the terminal
building.

— I'm here, Mere. Hush now. Don't cry.

Mere weeps on my shoulder. I could almost believe she is a
little girl again bringing her tears to me. Behind her in the
shadows, Koro waits, holding Kararaina, their baby. She is
bundled in a blanket and he raises it to protect her from the cold
wind. For a little while longer I hold my sister. Then gently I
break our embrace.

— My Mere, my sister, you're still a tangiweto . . .

She lifts her head. Her face is gaunt with grief. Her sad sighs
are the winds gathering round a hill at Waituhi. She brushes at my
own tears. I kiss her gently and put my arms around her.

— We go now.

Together we walk toward Koro.

— Tena koe, Tama.

— Tena koe, Koro, Kei te pehea koe?

— Kei te pai, kei te pai.

Little Kararaina starts to cry. Mere takes her from Koro and
whispers to her.

— Say hello to Uncle, Kara.

She is too tired. She puts her hands round Mere's neck and goes to sleep again.

— It's been a long day for her, Tama.

— A long day for all of us, Mere.

— You brought any luggage?

— Ae. A suitcase.

Mere turns to Koro.

— You get Tama's bag. We'll wait in the car.

I wink at Koro.

— Mere, she's just like Mum, I tell him. Always giving orders.

We laugh together. Then Mere and I walk toward the car. I open the back door and Mere lays Kararaina down, carefully folding the blanket over her so she won't get cold.

— We all sit in the front, Mere says to me.

I put my hand on her puku.

— Be a bit of a squeeze won't it? You're getting fat again.

— It's that Koro! she moans. He won't leave me alone. Don't you worry, we'll fit. Haere mai.

I shut the door. We wait for Koro. Mere starts to weep again. I put my arms round her. Dad used to cradle his children in this manner when they'd fallen asleep at a hui. No matter how tired his arms, he would have cradled us all like this even if the world was ending. He was a Kauri, my father. If there were storms I would shelter beneath his wide-spreading branches. But lightning has struck the tree. It has toppled to the ground with a cracking and splintering of branches. And I have no shelter now.

— Aue, Tama . . . Mere weeps. Dad, he was just lying there in the bedroom. Ripeka and Mum were with him, and Mum was stroking his hair. Me and Koro, we didn't know until late this morning. We were out at Mangatu and Ripeka had been trying to get hold of us all morning. Then Uncle Pita came to tell us.

I hold my sister closely.

— Koro reckons I went crazy. He says I screamed and when he tried to calm me I started to hit him and claw him. And Uncle, he was scared I might lose this baby I'm carrying. But I said I didn't care, I didn't care about anything or anybody, just Dad. I just wanted Dad.

I try to comfort my sister. In the back seat Kararaina stirs.

— We went to Waituhi straight away. Didn't even have time

to get changed. We still had our shearing clothes on. And I rushed from the car and Ripeka was waiting at the door and I said to her: Where's Dad, I want to see Dad . . . I pushed her away and ran into the bedroom and . . . Oh, Tama, he was just lying there, just lying there. And I don't know what I did or what I said, only that I cried out his name and held him to me. I wanted to die too, Tama. I just wanted everybody to leave me alone so that I could die too . . .

— Mere, be calm now, Mere, I whisper to my sister.

— He was so good to us, ay, she weeps, He was so good, and I kept on remembering how I used to be awful to him. All the quarrels we used to have and all the ways I used to hurt him.

— Don't think like that, Mere, I whisper. Turi turi.

But she still weeps, remembering.

— Tama, even now my heart is aching for Dad. It was horrible to see him lying there like that. Mum, she was sitting beside him, stroking his hair. Some of the kuias were there too, kneeling on the floor and wailing softly. Auntie Ruihi, she came over to me and we wept together. Mum started to cry too. So we held each other and I told her not to worry. She was sort of whimpering and I didn't know what to do except hold her and tell her I was there. All the time, more people were coming into the room, whispering to each other. Then Uncle Pita came in, and told Auntie Ruihi that we better get the body ready because he wanted to take Dad to Rongopai. She told Mum and Mum started shaking her head. She told them: No. She wouldn't let them touch Dad. And Uncle Pita, he shouted at her and said: Huia, it has to be done . . . But you know how stubborn Mum is. She said to them to get out. And Ripeka and I, we saw her shivering with anger. We calmed her down. It took a long time. After a while, she just went limp. She looked at me and Ripeka and tried to smile. And she whispered to us: You kids, you help me with your father. He doesn't want these other people to touch him. You help me, ay? So Ripeka and I nodded and we asked everybody to leave the room. Oh, Tama . . . Ripeka and I, we didn't know what to do. And Mum, she was suddenly so calm. She told Ripeka to wet some towels and bring a basin of water. Then we helped her undress Dad. He was so heavy, Tama . . . And Ripeka and I were crying. Mum yelled at us: Stop it! There was such anger in her voice. Then she turned away from us and began to talk to Dad, in Maori, so we wouldn't understand what she was saying. But I caught some of what she said. She was telling him not to fight her, to make his body loose. And as we washed him with the towels, she told him how she loved him, had always loved him, and why did he have to leave her? She didn't want him to go away, she told him. Why, Rongo, why? she kept asking. Ripeka and I, we couldn't help it, Tama the tears just came. But Mum didn't seem to know we were there. She just kept whispering to Dad, and loving him.

Mere's voice breaks.

— We dressed him after that. Dad, he'd gone loose for us. He wasn't heavy any more. Then Mum brushed his hair and kissed him. She smiled at us and said: Ripeka, Mere, you've both done well. And then she told us to leave her with Dad for a while. She wanted to be alone with him. So we went out, but even through the door we could hear her weeping and saying Dad's name over and over again: Oh, Rongo, Rongo, Rongo . . . And while we were waiting, Uncle Pita told us the hearse had arrived. I looked outside and I could see it just by the gate, all black and shiny, and people crowded round it. And the men, they were taking the casket out. Tama! It was horrible . . . Uncle went into Mum and closed the door. We heard her screaming in there, screaming at Uncle in Maori. And Uncle, he must have gotten angry at her too and I think he must have slapped her to make her come to her senses. Then there was silence. And Mum came out, holding tightly to Uncle, and she wouldn't look when the men brought the casket in. She just sat there, with the women. Then the men came out of the room where Dad was and said we could go in and see him. The women started wailing. We took him to Rongopai this morning . . .

I hug my sister close to me. Koro comes to the car with my suitcase. He puts it in the boot and steps into the car. He sees Mere weeping.

— Is she all right? he asks.

I nod.

— It's rough on her, she loved Dad so much.

— It's been rough on all of us, he answers.

He starts the car and switches on the lights. The night is filled with rain. The car draws away from the air terminal, the windscreen wipers flicking back and forth across the window. The world with my father is soon ending. A lifetime . . .

It is the world gone full circle. Yet, some time, the world must turn again. Another hour must begin, the hands moving away from the hour gone. A sun explodes, another brightens the sky forming nova. A new day. From the ruins of an old life, a new life must rise. Some day.

E pa, for you, I will build life anew. For Mere, for all my family, I will build a good life.

The lights of the air terminal recede. The car turns through Te Hapara. Mere becomes calm and together we watch the rain falling. Kararaina cries in her sleep. I look back at her to see that she's all right. I see a pile of clothes stacked against the back window.

— Are you staying out at Waituhi, Mere?

She nods.

— We've been round home collecting our things. Ripeka and Hata are already out there. Wiki and Matiu should arrive from Auckland sometime tomorrow.

The car turns onto the main road out of Gisborne. The headlights swing upon empty fields and point into the country.

— Ripeka and I, Mere continues, we went out to the house this afternoon after Dad had been taken to Rongopai. We went with Mum. She wanted us to help her pack Dad's things and she didn't want to be alone. All of his belongings, they have to be buried with him, ay. We took his photos from the walls. Even Dad's trophies, the ones he won at hockey and football, we had to get them too. And Mum, she kept on saying to us: See this one? He won that at Hamilton. This one he got at the tennis tournament at Poho-o-Rawiri . . . She's taking it hard, Tama. Later, she packed his clothes, all his things, and she was crying. Everything of Dad's is all gone from the house. All gone . . .

— And Mum, how is she now, Mere?

— Still the same, Tama. She's at Rongopai, sitting with Dad, at Rongopai . . .

— And the kids? Marama and Hone?

— They're scared, Tama. They don't understand. They just hold tightly to Mum, and they look at Dad and they don't understand. You'll have to tell them about Dad. I tried, but I couldn't tell them. I didn't know how, and I didn't know what to say. They cry. They don't know what being dead means.

Mere brushes at her tears. Koro looks at her and reaches out to press her hand. And the car swerves.

— Koro! You just watch the road! Mere says.

Then quickly, she presses his hand.

— I'm sorry, Koro . . . Don't you leave me, don't you leave me . . .

She is like a little girl, looking into his eyes.

He smiles at her.

— E hara! he whispers. What's wrong with you! I'll never leave you, you got all my money in your bank book.

Mere tries to laugh.

— Yeah, and I'll spend the lot if you don't watch out.

The car passes through Makaraka. The hotel is bright with lights and there is a burst of sudden laughter as we pass. Laughter and joy. That is not the world I know.

I watch the darkness, and it unfolds like a dream before me. I could almost believe that this was our family's old truck, and Dad was driving, and those headlights shining are the lights seeking the way home to the farm. And Dad and I are laughing and . . .

But Dad is dead. I look ahead, and there is only this night not any other night. I see Matawhero blur past through the rain. Dad used to sell his stock at the sale yards there. All those days, they're gone now.

E pa, there is only this darkness for me. The long Po has fallen, for you have taken the light with you. Let there be light again for me . . . Tears, do not fall. Heart, do not thunder so. Let me have peace from my sorrow.

Mere whispers to me.

— Tama . . .

— I'm all right, Mere. I'm okay.

We sit in silence for a while. The car crosses a long concrete bridge and on the other side of it, roads fork in different directions. We take the road to Patutahi. The windscreen wipers swing back and forth across the dark night.

— How are things at Rongopai? I ask.

— Everything's just about ready, Mere answers. The people at Waituhi have been working flat out all day. Uncle Pita's been in charge of everything, organising things. I don't know what we would have done if he wasn't there. He got some of the boys to put up a marquee near the meeting house. That's where the people who come to the tangi will sleep. Uncle, he reckons a lot of people will be coming. Everybody's been pitching in, ay Koro.

— Ae, Koro answers. We just dropped everything. Me and some of the boys went out pig-hunting to get some pigs for the hangi. A lot of people to feed for three days. Henare Tipene, he gave us a sheep. And your Dad's shearing gang, they dubbed in some money to buy tinned food.

— And Ripeka, Mere continues, she told Hata he better get the cookhouse ready.

— We're going out again tomorrow, pig-hunting, Koro says.

— Everybody's been busy, Tama, Mere tells me. Hay to get for the marquee. Blankets. Some of the people will sleep at Takitimu. That's where the people will be eating too. Uncle Wiremu and our cousins, they dug the pits for the hangi. When everybody found out about Dad they all came to help. Lots of spuds to peel. Just about all the women, even old Nanny Kiri came to the hall. And all the time, the trucks were arriving and more people were coming with more potatoes and pumpkins and mutton and . . . Aue, my hands are still sore . . .

— Lots of people coming, Koro continues. Lucky that the weather's been good for most of the day. It was hard enough getting the marquee up as it was. It'll be good and dry in there tonight. It only started raining this afternoon. We got the marquee up and the straw laid down for the people to sleep on, just in time. Ae, lots of people will come.

— Dad was a good man, that's why, Mere says fiercely. That's why all those people are coming. Even all Mum's family, they're coming too. Already there's some people at the meeting house come to see Dad and . . .

Mere starts to weep again.

— Tama, everybody's been so good to us. And they bring money or kai to help us out. Uncle Wiremu, he gave Mum his pay this week. Mum, she said: Never mind, you keep it for your family. But he told her not to be hoha and take it or else! Even Auntie Arihia, you know how flash we used to think she was, she even came down to the Hall. And she yelled out: Where's a knife, somebody give me a knife, I'll show you fullas how to peel spuds! And she sat down with us in her neat clothes and she was weeping and crying, but she wouldn't stop. And she got a ring from John. He said she had to come home, she had to come home. Auntie Arihia, she got wild and told him to go to hell, she wasn't coming home for him, there was too much work to do here.

— Even Auntie Arihia is at the Hall?

— True, Tama. She got the boys to set up the trestles in the Hall, she organised lots of things we'd never thought about like the crockery and knives and forks and things. You know Auntie Arihia, we always used to think she never swore. But she did! She kept everybody going, and she really ripped into some of the boys when she saw them being lazy. Afterward, I went up to her and I told her: Auntie, I never used to think much of you. And she started to cry.

— A lot of work been done today, Koro says. A lot of people pitching in. It didn't take long for Uncle Pita to get a gang out for the pig-hunting. He didn't even have to ask. The boys just came and said they'd give a hand. We went out the back of Te Karaka, but when I left them, they hadn't caught anything. They must be still out there, somewhere . . .

— Yeah, Mere says, digging him in the ribs. And you were late coming to pick me up. You stop off at the pub somewhere ay?

— Me? Koro answers. How can I when you got all our money! We smile at each other.

— Never mind, I tell them. At least you got to the airport on time and were there to meet me. If you hadn't been, I don't know what I would have done . . .

— Tama, Mere whispers. Kia kaha.

The car turns at the crossroad which leads to Patutahi. On the other side of it, a few miles further on, is Waituhi. Where father waits. Already I see him, lying on the marae at Rongopai. In my mind I see the meeting house ablaze with light. Mum is watching over Dad. Marama and Hone are with her. Some of the kuias are there too, ready to welcome the mourners whenever they come. Forms have been placed outside the meeting house on both sides of it. There, people are sitting, weeping and remembering Dad. Their tears mingle with the falling rain. And often, they lift their faces into the light shining from beneath the eaves of Rongopai where father lies, to call to him.

Further down the road, Takitimu Hall is being made ready for feeding the people who will come to the tangi. Uncle Wiremu is tending the hangi. The women are bustling in the Hall, preparing the food. In many of the houses, more women are making paraoa rewana and baking.

The lights are on in Waituhi and people run through the mud and rain busying themselves for the tangi. There is so much to do that there is little time to weep. It is best to keep on doing something, anything, to keep the grief away.

Aue. Aue . . .

This is the cry of sadness.

Aue. Aue . . .

This is the keening of women on the marae, waiting to welcome the visitors to the tangi.

Aue. Aue . . .

And this is the cry of my own heart breaking. E pa, he has gone from me. I am alone. For three days, I will see him lying still on the marae. For three days, I will remember how good he was to me. Then on the third day, he will be buried on the Hill.

Aue. Aue . . .

The call has gone out across this land. The tangi, it is the home-calling. This night the whanau are returning to Rongopai. My sister, Wiki, and her husband. All my uncles and aunties, all my big family, they come. E pa, I am coming too. Almost with you now . . .

Patutahi glimmers and fades past. The car crosses a small bridge. The road stretches away in front of me, endless and unending, toward Waituhi, where father waits. Above, in the night sky, the moon appears, wan and sliding between the dark clouds.

This is the night of my childhood ending. This is the night of my own life beginning. Father is dead and I am at once a man. So many things have been left undone by father. So many things to do now that he has gone. The calm of my life has been altered; my days shall be darkness until that time when I can fuse my world together again. I am the eldest.

The car lurches round a bend in the road. Kararaina wakes up and begins to cry. She lifts her hands into the air, wanting to be picked up. I reach over and get her.

— Turi turi, Kara, I whisper. It's all right.

But she just looks at me as if I was a stranger and reaches out for Mere.

— She doesn't remember me, I tell Mere.

— You've been gone from home a long time, Mere answers. She begins to soothe Kararaina, making soft sucking noises.

— What's wrong, baby? You done a mimi? No. Don't be scared. See your uncle? Kiss Uncle, give him a big kiss now.

Kararaina lifts up her head for a kiss.

— That's a good girl! Mere says. Your uncle, he's come all the way from Wellington! A long, long way! He's come home . . . No more cry now. Everything's all right.

The moon disappears behind a cloud. Darkness looms. Then there is the moon again, and the road curving round a hill, the hill of the Maori stockade . . .

— Aue, Mere . . .

— Kia kaha, Tama. Be strong.

And suddenly, the lights of Waituhi appear, streaming down the windscreen like falling stars. Mere clutches my hand. She looks up at me and the moon gleams in her tears.

— Tama.

I look ahead at the road. My heart is filled with sorrow. My tears fall quickly, and in my mind pictures of my father flicker. E pa . . .

The church spins past. The houses spin past. A group of people walk down the road, toward the marae. They step aside to let the car pass. The headlights swing over them as they clutch at their coats against the rain.

Ahead, the night opens. In a widening cleft of dark, Rongopai appears. The marae has been strung with electric lights. The gateway is open. People are huddled in the rain looking upon my father.

E pa, why have you gone from me? Why have you left me? Kauai koe e haere, e pa. Don't go away.

I close my eyes, tightly, tightly closed. For this is just a dream and when I open my eyes, father will be there to smile at me and open his arms to me. He will say: I knew you would come home, Son. I knew you'd come home to help me. And we will embrace one another. Then he will laugh and say: Come on then! Now

131

that you're home, there's plenty for you to do. No rest for my son! And I will answer: What's wrong with you, old man! And he will smile, and he will say: My son, I knew you'd come home . . .

All this will happen when I open my eyes. When the car slows down, when it stops bumping and swaying over the rough ground, I will open my eyes and see him, and I will be with him again. We will embrace one another and I will tell him: E pa, I'm home now.

The car has stopped. Now I will open my eyes.

So much light, so much blinding light. Where are you, e pa? I've come home to you. Mere, where's Dad? Mere?

— Tama. Dad, he waits.

Yes, Mere, I know. But where? And why am I weeping? I should be happy. Dad, he will come and he will say to me . . .

Koro opens the door. I step out. For a moment there is silence. I wipe my tears away. The rain stops. Then the wind moans. The women begin to wail, welcoming me. My heart bursts with sorrow. I lift my eyes and I see him.

— E pa . . .

And one step further now.

Twenty-seven

You are alone.

· Behind you all is darkness. In front of you the light blazes on the marae. See how the light arcs on the ground and diffuses into the night. Here you stand, still in the darkness. Perhaps you can turn away. No, it is too late. The kuias raise their arms beckoning you forward. Listen: the sound of their wailing is like a soft wind whispering.

Haere mai ki o tatou mate e.

Do you know what they say?

Come to our dead . . .

So take one step forward. There is no escaping the sorrow of the marae.

Haere mai ki o tatou mate e.

The cry echoes across the marae. The kuias are opening their voices to you. They fill the darkness with their keening. The sound grows louder and in its spiralling flight it gathers other carolling voices. Higher and higher it spirals, louder and louder, like voices caught in a whirlwind.

Your tears fall. The wailing has opened up your heart and you remember your father.

Come to our dead. Come. Come.

No, don't force the memories back. Let them come to you with their whispers of the good times you shared together. He was a good man. He lived only for you. Now he is gone. Remember him and weep.

Haere mai ki o tatou mate e.

Listen to the wailing. Why do you hold back the memories? Let them flow as your tears flow. And as you remember, call out to him.

— E pa. E pa.

And one step further now.

Rongopai rises up before you. The roof holds up the night. It is an old meeting house, painted with swirling colours. Beneath the eaves, the light blazes brightest of all. There, your father lies. Don't be afraid. This is the longest journey of all. It is the loneliest of journeys. Haere mai. Haere mai. Step into the light. Come.

On both sides of the marae the mourners are watching you. You must not falter. You must be proud. Step boldly, step firmly. Come.

Come to our dead . . .

Look: the kuias, the old women, assemble in the light and cast a shadow upon the marae. Their faces are veiled in shadows. Upon their heads they wear plaited wreaths of kawakawa leaves. They have threaded their gowns with sprigs of greenery. And in their outstretched hands, they wave small green branches.

Haere mai ki o tatou mate e.

The women moan and sway in time with the wailing. Their bodies quiver, their hands quiver, and the green branches cast fleeting shadows. This is the aroarowhaki, strange and tremulous, the giving up of the body to grief.

Come to our dead.

The faces of the kuias are filled with sorrow. For three days they will sorrow and the lines in their faces will grow deep with grief. Their eyes will be heavy-lidded with wanting to sleep. But always, they will watch over your father. They will not sleep. Every visitor to this marae will be welcomed in this same manner.

They will call and they will say: Haere mai. Come. Look upon our son where he lies. Share your grief with us. We are alone now.

You are alone too. It is too late to tell your father how much you loved him. All those words, soft and beautiful, will never be said.

Haere mai ki o tatou mate e.

Look: a woman steps forward from the ranks of the kuias. Listen: she begins to sing a lament. Her voice quivers like the outstretched branches she holds in her hands, then soars alone and disconsolate above the wailing. The waiata tangi; the song of sorrow.

> *Haruru ana*
> *Te Tiro a Whiro*
> *Taia ake ahau e te mate*
> *I muri nei ei.*

It is not the wind whispering; it is not the wind changing. It is a plaintive voice soaring.

> *Death comes, but I am*
> *not yet dead.*
> *I breathe, I live.*

Her voice sings above the marae, curling and fluttering like a wounded bird. She calls to others and from the darkness other voices come like a rush of wings to join in her lament. Listen: the words express the sorrow of this gathering. Your father has left them. This night is like the sea and they are gulls wheeling and crying above the waves, dazed and bewildered because he has gone. Open your heart. Let your sorrow too, wing upward to join with their sorrow.

> *I breathe, I live,*
> *I call ...*
> *But there is no sound.*
> *The tide ebbs silently away.*

Join them; call with them. Your father was their brother, son, and friend, not only your father. They were his family. Now that he is gone, they weep. Don't brush your own tears away. There is no shame in weeping. Let them fall, let them fall.

This lament brings you memories of your father. It sings of happy days when you were a child and he was with you. You trusted in him. If you were afraid, you went to him and your fear went away because he was there. You often played together: childish games at the beach or beside a river or at home before you went to bed. Wherever he went, you wanted to go. Sometimes he took you with him and you were glad. But sometimes you had to stay home and look after your mother and sisters. You were proud of him, and you wanted him to be proud of you. And you wanted to be like him, only like him.

> *Memories rise in the still air*
> *Like smoke from many fires.*

They were good days. There seemed nothing to fear as long as he was there. You were content. If there was a storm, you used to look out the window at the rushing clouds and the trees bending in the wind, and yet you would be calm because he was there. At night, if you were afraid, you needed only to call to him and he would come. He was always there when you needed him. Your life with him was a summer without end.

> *Kua makariri ke*
> *te okiokinga puehe kau?*

Now he is dead. Life has changed; winter has come. Although you are almost a man now you grieve like a child for him. You never thought that he could die. Sometimes, you were so interested in your own life you forgot that he was there. Perhaps you even thought you didn't need him. Now, you are alone. And you sorrow not only for him, but for yourself too. With his death, the world has changed for you.

> *Is this the same place,*
> *This place of ashes?*

Look around you: you know this place well. This is Rongopai, your meeting house. This is the house of the Whanau A Kai and this is Waituhi their home. You have happy memories of this place. Now it seems different, as if all happiness has fled away from here with your father and left only this darkness. And with this darkness come dark hours and you are bewildered by the sorrow they bring.

Pumau tonu atu
te rere anga awa
te tonga o te ra
nga maunga tu noa.

All the world should end now that your father is dead; but it is only your world which ends. Elsewhere people are laughing and enjoying life. Why is this so? There should be no happiness now that he has gone.

> *Yet the stream still runs*
> *And the sun rides over the sky*
> *And the mountains*
> *Are always there.*

No, the world does not end. Night still comes and after night, the day. The procession of days, seasons and years continues. You still live, you still breathe. He is gone, you are still here, to remember him and sorrow for him.

And one step further now.

Wait ... A voice rings across the marae above the wailing. The wailing fades away.

Haere mai, haere mai, haere mai.

The voice thunders again. And there, your grandfather is coming out of the night onto the marae. Your father was his son. He weeps now that his son is dead. He comes to you and calls to you and his voice is broken with grief. Then he rests and lowers his head. For a moment he is silent. Then he looks up, with dignity, and his body straightens.

— Haere mai taku mokopuna. Haere mai to koutou papa. Haere mai ki Rongopai. Haere mai ki te Whanau A Kai. Haere mai ki o tatou mate e ...

The words are phrased with ancient dignity. They ring the air with pride and sadness.

— Welcome, mokopuna. Welcome to your father. Welcome to Rongopai. Welcome to the Whanau A Kai. Welcome to our dead. You have journeyed a long way to honour your father. He sees you and he is proud. We too, have come to farewell him. We say

138

to him: Go now, e Rongo, travel from this place, haere ra e Rongo. His journey is a long one. He is sad to go and we are sad to see him leave us. But dying is a part of life. When we are born, we die too. Kia kaha, mokopuna. Have courage, mokopuna. There is a gap in the world now that he is dead. But we weep with you, all of us here, and you are not alone. Kia kaha. Kia kaha . . .

Your grandfather weeps to himself. Your Auntie Arihia moves toward him, but he gestures her away. She is afraid because he is a sick man. Then he begins to speak again. He turns to the assembly and addresses them.

— Tenei tangata, he tangata pai . . .

This man, he was a good man. He was a good son not only to me but also to the Whanau A Kai. He was quick to comfort, slow to anger. He was my eldest son and all of you here were his children. His aroha for you was boundless. He gave you love when you needed it, help when you asked for it. He did all things with aroha. To manawa, tona manawa; tona manawa, to manawa. His heart was your heart; your heart was his heart . . .

The mourners nod at the words of your grandfather: Ae, ae, they say. And they recall past memories of your father. There, brushing at her tears, is Auntie Hine. She is your father's cousin and she remembers how he looked after her when she was a young girl. Over there is Uncle Wiremu, the youngest of the brothers, recalling the times your father helped him and how good it was to be protected by him. Erana Tipene, she remembers how your father used to come and see that she was all right and that she had enough money to feed her children after her husband died. They remember and are sad.

Your grandfather continues to speak of your father. He was not a selfish man, your grandfather says. He gave his heart to the whanau, as was the Maori way. He was the shelterer from storms, the giver of food, a Kauri . . . And he spread wide his branches across the whanau to protect them from the wind and rain. That was why he was well loved, that was why his people mourned him.

— Aue, e Rongo . . .

Your grandfather calls to him. He turns to the meeting house where father lies and extends his arms to him.

— We are sad that you leave us, Son. We wait here, looking over you. And look how your own son comes to you . . .

His voice breaks with agony. His tears are bitter rain. Then he turns to you, your grandfather, and calls to you.

— Haere mai, haere mai, haere mai. Haere mai ki o tatou mate e. Haere mai to koutou papa . . .

Welcome, welcome, welcome, Come to our dead. Come to your father . . .

And one step further now.

But wait: your Uncle Pita has come to your side. He asks a question of you. You do not hear. He asks again. You nod and you hear yourself answering: Ae, uncle. You speak for me.

So lower your head now. Stand still and proud. And listen as your uncle speaks for you on the marae. Be calm.

He says you sorrow now that your father is dead. Your father gave you life and now your life has been taken away. You thank the assembly for sharing their grief with you. You thank them for the arrangements they have made for your father's tangi. You come to pay tribute to your father. He was a good man.

Your uncle's voice is soft and calm. And as he speaks, you weep.

Your father gave you everything, your uncle says. You owe him a great debt. When he lived you tried to make him proud of you. And you did make him proud. Now that he is dead, you weep. For without him, you must make your life alone without his aroha to guide you. Here, in sorrow you stand, and it is good to know that you do not stand alone.

The mourners look upon you and reach out to comfort you. Look up now and let them see your tears. They know how much you have loved your father; how deeply you grieve for him. Often they have seen you walking with him. Hear them as they whisper of their love for you: Tama, mokopuna, we grieve with you, and you are not alone. Kia kaha, our son. Kia kaha . . .

Your uncle grips your shoulders and smiles wanly at you. Then he resumes speaking.

— Aue, e konohi tana manawa. Aue, e konohi tana ropi. Ae, e tauhou ia ki tenei marae hei wa roa . . .

Aue, your heart grieves, your uncle tells the assembly. Aue, your body grieves. Ae, you have been a stranger to this marae for a long time. But this is your whanau, this is your home. Rongopai is your meeting house. Your father has called you and you have come. This is your home. Here lies your father.

Your uncle is ended now. His voice drifts away. The soft keening of the women fills the silence. Your grandfather looks up at you and his eyes are brimming with tears.

— Haere mai, Tama. Haere mai, haere mai.

Come, mokopuna. Come welcome.

And one step further now.

Your grandfather embraces you. It is a tight clasp. Weep with him. He is an old man; first his wife, and now his eldest son is gone.

— Aue, mokopuna, he whispers. Aue . . .

He loosens his embrace and brings your face close to his.

— Mmm. Mmmm.

It is sweet sadness to press noses in the hongi. It is sweet sadness to weep together. At the end of the embrace, your grandfather looks upon you and tries to smile. You had always thought of him as being strong. His pride was his strength and sometimes you were angry with him because he was so stubborn in his pride. Now, grief has snapped his spirit. He takes your hands and puts them onto his heart.

— E mokopuna, he says. You are my heart now. You are my eldest.

Once more you embrace. And again and again he whispers to you: I too, would wish to die. I too, would wish to die . . .

Comfort him. Tell him of your love for him. And now, look up. Look upon the mourners as they come to greet you. They come from the shadows and the light and they open their arms to you.

— Haere mai, Tama. Haere mai, mokopuna.

Come, Tama. Come, mokopuna. Come and press noses with us and let us join our sorrow. Haere mai. Don't be too sad. We also grieve with you.

Their faces are wan with grief. They are faces you know well, the faces of your family. They welcome you and weep with you. Auntie Arihia, your father's youngest sister. Uncle Kani, your father's best friend. Nanny Maata, sister of your grandfather. And her husband, Nanny Piripi, who tries to make you smile.

— Your father and me, he says. We argued a lot. Now he is gone, I feel lonely. Nobody to quarrel with now. Nobody.

They come, they come, to share their aroha with you. Auntie

Mina, she shows you her hands and laughs through her tears:
So many potatoes to peel, aue! Henare Tipene, he embraces you
quickly because his clothes are muddy from digging the hangi.
Nanny Kiri lifts her face up for you to kiss. She touches your tears
and then her own and nods her head sadly.

— Your tears, my tears, she whispers. For him, your father.

She wipes at her tears with her hands.

— See? she says, looking up at you. They still come, they still
come from my eyes.

Then she turns away.

This is your family. As you press noses with these people, you
recall the happiness of the whanau. For each of these people, you
share a private memory and affection. Auntie Ani, her cupboards
were always opened to you if you were hungry. Uncle Henare,
one night when you were small, he let you sleep in his bed with
him and Auntie Makareti because you were afraid of the dark.
Nanny Piripi, he whittled you a kaitaka, a spinning top to play
with. Your tuakana Arana, he taught you how to play the guitar.
Remember? And Uncle Pita . . .

— Aue, Uncle, you whisper.

— Kia kaha, Tama, he answers.

Of all the brothers of your father, Uncle Pita is the one you
love most. His calm is his strength too, just as your father's calm
was his strength. His heart and house was always opened to you,
and you often stayed with him. Remember now, the times you
used to come home and your mother would growl you and say:
Where you been? Don't you know where your own home is?
Most of those times, you were with Uncle Pita. He used to take
you out pig-hunting with him and his own sons. And when you
grew older, you went out shearing with him. He and your father
were very close and your father used to say: If anything happens to
me or if there are some things you have to know and I'm not here
to tell you, you go to Uncle Pita. He will help you.

Now, Uncle Pita is here with you. Look at him. His face is calm.
He does not show his grief, yet you know he grieves deeply for
your father.

— Aue, Uncle.

It is good to feel his strength. It is good to know that he is here
to guide you. He smiles, understanding.

142

— Not to worry, Tama, he says. Not to worry.

Kia kaha. Have courage, Tama.

They come, they come, your family. They press noses with you and their aroha flows out to you. Greet the family as they come, and look how they grieve with you. This is the longest journey.

Then the last hongi, the last sharing of grief, and you are alone. The mourners open a gap for you and the marae spills with light once more. The gestures of the aroarowhaki rustle softly again. The wailing too, begins to sigh with the wind.

Haere mai ki o tatou mate e . . .

The wailing grows louder and more decorative. It slides from one sound to another, dignified and slow-moving, fading at the end of the phrase and then soaring higher and catching the next phrase with a sudden burst of anger. It is the shrill sound of grief, bringing with it ineffable loneliness. But do not falter, do not hesitate. Haere mai, haere mai. Come. Your father waits.

And one step further now.

No, don't stop. If you stop, even for a moment, the grief will possess you completely, and you must complete this journey. You are your father's son, the eldest. You must make him proud, you must have courage. If you stop, you will be like an empty canoe adrift on the sea. Take up the oar; strike deep into the water.

Look: there is your mother, waiting for you. She sits, weeping over your father. With her are your sisters and the little ones, Hone and Marama. They wait for you. Your father waits for you. You mustn't falter now. Let your mother be your guiding star. Point your prow toward that star and let her know that you are here. Stike deep, strike deep.

Suddenly, the darkness is behind you. Rongopai has reached out with arms of light to enfold you. Look how the light shines brilliantly from the porch, enclosed within the peak of the sloping roof. The roof, it seems to move, seems to topple, and in falling would crush you . . . No, it is only your senses reeling, your heart breaking. Don't be afraid. Haere mai. Haere mai. Come.

There is nothing to fear. That's what your father told you, remember? He told you many stories about this meeting house.

Think back on them. He sat with you here, one day, and told you
of Rongopai. Listen to the wind. This wind also whispered here
on that day, long ago.

— This house, it is also the body of an ancestor, son. See the
koruru, at the top of the entrance? That is the head. The arms
are the maihi, the boards sloping down from the koruru to form
the roof. See the ridgepole? It holds up the roof and is the
backbone. And there, inside the house, those panels are the ribs . . .

Your father, he told you not to be afraid. The meeting house
would not harm you. You were one of its children. So bear
yourself with pride. The meeting house is not angry with you.
It opens its arms to you with aroha. And there, displayed on the
walls of the porch, are the photographs of your tupuna. They too,
are here to mourn your father's death. They are not angry. They
beckon you closer. Closer, toward the brilliant flower wreaths
banked high upon the porch. They too, seem to hold green
branches in their hands. They too, wear chaplets of kawakawa
leaves upon their heads. They too, have come to mourn with the
living for your father.

There, beneath them, your mother lifts her arms to you. And
Marama, she cries out to you.

— Tama! Tama!

Her voice rings the air with despair and at the sound, the waiata
tangi begins again.

> *Haruru ana*
> *Te Tiro a Whiro*
> *Taia ake ahau e te mate*
> *I muri nei ei.*

From this day forward you will always be alone. Your father
is gone now and the world is filled with darkness. He was a good
man, the axis of your universe, the sun giving light to your day.
Now clouds obscure the sun. All the world laments with you.
And this place has become desolate with ashes and sorrow.

> *I breathe, I live,*
> *I call . . .*
> *There is no sound, the*
> *tide ebbs silently away.*

The waiata tangi soaring. The wind gathering to mourn for your father. And there, shimmering in the light, your father is waiting.

One step.

And one step further now.

But wait: a voice cries out above the wailing. It sings with an indescribable fury and the words spill across the marae with fierce agony.

> *. . . kei whea i ara te toka whaiapu,*
> *Te homai nei kia ripiripia*
> *Ki te kiri moko e mau atu nei?*

Look: on the edge of the marae, half in light half in shadow, a woman stands. Her eyes are wild, her face is ashen with anger and framed with long black hair, matted with the rain. She wears a black gown and her thin arms reach out to you. You know this woman: she is Auntie Ruihi, a sister of your father's. Her love for him was great, and her body trembles with anguish now that he is gone. Listen: she sings of her grief.

> *. . . Where is the jagged rock,*
> *with which I might lacerate*
> *this wasted body I possess . . .*
> *Where . . . Where . . .*

She sobs to herself and covers her face with her hands. Then her eyes look out from between her fingers and she cries out her anguish to you.

> *Aue! Aue, e mokopuna.*
> *A, e rua i ara aku ringaringa*
> *Ki te whakakopa mai i taku manawa,*
> *E kakapa ana mehe rau kahakaha . . .*

Auntie Ruihi . . . When your Nanny Puti was buried, this woman wanted to throw herself into the grave too. You were a little boy then. You didn't understand about death. You stood watching your Auntie Ruihi as she screamed and fought against the men who held her back. She was possessed by grief and she cried out to your Nanny: E ma! E ma! Kauai koe e haere, e ma . . .

145

> *Aue! Aue, e mokopuna.*
> *A, both my hands are needed*
> *To clutch and hold my heart within,*
> *As it wildly flutters like*
> *the kahakaha leaf . . .*

Now this woman grieves again. First her mother, now her eldest brother dead. She comes, stepping slowly from the darkness into the light. Her gown is threaded with green leaves. The mourners make way for her. As she comes, she intones an ancient lament. The wailing bursts around her song. But her voice thrusts above the wailing.

> *Whakarongo ki te tai*
> *E tangi haere ana,*
> *Whakariri ai*
> *Te rae ki Turanga . . .*

She comes to you, her hands outstretched to you. In her eyes there shines such desperation that you forget your own grief.

> *Listen to the tides*
> *Lamenting as they flow,*
> *Surging sullenly by*
> *The headland at Turanga . . .*

She performs movements to her lament. Her hands move with intricate precision telling of the grief which aches in her heart. They are slow ritual movements, one gesture blending into another. She touches her breast with her palms, then turns the palms toward the gathering. Her fingers quiver upon her eyes, then flicker down her body, enacting the falling of her tears. With a bold sweep, she touches her lips with her hands, then lifts her hands, shivering the aroarowhaki toward the night sky. All the while, her body sways with sorrow, rippling a strange shadow on the marae. Then she opens her arms again and lifts her eyes to you.

> *Through the spray of my tears,*
> *I see you, my brother's son.*
> *Come weep with me,*

146

> *Our anchor is gone, and we are*
> *cast adrift at the mercy of*
> *the sea . . .*

The wailing soars around her. At the beginning of each phrase it bursts anew, like spray spuming higher and higher upon the face of a cliff. And she comes, with dignity and despair, through the waves cascading and the spray falling.

> *Our anchor is gone and we*
> *are cast adrift, at the*
> *mercy of the sea . . .*

Go to her. Embrace her. For you are her haven in the storm of the tangi.

> *Te ao o te tonga*
> *E whakina mai ra*
> *Haere ana koe*
> *te hiwi o Hikurangi.*

Listen: listen to the way she calls to your father. She is a gannet circling and calling for a companion. She swoops low over the water, touching the tips of the waves with her wings. Then she soars aloft, fluting her sorrow across the desolate expanse. And perhaps far away, she sees a sacred mountain . . . Hikurangi. She wings towards it, a solitary feather falling in a soft grey sky.

> *The clouds in the south*
> *I see before me,*
> *As you wend your way*
> *Over Hikurangi.*

And she comes to you and weeps brokenly in your arms. Hold her tightly. Her heartbeat, you can feel it pounding. Tell her: Auntie, it's all right now, kia kaha. Speak to her softly. Speak to her with aroha. You are her Hikurangi now.

> *Aue, aue . . .*
> *Ka whanatu te aroha*
> *I te pi to ngakau . . .*

Comfort her. Press noses with her. Once more, before she is gone.

Aue, mokopuna . . .
Aue, aue . . .

Listen as her voice dissolves away into the darkness. Aue, aue
. . . the whisper echoes, softly calling from the shadows.
And one step further now.

See? Almost there. On either side of you the porch extends.
Above you, the roof thrusts into the night sky. Around the
electric lights moths have gathered. The light is harsh and high-
lights the painted swirlings of the panels. Some of the panels have
decayed with the seasons and the paint has blistered and flaked
away.

There, in one corner, is a silken spider's web, cast between an
eave and a wall of the porch, beaded with rain.

Look downward from the apex now. The photographs of your
tupuna, your ancestors, are closer now. You know some of these
tupuna well. That woman there, she was your great-aunt. She
has the moko and when you were a child and you visited Rongopai
you would stand before her, lift the veil covering her face and
trace the spirals of her moko with your fingers. There, beside her,
an old kaumatua looks out upon the world with self-conscious
dignity. He wears a feather cloak fastened about his neck and he
has a greenstone dangling from an ear. That pendant has been
handed down through your family for many generations. Your
father, he showed it to you when you were a boy. It was deep
green as the river and gleamed as if with the sunlight sweeping
across the river. You held it and trembled, and it flashed with a
calm green fire.

And softly, the waiata tangi begins again.

> *Haruru ana*
> *Te Tiro a Whiro*
> *Taia ake ahau e te mate*
> *I muri nei ei.*

Look: see how the porch has been decorated with greenery.
It shimmers with the wind, like a forest in a dark afternoon.
Listen: you will hear a waterfall quietly thundering. And melting
into the sound, is the disconsolate twittering of the Piwakawaka

148

as it flees further into the forest. Follow after it; come closer. Don't be afraid. Haere mai. Haere mai.

> *Death comes, but I am*
> *not yet dead.*
> *I breathe, I live.*

The porch seems suddenly brilliant with its mass of flower wreaths. They are banked high upon the floor. The petals shiver and drops of rain fall from them.

And there, amid the wreaths, your father lies. Among a profusion of flowers. Among glistening white flowers.

One step further now.

> *Pumau tonu atu*
> *te rere anga awa*
> *te tonga o te ra*
> *nga maunga tu noa.*

Brush away your tears. Look up. Be proud. Look upon your mother and your family where they wait for you, their eldest brother and son to come. They sit round your father's casket on a wide flax mat which has been laid on the earth floor. Next to them are some of the possessions of his life: his silver sports trophies, his photographs, his suitcases of clothes . . . All these possessions will be buried with him.

> *I breathe, I live,*
> *I call . . .*
> *But there is no sound. The*
> *tide ebbs silently away.*

The children are crying, Hone and Marama. They are too young to understand about death. You didn't either, remember? When your Nanny Puti died, you sat beside her casket looking out into the darkness and there was such terror out there. The shrill ululation of the old women, the shadows which melted in and out of the night. Grief was all around you, too large to comprehend. You knew only that your nanny was going to be buried in the ground where it was cold. Whenever the wailing began to welcome visitors to the marae, you used to whisper to your nanny: Don't you be afraid, Nanny. Don't you be afraid.

Remember your terror. Now think how greater it must be for Hone and Marama. After your Nanny Puti died, your father was still with you. For these two children, there is no father now. For them, the light has been suddenly extinguished and this is no momentary eclipse. They do not understand the total darkness. They look out into the darkness and see you. You are the eldest brother, and they cry out to you. And from out of this dark night, you must bring them light again.

> Yet the stream still runs
> And the sun rides over the sky
> And the mountains
> Are always there.

Forget your own grief. You must look after your younger brother and sisters, your mother too. Father is gone but the family remains. Listen: Marama is crying for you again.

— Tama! Tama!

Open your arms to her for she has wrenched herself from your mother and comes running toward you.

— Tama! Tama!

Hold her closely, hold her tightly. Her body trembles with fear. And you must be a giant Kauri, spreading wide its sheltering branches.

— Tama . . .

Hug her tightly. Forget your own tears. Once you were a child and you witnessed the sorrow of the tangi. Your little sister must witness it too: the tangi of her father. You must take her hand in yours and walk with her. Her wounds will be deep; you must salve them. Long nights she will weep: you must comfort her. And when she cries out in her sleep, you must go to her and kiss her tears away. From the ashes of the tangi, you must merge your life with hers and reconstruct her world again.

Take her hand now. Look how your shadows join on the ground. Your hands reach out to each other, and slowly become one shadow. Marama looks up at you, both grave and trusting, and brushes her tears away.

And one step further now.

Once, father guided you like this. It may have been on a city street rushing with people. Or it may have been across a hillside during the night when you could not see your way. But you were not afraid, because your hand was in his. That was all that mattered; just being with him.

> Memories rise in the still air
> Like smoke from many fires.
> Is this the same place,
> This place of ashes?

Now he is dead and this place is a place of storms. Remember now, how you used to sit at the window, waiting for your father. It would be raining outside, the rivulets streaming across the window pane. In the window, would be reflected the flames of a burning fire, fire and water mingling. Your mother and your sisters would be sitting near the fire, your mother knitting, your sisters playing. But you would still remain at the window, looking out for him: Dad! Dad! And you would wave to him, and he would lift his hand to wave back to you. In your heart you would feel a sudden calm. Your father was home.

You are home now. But father is gone. Brush away the rain, brush away the tears. Your father lies still and you may lift your hand to wave to him, but he will not wave back. So go to him. One step. Now the next. Do not falter. You are almost there. See? Your sister Ripeka raises her arms to greet you and she sings of her sorrow.

> From this bitter place of ashes,
> My grief rises; from this place
> So changed now.

The mourners join her lament. These are the voices of the tangi. These people, they see your father lying here, yet they live on. The world relentlessly turns. Why is this so?

> Yet the stream still runs
> And the sun still rides over the sky
> And the mountains
> Are always there.

Look now, upon your mother. Your father was her world and she weeps because he is gone. She kneels close to the casket, brushing your father's face with her hands. Her tight embrace with him has been broken, and she is Papatuanuku the Earth Mother who reaches out to him to embrace him again. This is the day of separation of Earth and Sky.

And one step further now.

Your mother looks old in the light. Her eyes are red-rimmed with weeping. Her body is thin and wasted away with grief. But she is still beautiful. She is the Earth. Her hair is silver with the mists of the hills. Her eyes are like shimmering waterfalls. The contours of her face are the sculpted landscapes of earth. Her moods are the seasons. This is her winter unending, the most bitter season of all. Look: you will see the frost on her cheeks and the ice glittering in her hair and the cold wind blowing across her body. She has known other winters but they have been followed by thaw and sparkling sun. This winter is too desolate and despairing. No spring will follow.

She kneels by your father. In her lap, she cradles Hone, your young brother. Sitting close by her is Ripeka, and Mere has joined her. Soon, Wiki will be here too, to join you all. This is your family.

— E pa, kauai koe e haere e pa . . .

Dad, don't go away, Dad. When you go away, my world collapses and my life decays. No more the warmth of the sun in that forever sky. The sun is snuffed out. And I and my family are left calling for you in the falling darkness.

— E pa, kauai koe e haere e pa . . .

And one step further now.

And now you stand on the edge of the porch. The flower wreaths spread out before you, lustrous with the rain. The greenery casts flickering shadows in the light. Amid the flowers, photographs of your father sparkle with raindrops. And as the wind blows softly upon the wreaths, the air is filled with their thick perfume . . . the smell of beauty, the smell of decay and death.

No, don't turn away. Hold tightly to your heart so that the agony does not split it apart. Step firmly. It is not the ground which reels and sways but your body. Strike deep with the paddle, strike firmly, strike deep. Kia kaha; be strong. Do not despair. Now lift your head. Lift it high and look across the water to where he lies. Do not listen to the wailing. Be proud. Look up; look upon your father.

> *Through the spray of my glistening*
> *tears, I see you, my father.*
> *I weep, for the carved prow*
> *sinks slowly beneath the sea.*

Your sight blurs with tears. You see only an aureole of light, shimmering and glistening like a silver mist. Brush away your tears, brush away the wisps of the mist. There lies your father . . .

And in the night, a clap of thunder reverberates across the hills.

One step further now.

Do not listen to the rain falling. Do not listen to the women wailing. It is only the wind sobbing with rain. It is the wind shifting, the wind renewing.

The rain falls heavily, drenching you suddenly with cold. It rushes down the sloping eaves of the porch. The wind rustles the greenery with a sudden whirlwind. And the flower wreaths sparkle with raindrops.

Father . . .

No, don't stop your tears. For with tears, you remember him and honour him with your love. There is no shame in weeping. Look upon your father where he lies. Look with memory upon the times you shared together; those times never to be shared again. Look upon him.

— Kauai koe e haere, e pa

Kauai koe e haere . . .

And one step further now.

His face is calm. He lies as if he is only asleep. In sleep, he looks calm and younger than his years. His face is smooth and glistening. His hair is threaded with grey strands. His hands are folded over his breast, across the white coverlet. And the lower part of the casket is covered with a feather cloak, opening out like the wings of a giant moth.

— Dad . . .

Marama lets go of your hand to rush helplessly to your mother. But stand for a while, loving him. He was the calm point of your

153

world. Now he is gone and all the calm has gone with him. You walk alone.

One step further now.

And you are with your family, embracing Ripeka.

— Tama . . . she weeps.

        Tama . . .

Embrace her tightly, hug her close to you. Then kiss Hone and Marama too.

> *Death comes, but I*
> *am not yet dead.*
> *I breathe, I live.*

And now, your mother . . . She tries to smile at you, but her tears rush quickly down the slopes of her face like storm water from the hills. Her eyes are haunted with grief, her body ravaged with sorrow.

Kneel down beside her. With tenderness, she touches your face with her hands, tracing your chin, your cheeks, your brow.

— E ma, I'm here.

But she places her fingers across your lips. You do not have to speak. You are here and that is all that matters. Gently she caresses your lips and then her lips. And she curls her hands under your chin to bring your lips together. Lips, and then noses to touch . . .

— To papa.

To papa . . . she whispers.

And she motions you near to him.

Listen: the wailing has stopped. There is only the sound of the rain falling.

— Your father.

Your father . . .

Your mother's voice is strained with grief. Her gestures are small and helpless.

— To papa. Kua mate to papa. To papa.

She bends to him and brushes her hands through his hair. Then she puts her cheek upon his. She motions you closer and makes soft loving noises.

— Haere mai, haere mai. Mmm. Mmmm.

Bend toward him. Do not be afraid. See how your shadow falls across his face so pale and calm.

Whisper to him, tell him: Haere ra, e pa, goodbye my father. Go now, e pa, I am here. To look after the family now that you are dead, to do as you would want me to do.

Now, let your lips touch his.

His lips are cold. Yours are warm. Your tears fall hotly on his face. Now bend to him again. This is your father and you are his son.

One last kiss.

His lips so cold, so cold.

— Aue, e pa.

Aue, Aue, Aue . . .

And the wailing soars, rending this night and rending your heart and crying with the wind.

> *Death comes, but I*
> *am not yet dead.*
> *I breathe*
> *I live . . .*

Twenty-eight

The tangi marks the end of one life, the beginning of another.
Before it stretch the greenstone years of a boy with his father.
They were happy years; perhaps too happy, for anything following
can never hope to surpass them. They were possessed with aroha,
and that aroha created a world for me which I thought I would
never want to leave. Yet leave Waituhi and Dad, I did. But, I
always knew that that world was still there for me to return to;
that father would always be there. Waituhi still remains. But father
is dead. The greenstone has shattered. What comes after?

E pa, I am afraid.
Don't be afraid, Tama.
I do not have your strength, e pa.
You will find your own strength.
There will be times when I will need you, Dad. When I will
need to know that you are here. Times when decisions will be
hard to make. I may make the wrong decisions, e pa.
I have been wrong sometimes, Son.
I will need you, Dad . . .
You will find your own strength, Tama. Kia kaha. Kia kaha.

I was eighteen when I left Waituhi and went to Wellington. My
feelings, I suppose, would not have been too different from those
of the girl who boarded the train at Wairoa. She sits opposite me,
staring out the window as the train leaves Waipukurau. In her
eyes I see both sadness and eagerness. Sadness because she has

left home. Eagerness because going to Wellington or any big city is the dream of most young people who live in a small country settlement far from anywhere. How long will she stay in Wellington? A year, perhaps two, or maybe forever? Many of my own friends left Waituhi and have not returned. Their dream has become their reality. Even for Erana.

We'd made promises to each other, Erana and I, before she'd left Waituhi. I was sixteen then and she was a year younger. We'd write to each other, we said because we loved each other. When she'd gone the world had seemed empty. We did write, long letters at first. Then the letters from her became shorter, more terse and spaced further apart. When she came back for a brief visit there seemed nothing between us. She'd changed; I suppose I had as well. I went to the airport to meet her. Her parents were there too. But when she got off the plane she was not alone. I left before she could see me.

She came around home one night. We talked. We said goodbye to each other. I never saw her again.

The dream; the reality. I did not share it at first, perhaps because there was a greater dream to realise: the building of the farm, the breaking in of the land. All our lives our family had lived so much a gypsy life that we held fast to Waituhi. For us, Waituhi wasn't just a few houses strung along a country road; it was our home and we had finally come home to stay. Unlike my friends who dreamed of leaving, I didn't care that the work was hard. I would look inward and know that if I stayed, life would always mean hard work. That fences would have to be put up, scrub cut, cattle yards erected, sheep and cattle shifted from one part of the farm to another, mustering during winter, dosing, docking, lambing, shearing, haymaking, planting potatoes and maize, hoeing . . . It didn't matter to me for Waituhi was my home. I didn't care that my friends thought the life monotonous; for me, there was always a sense of contentment in feeling a rhythm beneath my feet. The heartbeat of the land. That season would follow season and that the rhythm would never alter. Knowing this brought me peace like no other I had known. And then there was father too.

I look at my reflection in the window of the train. I see only Dad's face, strong and calm, and the rugged contours of this darkening country rushing across it.

Waituhi was Dad; Dad was Waituhi. That also was a reason for my staying there. I could never think of one without the other. Even now, although he is dead, he still exists for me as Waituhi. And Waituhi, for him, was his world. During my first year away in Wellington he and Mum and the kids moved into Gisborne again because Mum wanted the young ones to have a good education. They did not sell the farm and Dad used to get into the truck and journey out to it every day.

— I don't know what's wrong with your father! Mum used to tell me. I never know where he is these days.

— You know all right, Mum, I would answer. You want to go back too.

— Me? I've had enough of the hard life, boy. Anyway, one of you fullas has to get some brains and seeing that you were too dumb at school, I guess it has to be your little brother!

For both Mum and Dad, Waituhi was inescapable. They pined for it and in the end, they returned. That was when Dad began to ask me to come back, come back:

— Your father, he's getting old, he used to say. You stay at home and help me, ay? Never mind about Wellington. Come home, Son. Come home.

I did not go home. I stayed in Wellington four years. I did not leave Waituhi for any particular reason. I had finished school when I was sixteen and the two years I spent on the farm were too busy to be dull. Yet, there was a certain restlessness in me. I saw my friends leaving Waituhi and I envied them. It was not easy to remain at home when it seemed that all the friends of my generation were going away. I wanted to go with them too. I was content yet discontent. Happy yet unhappy. What happened to me was something strange, something inexplicable. I did not leave out of boredom or anger for I loved Waituhi. I suppose the bright lights of Wellington attracted me. I spoke with Dad and told him I must go.

He drove me to the railway station at Gisborne on the day I left. Mum and the kids came too. Ripeka, Mere and Wiki were young girls; Marama and Hone were babies. Strange to think that the three elder girls would get married during my four years away from home. We were, and still are, a close family and it was not easy for me to leave my family. Only Wiki and myself have ever lived away from the family, away from Waituhi. On that day I left Waituhi I never thought that Wellington would claim four years from my life. I kissed my family and hugged them close to me. It must have looked amusing really; there they were, standing in a line on the platform and I went down the line starting from Dad who was the tallest to Marama who was still not at school. Ripeka wanted to come with me. She said it wasn't fair that I was going and not to come with me. Wasn't it supposed to be share and share alike? It wasn't fair! She made us all laugh and that was good because I was feeling sad and Mum and Dad were worried for me. Then it was time for me to board the train. Dad whispered to me:

— Remember, Tama. You are the eldest. Come home if anything should happen to me. The eldest always looks after the youngest. That is the Maori way. Haere ra, Son.

I came to the city. Both sad and eager, I came. On a train like this one, four years ago. I am twenty-two now.

I cannot explain why I stayed away from Waituhi for so long. Perhaps it was because life kept opening out, opening and opening like an unclenching fist, and I could not leave until the fingers were fully splayed. Whatever the reason, they were good years. I do not regret them. I immersed myself in the life they brought me and will always remember them with a fondness and also a kind of poignancy because although they were filled with excitement, they were also the drifting years when nothing and yet everything happened. I fell in and out of love. I made friends and lost them. My weekends were sometimes wild, sometimes calm. Always, life opening and opening outward.

Everything happened and yet those years were drifting years. They were aimless. Selfish. I did not entirely forget Waituhi and I went back to visit occasionally. Perhaps for the Maori hockey tournament, Christmas or a wedding. There were even times when Waituhi would come to me as a memory. I would remember the aroha, always the aroha of village life and family life, and I would be lonely even on a crowded street. Still I remained in Wellington. I changed, although I did not realise it. I grew accustomed to the aimlessness of my life. I thought the greater dream of my father had been accomplished. Whenever he said he needed me, I laughed at him.

— You don't need me, Dad! I'm hopeless, you always said I was!
— Tama, I do need you. I want you to come home. Your father, he's getting tired now. He's getting old. Come home. Come home.

E pa, do not be angry with me. I should have realised . . . But try to understand, e pa? I was having such a good time that I did not want to leave Wellington. I did not think you would ever grow old. You seemed so much a part of the universe, e pa. You were the sky, and the sky was always there. The sky does not grow old. I thought you and Waituhi would always remain the same, unchanged: that Time would flow round you both without disturbing you. Time passed only where I was, that's how I imagined it. But not in Waituhi, surely not. Waituhi was timeless. You were timeless. Yet, you did grow old, e pa. And the years passed where you were too. The family grew up. Ripeka, Mere and Wiki, they got married; Marama and Hone began to go to school. You became a grandfather when Mere had a baby girl. Why did I believe that you and Waituhi were timeless? E pa . . .

Four years; good years.

And then a telephone call from Waituhi, ending one life and beginning another. I returned to Waituhi. Now, I'm on my way to Wellington. But not to stay. I shall never leave Waituhi again.

I will need you, Dad.

You will find your own strength, Tama.

When will that be, e pa? Even though you are gone from me, the desolation of the tangi is still upon me. Your strength was my strength. In an aimless life where people walked in and out of that life, you were my only strength. I am afraid.

Kia kaha, Tama. Be strong.

Strong, e pa?

I am a nightwalker, searching for another sun. Alone in a twilight world, I seek another day. Rain is falling, darkness is falling. Darkness and rain; rain and darkness.

Twenty-nine

*And who are these people coming out of the sun? Is that the shrill
cry of welcome once more?*

> *Haere mai ki o tatou mate e . . .*
> *Haere mai. Haere mai . . .*

Around me, the mourners are stirring, gradually unfolding, to
peer into the sunlight. More visitors are coming. From out of the
sun they are coming. The old women of the marae open their arms to
join in welcoming the visitors. My grandfather lifts his head, dazed.

> *Welcome. Welcome.*
> *Come to our dead . . .*

Have I been asleep? I did not mean to sleep but I'm so tired.
So tired. I should have eaten something this morning. I have no
will to eat.

Is Mum awake? I must go and wake her. Tell her that more
people are coming to honour father.

— E ma, wake up, e ma.

She sits beside Dad, but she is not asleep. Her eyes are fevered
with the days of sun. With watching through the night, the flights
of falling stars across the midnight universe.

— I see them, Tama. I see them coming.

She looks into the sun. Her eyes brim with tears. She puts her
head close to father and whispers to him.

— See, Rongo? They come. Look how they come to you.

Her eyes are fierce with pride, her voice rings out with pride.

— Haere mai e te manuhiri! she calls. E te manuhiri, haere mai! Haere mai! Haere mai!

She is proud that her husband was so loved by his people. And I gaze upon her, proud that this woman is my mother.

What day is this? Is it the third day? When will the third day come? When?

The ritual of welcome is beginning again. How many times have I seen this same welcome? So tired. So tired.

And always the wailing, the winding together of the voices of the marae people and the visitors as one voice. I cannot sleep for the wailing. But I have no will to sleep, for if I sleep I might not wake for a long time and I will lose those minutes of gazing on my father. Time enough for sleeping after the tangi.

The wailing awakens Ripeka. She nudges Mere. They look out into the red haze of another day, another welcoming.

> *Haere mai e te manuhiri!*
> *Haere mai ki o tatou mate e . . .*

An old koroua is walking toward the marae. Between the vanguard of welcoming women he comes. He approaches in silence. Then he stands before father. He weeps softly. Then he looks up, trembling, and surveys the mourners. His voice is a mere whisper, short-lived.

— There is something I want to say . . .

He looks at father again. And again, he whispers.

— There is something I have to say . . .

Something . . . Something . . .

> *Haere mai ki o tatou mate e . . .*

The women are calling again.

I lift my head. Who is coming? What day is this? When will the tangi end? E pa, let me sleep for a while, just for a little while.

> *Come to our dead . . .*

Who is coming? When will it end? It is not the women calling. It is only the wind. Only the wind.

Let it be the wind. Let it be just the wind.

A car is approaching Rongopai. My mother shades her eyes with her hands to see who is coming. The car swings through the gate and drives slowly through the groups of mourners. A young girl hunches in her seat, hiding her eyes from father. The car stops. The door opens.

And my mother cries out hoarsely:

— Baby! Baby! Come to me, come to me . . .

Wiki, my sister, stumbles into the sunlight. Until Marama and Hone were born, Wiki was always called Baby. Her face is white with shock. She takes one step and falls. Her husband, Matiu, helps her up, and she sobs:

— Dad! Dad!

There is a storm on the marae. The mourners, caught up with her grief, sorrow with her. Ripeka and Mere cover their faces with their hands.

— Wiki! Baby! Come!

I go to my sister. She and Matiu have come from Auckland. I say to her:

— Don't be afraid, Wiki.

She clutches me tightly. Matiu and I support her. We walk through the mourners toward the porch where father lies.

> *Haere mai ki o tatou mate e . . .*
> *Haere mai. Haere mai . . .*

Wiki seems lifeless in our arms. Her feet drag on the ground.

> *Welcome to our dead . . .*

She begins to moan.

— I don't want to see him. Let me go, I don't want to see Dad. He's not dead. He isn't I know he isn't Let me go No I can't go any further Let me go Oh no Daddy He's not dead is he Tama Let me go Please.

— Wiki! Baby! Come to me, Baby.

Wiki looks up. She sees Mum beckoning to her. She sees father lying there. And she screams. Then she struggles away from us, almost falls, and runs toward her father.

— Dad! Dad?

She kneels beside him, her fingers clutching at the silk. Then slowly, her fingers trail long scratches upon the shining wood.

— Come to me, Baby . . .

The wailing soars.

Who are these people who come forward now? So many mourners, and so many speeches have already been said on this marae. Is this the third day?

More visitors are at the edge of the marae. The haze shimmers upon them. My grandfather welcomes them. Then from the midst of the haze, a man steps. And Mum weeps.

— See, Rongo? My own father comes. My people are here to mourn with your people. . . .

Mum's father points toward Rongopai. He spreads his arms and tells the assembly about Dad: how my father had visited the Whanau-A-Apanui and had taken away one of his daughters, my mother. This daughter was wilful. She wanted the stranger, and married him.

My mother's father pauses. Then he grasps at his heart.

The pain of her leaving was big, he says. I was angry with my daughter but I was more angry with the man who had stolen her away from me. For a long time there was silence between us. Then one day, she came back to see me and I could tell that she was happy. My heart melted toward this man. We began to know each other, and I called him: Son. Yes, he is my son too. He does not only belong to you. He is also here, in my heart. Now my heart is empty because he is dead. I come here to your marae to say: haere ra, to say farewell to my son. Haere ra, Rongo. Haere. Haere. Haere.

The speech ends. My mother's father comes forward. My aunties and uncles, my mother's sisters and brothers, follow behind him. Their children, my cousins, are with them. Together, they approach father. They look upon him.

Then one by one, they kneel beside Mum and press noses with her.

— Turi turi, Huia . . .

Don't cry, Huia. We're here now. Hush.

And Mum hugs her father tightly.

— E pa, e pa . . .

It is good to have you here.

> *Haere mai ki o tatou mate e* . . .
> *Come to our dead.*

More mourners are coming. I am so tired. Look, sun: look upon my face. Go quickly across the sky and let the night take your place. For in the darkness I may rest, may rest.

Who are these people who come to see father? I do not know them. Who are they?

— E ma . . .

— They are some of Dad's Pakeha friends. Go to them, Tama. Tell them not to be afraid. They do not know of the tangi. They don't know what to expect. Go quickly.

I cross the marae toward the visitors. Two couples stand there. The men are ill at ease. Their wives are hesitant. I smile at them.

— I am Tama Mahana and Rongo Mahana is my father. I am glad that you have come here to Rongopai. Welcome.

— We had to come. Rongo was our friend. We've brought a wreath with us. What can we say? We respected your father very much. He was a good man and we're sad that he is dead.

— I am glad you have come. You have made us feel very proud . . .

Is this the third day? What day is this? When will the tangi be at an end?

Marama and Hone hold tightly to Mum. They watch the kaumatua as he comes, afraid of him because of his appearance. His eyes flash fire. He wears a feather cloak and he has shark-tooth pendants in his ears.

— Don't be scared, Mum tells them.

— I'm not scared, Marama answers. Hone is scared though.

— Eeee! I am not either! Hone whispers. You're telling lies, Marama.

Mum smiles wanly and tells them to hush.

The kaumatua stops in the centre of the marae. He begins to speak in Maori: Ti hei mauriora . . . A torrent of words that are rough and loud. He speaks of the history of the whanau. He speaks

166

of my father. The assembly listens. Some of the people weep at his words and whisper:

— Ae, ae. That is how Rongo was.

Then suddenly, the kaumatua stops. Slowly, he unclasps the feather cloak from his shoulders. He lifts the cloak high, then drapes it upon Dad's body. His voice rises again.

— Haere ra, mokopuna . . .

Farewell, nephew. Go to Te Reinga, the world after this life. Go to Hawaiki, to your ancestors, to your tupuna. They will greet you there. Heart of the whanau, haere ra. Shelterer from the winds, farewell. Giver of shade, haere ra. Farewell to Tawhiti-Pamamao. E mokopuna, haere ra, haere ra, haere ra. Haere ra, Rongo. Haere. Haere. Haere.

With love he says the words. With love he looks upon my father. And with love, the mourners sing softly to father. Warmly and softly.

> Arohanui, e pa.
> Haere ra, taku hoa.

And warmly and softly, a waiata aroha begins.

> Haere mai ki o tatou mate e . . .
> Haere mai. Haere mai.

So much light, so much sun. And is that the shrill cry of welcome yet again? Which day is this? Has the sun risen once, twice, or is this its third rising?

The sky is a huge glistening eye, limitless and without depth. The sun is that eye's roving iris swinging from one corner of the eye to the other. Its gaze is baleful and without compassion. It beats down heavily upon the marae where the throng of mourners gathers. So many of them are here. Some sit on the long benches which ring the space around Rongopai. Others kneel on the wilting grass. Uncaring, the children play beyond the marae. An old kuia is asleep in the sun. A young woman rocks her child to sleep in her protecting arms. A boy is wandering back to the marquee where there is shade from the sun. My grandfather's face alone, stares blindly into the sun.

And always, the sun spinning, spinning, spinning across the sky.

When will there be an end to the long procession of mourners? They come, they still come. To weep over father where he lies, and then to weep with us, his family, where we watch over him. They bend toward us, to express their love and grief in the pressing of noses in the hongi.

The shadows still come, still bend. They whisper:

> *Haere mai, Tama. Mmm. Mmm.*
> *Kua mate to papa. E tangi ana ahau.*
> *Your father is dead. I weep for him.*

And as they bend toward us they leave behind a token of their aroha: a greenstone pendant to place with father in his grave, a present of money, or a small memento which father gave them once and is now returned to him.

Or a flower wreath to cover father with and to wither with him when he lies beneath the cold earth.

From where do they come, these long processions of mourners? From where do they come, these specks out of the sun?

A black veiled group is approaching the marae.

Suddenly, an old kuia begins to wail among them. The others with her join the lament. The wailing echoes from one voice to another, growing more intense and soaring higher and higher. And suddenly, the sound seems to pierce the sun. It shatters into ribbons of light as the mourners step onto the marae.

And my father's people welcome the mourners.

> *Haere mai ki o tatou mate e . . .*

E pa . . . Can you see them coming? Can you see them all? Do not go from me, e pa. Kauai koe e haere, kauai koe e haere, e pa. Can you hear me, e pa? Can you hear Mum whispering to you? The wailing has torn her heart apart and she is saying:

— Rongo . . . Rongo . . .

I will clasp you tightly to me and will never let you go. I will hold you closely and will never leave you. Like this, I will kiss your lips. Like this, like this. My tears will cool your body when the sun is high. My warmth will keep you warm when night comes. So stay with me, Rongo. Never leave me.

— Haere mai ki o tatou mate e . . .
— E Rongo. Aue, e Rongo.

In this place of death why do I still live? Why does the earth still turn in this place of sorrow?

E pa . . .

> *Death comes but I am not yet dead.*
> *I breathe, I live.*

Mum reaches out and touches my hand.
— Tama, you must be hungry. Go and eat, Son. Have some kai.
— I'm not hungry, Mum.
— Tama, I know you're hungry. If you're not, Hone and Marama must be. Take them with you and get them some kai. Take them to Takitimu Hall and feed them. And afterwards, play with them, ay? It isn't good that they stay here with me all the time. They must learn to laugh again; to forget. And Mere? Ripeka? You fullas go too. All of you, go. You're all still the same. Your father and I have no privacy with you fullas around.
Mum smiles at us. I sign to Ripeka and Mere to come.
— You'll be okay, Mum? Mere asks.
— Course I will!
— Do you want us to bring you something to eat?
— No. Now all of you go.
I leave the porch. Marama and Hone come with me. Mere goes to feed her baby. Ripeka walks to the truck where her husband, Hata, is waiting.
— Will Mummy be all right without us? Marama asks.
I nod for Mum is not alone. She has Dad. And also, some of the old women of the village look over father with her. Among them are Auntie Ruihi and Auntie Hiria, Mum's sister. Always there are women to keep vigil over my father. My grandfather, my father's father, is there too.
— You're going to stay with us now, ay Tama, Hone says.
— Yes, always.
— For ever and ever?
I nod my head. Hone smiles at me. Then his face grows puzzled and he looks back at the meeting house, to his father lying there. With alarm, he asks:

— Are you sure, Tama?

— Yes, I'm sure.

And Hone grins again.

— Don't be afraid, I tell him and Marama. Come on, give me your hands. See? I am holding them tight now and nothing will harm you. I will never let go, now or ever. So don't be afraid.

And I hug them close to me.

The smallest fern, even the mamaku that hangs of its own weight down, is stronger than I, much stronger than I . . .

— Wiki, hush now.

My sister trembles in my arms. I stroke her hair. I have never needed to comfort my sister before because she always sought father for comfort. But Dad is gone now, and I stand in his place. I am the eldest.

— Wiki? Turi turi, Wiki.

But she still cries. I am not yet a Kauri. E pa, the world dies with you and I die also. Yet this body still lives, still breathes, and this heart still beats. Why is this so? And is Wiki a reason why I must live? To look after her and my family now that you are gone?

— Wiki . . .

— Tama, my tears will not stop.

I hug her closer.

— My sister, do not weep. I am here.

I am not as my father was. I do not have his strength. But . . . Let the darkness come, I will not care. Let the sun blaze each day. I am home, e pa. And here I will stay.

— Uncle Pita? Where are we going?

I follow my father's brother to his truck.

— We have to get some more hay for the marquee. So many people have come and the ground is wet. The hay will keep the inside of the marquee dry.

I get into the truck. Uncle starts the engine and we leave Rongopai behind.

The road unwinds before us. We do not speak for a while. Then Uncle smiles at me, concerned.

— Don't take it too hard, Nephew.

I cannot answer. The truck hums along the road.

170

— Thanks for arranging everything, Uncle, I tell him.

— No need. I did what had to be done.

— There was so much for you to do. I should have been home to take care of everything. But I'm so hopeless at such things. Everybody has been good to me, to the family.

Uncle laughs.

— There isn't anything you could have done except get in the way.

I grin back and sigh ruefully.

— Are you home to stay now? Uncle asks.

— Dad said I must look after Mum and the kids if anything happened to him. Yes, I'll be staying. There's so much to take on though. The farm. Everything. And I'm used to the easy life now, Uncle. It was okay working for Dad, but now that he's gone, it's going to be hard. I don't know where I'll begin.

— You'll learn, Nephew. It'll be hard, but you'll learn.

We grow silent. The truck slows down and bumps through a paddock to a shed where hay is kept. Uncle switches off the engine. Then he turns to me.

— Tama, you seem to think you're alone. But you're not. Don't worry too much about the future. Don't take your father's death too hard. And if you feel it getting too much for you, you lean on me, ay? You lean on me . . .

I look away from my uncle because I do not want him to see my tears. And while I am not looking, he punches me in the shoulder.

— Hey! Enough of that! You're a man now!

— Yeah, I answer. And you're lucky that you're shorter than me, otherwise I'd give you a hiding.

Uncle Pita laughs. He gets out of the truck.

— I know what, he says. After we've finished here, how about you and me going to the pub, ay? I won't tell your Dad.

— I should have known we weren't coming to do some work, I answer. You just wanted me as an excuse to have a few drinks, I know you.

Uncle Pita smiles wanly at me.

— No, Tama. I wanted to get you away from Rongopai. You're taking it too hard. I wanted to talk to you. To tell you to lean on me. To tell you . . . so many . . . things . . .

With aroha, we look at each other. With aroha, we embrace each other.

Where are you, e pa? I call, but there is no sound. The tide ebbs silently away . . .

Mere, Hone, Marama and I are walking toward the old homestead. I am carrying Kararaina, Mere's baby, on my back. We are going home to get some blankets. More people have come to Rongopai.

The day is hot. Mere stops by the path and sits down for a rest. Kararaina begins to cry so Mere unbuttons her dress and Kararaina begins to suck at her breast.

— Eeeee! Hone yells.

— Go and play, Mere growls.

— Hone only wants to have some milk too! Marama says.

— I do not, Marama! Hone yells. Just wait till I catch you, I'm going to give you a hiding!

The two children run away, laughing and playing with each other. I pick a blade of grass and begin to chew at it.

— What's going to happen after the tangi? Mere asks.

I shrug my shoulders.

— Koro and I have been thinking, Mere continues, and we reckon we might come back here and stay with Mum.

— There's no need, I answer.

— I think Mum will need us, Mere says. She'll need to have somebody with her all the time, to talk to. Sometimes, to cry with. The house will be a lonely one now. Mum might have growled Dad a lot, but she needed him. She thinks she's strong, but she isn't; she's just stubborn! Yes, I think me and Koro will come back here. And Koro can give you a hand. You'll need some help with the farm, ay. It's settled then.

— You're a stubborn one, too! I say to Mere.

— No, Mere says. Her eyes brim with tears. No, I'm not stubborn. I try to be strong, just like Mum. But I'm not, you know. Dad was good to me. Now that he's dead, I keep thinking of how good he was.

I comfort Mere. Suddenly, Hone screams.

— Tama! Tama! Marama calls.

I run to where Hone is lying.

— Hone fell over, Marama says. He hurt his foot.

— Let me see, I tell Hone,

But he pushes me away.

— I want Daddy, he says. I want Daddy.

— Dad isn't here any more, Hone.

— He is so! Hone yells. You're telling lies, Tama! I want him, I want Dad . . . Daddy! Daddy? Daddy!

I hear him calling, his little voice calling. E pa, how will I explain to him? How will I ever begin to explain?

And I look up and see a hill far away. A hill upon which the sun blazes harshly. Where two shadows are bending. Bending and digging, digging and bending, in a family graveyard.

And a field half-ploughed, the plough lying on its side where father has left it, in which my little brother is calling.

— Come, Tama.

  — Where, Uncle?

  — To the hill, Tama. To the hill.

  — No. Let me stay here.

  — You must come. Now. We need you to help us. Haere mai.

My Uncle Pita waits for me. My mother cries at his words. She looks away from me as I leave. She strokes Dad's forehead, speaking his name over and over again. The other women on the porch begin to weep with her.

I follow Uncle to his truck. We drive toward the hill. The bus into Gisborne speeds past. There are no passengers, nor will there be any until the tangi is ended.

The hill grows larger, like a pyramid in the sky. The car stops at the gate.

  — Come, Tama.

The day is hot, the wind is warm. I follow Uncle through the sun and wind and green grass waving. The hill. The path. And I remember following after Nanny when she died, and hearing her rolling in the slow rising casket . . .

  — Come, Tama.

  . . . And my Auntie Ruihi screaming beside the open earth . . .

My feet are leaden, my heart is breaking. Above me, Uncle Pita is walking, crushing yellow flowers with his footsteps. Then he stoops to wash his hands at the gate . . . the gate to the graveyard.

— Come. Haere mai.

The graveyard is overgrown with gorse and long weeds. Somewhere, there is the sound of shovels digging into the earth. Digging. Uncle and I approach the sound. Hori and Koro see us and rest. Uncle motions Hori to give me his shovel. I take it. Then Uncle slips into the grave. I join him.

— Kia kaha, Tama, Uncle whispers.

I begin to dig. Slowly at first. The clay has not been reached yet. My tears begin to fall, warm and scalding. For this is where father will lie. Here, in this cold earth. Here. And he will be gone forever.

E pa . . .

Memories rise in the still air like smoke from many fires. Is this the same place, this place of ashes?

Father lies still. His hands are clasped upon a feather cloak. The cloak spreads across the porch like blood-gorged wings, curling slowly up and out toward the sky.

And I can only gaze in stricken agony at his magnificence.

E pa, you made my world and now you take it away with you. You gave light to my universe, the sun to my day. Yet, though you are dead, the sun still shines. But it is no ordinary sun, e pa. This is the sun of another world in which you do not walk with me. In this world, I must slough off my memories of you.

E pa, let me live. In this new life, I must be a man now. Not a child with his hand in his father's hand. I will be sometimes sad, sometimes happy, sometimes even, myself. I shall look after the family as you have taught me. I only fear because your world was so complete and I have little knowledge of how to build such another world.

Soon, e pa, you will be closed away from me. But stay a while longer. Stay here with me. Now, and after . . .

The flower wreaths shimmer in the hot sunlight. They glow with the colour of burning coals, with the crimson flickering of petals. And wild bees come to drink of the honey of the wreaths.

E pa, why didn't you teach me to be strong? I am a man now, yet

I am not ready for the world. You should not have let me love you so much. You should not have been so much a maker of my world. For at your going, my world goes too. It goes with you at the going down of the sun. And when the sun rises again, it rises upon ashes and wisps of smoke curling from a hundred fires.

Yet the stream still runs and the sun rides over the sky. And the mountains are always there.

Hone and Marama have finished having kai. Some of the other kids of the village have taken them to play outside. I sit in the dining room of Takitimu, listening to the cooks laughing and joking. Auntie Arihia comes and sits beside me.

— Hullo, Nephew, she says.

— Hullo, Auntie.

— Hey, Nephew, you're skinny! Are you sick or are you in love, ay?

She jostles me playfully and I smile at her.

— See? she yells to the women in the kitchen. I told you I could make him smile!

The women come out and sit with me.

— You haven't made him laugh though, Mrs Wharepapa says. She looks at me impishly. How can I make you laugh, Nephew? How can I make you laugh, ay? Shall I wiggle my bum? Will that make you laugh?

— If you wiggle your bum, somebody says, it might fall off!

— At least I've got a bum to wiggle, Mrs Wharepapa retorts. Not like you, Skinny Bum.

— I'd rather have a skinny bum than a fat bum!

And the women begin to squabble.

—Ara! Auntie Arihia says, triumphantly. We made him laugh, we made our nephew laugh!

The women smile at me. Auntie Arihia hugs me.

— We made a bet with each other that we could cheer you up, boy. You have to learn to laugh again. Don't mourn all the time, Tama. Life doesn't end. It goes on and on . . .

— Hey, Nephew! You're wanted on the telephone!

I see Nanny Whiti waving to me from the door of his house.

— Hurry up, it's a toll call.

I run to the house and pick up the 'phone.

— Hullo?

— Is that you, Tama? It's me here, Sandra. Oh, Tama, I've been out of my mind with worry wondering where you are and how you are. I only found out about your father this morning, and I've been trying to get you ever since. Why didn't you tell me, Tama? Why didn't you let me know?

— It all happened so quickly, I try to explain. I didn't have time to tell you. I had to get here as soon as I could.

— Why didn't you tell me, Tama? Do you want me to come up there?

— No. You wouldn't like it here.

— I'll come if you want me to.

— No, Sandra.

— Will you be coming back to Wellington again?

— I'm not sure. I can't make any plans yet. There's so much to do here.

— Well, when you do, will you give me a ring?

— Yes, I'll ring you.

— And I'm sorry about your father. That's why I rang up. To tell you how sorry I am for you. I liked your father when I met him. Tama, why didn't you tell me?

— Please, Sandra . . .

— I'll never understand you. But ring me when you return? Promise?

— All right.

— Goodbye then.

— Goodbye, Sandra.

There is a world outside this world of the tangi. People there are still living, still following the accustomed patterns of their lives. I have woven a pattern there which still exists. And after the tangi? What then?

That was another life. Another day.

I look out from the shadows of the porch to where the sun is blazing. There the mourners still sit, keening to one another.

Marama begins to cry. Mum soothes her.

— Go and play, Marama. You've been a good girl sitting here with me and Dad. But go and play now, you and Hone.

Marama looks at Hone. Then she nods.

— Will Daddy mind? Hone asks hesitantly.

— Daddy won't mind. He wants to see you two fullas being happy. Tell you what! You and Hone go there, on the edge of the marae and let Daddy see you play.

— Okay, Hone nods. He looks at Dad.

— How can Daddy see when his eyes are closed?

— He can see, Mum says.

— I won't be long, Hone tells his father. I won't go too far away.

He and Marama run into the sunlight. A dog begins to bark. It hurtles from the marquee and joins the two children. Marama yells with delight and plays hide and seek with the dog. She pulls Hone after her, and the mourners growl them amiably.

— Hey! You kids! Nanny Kiri says. Don't you come and hide behind me; if that dog doesn't bite you, I will!

The assembly watches and laughs. Other children appear. And suddenly, it seems that the afternoon sings with laughter. The dog barks, the children scream and scatter in the sun.

And then Marama turns toward the meeting house. Her eyes are bright. Her voice sparkles.

— Are you watching, Daddy? Are you watching?

I sit with the men beside the hangi pit. There are ten of them, all village men.

— Boy, Kani Heta says. I don't know where all these people are coming from! Looks like we'll have to go pig-hunting again. We have to feed them somehow.

— How about tonight, ay? Hoki Kahurangi says. Be a good moon tonight.

— Maybe for eeling, Frank Whatu says. But not for chasing pigs! Who wants to go chasing pigs at night time?

— It might do you a bit of good, Henare Rata laughs. It'll give you a rest from chasing the girls!

The other men laugh. Then Uncle Pita says:

— Yeah, there hasn't been this many people in Waituhi for a long time. Rongo, he was much loved. They just keep coming and coming. I don't even know some of them. It's good too, that Huia's people have come. It meant a lot to her.

The men nod in agreement. Arapera Jones rolls himself a cigarette.

— One thing about the tangi, he says. It might be sad, but it sure brings everybody together. It's good to be together for a change. Take my house: I've got my brothers back there with their kids, and my own kids too. There's hardly any room to move. But I'm enjoying it all, enjoying it all. Yeah, we're having a few beers at our place tonight . . .

He breaks off and looks at me. Uncle Pita laughs.

— Tama understands, ay Tama!

— Of course I do.

— We have a few beers, Arapera Jones continues, but it doesn't mean we forget the tangi. No, I won't forget your father for a long time, Boy. He was good to me. And he kept himself in good shape, that old fulla. Yeah, I can still see him now, running down that side-line in the game against East Coast last season. And there was I, with my big puku, jealous as hell!

The other men laugh, remembering.

— Ah well, Uncle Hori says. Although Rongo's gone, Tama is here. He'll take his Dad's place at football. Looks like he's pretty fit too, ay Tama?

— Fit maybe, I answer. But I'm not playing against any of you fullas. I'll get mangled.

— You want to put on some weight, that's your trouble.

— No, the trouble is that you fullas need to take some weight off, I answer.

The men laugh again. Then Uncle Pita gets up and stretches.

— Well! Let's have a look at the hangi, boys! Plenty of people to feed! Another day tomorrow!

We grab shovels and begin taking the sacking and dirt from the top of the pit. The ground steams.

Another day tomorrow; another life tomorrow.

There is a bitter wind blowing dust and ashes from the South. I can no longer see the stream, the sun, the mountains.

My Auntie Hiria, my mother's sister, approaches the porch. I greet her. She smiles at me.

— Tama, don't weep. You're a man now.

— Even men weep, Auntie.

178

— Ae. But save some tears for tomorrow.
— There is no tomorrow now that Dad's dead.
— Tomorrow will come. Weep then, Tama. Weep then.

The sun slants across the brilliant flower wreaths. It gleams upon
a portrait of my father. It is a photograph that was taken when he
was very young.

And it could almost be a photograph of myself . . .

My grandfather, my father's father, takes me aside.
— Be strong, Tama. Kia kaha.
— Yes, Nanny. I shall try.
— You are the first-born, the first son, as your father was and I
was, also.
— Ae. That is why I weep sometimes, because I am the first-
born. Am I strong enough, Nanny?
— Yes, mokopuna. You have always had the strength. But never
the test of that strength. Kia kaha. More mourners come and you
must welcome them.

Hata, my brother-in-law, takes off his shoes and comes onto the
porch. He sits with Ripeka, my sister, for a while. Then he whispers
in her ear.
— Where are you going? she asks him.
His words are too quiet for me to hear.
— Do you want me to come too?
He hugs her closely and smiles at her.
— No, dear. Your place is with your father . . .
And Ripeka leans her face upon his shoulder.

From where do they come, these long processions of mourners?
Which day is this? Is it the third day? And which night is this
approaching?

> Haere mai ki o tatou mate e . . .
> Haere mai. Haere mai . . .

*What night is this? Let this night be endless, endless Let the new sun
never rise . . .*

Which night is this? Is it the second night? No, let it be the first night. For if it is the second then tomorrow will be the third day, and in its afternoon father will be taken from me. E pa, stay with me and I am not afraid.

The children lie curled near Mum, sleeping with their heads in her lap, their hands tightly locked in hers. Father's face shines now, not with the sun, but with the harsh electric lights strung above the porch. The light cuts the darkness with a gleaming arc and within the light the mourners sit huddled in blankets.

A car swings round the road. For a moment its headlights dazzle my eyes. Then it roars past the meeting house, past the twinkling lights of Waituhi. Some of the whanau have returned home to their own houses to rest from the weeping. They will be sitting down to kai now, perhaps talking about Dad with the visitors who are staying with them. The night brings peace. The day will bring the grief to them again. So sleep well, my whanau, sleep well.

The moon rises, casting a calm glow over the land. Wisps of smoke curl from the houses like fingers clutching at the moon. Afar off I can see Takitimu Hall, silhouetted against the blue drenched sky. Some of the visitors who have come are sleeping there. Mattresses have been laid on the floor.

Here, near the meeting house, visitors are sleeping on hay in the marquee. Sleep well, sleep well, until the sun shines again.

My mother is still awake. She does not look toward the night. She sees only father, only father. The wind blows beneath the eaves of the meeting house. She shivers.

— Mum, are you warm?

She nods. She puts her hands across father's body and places her head close to his.

— I'm warm. Your father, he keeps me warm.

And as she cradles him, she whispers soft words.

— Rongo, Rongo . . .

On nights like this, like this we have helped each other. Do you remember? So many, many nights . . .

Which night is this? Is it the second night? No matter, it is still the tangi, the mourning of my father.

180

The night is clear. The night is filled with a deep and utter stillness. I am so tired, so tired.

But what is that sound? It is the long, clear whistling of a man walking in the hills. Listen, e pa. It is how you used to whistle when we were children. Listen: it is the song of the hills, soft and tender, echoing back from height to height. The sound ripples through the silence as if a stone has been dropped into a deep well. It is the song of the earth renewing. Of clear streams trickling over parched earth and leaves rustling in the wind. It is the plough turning the fields, the indefinable aroha between earth and man.

E pa, I was a child then, and I was afraid of the darkness. Yet I would not fear the night as long as the hills echoed your song to me. Never leave me, e pa. Never leave me.

My tears spill onto his body like night dew falling.

Never leave me . . .

A star blazes a sudden trail across the night, above a hill in Waituhi, across the face of the moon. The night brings peace. In that peace, I may rest.

A soft voice begins to sing in the night. It is an old woman singing. She sits among the mourners, swaying in time with her song.

> *E pari ra nga tai ki te akau,*
> *E hotu ra ko taku manawa . . .*
> *As the tide beats against the shore,*
> *So beats my sorrowing heart . . .*

Another voice joins in the song. And another and another. One by one, the mourners lift their heads to the light, looking toward the place where father lies. This is a night of their vigil. They sing to comfort each other through this long night. But most of all, they sing of their aroha for father.

Listen, e pa. And look, e pa: the song has brought others to the marae. The women are coming from the cookhouse, the men from tending the hangi. They pull their gumboots on and slip jerseys over their shoulders because the night is cold. They come, they come, to sit with the night mourners and share their blankets with them.

181

Tena ra, tahuri mai,
E te tau, te aroha . . .

The flap of the marquee opens, e pa. More people come for the lament is sweet to sing. They come in their pyjamas, they come in their nightgowns, to sit on the marae and sing to you.

Tenei ra, ahau te tangi nei,
Mohou kua wehea nei . . .

The people come, the people sit, filling the night with their song. They sing in unison, swaying and holding hands, looking at father.

Haere ra, mahara mai.
E te tau, kia mau ki a au.
Haere ra, ka tuturu ahau. Haere ra.

The song is ended. The people still remain. Someone yells:
— Hey! What's another song!
— Yeah, let's have another song, ay.
— Where's a guitar! Get a guitar!
A young boy runs to the marquee. He comes back with guitar in hand. He strums it, and another song bursts in the night.

Karanga tia ra, karanga tia ra,
Pohiri tia ra, nga iwi o te motu . . .

A joyful song, joyfully sung. An old woman stands up and begins to perform the actions to the song. Others stand up with her. The mourners watch and laugh as they sing.

All the long night they sing. My mother begins to sing with them. Song follows song.

Pa mai, to reo aroha . . .

No-one sleeps this night. They stay here, keeping company with father before the day comes again.

E pa, let the sun fall and the earth tremble. As long as my people are joined together, there is no darkness. As long as there is such aroha as this, I will not fear . . .

Is this the end of the night? Is this the beginning of my new day?
Which day is this, which night?

So cold, so cold. It is early morning and the world is filled with mist and the cold glitter of frost. The morning mist swirls in eddies upon the marae, drifting upon the small shapes of the mourners. A baby cries in the marquee.

Here on the porch, Mum lies beside father, her hands outstretched across him. She whispers softly to him.

— Rongo, I am here. I will keep you warm.

She brushes the frost from his eyelids. Her tears thaw the coldness from his cheeks. She shifts closer toward him, resting her head upon his chest.

And as she clasps him tightly, she disturbs the frost from the flower wreaths. They shiver and glitter with diamonds in the slowly rising light of another day.

Mist does not separate earth and sky; Death will not separate Earth and Sky.

From where do they come, these long processions of mourners? Is that the shrill cry of welcome once more? And what day is this? Which night is this? Why does the earth still turn in this place of sorrow?

— It is time, Tama.
— What did you say, Uncle Pita?
— This is the third day. This is the afternoon. It is time.
— The third day? The third day?
— Ae, Tama. The afternoon of the third day.

E pa . . .
   E pa . . .
This is when my world ends; this is when my life ends. This is when my world begins; this is when my life begins.

— Haere mai ki o tatou mate e!
   Haere mai! Haere mai . . .

Thirty

The mountains are coming closer. Clouds are lowering upon them swirling down with drifting grace, shedding eternal tears. The earth is a desolate sea, howling in darkness.

A train moves slowly into Palmerston North. For a quarter of an hour it stands at the station. Then it leaves Palmerston North. Away from the brightly lit city it thunders, toward the towering mountains. Far, far on the other side of them, lies Wellington.

Into the darkness. Into the night.

This is a silent world. People are weeping but I do not hear them. Women are wailing, but I do not hear them. All around me are the sights of people grieving, of despair and of distraught mourners. But no sound. No sound.

The church service, held for father on this marae, held in front of him, has ended.

And my grandfather, who led the service, has been the first to kiss my father before the casket is closed. The family has followed him, the old people, the young children, and father's children too. Each in turn has taken off his shoes and crawled onto the porch, to lie beside him and whisper his farewell.

I too, have stroked his hair. I too, have let my tears fall upon him. And I too, have kissed him.

Now, the whispered farewells are ended.

Uncle Pita speaks to me but I do not hear him. He motions me to follow him. He also motions to Uncle Wiremu and Uncle

Arapera, two of my father's brothers, and Kani Heta and Hoki Kahurangi, two of my father's friends, to join us. Together we walk through the grieving crowd toward Rongopai.

The mourners open a way for us. The women are gaunt, the men are grave. The children look at us, afraid. The crowd opens and there in front of me, Dad waits. *Tama you'll have to come home. Dad's dead.* The sun shines on the closed casket. It gleams on the silver inset upon which are inscribed the words: Rongo Mahana Born 1916 Died 1972. Part of the casket is covered with a feather cloak, rippling across the porch with the bronze fire of a moth's wings. At his feet, the flower wreaths are a blaze of dazzling colours. The photographs of Dad, displayed on the porch, flash in the falling sunlight.

Uncle Pita steps onto the porch. He bends over my mother where she kneels, her arms spread across the polished wood. *Mum was just lying there as if she was waiting for Dad to wake up.* He speaks to Mum. She shakes her head and clutches more tightly at father. Uncle Pita speaks to her again and holds her shoulders. My sisters too, they come to prise her away.

Her fingers claw at the casket as she breaks her clasp. Her head arches back, her hands reach up to tear at the sun.

And there is a storm among the mourners. Women gather round my mother, weeping with her. *Come home, Son.* Marama and Hone are afraid. Mum looks at them, dazed, and then gathers them into her arms. The children seem to calm her. She reaches for her black scarf and puts it over her hair. Wiki and Mere help her to stand. She sways, almost falls. *Come home, Tama.* But her face is calm now. She stands. She waits.

My shadow falls across the marae and each step I take is into that shadow. The dust swirls at my feet. Upon the porch, father is waiting.

Uncle Pita beckons me forward. I step among the flower wreaths toward him. I kneel on the other side of the casket. Together, Uncle and I lift the feather cloak from the casket.

The other men come onto the porch. We are the pall bearers. We wait while the hearse reverses slowly through the crowd toward father. The hearse stops, the door swings open. And carefully we lift father from the porch. *I must go home, Mr Ralston.* He is so heavy, so heavy. And although it is only a few steps to the hearse, it seems a long journey. The doors close behind him.

And people gather at the glistening windows, and palms press silently on the glass.

Another car draws up near the porch. The photographs of father, the flower wreaths and the feather cloak, are placed inside it. My mother steps into a funeral car. My sisters and brother step in after her. Mourners begin to move to the road. Already, some of them stream toward the hill where the graveyard is. Others are stepping into their cars. Headlights are being switched on, like a coronet of moons around an eclipsing sun.

I join my mother and my family. Mum sits in the back seat. Ripeka and Wiki are with her. Hone and Marama encircle her with their arms. Mere has gone to her own car.

The car begins to move. It follows the hearse as it slowly moves through the mourners to the gate. The mourners make way. Behind us, the other funeral cars begin to follow.

And glimpsed for a moment is the grief-stricken face of my sister, Mere.

The car bumps through the gate. It turns onto the road, following the hearse. *No, Mr Ralston, he was not an old man.* Far ahead, the road streams with people walking, slowly walking, crying out to the Hill, announcing that my father comes. People are clustering round the hearse. Auntie Ruihi is among them. Her lips are moving. She speaks to father.

I look away. Away from the road, away from the hill. I see the homestead and it seems to me as if I am there, watching from a window. I see people walking along the road which winds through the village. They raise swirls of dust. A long line of cars shines among them, more swinging into view. The cars come from Rongopai. They are heading for the hill. People are clustering there. People are streaming up the hill toward the graveyard.

The road unfolds through the green fields. This is my home, this is my whanau. This is Waituhi. *Where are you going, coz? I'm flying home, Kopua.* I look upon my village and suddenly the light begins to fade. A shadow advances across the landscape. It ripples across the houses. The wind and clouds are gathering at the hill. It always rains when a Maori dies.

The coldness strikes with a sudden blast of wind. The sky

begins to darken, a shadow across the sun. The sky comes to embrace the earth. No sound. No sound.

I look back. The cortege extends along the road behind us as far as I can see. Rongopai is for a small space of time, deserted. I look forward. Before me, the Hill is rising higher. People are stumbling toward the graveyard. At the foot of the Hill, a large throng of people wait. They wait for father to come.

The car begins to slow down. The crowd thickens at the windows. In front, the hearse comes to a silent halt. The doors swing open.

E pa . . .

For a moment, the world is a blur of rushing shadows. Black veiled faces mourn with soundless agony. Then, there is Uncle Pita with the other pall bearers, beginning to take father from the hearse.

I step from the car and open the door for my mother. We embrace. Then she breaks our clasp and gathers the children to her. Mere joins us. *Don't weep my sister. I am here now.* Together we walk through the bustling crowd to where father is waiting.

Uncle Pita motions to me. Before I go to him, I turn to my mother.

— E ma, be strong e ma.

But she does not hear. I take my place beside the casket. Father is so heavy. I can feel his body moving inside the casket as we carry him through the crowd.

My heart is breaking. My tears are falling. And a storm is gathering across the hill. *Dad waits for you at Rongopai, Tama.* The sky is thick with lowering clouds, surging and lowering. The day is darkening, becoming ashen. The air is shifting, swelling and subsiding. The mourners must struggle against the currents as they climb the hill. The wind and clouds are coming to farewell father.

Beyond the hill, the sun is shafting sunlight upon another world.

Uncle Pita signals a rest. We lower the casket to the ground. Each of us is lost in our own thoughts. My mother comes to rest her head against the casket. Behind, more mourners are streaming up the hill. *Dad waits, Tama.* Above, mourners are waiting at the graveyard. Waiting where headstones and crosses prick at the ashen sky. *Tama, he waits.*

Rain begins to fall. It splashes on my mother's face. It splashes upon my father's casket. Then Uncle Pita motions us to take him up again. He is so heavy my father. But one step. Then another. *And one step further now.*

Through the rain, carrying father. Through the press of mourners. The rain streams from their faces. The path is becoming muddy and trickles with rivulets of rain. On the path, a fallen chaplet of kawakawa leaves lies.

Ahead, the mourners gather round the gateway to the graveyard. *Haere mai ki o tatou mate e.* They open up before my father, waving sprigs of greenery in their hands. The mourners glisten in the rain. Their hair is matted and they lift their faces to the darkening sky. *Haere mai, haere mai.* The women sway and keen a lament. They raise their arms toward my father.

So heavy he is; he is so heavy. And as I am carrying him, my feet slip. My grandfather gives me his strength. He steadies father for me. Then he comforts me. *You must make your father proud, mokopuna.* And one step further now, through the gateway into the graveyard.

Here, in this place, lie my whanau, my family dead. Here, among the flowering gorse they lie, beneath simple headstones.

And father comes to sleep with them. This is the afternoon of the third day.

Strange, the wind has ceased a moment. Strange, the clouds are still. Nothing moves in this world except the mourners following through the graveyard after father. *There is no sound. The tide ebbs silently away.* But a further step forward now. Past the headstones to the place where father will rest. Until I am standing with him at the newly dug ground.

The casket is laid upon the ground. *Death comes but I am not yet dead.* The mourners press close to it. To one side, Mum is standing with my brothers and sisters. My grandfather is with them too. He embraces her and then addresses the mourners. He is saying farewell for them. The mourners nod at his words. They brush at their tears. Once again they come forward, one by one, to bend and say haere ra to father. They kneel in the mud and whisper to him. And Auntie Ruihi kisses the polished wood. *I breathe, I live.*

Then my sisters come to farewell father. Ripeka the calm one,

Mere the strong one, and Wiki the one whom father loved most. Finally, my mother bends to the casket. She caresses it softly. I join her. *Kua mate taku papa*. We link hands.

Uncle Pita motions me to help lower father into the ground. I take hold of the cord. It begins to rain again. Grandfather reads from the Bible, a hand raised in the air.

E pa, don't leave me . . .

Slowly, slowly the casket descends. Until the cord slackens.

The rain drives across the hill. The women clutch their scarves and the men bow their heads against the wind. So many are the mourning people who come to farewell father.

Petals fly loose from the flower wreaths. The leaves of the kawakawa chaplets swirl away in the wind. The black skirts of the women flap soundlessly in the storm. The mourners come forward to look upon father. Clay trickles upon the casket. *I bend toward him and my shadow falls across him.* My father's belongings, his clothes, suitcases of garments, cascade into the ground. So many photographs are thrown into the ground to crack and splinter across the casket. *E pa, farewell e pa*. One by one they fall.

And then the feather cloak falls, unfolding its glistening feathers to shimmer across father. *Your lips are cold, e pa.*

No sound, no sound. In the driving rain, I see my mother step forward. She bends to the earth and then she gathers some clay and casts it into the grave. And suddenly, there is a storm of sky and earth, of upraised hands casting crumbling earth toward father. The dirt rains upon him, upon the feather cloak.

And men begin to shovel earth over him.

Farewell, e pa. . .

Some of the women fling their kawakawa circlets to the ground. Auntie Ruihi struggles against the arms of Uncle Pita. My grandfather lifts his face to the bitter rain. Mere and Ripeka must hold Wiki back from the open ground. The dirt falls, *the rain falls*. The dirt falls, *the rain falls*.

I hold my mother tightly to me. She stretches forward for father.

And Earth reaches for Sky and Sky bends to Earth. One last fierce clasp in rain and wind and wind and rain. One last embrace of rage and fury and helpless grief. One last clinging of body to body, of Earth to Sky. One last meeting of lips to lips and tears to tears.

And then the slow drawing away, the slow tearing away, the slow wrenching away of Sky from Earth, of Earth from Sky, in the final, sorrowful separation . . .

    Farewell, e pa. Haere ra, my father.

Thirty-one

If anything should happen to me, you must look after the family, Tama.

Yes, Dad.

You must come home. Your mother will need you. Your brother and sisters will need you too.

Dad, I will remember.

You are the eldest, Son. The eldest always looks after the younger ones of the family.

I understand, Dad.

I was taught that when I was a child. I teach you the same thing now. Never forget.

E pa, I will never forget . . .

Good boy, Son. You make me proud, ay?

I will be your son, e pa. I will make you proud, e pa. Haere ra, e pa. Haere ra.

Thirty-two

The window streaks with rain. The train leaves the platform at Levin. We are nearing Wellington. It is past seven o'clock now. In a short while my journey will be over.

The train curves into the dark bleakness ahead, breaking through the rain. The carriage rocks and sways like a canoe adrift. The mountains are the ridged backbone of a whale plunging. The landscape is the turmoiled waves of its huge tail flukes descending. Another sheet of rain dashes against the window. The streaming raindrops scatter through my reflection.

I am Tama Mahana, and my father is dead. This is the end of my journey but it is also my journey beginning. It is a journey out of the upheaval of the tangi. The tangi is over. The hands of the clock stand at the beginning of another hour.

Father . . . After his burial the world seemed to stand still. There seemed a sudden calm. In that world I walked in numb despair. The tangi was over, but there was still so much to do.

I went to see the mourners who had come. I went to thank them for coming. I went to Rongopai and kissed them. For them, the tangi was over, but not yet for myself. In the marquee, the visitors joked and laughed with each other. They waved me to join them.

— Don't be sad, Tama, they said. The time for grieving is over. You must go on living now.

I wandered on the marae and wondered why it was so calm. This was another day, but this was the same marae. This was the sky of another day, but it was still the same sky. Only a few flower petals and drying leaves remained to remind me that here, my father had lain.

I saw smoke curling from homes in Waituhi. Children laughed in the sun. The bus into Gisborne idled past, and was filled with local people going into the city.

Life was renewing. But not yet for me.

The train speeds across the night, closer to Wellington. There is a sudden glimpse of traffic trickling along a wet shining highway. The fluorescent lights of a roadside cafeteria snap on and off with a bold orange glow.

The girl from Wairoa strikes a match. She bends her head to catch the flame to her cigarette. Her eyes are filled with excitement. She leans back and looks out the window upon the lights of Wellington approaching.

The night after the tangi, the visitors assembled at Takitimu Hall. This was the farewell night. Outside, the hangi gushed steam through the darkness. The smells lingered as the men began to take the food out. Inside the Hall, the women joked and made the tables ready for the kai. Ripeka, Mere and Wiki helped in the kitchen. My mother sat with her sisters who were trying to make her happy. The crowd overflowed from the Hall, outside onto the grounds. Groups were drinking. Children were playing in the darkness. Hone and Marama were among them. Then the kai was ready. Auntie Hine yelled out:

— Haere mai ki te kai! Haere mai!

And they all came into the dining hall, warming it with their laughter.

I watched them, not understanding. My father was dead. Yet, there they were, these same people who had mourned him, happy now. They saw that I was still unhappy.

— Tama, let your father rest, they said. Come. Eat. Haere mai.

Together, they tried to make me forget. They told me jokes, they told me to join in with singing the joyful songs of our people. For while we were eating, we also had a concert. Somebody would sing a song and others would join in.

Then, when it was getting very late, the tables were cleared and put away. The cooks came from the kitchen. The speeches

195

were said. My grandfather spoke first, thanking the visitors for coming. My mother's father answered on behalf of her people. Then Uncle Pita spoke. And so it went on. Sadness came to the Hall when the speeches were finished. I spoke too. And then somebody began to strum a guitar. One last song before departing.

> *Tahi nei taru kino*
> *Mahi whaia-ipo,*
> *Ke te wehenga*
> *Aroha kau ana . . .*

In the morning, we would be leaving one another. Some of these people had come from Auckland, some from Wellington. The whanau would be loosening hands and going away. Perhaps not to see each other, not to be united again for a long time.

> *Oh how it grieves me*
> *To look within your heart,*
> *And think of parting,*
> *Which brings such sorrow . . .*

So now we sing to one another, because this may be the last farewell for some of us. We sway together and we sing of our love for our whanau. And we say to each other: no matter how far away from here we go, we will always leave our hearts here. Always remember us. Always remember.

> *Haere mai ra*
> *Kia hau nei ra,*
> *He aroha tino nui*
> *Haere ra . . . .*

We sing of Maori aroha. We say: to manawa, e taku manawa. Your heart is my heart. When you are sad, I am sad. When you are happy, I am happy. When you need love, I will give you love. Your tears are my tears. Your laughter is my laughter.

> *There'll be a welcome*
> *when you return,*
> *You know my heart is yours,*
> *come, haere mai . . .*

This is what aroha is. No matter how far we or you go away or if the world is grey, always remember: we are all family. Until we meet again, or until the sun shines again, let us enjoy each other's company. We may not meet until the next homecalling . . .

The carriage is filled with the stirring noises of the other travellers. A woman wakes her small son who has been sleeping in her arms. An old man wakes from dozing. Three young men put away their playing cards. The Maori girl looks at her reflection in the window and begins to comb her hair.

The visitors began leaving Waituhi in the morning after our gathering at Takitimu Hall. All day long there was a steady departing of cars. It was sad to see them leave. They were sad to leave. I had welcomed them here. The village had welcomed them here. Now, the village and I were farewelling them.

— Tama, if you need us you need only call and we will come.
— Look after your mother, Tama. Kia kaha, Boy.
— Why don't you send Marama and Hone to us for a holiday? It's about time we had our mokopunas to live with us.
— Aue, Nephew. My heart still aches . . .

Gradually, they left Waituhi. The tempo of village life began to return to normal. But there was still so much to do. In the following days, Uncle Pita and I, helped by the other men, pulled down the marquee and returned the hay and bedding. The women of the village had a huge dish-washing session at Takitimu Hall. Afterward, they scrubbed the floors. The left-over food was divided equally among them.

Then Takitimu Hall saw another gathering. This was for the village people. We sat around and talked quietly to one another. Uncle Pita and the boys went down to the pub and brought back some beer. We were all very tired. It had been an exhausting time. We talked about Dad. Then we talked about how good it had been to see our family gathered together again. Finally, we left the Hall for our own homes. Auntie Ruihi to her children. Uncle Pita to his farm. The hangi was closed for the last time. It hissed and steamed as we dampened it. Then, my grandfather quietly closed the door of Takitimu Hall. Life was renewing.

Yet my father's family still grieved.

A week after the tangi, we all gathered at the homestead: Grandfather, Dad's brothers and sisters, myself and my brother and sisters. Together we talked about the future and what had to be done. My Uncle Arapera thought it might be best if Mum sold the farm. Uncle Pita answered:

— No. Tama will look after it.

— Yes, Mum continued. Tama and I.

— And don't forget me and Hata! Ripeka interrupted.

— Huh? What about me as well? Mere asked. How much are you going to pay us, Mum?

We all laughed. After a while, my grandfather and my father's brothers and sisters left the homestead.

— Don't you worry if things go hard for you, my grandfather said. We're all here to help you. Even me. I'm still good for putting up a fence yet. Okay, so I'm an old fulla, but I got something over you, mokopuna. I'm wise.

— And speaking of fences, Auntie Ruihi said, you better do something about the one near the main road. And then there's the spuds to dig up, and the well which your father was going to put down in the far paddock, and . . . Aue! I bet you'll be like your father. I may as well do it all myself.

Uncle Arapera, Auntie Arihia, Uncle Wiremu, I said goodbye to them too. Then it was time to thank Uncle Pita.

— You are the eldest in your family, he told me. Now that your father is dead, I am the eldest in my family. Tama, if ever you need me, you lean on me.

We embraced and closed a gap in the world. Then Uncle Pita gave me the gifts of money which the mourners had left for our family.

— This is from our people. It is to pay for the tangi, for the funeral.

My mother wept.

— Turi turi, Huia, Uncle said. Be proud. You should be proud. He left then. The homestead grew silent. Night approached. Mum said to Marama and Hone:

— You come and sleep with Mum tonight. She's a big baby, she doesn't want to sleep in her big bed all alone. You come with me and keep me warm, ay?

One by one, my sisters and their husbands would go to bed too. Often I remained alone after everybody was asleep. Like Mum, I felt the night encircling me with loneliness. I would go out onto the verandah and watch the clouds scudding silently across the face of the moon. Far away, the lights of Waituhi would be glowing like many lamps twinkling in the night.

I would hear my mother where she wept in the bedroom she had shared with Dad, her voice whispering disconsolately through the darkness.

— Aue, Rongo. Oh, Rongo, Rongo, Rongo ...

And then I would hear Marama saying:

— Don't cry, Mum. Don't cry.

Sometimes, listening to my mother's sadness made me recall so many memories of Dad that I remained on the verandah to watch the morning burst across the hills. And there was one beautiful morning when both Mum and I watched the sun rising. We sat on the steps and we were silent. Then Mum said:

— We'll be all right, Son. Don't you worry. We'll be all right.

The train stops briefly at Paekakariki station. In half an hour, it will reach Wellington railway station. Some of the passengers get off the train. I see them dashing away through the rain. This has been a long journey. It is almost over now.

The nights following the tangi were the worst times for my mother. She was kept busy during the day with running a household of sons and daughters and two small mokopunas. We all tried to make Mum happy, even if only for a while. Sometimes, it seemed as if nothing had changed at all. We sat together and talked and laughed. And the children played among us. Hata and I had already begun to make plans about the farm. Mum would shake her head and say:

— Your fullas' schemes will never work! Aue! I had to teach Rongo; and now, I have to start all over again with you fullas.

We made Mum too busy during the day for her to be unhappy. But with the night, the memories came. When the time came to go to bed, Mum would begin to weep. Always, she beckoned to Marama and Hone.

I look out the window. The landscape is dark; the night is here. How long will it be until my morning breaks? The rain streams down the glass and the gathering lights of Wellington are fires stippling the darkness.

Slowly, life was beginning again. The call to go on living became more insistent. One Friday night, I made my first visit after the tangi into Gisborne. Marama and Hone were with me. We walked the crowded streets together. I wanted to make them happy. They would run toward a shop window and look with wide eyes at the toys. Marama wanted a colouring book. Hone decided he'd have a toy truck. They wanted ice creams so I bought them an ice cream each. They wanted some lollies, so I bought them some lollies. Then they got too ambitious and wanted to go to the pictures.

— No, I told them. I'm broke enough already.

So we kept looking at the shops instead. It was good, because I met many of my friends.

— Gidday, Tama! they would yell.

I met Kopua, my cousin, whom I'd not seen since I'd met him last at Wellington Airport. He'd been at the tangi and yet I couldn't remember having seen him there.

— I was there, he said. And afterward, I thought to myself: well, you're back home, so you might as well stay home. So here I am!

Kopua wanted me to have a few drinks with him. He insisted so much that I finally gave in. I told Marama and Hone to go and buy some fish and chips and wait for me at the truck.

I met more of my old friends in the pub. Some of them didn't know that Dad was dead. I didn't tell them. It was Friday night and I didn't want them to feel sad.

— How long are you staying in Gisborne? they would ask. When are you going back to the big smoke?

— I'm not going back. I'm home to stay.

— Not going back? Hey, that's beaut! Come to our party next week.

I promised to get in touch with them later. There was so much to do before I could ever join them again. Then I told Kopua that I'd had my few drinks and it was time for me to go. He argued a bit at that, but then said he would come round to see me the next weekend.

I left the pub and went back to the truck. Hone and Marama were not there. I felt panic-stricken. I rushed through the crowded streets looking for them.

— Hone! Marama!

I saw Auntie Ruihi among the crowd and asked her:

— Have you seen the kids?

But she hadn't. She said she would look on one side of the street and I better look on the other. We would meet at the truck. I pushed through the crush of people, looking for them. Everywhere, people were happy. I wished I'd never gone to the pub.

Then I saw them. My anxiety dropped away. I strode to the truck. They were sitting in the front waiting for me and Marama was saying:

— One for you and one for me. And one for you and one for me . . .

— Just what do you think you fullas are doing? I asked.

— We're sharing our chips, Tama, Marama said.

— And where have you fullas been! It doesn't take this long to go to the fish shop and back.

— There was a big queue and we had to wait, Marama replied simply. Those fullas were mean. They kept pushing me and Hone right to the back, ay Hone.

—Yes, Hone agreed. Now hurry up and finish sharing the chips, Marama. We got up to one for me.

— Not! The next one is for me.

— Eeee! You're a liar, Marama.

They continued to squabble. Auntie Ruihi arrived at the truck. She shook her head and looked at me.

— I don't know, Tama Mahana. I don't know . . .

I took Marama and Hone home.

The train jolts to a stop at Porirua. The girl gets her suitcase from the rack. She smiles at me before walking down the aisle of the train. I watch her through the window. She stands there, hugging her coat to her to keep out the cold. She stands, she waits. The train departs from the station.

The tangi was my night, dark and all-encompassing. But light was coming to scatter slowly away the night. A changed sun was leaping into a changed sky. The wind was sighing with new breath. One morning, I heard the Piwakawaka chirping:

— Forgive me, Tama. Live again, Tama.

His fluted notes welcomed in the dawn; Hinetitama who became Hine-nui-te-Po. So Hine of the long night becomes Hine the dawn maiden. So one night ends and another day begins. Life was renewing.

I went out that day and walked alone to Rongopai. I stood on the marae and saw the roof of the meeting house still holding up the sky. Then I walked along the road and up the hill to see my father where he lay in the graveyard. The earth above him was strewn with wilting flowers and scattering leaves. From his grave, I could see right across Waituhi to the surrounding hills. The village, the meeting house, my family ... And I whispered to father:

— E pa, you are still here.

Through a tunnel the train rushes and suddenly Wellington Harbour appears. The sea is calm with a metallic sheen. The inter-island ferry is steaming out toward the Heads. Its glittering lights are reflected in the water.

The train follows the railway track as it curves round the harbour. Wellington is ahead, stack upon stack of glowing lights rising upon the hills. Soon the train will rumble into the station. Once again, a thousand destinies will be set in motion.

It was time to live again. The tangi was over. Our family talked things over one night. It was decided that Mere and Koro would stay with Mum and me at the homestead. Hata already had a good job in Gisborne and he and Ripeka owned a State house in the city. Wiki and Matiu, of course, would be returning to Auckland.

Wiki cried when she left Mum. We waved and waved until the car had disappeared. She is coming back to us at Christmas. As for Ripeka, well Gisborne was really only down the road. She promised to come out and see Mum as often as she could.

So we were left: myself, Mum and the children, and Mere and Koro and the baby. We had no time for feeling sad that our family was separating. Came the morning after Wiki's departure, and there was Mum, already in her gumboots, shouting through the house:

— Come on! Time to get up! There's a lot of work to do!

I groaned when Mum pulled me out of bed. But she was insistent.

— Come on, Son! Get up. I don't know, you're just like your father was. Shake it up, shake it up!

Breakfast was a merry affair. There was Mum, bustling around us, telling us to get a move on and take your time but hurry up. Mere winked at me. It was good to see Mum in such a mood. It was just like the old times.

After kai, Koro went to the shed and drove the tractor to the potato paddock. Mum, Mere, myself and the kids followed after him. When we reached the gate, Mum paused for a moment. Dad had been discing this paddock before he died. Her eyes glistened. Then determined, she strode into the paddock.

— Come on then! What are you fullas standing around for! There's work to do.

Koro began to turn the ground. The potatoes were lifted out by the steel blades of the plough. We followed after him, picking up the potatoes and putting them into sacks. Mum and Mere joked with one another.

— Hey, Mum! Mere would say. You left a spud behind.

— You left it behind. Not me.

— Don't you talk to me like that, Mum, or else I'll find another job. Anyway, how much are you going to pay me?

— Pay you? With what!

— You mean you got no money? Ah well, I tell you what: you give me the farm when you die, ay?

— Me, die? You'll be waiting a long time, Girl. Your mother, she's never going to die. Never.

Wellington. The train comes slowly to a halt. The engine whines down into silence. The noise of people rushing and bustling on the platform rises. I watch them from the window. I see people stepping down from the train and being greeted. I look away. Nobody will be here to meet me. Sandra and this life are not now my life. My life is in Waituhi. To Waituhi, I shall return.

I stand and reach for my coat. It has been a long journey and I am very tired. I walk down the aisle and step off the train into the crowd. Chapters begun, chapters ending, chapters continuing. A thousand destinies . . . My suitcase is in the luggage compartment. I join the people milling around it.

— Yes, that's my case. The brown one.

— . . . and mother told me to tell you . . .

— Is it always this cold, Betty?

203

— Thank God I'm here. It's been a long trip ...

A porter puts my suitcase on a trolley. I elbow through the crowd and pick it up. Then I walk along the platform and through the concourse. My footsteps are drowned by the noise of people rushing and clattering in the station. They belong to another world ...

For a moment, I pause on the steps to the railway station. I am half in light, half in darkness. Shadow and light, my future. It is raining heavily.

E pa, one day I will build my world again. One day. See, e pa? No more tears. You are still here with me.

I walk out into the night.

My mother was the Earth.

My father was the Sky.

They were Rangitane and Papatuanuku, the first parents, who clasped each other so tightly that there was no day. Their children were born into darkness. They lived among the shadows of their mother's breasts and thighs and groped in blindness among the long black strands of her hair.

Until the time of separation and the dawning of the first day.

Epilogue

Mourners are making their way down the hill from the family graveyard where we have laid our father to rest. They are streaming away through the sunset.

Together, we have stood beside his grave. We have listened as our grandfather blessed the ground into which our father was lowered. We have urged the diggers to work quicker with the chanting of a haka. We have told them to put their strength to the spade, so that our father is more quickly embraced by Papatuanuku, the Earth.

Then, weeping, we have lain the flower wreaths upon him. And together, we have listened to a pakeke intone an ancient lament.

It has rained; and we have all waited through the rain and then the burst of sun beside the grave of our father. We have not wanted to leave him.

Now, the sunset has come. When it first drifted through the clouds, we had begun to sing hymns. Softly. Quietly. Trying to find peace with ourselves. Trying to calm our sorrow for our father.

Now, we are leaving him. My mother's arm rests on mine. My sisters and the little ones follow closely with her.

People stream before us; people follow after us. I guide my mother to the bottom of the hill.

Suddenly, she lets go of my arm. She turns to face the hill where our father lies. The setting sun shines full upon her. The many emotions of sorrow flicker on her face. The tears spill quickly.

Then, from a well of strength within her, she calms her sorrow. With an angry gesture, she flicks her tears away. With pride, she looks upon the hill. And slowly, she lifts her arm to our father.

— *Haere ra, Rongo! Haere! Haere! Haere!*

Her voice is strong and ringing. It is fierce with pride and breaks the silence of the departing mourners.

— *Haere ra, Rongo! Haere! Haere! Haere!*

All faces turn back to look at the hill. And many hands lift in the air and many voices join my mother's voice.

— *Haere ra, Rongo! Haere! Haere! Haere!*

Farewell, Rongo! Farewell! Farewell! Farewell!
It is a cry of aroha, swelling louder and gathering in strength. It is an acclamation for our father.
It is the final farewell, echoed by earth and sky.
It is a roar of pride, before the slow descending of the sun.

Whanau

FOR TE WHANAU A KAI
AND JOY

One

An Irishman, a Scotsman and a Hori
Were sentenced to be hung one sunny day.
The Irishman said: Hang me from an oak tree.
The Scotsman said: Any tree will do.
Then the Judge turned to the Hori
And asked: What will be the tree for you!

It is four o'clock, Sunday morning. The sky is lightening with the sun, a pale wash spreading above the foothills. The clouds are pink-streaked, steaming from the valleys. Shadows remain on the lowland, gradually receding as the sun rises. They linger on a small wooden bridge. Then first light touches the wooden spars and criss-cross shadows are cast upon an old truck as it rumbles over the bridge. The headlights are still shining.

A man and two women are sitting in front. One of the women has a sleeping baby on her lap. The man's eyes are squinted and bloodshot, and his hands grip the steering wheel tightly as the road momentarily blurs with brilliant sun. In the lapel of his black suit he wears a wilting carnation.

— I sure can't wait to hit that bed, Charlie Whatu yawns.

— Well make sure you don't hit the bend first, his wife says sharply.

— It's sure been a long night, Charlie says.

— For you and me, yes, his wife smiles. But not for those fullas on the back!

Her eyes twinkle as she looks in the rear vision mirror.

— We're not as young as we used to be, says Maka, the other woman with the baby. I'm so tired my eyes are falling out. Not enough sleep, that's the trouble.

— You mean too much booze, *that's* the trouble! Charlie laughs.

People of the village of Waituhi huddle together on the tray. They are past caring about their neat clothes, the clothes they put on for special occasions. The dresses are crumpled, the suits stained. And who cares if the lipstick has smeared or the hair's gone haywire; you can't keep beautiful all the time. Soon be able to sleep it off, close those bleary eyes and lose the old haggard look. But until then, keep those blankets tucked under because that wind is bloody cold and keep singing to the guitar:

> *Won't you hang me from my favorite tree?*
> *Said the Judge: Oh what tree can that be?*
> *It's my dying request, it's the tree*
>   *that I love best,*
> *Won't you hang me from a gooseberry tree!*

There are eleven adults on the back of the truck. Only seven are still singing; the other four have flaked out under the blankets where three children are sleeping. They're haurangi, those four! Couldn't take the beer at George Karepa's wedding yesterday. Man, a good wedding it was too. Plenty of kai, plenty of booze and plenty of dancing. Terrific band too, those 'Condors'. Trust that Charlie Whatu to want to come home so early. Trust him to be the owner of this truck. He sure is haddit spoiling all the fun. Not to worry: you don't have to be at a wedding to enjoy yourself.

> *Said the Judge: Oh but surely you know*
> *That a gooseberry tree is too low?*
> *That's all right with me, says Mo,*
> *I will wait till it grows*
> *To the size of a big apple tree!*

2

The song ends with laughter. Eyes light up with pleasure and voices punctuate the steady drone of the truck's motor.

— What's another song! Hine Ropiho yells. She's twenty-four and is still feeling happy; not like that Jack, her husband, or that Mattie Jones. Both of them are out to the world, sleeping the beer off.

— Ne' mind about the song, Sam Walker interrupts. Just pass that bottle over here ay, Hine. I know you're tryin' to hog it all in your corner!

— Too right, too, Hine answers. What's wrong with the bottles you got in your corner, Sam! You ain't getting my bottle, that's for sure. Come on, Joe, play another song!

— Wait your hurry, Joe says.

Hine leans back against the side of the tray. She is blissfully tired. For one day she has been happy, one solitary day among all those days stretching backward and in front of her. But not to worry about the grey days ahead and Jack . . . Time enough for that.

— Jeez, she whispers, it was a good wedding all right.

— Yeah, Sam Walker answers.

— Hey! Joe says. Let's go back, ay?

— Why not! comes the chorus.

— The party's bound to be still on, Sonny Whatu says. Dad's a bloody nuisance wanting to come home. Bang on the roof and tell him to turn his precious truck around. It's going the wrong way for the party!

— Hey, Charlie! Sam Walker yells to Sonny's father. Charlie! Charlie, you deaf bastard.

— What's up back there! Somebody want to get off and have a piss? Can't you fullas hold your booze!

— Charlie! Hine Ropiho yells. You just turn this truck around or I'll give you a good hiding. We want to go back.

— Aaargh, catch a taxi then, Charlie Whatu answers. Next time, I'll leave you fullas behind and you can all walk home.

— Oh Charlie, sweetheart, Hine says. Don't you love us any more?

She grumbles to herself.

3

— We should hijack this truck, Sonny Whatu says.

— And fly it to Cuba? Sam Walker asks.

— Man, yeah, Sonny grins.

— You'd better wake up both of you, Hine grins. This old truck get to Cuba? Huh! Even if we could get Charlie to go back to the wedding we'd be lucky if we got halfway there.

— Halfway? Sam asks. You sure would be lucky!

Hine nods in agreement. Then she sees a little head pop out of the blankets beside her.

— Huh? I thought you was asleep, she says.

— You fullas making too much noise, her son answers. Are we home yet?

— No, Boy Boy. You go back to sleep. Pull the blankets over your head. We'll be home soon and you can have a long moe in bed.

The head disappears. Sonny Whatu yells:

— Come on, Joe, attack that guitar! Don't let the old man spoil our fun.

Then he sees that Mattie Jones is waking up too.

— Hey, look at this! he laughs. Sleeping Beauty is coming alive again. Give us a kiss, Mattie.

— Keep your fucken hands off me, Mattie Jones answers. Her voice is hoarse with pain. She pushes Sonny away and lifts her head to the sun.

Her face is startlingly beautiful. Her eyes, deep brown, swim with tears. She flicks them away and fingers the purple bruise on her cheek. Then she moans.

— Oh, Jeez, I'm going to be sick again.

— Not over my dress, you don't, Hine snaps. That'll teach you to drink too much.

Mattie moans again.

— What's the time? she whispers. That isn't the sun, is it? Oh my God, it is too! I feel like a bloody wreck.

— You sure look like one! Sam Walker laughs. He puts his arms around her. What were you up to last night, ay Mattie? What'd Blacky do to you after the dance! Did he hit you, ay? And did he give you that black eye?

4

— Blacky? Blacky who! And what black eye; that ain't a black eye, that's my mascara. And I never went with no Blacky last night, did I Hine?

— Can't you remember, you dumb moll? Hine grumbles.

— No, and I don't want to, either, Mattie answers vaguely. Anyway, Hine Ropiho, you were supposed to look after me. Big friend you are.

— Don't blame me, Mattie. What you do is your own business. If you want to make a fool of yourself, that's your worry. I was too busy holding up Jack to worry about you as well.

Hine looks down at her husband with disgust. She boots him.

— Jack? Wake up! I'm not carrying both you and Boy Boy to bed.

Everyone laughs. Then Sonny Whatu asks:

— You think George Karepa will bring his missus back here with him?

— Back to this one-horse place? Sam Walker answers. Not likely! Him and Alice are off to Wellington.

— Lucky bastard, Sonny whispers.

— Nothing for him here, Sam continues. What's he want to come back here for! No, he's after the big money and good on him too.

— Boy, it was a good wedding . . . Sonny sighs.

— Yup, Sam says. Another fulla gone down the drain. Hey, Mattie! You were hot on George once, weren't you!

— Damn George Karepa! she spits.

— He ditched you, ay Mattie? Sam teases.

— What do you mean he ditched me? Nobody ditches Mattie Jones. If you want to know, I ditched him so there. Jeez, I feel sorry for Alice . . .

— Why, Mattie? Sam chuckles. Has George got a big one?

— Shut your mouth, Sam.

— Come on, Mattie, Hine interrupts. Don't take any notice of Sam. He's only joking.

— Well he can keep his damn jokes to himself, Mattie whispers, tears springing in her eyes. All you fullas, just leave me alone ay?

Sam laughs. He hugs Mattie close to him.

— Can't you take a joke, you stupid moll? he asks. Cheer up, Mattie. You can cuddle up to me any time.

— You stink, she answers in a softening voice. Oh, Jeez, everything's gone wrong . . . and I feel groggy and . . . when are we going to get home? And somebody tell that sun to go away? Hey, Charlie! Can't you make this truck go any faster?

Sam grins. He grabs the guitar from Joe.

— Listen to Mattie giving orders! Come on, boys, let's sing her a song!

> Show us the way to go home,
> Mattie's tired and she wants to go to bed.
> Oh, she had too much to drink about an hour ago,
> And she wants to go to bed instead.
> Wherever she may roam, on land or sea or
> Anywhere you want her to, you can always
> Hear her singing this song:
> Show me the way to go home . . .

Wanly, Mattie smiles. And the others whoop and laugh together. The truck sways round a corner. Ahead lies the village. Home.

— Home sweet home, Charlie sighs.

— Bed sweet bed, his wife grins.

She looks out at the village. All her life she has lived here. She has never known any other life except village life. Yet, her breath still catches at this first sight of it, so bright and beautiful in this morning sun. Home.

— Home! Hine Ropiho yells.

— Yeah, back to the sticks, Sonny Whatu growls moodily.

Back to the nothing place, the nowhere place. Back to the boredom and a life which is a wash of grey without any bright colour. Back in Waituhi. Back in the middle of silence.

Quickly, Sonny wipes the greyness from his mind. He strums a loud chord on the guitar to get rid of the silence.

— Hey! It's been a beauty night. A big hui. A wedding. George Karepa, he was one of the crowd. Now he's married and going to the big smoke too. Wellington, that's the place all right . . .

6

Two

The village is sixteen miles from the city, on the outskirts of the farming district where mountain ranges break the blue of sky. Huddled close to the foothills, it is far from the main arteries of traffic pumping commerce to and from the city. It is a backwater place and there is no reason why it should be here except this: the Whanau A Kai live here. This has always been their home and this will always be their land. It is their hearth. Their parents lived here before them and *their* parents before them, and so it has always been.

The Whanau A Kai, the family of Kai, an ancestor, are the tangata whenua. They are the children of this land. They live close together, clustered around the meeting house, the painted Rongopai, which is the heart of the village. Even before Rongopai was built they were here. In those times the tangata whenua were many; their number is small now.

Unless you have a car, the only way to get to the village is by the bus which leaves the city every afternoon after the clock tower has chimed five and factories have spewed out their employees from closing doors. The bus is driven by a man of the village who would be surprised to hear you ask for a fare. Very few strangers travel on the bus. He may ask you: Have you relations in the village? And if you've none, he'll say: Well, where will you stay? And he will grin as he tells you there are no hotels, no boarding houses, no nothing out there! Then he'll probably tell you you'd better stay at his place for the night and catch the bus back to the city with him in the morning. There's no chance of getting back from the village tonight; that is, unless someone is going to the pub or the pictures. The bed is yours if you want it. Come. Haere mai.

You'll find that the passengers will stare at you as you step onto the bus. Don't be afraid, because they are really shy with strangers. However, if you smile they will smile too. And you are then not strangers any more. They will ask you: What you want to come to our one-horse place for! And after they have asked you, tell them you want to see the meeting house, Rongopai. That will make them proud, so proud. And they will look at you with love, with aroha, for you have honoured them.

More village people will board the bus. The young girls will glance sideways at you as they pass down the aisle, and will giggle into cupped hands. The kuias, flax kits full with shopping, will heave themselves into seats and gossip openly as if they don't care if you hear them. But you will see them nudging one another if the gossip gets too racy. The men from the freezing works shout and swear and then look at you and wink before shouting and swearing again. One by one, the children will edge closer to you, to look at you with big eyes.

Then the bus moves away from the city. Clouds of cigarette smoke fill the air. The sound of people talking, arguing and laughing grows louder. And you'll become the centre of attraction. Talk with these village people, laugh and joke and sing with them. You are one of them now.

These village people, you will remember them all: the kuias in their black scarves and old dresses, the men in their black singlets and parkas, the bright and sparkling children. Some of them will claim more of your interest than others: the girl who is typist for a city accountant, the fortyish-looking man with the loudest laugh of all, the kuia who sits smiling, simply smiling, the high school boy who dozes among the songs and elbows of the back seat . . . They are of all kinds, these people. You'll remember them with

8

affection. And you'll find when the bus reaches the village that breaking away from them will be sad. Some will say: Haere ra, e tama. Goodbye, son. But others will tell you: Come over to our place for kai, ay? And if there's a cheeky one, he'll add: As our guest, not as our kai . . . So there is no breaking away really. And if they offer you their home and their aroha, then feel proud, e hoa. Feel proud that you've come to know these people. You will be one of the lucky ones, for many people are indifferent about villages like Waituhi.

They are the people who happen across the village by accident. For them, this would just be another *Maori* place. A wop-wop village out in the sticks. Lost in time and space, that's us. A couple of muddy roads, a meeting house on a corner, paddocks of maize and old wooden houses, that's us. And not worth stopping at either because there are no shops, not even a Maori concert group waiting on the side of the road to entertain. And worse still, no hot springs! Nothing, though Rongopai is famous in its own way. Nothing but a bump in the road and a bend of houses, easily forgotten.

Ae, many cars pass through the village, but few ever stop. Nothing registers as they blur past, not even the children sitting on a fence, waving, or the farmer silhouetted against the skyline whistling his dogs to heel. Nothing.

But there are the few, the very few who, although they may not stop, at least slow down as they drive through the village. Perhaps they are families on Sunday drives, pleasantly surprised at having come across this village they never thought existed. For them, there had appeared to be nothing except miles and miles of paddocks and bush on either side of a shingled road leading nowhere. Then suddenly, ahead is a sharp corner, curving into the foothills. They turn the corner and straight ahead lies the village, below a crown of rugged hills. To the right is a small wooden church with roof steeply slanted. Then on both sides of the road begin to appear the village houses, some almost hidden in the maize paddocks, others seeming to be planted in furrows along with the potatoes. On the left at the first bend is Rongopai, its painted eaves sloping to an apex which thrusts like an arrowhead at the sky. Beside it is an old iron cookhouse. And it is here that scrub-covered foothills begin to crowd the sky. The road winds around the bottom of the hills. More houses appear and some have muddy roads leading to them. The houses look very old with rusted roofs and paint peeling from the weatherboards. Curtains flutter from broken windows. Some of the windows are boarded up. Flax and flowers grow wild in the gardens. A drab place relieved occasionally by the shocking pink or lurid green of a house newly-painted. Long grass tangles in the barbed wire of falling fences. Cattle and sheep graze close to the rusting hulks of old farm machinery. Ae, a seedy-looking village, but exciting to come upon unexpectedly.

Then there is another bend in the road and on another hill to the left is the Community Hall. Further above it, tiny crosses mark the place of the village graveyard. Beyond the bend is the green country again.

And perhaps these people, these Sunday families and others slowly passing, see some of the village people. Perhaps an old koroua with his mokopuna shepherds sheep to the side of the road to let the car through: the old man waves his stick at the sheep and the young boy gives shrill barks, pretending he is a dog. Maybe two boys gallop their horses alongside the car, racing it and finally farewelling it with shouts and laughter. A woman is sitting on her front verandah, cross-legged and sleeping in the slanting sun. In a field of maize, children help their father with the maize-picking. And above the graveyard, a paper kite is flying, spearing at the sun. Perhaps. Perhaps . . .

And perhaps it is an early Sunday morning, and some of the village people are returning home.

The people and the village; the tangata whenua and the Whanau A Kai. Here they both are, in this place. . .

Three

The old truck lurches round the corner. Crouched in the drain, two girls listen until the sound of the truck fades into the distance. Then one of the girls clambers back onto the road.

— Come on, Janey! she says. I'm not going to wait for you all blinkin' day.

The other girl stares back, frightened.

— Is it really safe? Have they gone now, Hana?

Hana Walker puts her hands on her hips and sighs.

— Hurry up, won't you! It's cold up here.

She waits while Janey Whatu climbs from the drain.

— You think Dad saw me in the ditch? she asks. You think he saw us, Hana? I'm sure he looked out the window and saw me. He's going to kill me when I get home. What am I going to do?

— Look here, Janey Whatu! Hana says. He won't even look to see if you're in bed! Anyway, we won't be long getting home now. If he's waiting for you, tell him you've just been to the lav.

— In my best clothes? Janey Whatu wails. He'll never believe that. I'm going to get a good hiding for sure!

— Janey Whatu! Hana snaps. If you don't shut up and start walking, I'll give you a hiding myself! Now let's go!

She starts off down the road.

— Well? You coming, Janey? Or are you going to stay there beside that ditch!

Reluctantly, Janey Whatu follows. She is the younger of the two girls. She's thirteen, Hana is a year older.

Last night, Janey was supposed to have come home from the wedding with her Auntie Mere. Instead, she went with Hana to a city dance. Hana had been bored at the wedding. She knew all the boys there and they were just kids. She wanted to meet her boyfriend, Henry, at the dance in the city and had asked Janey to be her mate and come with her. So Janey'd told Auntie Mere that Dad had said she could go. The two girls had hitched a ride in to the dance, but Henry hadn't turned up. Hana had gotten wild because Henry had a car and she'd hoped he'd take her and Janey home after the dance.

— What shall we do? Janey had wailed as the dance neared its finish.

Hana had looked through the blue smoke and flashing lights of the dancehall, trying to pick out likely boys who would take them home. She had seen a Pakeha boy whom she knew had a car. A neat car, bright red with pennants flying from the aerial.

— Don't you worry, she had told Janey.

Then she had trained her eyes on the boy until he had turned to look in her direction. And she had tossed her hair in a supposedly sexy way, or like Raquel Welch did it in the movies, and had winked at him.

— Hana! Janey had whispered.

The boy had ambled over to Hana. They had danced. Or rather, Hana had danced while the boy jerked to the music. That was the trouble with Pakehas, they couldn't follow the music. And after the band had crashed and pounded itself to smithereens, the boy had introduced Hana to his mate. And the mate had danced with Janey.

Hana had grinned triumphantly at Janey.

— No trouble, she had said. These guys will take us home.

Janey had her doubts about that. And she hadn't liked the boy she was with. He looked like one big pimple. Her doubts had proved correct, for the two boys had driven the girls up Kaiti Hill. When Jim had started mauling her, Hana had slapped his face and pulled Janey from the car.

— Enjoy your walk home, bitch, Jim had yelled as the car roared down the hill.

Hana had picked up a big stone and thrown it at the Holden. She was going to tell Sam, her brother, about that fulla. Sam would really mangle him.

The girls have been walking for over two hours. Janey has been crying on and off, and Hana is sick of her. What a crybaby Janey is. Well, now that her Dad has beaten her home, she's really got something to cry about.

— Oh, what's wrong with you now, Janey Whatu! Hana snaps.

— Look at my dress, Janey weeps. There's mud all over it.

— Well it wasn't my idea to jump in the drain! Hana snaps again. She sees the funny side of it and giggles to herself. Then she grows angry again.

— Oh, stop bawling, Janey, won't you! Anybody'd think you had your hiding already. That's when you should start crying, not now. I'm never taking you with me again.

— I only came as a mate, Janey continues. I wish I'd come home with Auntie.

— Yeah, Hana groans. So do I.

— It's all your fault anyway, Janey continues. You said Henry would be at the dance. And you said he'd bring us home. You said we'd be all right and my Dad wouldn't find out, that's what you said, so it's all your fault, Hana.

— Blinkin' Henry! Hana seethes. I'm not going to speak to him again, that's for sure. He can go drown himself for all I care. I'll even push his head under the water for him. Yes, and I'm going to tell Sam about that Pakeha fulla. Sam and his mates, they'll kill that fulla.

Hana gloats to herself. Sam can scrap up large and a lot of fullas are scared of him. That Pakeha fulla better start running.

— This has been an awful night! Janey wails.

— Yeah? Hana says sarcastically. It didn't look as if you hated that fulla who was kissing you in the back.

— Him? Janey answers with disgust. He stuck his tongue in my mouth. I should've bitten it off. And he smelled stink too.

13

— Funny, that, Hana says. Pakehas always smell different.

Silence falls between the two girls. They pass the church and Hana looks up with narrow eyes at the steeply slanting roof. There'll be morning service today. She'll be going with Mum and Dad. They'll make her. They always make her.

— Soon as I finish school, she promises herself, I'm going to do what I want to do, not what anybody tells me to do. And I'm getting as far away from this place as I can. And nobody will stop me. Nobody...

— What you saying? Janey asks.

— Nothing, Hana answers. I was talking to myself...

She looks around her at the village. What a dump. What a waste of her life living here. And trapped here, that's what she is. School is a drag and nobody goes to church any more, do they? And why do Mum and Dad want to keep her at school? Who cares about having a good job! Any old job will do, the further away from here the better. She wants to have a good time *now*. All the other kids leave school early, so why can't she? Yes, and once she gets away from here, she'll buy lots of dresses and go to all the dances. She'll never go to bed; why sleep when there's so much to do? At home, her bedroom walls are covered with pictures of film stars ripped from magazines, showing the kind of life they have. Her radio is always on full blast, for only when it's on loud can she forget this hick town. She reads all the fashion books, wishing she could look like the women in them. And she envies her older cousins when they come back to the village from Auckland or Wellington. They tell her of the fantastic time they're having. And when they leave, she wishes she was going with them too.

There's nothing here for her. Getting away from the village is like a fever. One of these days, she'll make it. Roll on, that day! Perhaps, she just might come back now and then in her neat clothes and maybe she'll even have a car and a chauffeur. And she'll step out in her furs and diamonds and she'll be just like a queen. But if she does come back, she'll never come back to stay. No, it'll be just a visit, the shorter the better.

Janey Whatu begins to wail again.

— Oh, cut it out! Hana yells.

She tries to recall her fantasy, but it has gone. Old wooden houses on either side of a gravelled road have taken its place. She closes her eyes and whispers:

— One of these days. Yeah, one of these days . . .

Four

Two girls, walking swiftly home through an awakening village . . .

It hasn't changed much over the past few years. Although it is near enough to the city for shopping, work, school, sport or for going to the pub or pictures, it is far enough away to remain as it has always been. The generations are marked only by the houses which decay and the old people who pass away. No, to look at, the village hasn't changed much at all. But its children, *they* have changed.

Once, many of the Whanau A Kai lived here. They lived in small whares thatched with raupo built around a hilltop meeting house which was destroyed long ago; the serrated silhouette of the terraces, and scattered cooking stones, are all that are left of the Pa. They are the only reminders of the time before the Pakeha came. With his coming, a way of life changed.

But it did not change entirely. The Whanau A Kai continued living off the land and living as a family one with another. They continued to live simply, though some built large homesteads. At least, that is village legend anyway. It is one of many legends, of a time of prosperity when the land was still our own and the Whanau A Kai had pride. That was in the dreamtime before we were stripped of our dignity. The dreamtime . . . .

A dream built on other dreams. Built on pride and the obstinate need to believe that once there *must* have been a time when the village blazed briefly with beauty. There must have been, surely, somewhere, such a time. A time to look back to and to escape to from the shame and poverty of the present.

For now there is nothing. There are no great homesteads to give even credibility to the legend. Even the oldest houses in the village do not have that aura of greatness which the large homesteads must have had. They rot in overgrown fields and are used for storing hay and farm equipment. Starlings and sparrows have their nests in them. The elaborate cornices of the verandahs are spun across with spiders' webs. The wood is riddled with borer. Mice breed in the straw-strewn wind-invaded rooms, scratching sharply at the ripped and yellowing wallpaper.

Nothing is left of the greatness. Not much is left of the family land, Maori land.

Ae, but there must have once been a lot of land which was ours. We tilled it together and lived upon it together. But it passed from our hands, sold or taken in large chunks from us. The individual families of the village grew large and the land that was left could not support them. The families splintered as the land splintered. Some left for better money and a better life. Few returned.

The tangata whenua began to leave their land. Yet, the Whanau A Kai still lived on. A new generation built more modern houses. Even in this generation new houses have been built. But the younger people continue to leave and the village is aging. There is nothing for them here. The Pakeha way of life is forcing the links even between heart and heart apart. But the village does not die yet.

Of those who are left in the village, there still remain a number who cherish the ideals of family living and family aroha. Once, the people who felt this aroha for the old ones and the hearth land sprang from the soil in great numbers. But when times move onward, always something is left behind. It is good that some still remain to love the old people and the land. Time enough for leaving . . .

No! Why talk about leaving the village! These people will

17

never leave because they and the village are inseparable. They have been too steeped in family life. All their relations are here. This is their home, their family. They give life to the village; the village gives life to them. Away from it they will wither. The land is in their blood and they are the blood of the land. They will remain here because blood links blood, and blood links years, and blood links families now and over all the years past. It is good to remain *family*. There is such aroha in belonging to each other. It is growing up together, living all your years together and being buried next to one another. You are never a stranger. You are never alone. That's why it is good to stay here.

But the people who feel the aroha strongest are themselves old, with emotional ties with the past. And when they die will their children feel such aroha for the land? Most of them leave. And of those who remain in the village, few will do so for the sake of aroha. Some will stay because they have no inclination to leave; they are the lazy ones, as lazy here as they would be anywhere else. Others will stay simply because they have good jobs as shepherds or farmhands in the district or in shops and factories in the city, and only because of the jobs. And then there will be the ones who feel not aroha but an obligation to the old ones.

Some leave and are loath to go. Others go gladly. Better to stay in the city or even take the long day journey by train or bus to the bright lights of Auckland or Wellington. Ae, many of the school children of the village will later make that journey. Yes, many of them . . .

Five

From the kitchen window, Pita Mahana sees the two girls passing.
That niece of his, that Hana, has been up to her tricks again. A
good boot up the behind is what she needs. But that cousin of
his, Hepa, will be soft on his daughter as usual. She'll probably
spin some yarn and he'll believe her. Believes the best about
anybody, that Hepa. And who's the kid with Hana? Looks like
Janey Whatu . . .

— Pita? You there?

Pita Mahana holds the telephone closer. It had woken him with
its ringing. He'd pretended not to hear, but Miriama had kicked
him out of bed to answer it. And that's when he'd seen the two
girls sneaking home.

— Who's that? Pita asks.

— It's me, Jack here. One of our shearers hasn't turned up.
Can you come out and take his stand?

— Hold on, cousin! Pita groans. I just got home a few hours
ago.

He looks at his watch. Not even five o'clock yet.

— How come you're shearing on a Sunday! he continues. This
is supposed to be a day of rest.

— No rest for us hard workers, Pita! We need you out here.
Jim Franks put in a nightpen last night, so I rang up some of the
boys and they're all out here except young Sammy. It's our last

19

shed and the sooner we finish the shearing the better. And I don't
want to lose the contract with Jim Franks. He wants his sheep
finished by tonight because the trucks are coming in the morning.
So we need you, Pita.

— Where are you fullas?

— At Mairangi Station.

— Way the hell out there?!

— Yeah, I know. I would've rung someone else, but I didn't
know who else . . . Never mind. You go back to sleep.

— Cut it out, Pita growls. Who d'you think I am? We aren't
cousins for nothing. All right, what time do you want me to be
there? I guess I can keep my eyes open until tonight.

— Can you make it here by eight?

— I'll try. You got enough fleece-os?

— The more the merrier, cousin!

— Okay. I'll bring Miriama with me. And Waka as well. He
might as well make some money instead of bludging off me all
the time, ay.

— Thanks, Pita. Well, I better get back to the shed and start
cracking my whip. I don't know, everyone is half asleep this
morning.

— The wedding was too good! Pita laughs.

— Yeah? Well I was there too and I'm still fit as a fiddle.
These young fullas can't take it like I can.

— What a blowhard you are, Pita smiles. I can feel the wind
from here.

— Yeah. Well, you're coming then? Good. See you soon.

The phone clicks into silence. Pita puts the receiver down.
He yawns. Maybe his cousin is still feeling young, but Pita
Mahana sure feels old this morning. Too many kids to look after,
that's the trouble. Too many worries. No wonder he feels worn
out. Still yawning, he walks down the passage to the bedroom.

Pita Mahana is almost fifty. He married Miriama Wanoa when
he was eighteen. Their romance had been short and sweet and
he had brought his bride back to the village. Here they'd begun
their life together. It had been hard, but it had been good too. The

20

babies, it seemed now, had come just about one a year. Then after the ninth had been born, the boy Waka, Miriama had called it quits.

— This body, she had whispered, it needs a rest now Pita. It's tired, very tired . . .

That was seventeen years ago. And over all those years, Pita Mahana has slaved his guts out to support his family. The whanau land itself could not support his family alone, so he'd taken on labouring jobs. Sometimes scrubcutting, sometimes fencing. In summer, he and his family used to go out shearing. Sometimes, after the local shearing was finished in the district, he took his family down to the South Island to shear there. Occasionally, they went to Hastings to pick fruit. But sometimes, there were no jobs for him over the winter.

And yet, he'd not worried much at first. Something always turned up. And the other brothers, particularly Rongo, had lent him money if he needed it. His kids had been easy to keep then; they'd not wanted much because they'd not been accustomed to having much. Four walls, a roof, some kai and later a television, that's about all. All of them are married now except Waka. Only he and four mokopuna live at home. The mokopuna are the children of some of Miriama's nieces. The usual story. They were Miriama's children now. Although her body had been tired, her heart had pined for the sound of young laughter, especially after her own children had started leaving home.

Life continues to be hard for Pita and Miriama, but they've known nothing else but a hard life. Lately however, things have got a little worse. Age has crept up on them all of a sudden and they are beginning to feel their years. The man who could once shear three hundred sheep a day with ease, now finds it a struggle. His back is giving him trouble, but he must keep working. His children forget he's an old man and are still dependent on him although they're married. Four of them still live in the village and are they hoha! Sometimes they can't pay their bills or meet their hire purchase or mortgage payments. Not to worry, because there's always Dad to borrow from. Always Dad if their bedroom suite or car is to be repossessed. Unlike their parents, living the simple life is not enough for them. They want more than four walls and a roof. There must be wall-to-wall carpets, the most expensive wallpaper, a freezer . . . All the knick-knacks of modern living. So they sign on the dotted line, promising to pay so much every month, and who cares if they can't keep up the payments! Dad'll always help out. Why, he's made of money.

Aue. Never mind: Pita Mahana didn't have all his kids for nothing. Once they're on their feet, they'll look after him and Miriama. That's the way things have always been in the village isn't it? That'll be the way it will be, won't it? Yes, the eldest look after the young ones, but when they are old, it is the young who must then look after them. But why worry about it. He, Pita Mahana has many good working years left in him; and Miriama likes her 'holidays' down South. Time enough, time enough . . .

— Who was that on the phone? Miriama asks sleepily. .

— Jack, Pita answers. He sits on the side of the bed and strokes Miriama's hair. By Jeez, she's a handsome woman . . . Her hair may be grey but her face is still beautiful, with the clear skin and strong cheekbones of her own Tuhoe people.

— What did he want? Miriama asks again.

— One of his boys let him down, Pita says. He wants a hand at the shed.

— He's got a nerve! Miriama grumbles, sitting up. Doesn't he know it's Sunday?

— I have to go, Pita says. You want to come?

— I'm coming all right! Miriama answers, brushing at her eyes. Don't you think I'm letting my car out of my sight. I know you, you'll lend it to somebody and I don't want any more dents in my car!

— Whose car? Pita laughs.

— My car, Miriama says. I worked hard for that car and don't you forget it, Pita.

Her husband slaps her playfully on the bum.

— You better hurry up then, or else I'll pinch your car. Make a feed for us, ay? And for the kids too. We better take them with us otherwise they'll get up to mischief while we're away. I'll go and wake Waka up. If he thinks he's sleeping in while the rest of us are working, he's got a big surprise coming!

Miriama pulls back the blankets and puts her feet on the floor. Then she winces and bites back the tears.

— Pita . . .

He cradles her in his arms.

— Still sore?

— Hurts, Pita . . .

— Well, you know what the doctor said, dear. He said you got to exercise that arm. Otherwise you're going to lose it.

— But it hurts . . .

Pita kisses Miriama softly. He begins to stroke her arm, her arm almost dead with arthritis.

— You feel me? he asks.

— A little . . .

— Well you better start showing that arm who's boss! he whispers. You do what I told you. Put your fingers on the wall and start making them crawl up. Go on.

— But it hurts. It makes me cry . . .

— Come on, try . . .

And painfully, Miriama lifts her bad arm to the wall with her good arm. She tries to move her fingers, and gasps out:

— It hurts, Pita . . .

— Good! he answers. If it hurts, there must be a little life still there. You have to work that arm, Miriama. You have to work it hard. And if you don't, I'm not taking you out with me any more!

He grins to himself as he sees Miriama forcing her fingers to move.

— Yes, he says, get your wild up with that arm! Get angry at it and you'll be all right. Now you just stay here for a while. I'll go and get Waka out of bed.

He kisses Miriama again. Then he walks down the corridor to Waka's room. Hullo, what's this? The door is locked and there are no locked doors in the Pita Mahana house! Immediately, he bangs loudly on the door.

23

— Open up, Waka! he yells. I know you got somebody in there! Open this door and be quick about it!

He hears whispered voices behind the door.

— Go 'way, Dad!

— Just open this door! Pita thunders.

The door opens. Waka is standing there, frightened. And in the bed, a girl is hiding beneath the blankets.

— Come out! Pita says. I know you're under there!

And slowly, a head emerges, gives a small cry, and disappears under the blankets again. Ani Jackson, one of the girls of the village . . .

— We're going to get married, Dad! Waka blurts out.

Pita looks him over. Seventeen years old, this son of his. By Jeez . . .

— Well, he says, if you want to get married you better come out to work. When you got enough money to buy your girl some pants, then you can get married.

He strides from the room and back to Miriama.

— That bloody kid, he says. He's got a girl in his room.

— Ay?

— That girl of Hone's. Ani, the one with the big eyes.

— But she's a relation, Pita.

— Not that closely related. Waka says they want to get married.

Miriama starts to weep. Pita puts his arms around her. Inside he is chuckling to himself.

— Turi turi, he whispers, Plenty of time to cry when Waka and his girl start bringing the babies here for you to look after. Then you'll be sorry.

— How come we got such hoha kids? Miriama sobs. How come they always get into trouble? They sure don't take after my side of the family. All you Mahanas, all of you are a wild bunch. You fullas should've been drowned in a river!

— Don't start blaming my side of the family, Pita grins. Come to think of it, I can remember a Rotorua girl who was running wild until I made a good woman out of her.

24

— Don't you tell lies, Miriama growls, hitting him. Then she sighs. What we going to do now?

— Better drop into Hone's and tell him about the kids.

— He's going to be wild, Miriama says. He's not going to like it, I know.

— Nothing he can do about it, Pita shrugs. Nothing we can do either. Those two've done it themselves.

Miriama nods. For a moment there is silence. Then Pita asks:

— Your arm all right?

— Yes . . . Miriama answers. Then she tells Pita to wake up the mokopuna and get them ready for the shed. She goes to the kitchen and begins to make the kai: puts the electric jug on, makes some porridge in a big pot, slices some Maori bread and sets the table with butter and strawberry jam. That should do the kids. They can have a big feed at Jim Franks' place. She sits down and decides to have a smoke. She lifts her arm and . . .

The *pain* . . . And what will happen if the arm is really dead? Are you dead, arm? Are you lost to me? Will I now have to work in the paddocks with one arm? And how will I throw the fleece on the table? Arm, I live by you; don't go away from me . . .

Carefully, she nurses it. And as she does so, she thinks back on her life. There are few regrets really. Perhaps the biggest is that the Pita Mahana family have always been poor. If they'd been richer, maybe she'd have pushed the kids more and made them stop at school and get better jobs instead of following their father into seasonal work. No good this living from job to job, season to season. You could do it in the old times, but not now. These days, you need more money to live. Never mind. Pita might strike the double or win the Golden Kiwi and then give the kids some money to help them stand on their feet. . .

A noise sounds behind her. Miriama looks round. Ani Jackson, standing there. For a moment, the two look at each other. Then Miriama opens her arms to the girl.

— Haere mai, she whispers.

And Ani rushes into her arms. She weeps. And then she looks up at Miriama. In her eyes, pain. In her eyes, bewilderment.

Miriama has seen that look before. She brushes away Ani's tears. It is a bewildering time for a girl who has been made a woman by a man.

— Kei te whakama koe? she asks.

— Ae, Ani whispers.

— Kei te mamae koe?

— Ae . . . Kei te mamae au, kei te pouri au . . .

— Kaua e tangi, Miriama soothes. Kaua e . . . Ah . . .

The girl becomes calm. The two women begin to talk: about love, about life, about love and life between a man and woman. The older woman advises. The girl listens. It is both sad and joyful: sad because the girl is no longer a girl and joyful because now she is a woman.

— We'll speak with your father, Miriama says. He'll be angry, but in the end he'll understand. Then you will come and stay in this house. That son of mine! Never mind. It's done now. And don't worry about your Dad. Just leave him to me. You are my daughter as well as his now . . .

Six

— Hey Maka!

— Who's that?

— Mere. Open up!

— Crikey dick, you're up early. What you want?

— I got something to tell you. Hurry up and open this door.

— At this time of the morning you've got something to tell me? You must be crazy! Don't you ever sleep? Can't it wait? Look at the time! Only six, and I just got home with Charlie Whatu a while ago. Oh, stop hammering, I'm coming, I'm coming!

— About time you opened the door, Maka. Damn cold outside.

— Hurry up and come inside then. I'll put the heater on. Now what's all the fuss!

— There's going to be a wedding, Maka.

— Ay? You're a bit behind the times, Mere. The wedding was yesterday.

— I don't mean George and Alice's wedding. I'm talking about Waka and Ani getting hitched.

— What you talking about, Mere!

— That nephew of yours, Waka. And Hone's daughter. They're getting married.

— You sure you're still not asleep, Mere? First time I ever heard about it. Ani's too young to get married.

27

— You should get new eyes, Maka. Yeah, and Ani's going to stay with Pita and Miriama.

— How come you know all about it!

— Miriama told me. She was at Hone's place.

— Hold your horses, Mere, I'm not with you. How come Miriama was at Hone's?

— Well, you know I always get up early in the morning even if I been on the plonk. Yeah, well today when I got up I just happened to look out the window and I saw the Mahana's car outside Hone's place. Pita and Miriama got out. Waka and Ani was in the car. Yeah, well as soon as I saw Ani, I knew something was up. I mean half past five in the morning! So I went to have a look see, ay. And Waka, he sure enough had that guilty look.

— Crikey dick, that nephew of mine! I knew something like this would happen. I just knew it.

— Yeah, well Ani was crying, so I got in the car to cheer her up. I mean I like that kid, no matter what she's done, ay. And we was sitting there and Miriama and Pita knocked on the door. Hone came. Pita spoke to him — I couldn't hear what they was saying — and next minute Hone got his wild up. Miriama took him by the arm and they all went inside. Yeah, and you should've heard the racket, Maka. Everybody was shouting and that poor Ani, she couldn't take it. She opened the car door and ran inside the house. That's when things quietened down, ay. You know how much Hone loves that kid. Soon as he saw her, he must've forgotten to be mad.

— Poor Hone . . .

— Anyway, Maka, they all came out the house then. Hone was crying and you and I know it's got to be something terrible to make him cry. He came over to the car and Waka got out. And Hone took a swipe at him and said: You better look after my girl good, Boy! Yeah, well Waka said he would and Hone said he just better, that's all. And then Miriama told me herself about the kids. They've taken them shearing today.

— Ah . . .

— So what you think of that, ay Maka?

28

— Nothing much.

— Ay?

— Just what I said, Mere! What a cheek you got coming here just to tell me that!

— But I thought you'd want to know!

— Yeah, well now I know, ay.

— But they was caught at it!

— So what! They're going to get married aren't they? I'm happy for them, really happy. Goodbye, Mere.

— Ay?

— I said *goodbye, Mere*! See you later. Much later . . .

Seven

Flick. Flick. And with each flicking of her hand, the light cord swings a wide arc in the room. Hana Walker watches moodily as it swings a thin shadow on the ceiling. She lies on the top of the bed, still dressed in her good clothes. Why bother to change? What's the use? In half an hour, Mum and Dad will be getting up to go to church. And she'll have to go with them. Naturally. Of course.

And she'll have to sit there, dutifully between Mum and Dad, and listen to some dumb priest and sing those blinkin' awful songs. And there's no chance of escaping either. None at all. What a drag.

It had been easy for Hana to get into the house without Mum and Dad knowing she'd been out all night. It was always easy to sneak in: just lever up the window and hop in. Nothing to it. Why, she'd done it plenty of times. Something to laugh about. But why was she always ashamed? And why is she ashamed now?

— Be home early, Hana, won't you?
— Yes, Dad.
— You promise?
— I promise . . .

He had kissed her. He had told her to have a good time. Why did he trust her so?

They should give her up; she'd never be like Frank, so they

30

might as well stop hoping. She'd be more like Sam, her other brother. Sam and she, they had the bad Walker blood. . .

The telephone rings. Quickly, Hana jumps from the bed. Perhaps it's Henry! Well, too bad if it is. She's not running to the phone. Let it ring a little longer, that'll teach him. She waits for a while and then walks down the corridor and picks up the receiver.

— Hullo?

— That you, Hana?

— Oh . . . Yes, Mere, it's me. What do you want?

— Is your Mum up yet?

— No.

— Jingosh, nobody's up around here!

— Can I take a message?

— Never mind. I'll ring her later. It's about Ani. It can wait. Goodbye . . .

Hana hangs up, She hears Dad calling her:

— Who was that, Hana?

— Mere. She wanted Mum for something.

— Hana? Mum calls. You're up early, aren't you?

— I couldn't sleep, Mum.

— What's the time?

— About seven.

— Put some water on the stove, Hana? I'll get up soon and make breakfast.

— All right, Mum, Hana answers. She feels strangely sad as she wanders through the kitchen. Linoleum floor. Stainless steel bench. Bright curtains. Flowers in a vase. Clean. Perfect. Just like a Pakeha home . . .

And she is out of place here, puzzled by their values and the hopes mirrored in them of her parents. Their preconceptions of her: that she'll be like Frank, the clever one at University, the one who is doing something to prove the Maori is just as good as the Pakeha.

I can't do it, Dad.

You can, Hana.

31

I'm like Sam, Dad.

Sam was a coward, Hana. He gave in. He was weak with his drinking and his gambling and his smoking. He showed the Pakeha just what the Pakeha wanted to see. That the Maori is a no-hoper.

Please, Dad. I can't . . .

Yes you can. You can be like Frank. You must think of other than yourself. You must do it for your people. Stay at school for them. Get educated, do good work, for them.

Dad, you ask too much of me.

I ask only that you make me proud. That you make the Maori proud. . .

Hana rushes to her room. She flings herself onto the bed.

— I can't do it, Dad, she whispers. You will make me hurt you . . .

She turns her head into the pillow. She was going to be a failure, just like Sam, and she felt ashamed. Like Sam, she would leave this house, unable to look Dad in the eyes. Perhaps she would even try like Sam had done. He'd gone to Wellington to work in a Government job. He'd returned, defeated.

Hana sighs. At least Mum and Dad will still have Frank to be proud of.

— Hana?

She looks up. Dad, standing at the door. Dad, a member of the district Maori Council. Dad, proud of his status among his Pakeha friends.

— You all right, Hana?

— Yes, Dad. I couldn't sleep. I've just been lying here, thinking. That's all.

Her father sits on the bed beside her.

— What have you been thinking about?

— Oh . . . things . . . Oh, Dad . . .

She hugs her father closely.

— Are you ill? Do you want to stay home today?

And Hana's heart leaps. Oh yes, yes, please let me stay home. Today and all other Sundays. And let me be myself. Let me be myself.

The words spring to her lips. But she does not say them. Dad loves her; she loves him. She cannnot hurt him. Not yet. And if she does hurt him, it'll be far away maybe in Wellington, where he cannot see. . .

— I'm all right, Dad. I'll come with you.

Keeping her parents happy and not hurting them, that's the good thing to do. Living a lie is a very small price to pay . . .

Hepa walks back to the bedroom. He is in a thoughtful mood. He sits on the bed beside his wife, Dinah.

— Something's wrong with that daughter of ours.

— Oh?

— Yes, something's bothering her. I've sensed it for some time now. Something.

Dinah shrugs her shoulders.

— Could be many things, Hepa. All girls get restless at her age. Our little girl is becoming a woman. Her body stirs.

— Do you think I'm hard on her?

Dinah pauses, measuring her words carefully.

— As hard as any father who has an only daughter.

— Then you do think I'm too strict.

— Hepa . . .

— No, don't turn away, Dinah.

Dinah gives a slight smile, sad and tremulous.

— You're not strict, dear. But . . .

— Yes?

— You're too ambitious for her.

— And that's wrong? Hepa asks incredulously.

Quickly, Dinah steps out of bed. She begins to put on her dressing gown.

— I have to see about breakfast, she says.

— But is it wrong? Hepa asks again.

— Dear, you have some kind of dream for her. But is it her dream too? You expect her to live that dream for you. But does she want to? That's the question you should be asking. Only you have the answer, Hepa.

33

Hepa begins to reply, but Dinah places her fingers on his lips.
— No, Hepa. You must find the answer yourself.

She goes out of the room.

Alone now, Hepa remains sitting on the bed. He picks up a magazine, flips through it, then puts it aside. His thoughts bother him.

Hepa Walker is a man who occupies positions of prominence in both Maori and Pakeha society. Yet, to judge from his early life, you would not have thought his present prestige possible. Born in the village, he had been the third son of a large family with little mana. No silver spoon for him. His boyhood had been filled with hardship. His father had pulled him out of school because he'd needed the boy to help him in scrubcutting. Even if Hepa had remained at school, his academic achievement would have been mediocre. At thirteen, Hepa had had a shearer's handpiece shoved into his hands. By the time he was eighteen, it seemed that he was destined to be a labourer for the rest of his life.

Then the Second World War had intervened, and Hepa had swapped handpiece for rifle and had gone to fight overseas. His qualities as a leader of men had not gone unnoticed and his promotion to Lieutenant in the Maori Battalion had been rapid. He had been well-liked by his men and had gained their respect as a fighter. Fearless in battle, he had distinguished himself at the capture of Takrouna during the Tunisian Campaign.

At War's end, Hepa had returned to the adulation of New Zealand. He had received a hero's welcome from the village. Confident and assured, he had gained mana not simply because he'd been to the War but also because he now spoke with authority and skill. A leader in the War, he had become sought after as a leader for the Maori people during peacetime. It was expected of him. He had found himself assuming a role which, surprisingly, the War had prepared him for. As a spokesman on Maori affairs.

He had been a good spokesman too, and a respected leader for the district. His marriage to a high-ranking daughter of the

34

Waikato had increased his prestige. He and Dinah had become respected guests at huis, large gatherings throughout the country.

In spite of his poverty-stricken background, Hepa had risen to the top of Maori society. Wisely, for he was not suited to it, he had resisted any indulgence in national politics. Certainly the thought of being a politician was an attractive one, but Hepa was aware of his personal limitations. Anyway, as a district spokesman, he already had enough to do.

Hepa's rise in Pakeha society, by contrast, had taken him longer. It was here that his background told against him. He had not been educated into a business career and had not even been aware of the qualities, social and personal, which were required if ever he was to prove acceptable to Pakeha society. His progress had been marked by one social gaffe after another, but his saving grace had been an honesty which had led his Pakeha friends to overlook his deficiencies with good humour. They had tolerated him, he was quite a fine chap really, and anyway they needed a Maori to sit with them at their opening ceremonies — of a new post office, new municipal building, new school — and to appear with them in the social pages of the local newspaper. Yes indeed, one had to remember to include a Maori on any guest list, for the Maoris were important to the community weren't they? And wouldn't they be proud to see how well they were becoming integrated into society?

And so Hepa had found himself being groomed to fulfil a particular social role. Truthfully, he had enjoyed the process for he, like his Pakeha friends, believed that the future for New Zealand lay in the integration of the two races Maori and Pakeha.

One particular incident had convinced him of this. He had been invited to a lecture given by a Wellington economist at which that learned gentleman had illustrated with graphs, statistics and demographic projections that more movement of Maoris from the lower classes into the middle class bracket was necessary to promote the quicker integration of the Maori into the European way of life. At first, sitting there, Hepa had felt both rage and embarrassment. But as the lecture had continued, he had found himself agreeing with the economist. When you thought about it, more middle-class Maoris would solve many problems, many inconsistencies in the present situation. The crime rate would go down, wouldn't it? The social differences would be minimised, wouldn't they? The intangible and never-to-be admitted discrimination between Maori and Pakeha would disappear, surely? All this would happen, yes, when the Maori rose from lower to middle-class stature.

Hepa had taken a long and critical look at his own way of life. It was not that it was wanting anything; just that it could be improved by at least another car, a cocktail cabinet, a few pieces of crystal and a classical record collection. These had been purchased, but they had given only a semblance of middle-class standards. Actually attaining the attitudes that went with them was much harder.

But he has made it. A personnel officer in a local city firm, Hepa can socialise with the best of them. He plays golf on Saturdays, drinks in the best bars, attends the best church, and is on first-name terms with the district elite. In every way, he is a success.

Make no mistake though, he has not become a brown Pakeha. It isn't as logical as people think, to assume that if you walk into a Pakeha life you walk away from a Maori life. That if you credit yourself in the European world you debit somewhere in the Maori world. No, Hepa Walker continues to be proud of his Maori blood. But he is also concerned with the future of his people. Their salvation, as he sees it, is in education. Through education, they will start moving up from lower to middle.

So why should his hopes for Hana be wrong? How could anyone possibly say his ambitions for her are too strong!

Moodily, Hepa walks to the bathroom. He runs the shower, testing it with his fingers. Satisfied, he takes off his dressing gown.

His son, Frank, at university in Auckland, making his father proud. His other son, Sam, a no-hoper. You only have to look at the difference between the two of them to know Hepa Walker is right with his ambitions for Hana. So the Pakeha way, the 'you have to get on' way may be hard. It has to be taken, you have to

36

push yourself to take it, otherwise the Maori will always be second class, second rate.

Hepa Walker steps into the shower.

Once, the Maori race was a warrior race. There may not be any need for mere and taiaha in these days, but the warrior strength and tenacity is needed more than ever before to master the skills of the Pakeha life. The sooner more Maoris realised this the better . . .

Eight

—There they go again, Annie Jackson says. Right on the dot of eight as usual.

— Who? Kepa, her husband asks.

— The Walkers of course! Off to church while we sit around on our bums.

— Well, ain't Sunday s'posed to be a day of rest? I'd rather sit around here than in a church all day. Bugger that for a joke.

— Yeah? Annie Jackson snorts. Wouldn't be so bad if it was only Sunday you sat around on. When you going to find a job ay, Kepa? And when am I going to see some money from those two no-good sons of yours, that Mana and that Sammy!

— Tomorrow. I'll get a job tomorrow.

— Hah! I'll believe it when I see it. And wasn't that Sammy supposed to go shearing at Mairangi today?

— He can't help it if they don' come around an' pick him up.

— They came all right! But you need a bomb to get him out of bed. Boy, I'm starting to forget what a dollar note looks like!

— It's brown like your arse.

Angrily, Annie Jackson turns on her husband. For some time now, she and Kepa have been getting on each other's nerves. Pick, pick, pick on each other, that's all they seem to be doing these days.

38

Then through slanting sunlight, Pene comes laughing. Pene, eight years old, the youngest son.

— G'morning Mum! G'morning Dad!

— What you so happy about, Tutae? his father growls.

Pene just grins at him until he is all teeth. Then he kisses his mother.

— About time you were out of your pyjamas, isn't it? Annie asks.

— Okay, Mum!

— And you better get your Nanny up for his kai, ay?

— Okay!

And he skips from the kitchen, back to his room. Annie sighs. Kepa looks across at her.

— Sorry, Missus . . . he says.

— Yes . . . she answers. She smiles at him.

— Tomorrow . . .

— Ae, tomorrow Kepa . . .

And in the corridor, Pene is carefully tiptoeing into his room. Not only his room though, because his two big brothers sleep in it too. How come they're so untidy? The dirt must just love them! And they're still sleeping too; sleepyheads they are. Mana snoring from the bottom bunk and Sammy dangling from the top bunk . . . Pene sighs and shakes his head. He starts to clear up the floor. You'd think that Mana and Sammy would know that clothes are put in the drawer, not on the floor. Didn't they ever go to school?

Pene looks around, satisfied with his work. He shuffles out of his pyjamas and puts them away. Then he puts on his old clothes. Where are his boots? On hands and knees he searches for them. There they are: underneath Mana's bunk. How come they got there! That Mana must have kicked them there. Gently, Pene lifts his brother's head out of the way. Mana thrashes and snorts and makes funny noises in his throat because he likes sleeping with his head over the side. Sounds just like a pig who doesn't want to budge. But Pene just pushes his face out of the way again. He gets his boots and puts them on. Then he sniffs and his nose curls up. Pooh, this room is sure stink. Smells of toe-jam. You'd think that Mana and Sammy would know that socks have to be washed now and then. Better let some fresh air in around here. Open the window wide so it can flow . . .

— You want me to freeze to death? Mana yells.

— You fullas make this room stink, Pene says.

— Just you close that window and be quick about it! Mana continues.

Meekly, Pene obeys. Mana is unhealthy. He won't freeze, not with all *those* blankets on. Gosh, he doesn't like fresh air, he doesn't like the curtains open so the sun can shine in . . . The stink air and the dark must just love him!

Shaking his head, Pene leaves the room, shutting the door behind him. In the room across the corridor is his Nanny Paora. Old, old Nanny Paora. Hundreds and hundreds of years old, that's Nanny Paora. Lying there, staring at nothing.

And reaching up to catch the light as Pene opens the curtains.

— Eeee! Nanny! Pene laughs. You're too old to catch the light! You're not fast enough! I catch it for you, ay? I catch it! I catch it!

He darts around the room, hands outspread, following the sunlight as it ebbs and flows with the patterns made by the fluttering curtains. Hands wide and mouth wide with laughter, while Nanny Paora slowly grins with soundless delight. Then Pene jumps and brings his hands together with a sudden *clap*! And he glances at his Nanny and whispers:

— Quiet, Nanny, you must be quiet. Or else the light will get scared and fly away. Shhhhh. Shhhhh. I bring it to you. Shhhhh. Now . . . *there* . . . See, Nanny? See the light?

And it really does seem as if there is a small ball of light shimmering in his cupped hands. Shimmering, scattering ribbons of colour, becoming brighter and brighter. And Nanny Paora looks at the light and his face softens. It is so beautiful, shining there . . .

— I let it go now? Pene whispers.

Nanny Paora looks at him. He nods slowly. And Pene lifts the light to his lips, blows gently, and the light floats softly away like a glistening dandelion-seed.

There is silence for a moment. Then Pene grins:

— You want some kai, Nanny? You got a hungry puku?

Nanny Paora grins back.

— Okay! Pene says simply. Put your arms around me, Nanny. Now hold tight. You holding tight? Okay! Now shift your legs onto the floor. One leg. Now the other one. There we are. Now stand up, Nanny. I take your pyjamas off you quick or else you'll get cold, ay. Now we put some clothes on . . .

And slowly, Pene dresses his Nanny.

Nanny Paora is Pene's great-grandfather. He was born a long time ago in a different age, a different time. A strange, almost incomprehensible age, long past, long ago. Across the dim mists of his mind, the memories of that time sometimes flicker like shadows, vaguely stirring, slowly gathering and suddenly breaking through . . . And the old man *speaks* . . . Of a dreamtime . . . And an age lost . . .

Pene lives for these times when his Nanny dreams. For his Nanny takes him into his dreams and he becomes a part of them too. This old man, this solitary whale stranded in an alien present, has that power. For there have been many times when together, walking through the village, the past has enfolded them.

— Te Kooti coming . . . mokopuna . . . Te Kooti . . .

The light dimming, then brightening upon another day. And young men are building Rongopai and women sit in the sun weaving mats for that painted house.

— Building . . . for Te Kooti . . . Rongopai . . .

And on another day, an old woman dissolves from the dreamtime, dust swirling around her bare feet. Thick long hair and large black eyes has the woman; and the moko is on her chin like the soft green swirls of a calm river. Around her shoulders she wears a long cloak made of feathers. And her smile as she passes brings tears to an old man's eyes.

— E ma . . . E ma . . .

Again another day, and the village is a nest of small thatched whares. The hills are overgrown with scrub. Along the road a procession of people are coming, laughing and singing. And as they pass, an old man and a boy join them. Before the procession

41

is a painted house and smoke curls from the cookhouse beside it. Children run through the grass. Old men stand around a pit steaming with food. Women gossip in the sunlight. And the old man stays to talk with them while the boy plays with the children . . .

— A hui . . . mokopuna . . . Happy . . . time . . .

The dreamtime; the long ago time.

— There we are, Nanny! Pene smiles. All dressed now. Come now. We have some kai now. Come.

And together, they go toward the kitchen. Pene sits the old man by the stove so he can get warm.

— Not too close, Dad! Annie Jackson warns the old man.

He smiles at her. Although she calls him Dad, he is really her grandfather. But when she was a young girl, Nanny Paora and Nanny Moana had brought her up. In their old age, they had brought her to live with them. She and her cousin, Rosie. Both made sisters by the two old people. And Annie Jackson looks after the old man now.

— How you today, Dad? Kepa Jackson asks. You have a good moe? You enjoy the wedding? Eeee! I saw you looking at all those young girls!

Nanny Paora grins.

— Hey! Kepa laughs. The old man understood!

— Course he did, Annie sniffs. He's not dumb, are you Dad?

The old man continues to grin. Annie puts a plate of corn beef and puha in front of him. She puts a tea towel round his neck.

— Kai time, now, she tells him. Here's a spoon; attack that kai!

Nanny Paora begins to eat. Slowly at first, but then more quickly. And Pene laughs and says:

— Nanny likes puha, doesn't he Mum! Just look at him hoeing in! He's scared the kai will run away, aren't you Nanny!

Annie Jackson smiles. Dad and Pene are just a couple of kids. It's lucky Pene and he get on so well. Pene doesn't mind staying home on a Friday or Saturday to look after the old man while she and Kepa go off to town or to a party. As long as she brings Pene

42

some comics and lollies back from town, he's happy. Funny that Pene doesn't think the old man's a nuisance . . . Maybe one day . . . He can't be nursemaid all the time. The old man might be Pene's best mate now; but what about when the boy grows older? Will he still love his Nanny so? No need to worry about it. By that time, Nanny Paora might have gone from them. He's lived a long life. Everybody's been lucky to have him so long . . .

The thought makes Annie frown, because it brings Rosie's face before her. Rosie.

— *My name is Rosemary; that's my proper name and I wish you would use it, Annie.*

— *Huh! It might be proper, but you're still Rosie around here. Don't think it makes you a different person to be called Rosemary. Not around here it doesn't.*

Rosie of the airs and graces. Rosie the porangi one. Fancy wanting to put the old man in a home . . . He'd given her everything and yet she tried to do that *thing*. That big-shot husband of hers must have had something to do with it. When Nanny Paora had come down with his stroke and had gone to live with Rosie, everybody in the village had thought it was the best thing to happen. Rosie had a big house and lots of room. So they hadn't stopped her from taking the old man. They thought she loved him. And then they'd found out that Rosie had taken him to a home . . .

Yeah, well she, Annie Jackson, had fixed them up, that Rosie, that husband and those doctors. She'd been real wild all right. Kepa had driven her to the home and she'd thundered through the entrance:

— Okay! Where is he! she'd yelled at the receptionist.

— Pardon? the woman had answered, taken aback.

— My father! I've come to take him out of this damn place.

Annie giggles to herself as she remembers. Boy, she must have been awful. But pae kare, she showed the lot of them. Yeah, and that stuck-up doctor who wanted her to produce proof she was Dad's daughter, she fixed him good and proper. And that Matron too, or whatever she called herself. Yeah, Annie Jackson made *them* hop around for a while.

And she could have cried, seeing the old man sitting there, so lonely. She'd dressed him and told him:

— You're coming home, Dad.

And all the way out, those doctors and nurses kept arguing that she couldn't take him out and that she had to sign this or that form . . . And she was so *mad*, so mad and angry. But when they had gotten into the car, she and Dad, all her anger left her, and she wondered whether it had really been her who'd gone in there. She'd shivered:

— We won't be seeing that place again in a hurry, she'd said to Kepa. And he had laughed:

— Don't you worry! They'll never let you in there after your performance, even if you begged for it.

— Me? Beg to get into that Pakeha place? Not likely.

It had been good to bring the old man home to the village. Everyone had been overjoyed to see him back. They'd kept coming over to see how he was and they'd had a big party that night. But there had been one thing more that Annie had to do. She'd rung Rosie. Rosie.

— You had no right to take him out of the home! Rosie had screamed.

— You had no right to put him there in the first place, Rosie!

— No right? I had every right! And I'm coming out there to get him, Annie.

— No you don't, Rosie. If you take him away from me, I'll take you to court. Yeah, and I'll fight you for the old man. And you wouldn't like that, would you . . . You wouldn't like your name in the papers . . . *He's staying here*.

— But he needs a nurse to look after him, Rosie had said.

— A nurse my bum! He doesn't need a nurse; he needs a family. And that's what he has out here. I'm telling you, Rosie, Dad is staying here. I'm not letting you take him away, now or ever. You try it, and you'll have the whole Whanau A Kai to answer to. And even though you and me are the same bones, pae kare Rosie, I'll fight you if it comes to a fight. And even if I lose, I'll never give the old man up . . .

44

Annie Jackson trembles as she remembers that conversation. It had been ugly. It had been awful.

But all over now. The old man is here, in the village where he belongs. Yes, belongs: not only to Rosie, not even only to her, Annie Jackson, but to everybody. He may not be getting any better, but he isn't getting any worse either. Old, that's all that's wrong with him. And that's no reason for Rosie trying to put him away . . .

— Nanny's eaten all his kai, Mum! Pene calls.

— You finished yours? Annie asks.

— Course! Pene laughs. See? I licked it clean, too.

Annie nods. She sees Pene whispering to Dad.

— Mum! Nanny wants to go for a little walk.

— How d'you know, Pene!

— He told me, didn't you Nanny!

Annie wonders, undecided. And Kepa moans and says:

— Oh, let the boys out, Annie. You can't keep them cooped up all the time.

— All right, she sighs. But don't think you can get out of doing the dishes all the time, Pene Jackson! Just count yourself lucky this time. And you better mind your Nanny. Don't walk him off his legs. And don't you dare leave him to play with your mates.

— Nanny's my mate, Mum!

— Yeah, well you just remember that. You stay with him all the time, you hear?

— Okay, Mum, Pene answers. Come on, Nanny. Come on, before Mum changes her mind.

The two of them leave the table. Pene leads Nanny Paora outside. Annie smiles as she hears Pene saying:

— Hold your leg up, Nanny. Not that one, the other one! This shoe is for your left foot not your right foot. Don't you know which is your left? No, Nanny, give me your *left* leg! If you think I'm going to put your right shoe on first, you're out of luck. I'm the boss of us two! I don't know . . . Why are you so dumb, Nanny? Right, now don't move yet. I got to tie your laces. Boy,

45

you're hopeless. How come you can't tie your laces yourself! Even babies can do that. There! All done. Now come on, Nanny. Come with me, Nanny . . .

Annie looks out the window. She sees Pene guiding the old man around the potholes of the drive. Then they reach the road and Pene looks back. His grin flashes in the sun. He waves and then lifts his Nanny's hand to wave too.

— Wave to Mum, Nanny. Wave your hand . . .

Then he turns and hand in hand, he and his Nanny walk slowly along the road.

— Nice day, ay Nanny. See the sun? Isn't it bright! Makes your eyes watery looking at it, ay. Watch out for that big rock. You might fall down and break your bones. Big rocks must just love you, Nanny! They must want you to fall down, ay. I don't know: how come you got soft bones? My bones are harder than yours. Hey! Whose car is that over there, Nanny? It's Uncle Rongo's car, ay Nanny! Shall we go and say gidday to Uncle? You want to say hullo to him? Come on then! Quick! No, too late, Nanny. He's turning into the paddocks. How come you're so slow, Nanny? Even a baby can run faster than you! Never mind. We wave to Uncle Rongo. We wave and shout out loud. You ready? Ready, get set, and now sing out loud Nanny. . .

Nine

Rongo Mahana shuts the gate and walks back to the Holden. He hears Pene shouting to him and sees the boy and Nanny Paora waving from far away. Smiling, he waves back and then steps into the car. Carefully, he drives it down the muddy track leading from the road to the potato paddock. The car lurches and slides in the mud.

— Pae kare, Rongo mumbles, one of these days I'm going to get some gravel and fix this track up for good! Yep, one of these days, maybe even next week . . .

Next week? Who does he think he's kidding! It's always next week with Rongo Mahana. Full of good intentions, that's him. The next week man, that's Rongo. It's not that he's lazy; only, when that next week comes, he's always busy doing something else. A busy man, that's Rongo! Busy trying to catch up on all those next weeks, the hundreds of them he's been telling his wife, Huia, about all these years.

— Might fix that fence next week, dear.

— Yes, Rongo.

— About time I fixed it, ay.

— Yes, Rongo.

— Pae kare, it's about time I got down to it, dear.

— Yes, Rongo.

— But I really will fix it this time, dear.

— Yes, Rongo . . .

Mind you, he does get things done finally. And this track? Well, if he doesn't get it done next week, it doesn't matter really. It's not a main road anyway.

The Rongo Mahana family live in the city, in a tidy wooden house in a tidy wooden suburb. They have lived there three years now. That Huia, that hoha wife of Rongo's, had suddenly decided it would be best for the kids. She's wanted them nearer to the schools, nearer to the library and away from the no-hopers of the village. She wasn't going to see *her* kids going to the pack and growing wild, not on your life! No, her kids were going to get the best — whatever that was — and be nearer to civilisation. You think she slaved all her life for nothing? Think she went out into the paddocks picking maize all day for fun? Well if you did, just you think again. She's done everything for her kids. Suffered for them. Fought for them. And she'll keep on fighting for them. Because she's known what it's like to go to school in rags, to know nothing and have nothing, and to be laughed at for being so poor . . . She's known it all, known it all. And she's making sure that her kids don't feel the pain and the hurt of being dirt.

Rongo smiles to himself. Pae kare, that Huia, she had done it too! She'd pushed him and she'd pushed her kids. And now, the Mahana family can hold their heads high in this world. It hadn't been easy, but they'd made it.

And yet, neither he nor Huia could ever break the emotional link between them and the village. Never. For didn't he come here almost every week on some pretext or another? And didn't Huia sometimes come with him to bend beside him in the fields? Yes, there was no doubt about it. Someday, maybe when the kids had found their own ways in the world, he and Huia would return. This is their home. This is their heart.

There's still a lot of good years ahead. Fifty-five he might be, but Rongo Mahana is still young enough to start life out here again. Okay, so he's got a few grey hairs but he's still got his wind and that's what counts. Yeah, some of his mates around here must be jealous of him for sure! But they only got themselves to blame; pot bellies just don't grow on you, they get put there by the big eating and big boozing. Yeah, they sure get jealous when he trots out onto the football field.

— Hey! Rongo Mahana! they yell. What you think you're doing out there? Get off the field before you get hurt!

He's shown them up though. Like in that game last Saturday when Marist had been short and the reserve hadn't turned up. And who'd come to the rescue? Young Rongo Mahana himself, just raring to go! That had been a good game too. Yeah, and even though he'd been the fullback (you might get hurt, Rongo, so we'll put you in the back) it had been he who'd got that try which had clinched the game for Marist. Charlie Hickson had passed the ball to the inner who'd passed it on to the centre, who'd spun it out to the winger. And that winger was getting all bunched up by that Coast team so he, Rongo Mahana, had blazed all the way from the back — must have been fifty yards at least — to help him out. But you think that winger would let the ball out?

— Pass it out! Pass it out! he'd yelled.

But that kid didn't want to give the ball to an old man. The nerve! Yet he, Rongo Mahana, had nearly made the All Blacks just after the War.

In the end that kid just had to let the ball go. Pae kare, it had been a bad pass too, but he'd managed to scoop it up. In front of him those big forwards of the Coast team were waiting just to tear him to pieces, to make mincemeat out of him. And he'd heard Mere, his daughter, yelling out:

— You fullas leave that old man alone! I'll kill you fullas if you touch him!

Huh! She shouldn't have worried. It had been chicken-feed to get past them. A sidestep here, a fend-off there, a little of the old magic Mahana footwork, and off he'd streaked — it must have been another fifty yards at least — to score a try right under the goal posts. And who dared to call him an old man after that little exhibition? Nobody, that's who. And those old fullas from around here, they knew when they were beaten. Ah, if only Tama, his eldest son, had been there to see him dive over for that try. He would have been proud of his old Dad. Never mind: he'll be back soon on holiday from Wellington. Tama and he together again; the stories they'll have to tell each other . . .

Rongo Mahana stops his car at a corner of the paddock. He gets out and takes some sacks out of the boot. For a moment, he looks over the paddock, the long rows of potatoes, a few of pumpkins and marrows, and the tall maize glistening yellow and green in the sun. A big paddock, stretching back to the road. One of four paddocks in the village which together form what is left of the Mahana land.

— Well, Rongo says to himself, may as well get started!

The Mahana land . . .

Until last year, the Mahana clan would get together at a family meeting, dub in some money and buy seed to plant in the family paddocks. Then they would fix a time for the planting, calculating it the old way by the shape of the moon and the position of the stars in the night sky. Once that was done, they would all come together at the planting.

It used to be a good time. A family occasion. A gathering of the Mahana clan. Kids and all would come to follow the tractor and plant the seeds in the furrows. And although it was hard work it didn't seem to take long because everybody was too busy chucking off at each other to think of how hard the work was.

— Hey! Cover that plant properly with the dirt, ay!

— Worry about your own plant! And while you're at it, don't you know how to plant in the straight line?

— Who says I'm not planting straight! It's not me, it's the furrows that are crooked.

— Don't blame the furrows, ay! You must have had too much to drink last night!

— Me?

— Yes, you! And just look at that son of yours! Hey, Boy! You only have to dig a small hole for the plants. You think you're going to China?

— You watch your own son! He's not watering those plants at all!

— So? What with your boozing last night, you got enough water in *you* for all the plants!

And so it would continue all that day. The laughter and the light-hearted exchanges, and the constant bending into the planting. And at smoko times, the clan would all rest beneath a willow tree and eat some kai. Then back to the work again until night had fallen.

Sometimes, the planting would take a whole week, depending on how many paddocks the clan had decided would be planted with seed. One week among the very few weeks that all the Mahana families became one family. A happy week of shared muscle and sweat. Of laughter. Aroha. Until the planting was over.

Then would come the waiting time. The waiting for the maize and potatoes to grow. And each Mahana family would come out to the land to weed the growing plants and water them when it was their turn.

But once the crop was ready, the Mahana clan would come together again. They would gather at the harvest and there would be fulfilment of family reaping a shared labour.

This day, Rongo Mahana has come for this year's harvest. He has come with spade in hand to this paddock. He has come alone; he has come in sadness. There is no sense of fulfilment.

For last year, Rongo Mahana planted this one paddock by himself. And this day, he has come alone to the harvest.

— Times are changing . . .

Rongo throws the sacks on the ground. He sits on one of them and unlaces his shoes. He puts his boots on. Then he stands with spade gripped in his hands and pushes it into the earth to uncover the potatoes clinging to the roots of an upturned plant. He bends and pulls at the potatoes, his fingers searching the soil for any others which have not been exposed by the cleaving spade. And he piles them in the furrow between this row and the next before thrusting the spade again beneath the next plant in the row. Spade turning earth, body bending and fingers scrabbling in the dirt. Spade cleaving earth, body attuning itself to the rhythm of the work. Plant after plant being upturned.

— Good spuds these . . .

Losing himself to the rhythm of the spade. Trying to forget the loneliness of the digging. Moving up the row leaving potatoes strewn in the furrow. His heart racing, the sweat beginning to bead his face. And an aching beginning in his bending body. Alone in the paddock. A solitary speck amid the expanse of furrows cut into the earth. Alone. Alone under the hot sun.

And then the spade slips to cut into the roots of a plant and slice into the potatoes beneath. And with despair, Rongo grasps them and flings them at the sun. And the rhythm of this man to the land is destroyed . . .

A big clan, the Mahanas. Once they all lived here in the village. Seven brothers and three sisters. Rongo, the eldest. Growing up together, sharing life with one another. Marrying and bringing up families here. Until the land could not contain them all; until they began to leave the land. Of the ten families, only Pita and Miriama and Rawiri and his wife Teria, remain in the village. Rawiri and Teria and their seven children live in the old home, Mum and Dad's home. Rongo and the eldest sister have brought up their children in the nearby city. The rest of the clan are scattered throughout the country. A brother at Mataura in the South Island. Another brother in Hastings working the orchard during summer and odd-jobbing through winter. Two brothers and two sisters living in Wellington, their children assembling engines or shifting endlessly from job to job. And another brother in the freezing works in Hamilton. Scattered. And the times of their gathering together as a clan are fewer now.

Times are tightening up. During the first years when the Mahana families had begun to leave the village, they would still come back when called for the planting, the harvesting, the family shearing. And when the village itself called them for the big huis or the tangi, they would return. That was when there were a lot of labouring jobs around, when you could tell the boss you were leaving and know that you'd be able to get another job easy when you returned.

But the gypsy life too, is diminishing. And it seems you need

52

more money to live on these days. There is security in having and keeping one job, in having permanent employment. And living in the cities is nothing but an attractive trap. It binds you to itself with contracts: with high mortgages or steep rents, with hire purchase payments and threats of repossession. And it asks more of you: more of your money and more and more for things you did not really want. A Venus flytrap. And once you're caught, you can never escape. You must keep working and keep working to keep up the next payment. You can't afford to take a week or two off for something as ridiculous as the family planting.

Yes, ridiculous, that's what it is. And you say you want five days off to go to a *funeral*? Ridiculous! No, definitely not! No! You see our point, don't you? I mean the Company comes first, doesn't it? Heavens! What would happen if all you Maoris took off five days! The Company would be ruined, absolutely ruined. The quotas wouldn't be met, production would grind to a halt . . . And by *your* action, you would be putting *other* people out of work. The people who are waiting to assemble our product, the people who distribute it . . . It would be utter chaos. Can't you see that? No, definitely *no*. The Company cannot allow you five days off. If you persist in your intention, then we must terminate your services. And I'm afraid there would be little likelihood of your job being here for you when you returned. We have a long waiting list of applicants you know. I'm sorry, but that's the way it is. You Maoris will just have to learn to live with the times. You do understand our point of view don't you?

Yes, that's the way it is. So better to stay and not listen to the hearth calling you. Better to stay at the bench in the production line. Better to live with the times.

Rongo Mahana sighs. What's the use of feeling sad? What's the use of feeling angry? Can't do anything about it. Can't do anything at all. Pae kare, it's lucky there are at least *some* factories that understand the Maori way. But will they always be so understanding? Probably not. Things don't last forever . . .

The spade thrusts into the earth again.

And could you really put all the blame on the Pakeha life?

Blame it for changing the Maori? That sister, that Ruihi, she'd promised to come out for the planting last year. And she broke her promise. Don't know why, don't know why.

On that first day of the planting last year, Rongo Mahana had waited alone in the paddock. He'd hoped that somehow, the others of the family would be able to come. Even though they'd told him they couldn't make it, he had still kept on hoping. The sun had sprung quickly in the sky. And he had felt his heart breaking. The time of the family planting was over but he had been too stubborn to realise it. He couldn't blame the others for moving from the village and destroying the rhythm of the land. He couldn't blame Rawiri and Teria for being in Hastings while he waited here alone, nor Pita and Miriama for being away shearing. He could only blame himself for waiting, for being so stubborn. For hoping.

And then he had not been able to wait longer. He had felt the earth crying out for seed. He had felt the yearning of the land for peace, for it had become accustomed to the rhythm of the yearly planting. And there had been a crying out of his blood too. The rhythm of the land and the rhythm of his blood had been one and the same. And he had begun the planting and both blood and land had gradually become calm. And he felt the strength of the land calling him. He had made a promise to himself and the land that day. That every year he would return to bring peace to the land and to himself. Even if it meant pulling himself along the ground by his hands, he would do it. Crawling on hands and knees, he would do it. One row after another. Slowly. Painfully. Until it was done. And the tears from his eyes, it would be they which would water each green shoot.

A promise this, which Rongo Mahana remembers now, on this Sunday as he harvests alone. And when I am dead, what then? he asks himself. Who will come to bring peace to the land?

He laughs to himself and pats the earth affectionately.

— Don't you worry! he says. For Tama will come to you when I am gone. . .

Tama, the eldest son of Rongo. In Wellington now, confused

54

between two worlds. But the pull of the land in his blood will be the stronger. And he will come back. He *will* return.

Rongo Mahana decides to have a little rest. He sits on the ground and looks back over what he's done. Not too bad for an old man. And the spuds are good this year. How many sacks should he fill today? Better dig up as much as he can today. Take some round to Rawiri and Teria. Maybe they'll be able to give a hand with the digging tomorrow. No, tomorrow's Monday and they're both working. Ah well, that Huia, that lazy wife, she can come out here tomorrow instead of sitting around the house.

— Well! Better start again! Rongo says to the land. Times may have changed, ay land! Me and you are getting old. But pae kare, we're not giving up yet, ay?

And his laughter is a challenge ringing from his lips . . .

Ten

Sam Walker's bach. A tin shack behind his Auntie Maka's house. It is dark inside, but enough light streams through the cracks of the closed door and between the slats of the boarded-up window to light up the room.

Once, it used to be a kitchen where Maka would cook over an open fire. That was when the kitchen in the house in front of the shack became too small to cope with all her growing kids. So her husband, now dead, erected the shack. All of her kids have grown up and live in houses of their own these days. The kitchen fell unused until Sam, that nephew of hers, had asked her if he could stay there. She'd said yes, knowing it would be better for Sam and his father, Hepa, if Sam didn't live at home. If Sam hadn't come to stay, it wouldn't have been long before he and his father had a row. At least his coming to live in the shack saved that happening.

It is big, this one-room shack. Big and dark and cluttered with rusted pots and pans. From the ceiling hangs a rusting tilly lamp. A big black pot still hangs from a wire hook in the unused open fireplace. Beneath it, empty beer bottles and cigarette cartons are stacked. In the middle of the room is a long table, stained with candle grease and food. A bed has been squeezed into one corner. Next to it is a chest of drawers with a broken mirror on top. The cupboard where food was once kept is bursting with clothes.

A few pictures cut from magazines are sellotaped to the tin walls. A broken beer bottle lies on the dirt floor.

And scattered throughout the room, in various attitudes, are eight people, their faces haggard with drinking. Among them is Mattie Jones, sitting with Sam on the trestle beside the table, her hands limply outstretched across the table where beer bottles shine darkly in the light. She is sleeping, her head resting on the tabletop, her face bloated with beer and fatigue and yet, still startling in its beauty.

The air is hazy with cigarette smoke and stale with the smell of sweat. But the party isn't over yet. For sprawled in a corner, Sonny Whatu boozily strums at his guitar. No, not over yet. Not yet. Yeah, think they're going to stop the party because Dad wanted to come home early? Nah! Good old Sam for telling everyone to come around his place to finish off the beer . . .

Good old Sam, yeah, good old Sam. The village clown, that's Sam. No party is complete without him. A pub without Sam is an empty one, yeah. Wherever he is, that's where the fun is at. Where the laughs are loudest, the fights are fiercest, that's where you'll find him. The centre of attraction, that's Sam.

Sam, good old Sam. A chip off the old Walker block. Not like that cissy brother of his, Frankie darling, farting hot air at that university in Auckland. Not like that stuck-up father of his, Hepa Walker, Mister Walker Sir. No, good old Sam, with the bad Walker blood. Good old Sam who knew exactly what he was, a no-hoper, and that nothing he could do would ever change that. Good old Sam, handsome once and young, who tried to walk as his old man walked. But his legs were the bad Walker legs which led him into trouble. Good old Sam, he went to Wellington, bashed a taxi-driver over the head and ended up singing the jail-house blues. Good old Sam, bad news for the cops, bad news for his Dad. Good old Sam with good old Mattie. Two of a kind, the bad kind. Both of them back here where they know they belong. Back here, because there is nowhere else to go.

And Sonny sings:

Down the road I walk and there comes Mary,
Hair of gold and lips like cherries,
It's good to touch the green green grass of home . . .

A sliver of light stabs at Mattie's closed eyes. She winces and moves her arms. A bottle upturns and the beer flows quietly out to trickle through her hair and around her face. It follows the curve of her neck and spills onto her dress. She frowns in her sleep. But she is so tired, so tired . . .

She shivers as the beer seeps through to her body. As she moves the light strikes her closed eyelids again. And in that halo of haze and amid the beer bottles gleaming, she suddenly awakes. For a moment she is still, gaining strength. Then she brushes her wet hair back from her forehead and hoarsely moans.

Where am I . . . Where *am* I . . .

And gradually she remembers.

Remembers George and she and the Wellington years. The good years. Okay, so they had fights and so they quarrelled, but she loved George. And he loved her. And they would lie in bed together and they were happy. They were so happy. Yes, he loved her, *he loved her* . . .

She groans and tries to bite back the memory. Harder. Harder. Until blood seeps from her lips and she sweeps her hands across the table in anger. Glass shatters, beer spills. And she pushes against the table and stands.

— Look what you done! someone yells.

— Shut your mouth, Mattie whispers. Her head whirls and she sways uncertainly. What's the time? she wonders. She peers at the clock, standing among the beer bottles on the table. The little hand is on the ten — or is it the nine — no, the ten . . . Jeez, she's been drinking for over six hours. And where's that Hine Ropiho gone? Where? Take me home, Hine, take me home . . .

— Hine? she calls.

— Gone home, a voice answers. Her and Jack, they both gone.

— Then I'm going home too, Mattie says.

She stumbles to the door, but before she can open it, Sam

Walker grabs her round the waist.

— Stay, Mattie . . .

She wrenches herself away from him.

— Keep your fucken hands off me! She screams. All of you, keep your hands off me.

And she pulls open the door and staggers out into the sunlight. The brilliance strikes into the darkness behind her eyes uncovering pain . . .

— Hey, Whetu! I know that fulla over there.

— Where, Mattie?

— There, by the bar, with that Pakeha girl.

— That's George Karepa. With Joyce.

— I thought I knew him! He comes from where I'm from.

— Yeah, Mattie?

— But he wouldn't remember me. I was just a kid then. He wouldn't remember me, you think Whetu?

— Dunno. But I'd stay clear of him if I was you. He's big trouble, George Karepa. Stay clear of him, Mattie.

Shading her eyes from the sun and swaying she stands. Casting shadow across her mind. Trying not to remember. But not enough shadow, not enough dark and light still streaming through as if from a crack in an opening doorway.

And Joyce is standing there.

— So this is your new bitch, Joyce yells. So this is the slut who stole you from me, ay?

Joyce is drunk. In her hand she holds a glass which she throws at Mattie. The glass shatters on the wall.

— Get out, George says. Get out Joyce.

Joyce sneers. She walks slowly towards Mattie.

— So you're the one, ay? So you're the bitch? Yeah, you had to wait for my back to be turned, didn't you! Bitch. Bitch!

And she lashes out at Mattie. But George stops her. He raises his own hand and the cracking sounds as he hits Joyce in the face stun the air into silence.

Then staggering from the doorway through the hot sun. No, seeing Rongo Mahana as he waves to her. Remembering those few months, those good months, when she and George lived together in a small flat in Newtown. Those happy months. And then the long lonely times of waiting for George, always waiting. Waiting through nights. Then days. Then weekends. Alone. Always alone.

And knocking on door after door, doing the rounds of the party houses, trying to find him.
— You seen George?
And seeing the same look, that guarded look, in eyes looking into the darkness at her.
— No. Haven't seen him.
Looking and waiting. Waiting and looking. Making up. Making love. Then waiting again. And looking again. And finally, finding him.
And wanting to kill him and the girl cowering beside him. Clawing at his face, hitting at him and not caring about the blood drawn from her face by the ring on his bunched hand.
— Get away, Mattie . . .
And laughing in his face.
— Mattie, we're finished . . . I'm finished with you.
Laughing. Crying. Her heart bursting with grief. But standing erect, remembering her pride.
— You finished with me, George? Oh no, you got it wrong, Karepa. You belong to me until I say I'm finished with you. And I haven't finished with you yet. Not yet.
And walking away. Moving out of the flat. Moving through grey days and morning sickness. Alone, but not alone.
— You belong to me, George Karepa . . .

Through the gate and down the road she stumbles. And a car coming behind her swerves to avoid her and a horn blares to cut across her mind.

And Kararaina is crying in a small boarding-house room.

60

— Don't cry, baby. Please don't cry . . .

Hugging Kara close to her, fearing the footsteps of the landlady coming yet again to complain.

— Kara, please be a good baby. . .

Refusing help. Too proud to admit to her boss why she is always late for work. Not letting Mum and Dad know about Kara. Lonely in one room. Getting the sack. Finding a new job. Borrowing money to live. Lonely. Always alone.

— Kara . . . Please, Kara . . .

And finally, forgetting pride. Ringing home.

— Dad? Dad? Please come and get me . . .

Staggering down the road. And the world is a daze of whirling sunlight and hills. Remembering the long trip back here and her mother's tears, glad her daughter is home. And beginning to live again. And trying not to remember.

— Auntie! Auntie!

Mattie looks up. She sees Kara running toward her. And she crushes Kara in her arms.

— Auntie? You all right, Auntie?

And Mattie smiles wanly.

— I'm all right, Kara. But I'm very tired. You lead me home? You lead your Auntie home?

— Yes, Auntie.

And Mattie kisses her daughter.

No matter if you're married, George Karepa. You belong to me . . .

Eleven

— Maka? You up yet?

— Yeah, I'm up. Come on in, Mere.

— You had a good sleep?

— You trying to be funny, Mere? What with you waking me up early this morning and those boozers out the back having their party, I feel a proper wreck. And don't you start getting smart, either, Mere! You don't look so hot yourself today.

— I haven't even said a word, Maka.

— Maybe, but I can see you laughing in your eyes. Crikey dick, fancy coming around at half past five in the morning just to gossip. One of these days I'm going to do it to you and see how you like it. I like my lie-in. How do you think I keep beautiful!

— Eeee, Maka.

— Well, more beautiful than you anyway, Ugly. And don't answer back or else you won't get a cup of tea. How come you always time it right, Mere? And don't ask for the sugar because I haven't got any. You borrowed my last sugar yesterday.

— Oh . . . Sorry, Maka. I'll pay you back tomorrow.

— I'll believe it when I see it.

— Yeah, well . . . Hey! I saw that niece of yours a while ago.

— Which one?

— That Mattie. Running down the road and she was as drunk as a skunk. Almost got run over too. By a car, you know.

— Not a horse?

— No, a car and . . . Eeee! You're just having me on, Maka!

— Well, what else would run you down these days! You must think I'm dumb, ay Mere. Anyway, nothing wrong with going home drunk. You and me have rolled down that road plenty of times. Come to think of it, we fell in a ditch once. You fell in and pulled me with you.

— Not! It was you who fell in first.

— Now don't you argue with me, Mere. I was there, and it was you who fell in first.

— I'm not arguing, Maka. But you're wrong and . . .

— Just drink your tea, Mere.

— No good without sugar in it . . . Boy, those fullas out the back are kicking up a racket.

— You don't have to tell me that, Mere! I've been hearing guitars in my head all morning!

— Well, why don't you go and tell them off?

— No . . . Let them be happy . . . That Sam needs to let off a bit of steam.

— Yeah, I guess there was no parties in prison, ay Maka.

— Not for him, no. Two years he got. And then when he come home, his father wouldn't even let him forget it. That Hepa, you'd think he'd know better being on the Maori Council. But no, pick, pick, pick, all he could do was pick at Sam. Telling Sam he was no good and disgraced the Walker family. If he doesn't watch out, that Hepa will talk that Hana out of the house too. And knowing what she gets up to these days, I wouldn't be surprised if she got on to the wrong side of the track too.

— But two years, they gave him. Two years.

— Yeah, and his mate and him only did it for fun. You know, pretended they didn't have any money to pay for that taxi. And next minute, that driver was calling up the cops. No wonder they slugged him over the head. Crikey dick, that Magistrate must have had a stone for a heart. Never mind. Let's not talk about it. Sam's back here now. He'll be all right.

— Good boy, that Sam . . . Well! I finished my tea. I'll be off now.

— Huh? Already?

— Yeah. I only came around because I'd run out of tea. You wouldn't by any chance be able to . . .

— *No*, Mere! First sugar and now tea, I don't know how I put up with you.

— Well, see you Maka.

— The later the better.

— And Maka . . .

— What!

— It was you who fell in the ditch first . . .

Twelve

The sound of Charlie Whatu snoring is like an engine revving up, then coughing into silence and then revving up again. And Andrew, his son, grimaces to himself. Even outside the house you can't get away from the racket.

Andrew is sitting on the steps in front of the house. The sun is warm, but Mum and Dad are wasting away the day as usual. They sure love their sleep. Trust them to wake him up when they got home early this morning. And then, just as he'd almost dropped to sleep again, that Janey had woken him again with her noise. If she was going to make a habit of sneaking home, he wished she'd do it a little quieter. No, there was no peace around here.

He picks up his book and tries to continue reading it. But it's no good because Dad is snoring too loud. With a sigh, he puts it down. From afar off he hears a guitar plunking away. Sonny, boozing at Sam Walker's place. Every weekend it's the same. When you go to sleep, the last thing you hear is a guitar. And when you wake up, that blinking guitar is still at it. They're all wasters around here, wasting away good sunny days.

Andrew sighs again. Then he lifts his face to the sun and closes his eyes. Gosh! That sun is good! And the warmth stirs his blood and he murmurs:

— Mmmmm . . . Josephine, honey . . .

His lips pucker and he reaches forward.

— Gidday, Anaru! someone calls.

Startled, he opens his eyes. He sees Mere passing. She is laughing. Embarrassed, he says:

— Oh, hullo, Mere.

And he watches as she walks down the road. Big fat Mere. Just imagine kissing *her* on the lips!

Shuddering to himself, he closes his eyes and thinks of Josephine again. Now where was he? That's right, he was just about to kiss her before he was rudely interrupted. Mmmmm, Josephine. His honey. And one day, he'll tell her that she is. Not yet, though. And why not? Because he's too dang scared, that's why!

For Josephine is a Pakeha girl. To make it worse, she's brainier than Andrew and her father is rich. What possible chance has he got? His own dad is poor and Andrew himself, though intelligent, is just not in the same class as Josephine. And, of course, he is Maori. No matter that their aspirations and outlook are the same, he is Maori. No matter that they both aim at university, he is Maori. Not much use even beginning a relationship when you considered it. No, not much use at all.

The future seems tied up in knots. It's a strange world out there, outside the village. A European world. Where there is no family. Where they cannot help you. How lucky Mum and Dad are to live here.

Andrew sighs to himself. Where, he wonders, did he ever get the ambition to keep on with education? Why hasn't he left school like his mates? And why on earth did he have to fall in love with a Pakeha girl! It would have been better to go for one of the girls of the village like his cousin Waka has done. Waka and Ani, getting married. Dang it, if he was in love with a girl from around here, he wouldn't be worrying himself on a beautiful morning like this.

Then who or what was it that gave him the drive to get on with education?

It doesn't matter really, whoever or whatever it was. All that matters is that he cannot do anything about it. It is already too late to step back because his curiosity about the world compels him forward. He is caught in between, a Maori forcing himself against the values of a Pakeha world. And as he steps further into that world, he cannot help but change. He cannot help but worry.

— Dang it! Andrew mutters.

And he hears Dad chuckling behind him. There's no privacy around here.

— Spying on me again ay, Dad?

— What do I want to spy on you for! Dad replies.

— Because you're nosey, that's why!

His father hits him playfully.

— You must have something to hide ay, Son? You want to tell me about it? Not that I'll be able to help you much. After all, you're the brainy one of the family. As for your father, he's dumb.

He sits beside Andrew on the steps.

— I don't want to talk about it, Dad. And don't say things like that.

— Like what?

— Like being dumb, Dad. Because you aren't. You're much brainier than me, and you just don't know how lucky you are . . .

— Me lucky? Charlie Whatu snorts. How come I didn't get the double at the races yesterday then!

— That's not what I mean, Dad.

There is silence for a moment. Then Charlie Whatu nudges his son.

— Come on, tell me what's biting you.

Andrew tries to change the subject.

— Don't you think you better get dressed he says abruptly.

— Aren't I decent enough?

— Not with your legs open.

— Oops! Scared of the competition ay, Son?

— Don't make fun of me, Dad . . .

Charlie Whatu looks curiously at his son. Pae kare, who would have thought that he would have such a serious boy for his son! Something was eating him. Something was on his mind. Something.

— Tell me, Anaru . . .

67

And Andrew, haltingly and with embarrassment, decides to tell his father about this girl, Josephine. Then he tells his father about the doubts he has of himself. He asks his father's advice.

— Boy . . . his father begins, scratching his head. You're always thinking up problems for yourself. Okay, so we're poor and maybe we haven't got as much brains as other people, but we're still the same as them, the Pakeha. We're not lower class, we're not any of those things you think we are. And if that girl loves you, then she loves you for yourself, not because you're Maori or Pakeha. Just be yourself, Son. Be yourself.

— But I don't know who I am, Andrew says. Sometimes I'm Maori, sometimes I'm Pakeha, sometimes I'm half and half. You just don't understand, Dad.

His father muses for a while.

— Maybe I don't understand, he admits. I know in my heart that I'm Maori. The world hadn't changed too much when I was a boy, so my whole upbringing was Maori. But you? Well, you live in a Pakeha world and perhaps your Mum and me should have taught you more about your own people. Except that we could see it would be no use. You're a throwback, Son. You feel the old Maori in your blood and it fights with your Pakeha learning. You have to make your own decision about who and what you are. Maybe you'll be able to live in both worlds without feeling a stranger in either. . . Whatever happens, I can't help you and I feel sorry.

Charlie Whatu grows silent. Then suddenly, he laughs.

— Just listen to me telling my brainy son about life! It should be the other way round, ay?

— Don't Dad, Andrew pleads. Don't say things like that. You are proud of me; but I envy you.

— What the hell for? Charlie Whatu asks. I don't know anything! And look at my hands: all they know about is the soil. All they've done is labouring work. Fencing and digging post-holes, that's been my life. This head, it's got nothing in it. These feet, they'll always be stuck right smack in the centre of this village. You shouldn't envy that.

— But I do, Dad You're content; I'm not. You know about the earth; all I know about it is from books. Your life is here and you only want to stay here; I don't know where my life will lie. But wherever it is, it will not be as happy as yours . . .

Charlie Whatu looks at his son and shakes his head.

— I don't understand you, Son. This village belongs to you; you belong to it. You think I am content here? You better think again! I stay here because I'm no use anywhere else.

— Don't tell lies, Dad.

His father chuckles to himself.

— Can't put anything past you ay, Son! I'm only trying to make you happy. I'm not doing very well, am I? Never mind. Very soon you may not have to be worried about being Maori.

— What do you mean?

— There's been some new zoning laws, Son. You think the only problems are outside Waituhi. But they're coming in here too.

— No . . .

— We're not allowed to build on less than ten acres now.

— Oh, Dad . . .

— That means if some of the old houses burn down, or even Takitimu Hall, we can't rebuild them.

— No . . .

— And so what happens? All the old houses get older and when they are condemned, we can't rebuild them. Ten acres must be between us and the next house. The family is breaking up.

— Dad . . .

— That's why your cousin, George, had to build his house in town. He wasn't allowed to come back here. Because of the laws.

— But why, Dad? Why?

Charlie Whatu strokes his son's head.

— I don't know, Son. I just don't know. But don't be too sentimental about it. People thought the Maori was going to die out a long time ago. We might've been bought off our lands with a coupla blankets once, but we haven't sold our souls yet.

There is a gleam in Dad's eye. Then he slaps Andrew on the back.

— Enough of this talk. You'll get that girl and plenty of others too.

— Why, Dad? Why are they doing it?

Charlie Whatu looks at his son, strangely.

— I shouldn't have told you, Son. You take things too hard.

Andrew just sits there, not saying anything.

— Tell you what! Charlie Whatu says. You always used to moan and groan when there was some cleaning up to do round the meeting house. Well, today there's some cleaning up to do and . . .

— Let's get started! Andrew says furiously.

And Charlie Whatu chuckles to himself.

— That's the boy. That's the way . . .

Thirteen

— We better be going home now, Pene says.

He and Nanny Paora are sitting on the hill just above the meeting house. They've walked a long long way this morning. Nanny Paora was sure fit today! He just kept on walking and walking and even when they got to Uncle Charlie Whatu's place, he wouldn't stop. That was where Pene wanted to stop for a while, but Nanny, he was very stubborn today. Nothing that Pene could do or say would persuade Nanny's feet to turn in the direction of Uncle Charlie's place. In the end, Pene had just stopped in the middle of the road, arms akimbo, and shouted to Nanny:

— Look here, Nanny! Just where do you think you're off to? That's not the way to Uncle Charlie's house!

But Nanny Paora was already disappearing down the road.

— Just come back here right this minute! Pene shouted, stamping a foot on the ground. Nanny, you just listen to me! I'm the boss, not you! All right then: you go your way and I go mine!

Nanny Paora kept pretending he couldn't hear. He kept plodding on down the road. Pene had sighed. Where was he heading for now!

— All right, Nanny. You win. We go your way.

And he'd growled his Nanny all the way to the old homestead.

The old homestead was where Nanny Paora used to live when he had been a boy. When he got married to Nanny Moana, he had taken her to live there too. He had lived there even after Nanny Moana had died. Then he had suffered a stroke. That was when he had first stayed with Auntie Rose and then with Pene's family. The old homestead was deserted now.

Pene has heard a lot of stories about the old homestead from Mum. They were stories of the days when Nanny Paora had been younger and very important. Although Nanny isn't young any more, he is still important.

He is the only one of his generation still living in the village. He is the oldest Maori in the district. He is very, very, very old. And that is why everyone in the village respects him. To the mana of his lineage has been added the mana of his age. But the greatest mana of all is that Nanny Paora is also one of the few left in the country who is full-blooded Maori. It is something to be thought of with awe and respect.

And today, Nanny Paora had wanted to see the old homestead again. Strange that he would want to do that, because he usually never wanted to walk that way . . .

Most times, Pene was puzzled at why his mother loved the old homestead so much. In her stories to him about it, she made it seem like a palace, a place of beauty and serenity. She could never make Pene live her dreams like Nanny could do. And all Pene saw when Mum talked of the old homestead was just another old house, its verandah ripped away, the sheet iron roofing missing in places, and the windows closed to the world because they had been boarded up.

But when Pene was with Nanny Paora, then he saw the old homestead as it used to be. There was something magical about Nanny Paora. He could roll back the years and take Pene with him to live some magical moment, some strange and fascinating experience that, it seemed, had been waiting in the backwater of the years to be lived again.

But Nanny Paora and Pene had not stayed long enough at the old homestead. And Pene was glad because the moments were always sad. Today, he had seen an old kuia drawing water from a well near the old homestead. Nanny Paora had cried out:

72

— Moana . . .

Then he had drawn the edges together over that moment before it eddied too strongly around him. They had left the old homestead. They had come to the hill above Rongopai.

— Nanny? Pene says again. Are you awake yet? We better be going home now. Mum will be wondering where we are.

But Nanny Paora is still having a moe. He is tired out after all the walking. That will teach him!

Pene chews on a long straw. He decides to let his Nanny sleep for just a while longer. He wishes he still had some wild blackberries to eat.

The wild blackberries had been the main discovery of the morning. After Nanny and Pene had sat near the meeting house for a while, they had gone to look at the old cookhouse nearby. Pene had decided to have a look inside and had left his Nanny sitting at the door. The old cookhouse was where all the kai had been cooked whenever there had been a hui at the village. There had not been a hui for a long time. After he'd explored the cookhouse, Pene had returned to his Nanny.

And he had found the old man sitting in the long grass eating something.

— Nanny! he had screamed. What you eating? Let me look, let me see. You might get poisoned.

He had grabbed his Nanny's hand. Blackberries! Hmmmm. They tasted all right; they *were* all right! And there was a whole big patch of them growing near the fence!

— Eeeee! Nanny; Pene had giggled. Trying to keep it a secret ay, Nanny? I know you, you want to hog everything for yourself. Well I caught you, I caught you!

The old man had giggled too.

— Ae . . . caught me . . . mokopuna . . .

And they had both sat in the blackberry patch, making their mouths red with the fruit.

Then Pene had collected some for eating on the way home. He had washed his Nanny's face to get the red stains off, and then

73

had washed his own. One moment he had been talking to his Nanny; the next moment, the old man had disappeared.

— Where are you, Nanny?

He had heard his Nanny sighing sorrowfully.

— Nanny? Nanny?

And he had seen the old man walking slowly away from the cookhouse. One step. And one step further now. Toward the meeting house. Toward the painted Rongopai. Walking slowly through the sunlight. His arms outstretched.

— No, Nanny . . .

Toward dark shadows waiting on the porch.

— Come back, Nanny . . .

Toward whispering shapes calling.

— Don't listen, Nanny . . .

One step. And one step further now.

And Pene had rushed after the old man and grabbed his arms.

But it had seemed as if Nanny Paora hadn't known he was there. He had kept walking toward the beckoning shadows, his lips trembling with sadness and his voice sighing with sorrow.

— Nanny, don't listen . . .

And with panic, Pene had reached up and put his arms around the old man's head, closing his eyes from the vision, closing his ears from the calling.

There had fallen silence. The shadows had faded away. Pene had whispered to his Nanny:

— Don't cry, Nanny. Come away now.

And all the time they had walked away from the meeting house, he kept on whispering:

— Nanny, don't you leave me. Come away. Come away . . .

— All gone . . . my people . . . all gone . . . . Nanny Paora had sorrowed.

They had left the meeting house. They had climbed the hill above Rongopai. Here, Nanny Paora has been sleeping, curled up in the waving grass.

At last, Pene hears his Nanny stirring.

74

— Awake at last! he laughs. Did you have a good moe, Nanny? You love your sleep, ay. But we better get home now. Mum might give us a hiding if we stay here any longer.

He gets up from the ground and helps the old man to his feet too. They walk down toward the road.

And Pene shivers and hurries his Nanny past the meeting house. Then suddenly, he sees something bright in the air.

— Oh, look Nanny! Look!

He points to the sky. A kite is soaring, almost to the clouds, and its long tail bobs with coloured streamers. The kite swoops and curls with the wind currents. On the other side of the road, a group of children shout orders to their brother about flying the kite.

— It's a good kite, ay Nanny! Pene breathes. See how it flies!

His Nanny smiles.

— Good . . . kite . . . mokopuna . . . Tupurupuru he was . . . caught by two such . . . kites . . . Magic were those . . . kites . . .

And as the boy and old man walk along the road homeward, Pene recalls the story about Tupurupuru. It is a story he has heard many times before. Of how this man murdered twin sons of Kahutapere their father. Kahutapere, after several days searching without success for their bodies, became certain that some tragedy had happened. He made then two kites, Tara-ki-uta and Tara-ki-tai, named after the twins. The priests of the village chanted incantations over the kites. Then the two were sent into the air. They rose to a great height; they hovered over the Pa of Tupurupuru. Once, then for a second time, they dipped themselves over the Pa. It was a sign that someone there was responsible for the death of the twins. Tupurupuru was killed. The twins were avenged.

His Nanny first told Pene that story many years ago. Nanny knew many stories. And when the old man died, who then would know the stories, whakapapa and history of the Whanau A Kai? Nanny Paora . . . the only one of his generation left. Stranded here. Alone.

The kite dancing, the kite swooping through the air. Pene looks up at it and wonders what the world must look like from up there . . .

Fourteen

Teria Mahana stands at the back door of her house. Where the heck have her kids got to! She shades her eyes against the sun and sees them playing in a paddock near Rongopai. She breathes deep, expels and booms her voice across to them.

— Haere mai ki te kai!

It is a big voice which suits this big woman. And the children look at each other and sigh:

— Big Mama's callin' . . .

They pretend they haven't heard their mother. Her voice booms out again like a cannon.

— I said come and get it and if you kids don't come you sure will get it from me!

The kids moan to one another. Big Mama's always spoiling their fun. And just when they got their kite way up high too.

— Better do as your mother says, one of them sighs to another.

— What do you mean *my* mother! She's your mother too!

There are seven children in the paddock. Thirteen year old August is the eldest; he begins to pull the kite earthward. Like his sister and brother, June and July, he has been named after the month in which he was born. The twin boys are called Anzac and Crete because Dad was in the Second World War. One of the other girls is named Daisy after an auntie, and the youngest girl is called Hope because Mum hopes she won't have any more kids.

Seven are enough, thank you very much! And that father of theirs, Rawiri, better get used to it.

In looks, the kids are very alike as if they'd been mass-produced. But what can you expect? They followed each other so quick and fast that there probably wasn't time for Teria Mahana's body to make them look any different from each other. June, July and August were born one every year, give or take a few months. Then there was a gap of two years when Teria had been able to fight off her husband and dim that gleam in his eyes. However, he soon made up for lost time and the twins, Anzac and Crete, arrived. Daisy and Hope had followed soon after them. And after Hope had been born, Teria's doctor had told her to call it quits and not have any more kids.

— You should be talking to that Rawiri, Teria had said to her doctor. He's the one who should call it quits. No sooner do I get out of Maternity than I'm flat on my back again.

Funnily enough, Teria hasn't had any more children. Hope is four now and there's no sign of another baby on its way yet. But you never know: that Rawiri sure is cunning!

The kite falls to the earth. Anzac runs to it and holds it in the air while August winds the string in. August, he made the kite himself. His other brothers and sisters think he's hang of a clever! Yes, and he's promised to make them all a kite each. Then they'll be able to have kite-fights with their kites and that'll be beaut fun!

The children bustle around their big brother while he folds the paper tail up. He puts the kite under his arm.

— Let's get home to Big Mama, he says.

And the kids race to the house. Across the paddock, over the fence and through a flock of grazing sheep they run, yelling war-cries Indian style to each other. And Teria shudders. Heck, those kids of hers are sure a wild bunch . . . She braces herself to meet them and plants her body firmly in front of the back door. The screaming and yelling grows louder as the kids close in on her. And suddenly, they burst into the back yard like wild horses.

— Whoa there! Teria booms.

The children crash to a halt, stamping and whinnying to one

another. Teria waits for the commotion to die down. Then she lifts her right hand and points determinedly at the outside tap.

— Wash first; kai after!

For a moment, she can feel the rebellion of her children. Quickly, she knits her eyebrows into a fierce look and a silent battle rages. Her hawk-eye glare proves too strong for the kids this time. They turn and shuffle toward the tap.

Teria folds her arms. Now that she's got the kids under control, she has to keep them there.

— No cat-washing! she booms. Get that soap and water behind the ears, scrub those hands, those feet, those fingernails; and about turn! atten*shun*! and forward *march*!

Meekly now, the children troop forward past their mother, into the kitchen. Teria sighs: Heck, one of these days, her kids are really going to eat her! Not yet, though, because she's still the boss around here.

She inspects them all as they pass. Just as well they all had their hair cut for the wedding yesterday; makes it easier to see if they've washed behind their necks. Yeah, and they're all present and accounted for, so . . .

The children seat themselves at the table. They look up at their mother as she heaves herself into her chair at the head of the table. She looks at them all and:

— No talking! she booms.

The children look at each other, puzzled. None of them were even talking! Big Mama was laying down the law.

Teria looks over her children, satisfied that they're completely under control now. But she's still wild with Rawiri for leaving her at their mercy. Trust him to go out shearing with Pita and Miriama! At least he could have taken some of the kids with him instead of leaving them all at home with her. Yeah, and when he gets back from Mairangi with Pita, she'll give him a good hiding too!

— Now, Teria begins. Before we have our kai, I've got something to ask you kids and no crooked answers. *Which one of you mongrel kids pinched my chocolate*! Don't all speak up at once.

78

It was sitting right on the bench there when I got up in the morning. Now it's gone. It hasn't got legs, but you fullas have. Yeah, and you fullas have got hungry mouths as well. So which one was it! Which big mouth ate my chocolate! Well? I'm waiting, I'm waiting . . .

The children stare blankly, pretending they don't know who the culprit was. But they know all right: it was Hope who pinched Mum's chocolate.

— It was you, wasn't it Mischief! Teria says to August.

— Don't look at me, Mum.

— Then it must have been you, June.

— Who me? I hate chocolate, Mum.

— July, I saw you eyeing my chocolate!

— I was not, either!

— Well then, it must have been you twins, ay? Yeah, you two took my chocolate, I can tell from the guilty looks in your eyes!

— Don't blame us, Mum.

— Well, must be you, Daisy, or you, Hope. Hope, did you eat my chocolate? And don't try to hide under the table. It was you, wasn't it!

But before Mum can growl Hope, Anzac pipes up:

— It was me, Mum.

Then he gives Crete a nod, and Crete says:

— No, it was me, Mum.

— It couldn't have been you, Daisy smiles at Crete. Because I took it!

— Not! July grins. It was me!

— And me! yells June.

— And me too! August says.

The children nod silently to each other. All heads turn to their mother, seven voices each count silently, one, two, three and:

— We all took it, Mum! they say in unison.

Yeah, and what has Big Mama got to say to that!

Teria quietly groans. Heck, her kids sure are cunning. But she'll fix them!

— All right, she answers, baring her teeth. If you all took my chocolate, then you all get a hiding, ay! After kai, you fullas get a branch from the willow tree at the back. Not a twig; a branch. I'll teach you fullas, I'll teach you!

She beams at the sight of those falling faces. Take that! Think they can get one across their Mum, do they? Think they're the bosses around here, do they? Yeah, and they know very well that their Mum likes to read her magazines in bed and eat chocolate while she's having her read. Come to think of it . . .

— Any of you kids seen my True Confessions?

Startled, August looks away. Jingosh . . . That must have been the magazine he ripped up and made the kite from.

But before Teria can ask more about the magazine, a car turns into the driveway. The children are saved by the horn.

— It's Uncle Rongo! they yell.

They start getting down from the table.

— Hold it! Teria booms. Sit down the lot of you! Just wait here, don't touch anything, just *wait*.

She goes out the door. Seven pairs of ears listen like long wave antennae.

— Tena koe, Rongo.

— Hullo, Teria. That brother of mine in?

— He went shearing out at Mairangi this morning.

— By golly, I must be hearing things! Never mind. I didn't want him for anything. I just came around with some spuds for you fullas.

— You shouldn't have, Rongo.

— There's a coupla sacks in the boot. Good to see you, Teria.

— Good to see you too, Rongo. You had kai?

— No.

— Well come inside. The boys can bring the spuds in. Hey! That reminds me: Auntie Miro wants to see you some time.

— What for?

— About the hockey tournament for this year. But come and have kai first.

Teria and Rongo enter the kitchen. The kids yell:

— Gidday, Uncle!

80

He kisses the girls and winks at the boys.

— You fullas look as if you've been scalped, he laughs.

— Mum did it to us, Anzac tells him. She got a bowl, stuck it on our heads and cut all our hair off.

The boys look moodily at their mother. How would Big Mama like it if they did the same thing to her?

Lunch begins. Teria puts another plate on the table. Everything seems to be there: the bread, butter, jam, salt, more corn beef and potatoes in the pot, more puha too . . .

— All right, Daisy, she says. Your turn to say Grace.

— Our Father which art in . . .

— I said Grace, Stupid.

— LordblessthisfoodAmen, Daisy says hastily.

And everyone gets stuck into the kai. What do you know: the kids are using their manners today! Must be because their Uncle is here.

— How's Huia? Teria asks.

— She's all right. Still got her cough though.

— Yeah, I thought she sounded crook at the wedding yesterday. Hey! Did you hear about Waka and Ani?

— Mmm, Rongo nods. Kids sure grow up quick these days.

— Well I hope I get rid of all my kids early! The sooner the better. And Boy! roll on tomorrow! The only time I get peace and quiet is when they're all at school! I sure feel tired today.

— How's Rawiri doing?

— He's working at Golding's farm now. His fifth job this year, but we manage. Don't know how, but we do. Though I sometimes wonder how the heck the old people managed to keep their big families. I'm finding it hard, and yet my family is small compared to some of the old families.

— Times were different then, Rongo answers. As long as you had maize in the paddock, potatoes, a few cows, you were okay. You didn't really need money. Wasn't much you wanted in those days, wasn't much you could spend your money on. Mmmm, this corn beef's good.

— You want some more, Rongo?

81

— Pae kare, yes I'll have some more. I'll help you with your diet! You're sure getting fat these days.

— Me, fat? Teria grins. But that Rawiri likes me this way. The bigger the better, so he says! And you kids, no smart cracks from you either. You fullas finished?

— Yes, Mum.

— Well go and lose yourselves now. But don't go too far because you have to do the dishes. Anzac, you and August get the spuds out of Uncle's car.

— Can't we stay, Mum? Daisy asks.

— No. Me and Uncle want to talk and I don't want any big ears flapping around here.

The kids moan loudly.

— See you later, Uncle, they tell Rongo.

They troop outside and Teria sighs with relief. So do the kids: Big Mama will probably forget all about her chocolate now and so won't give them a hiding! Thinks she's the boss, does she? Thinks she just the queen around here does she? They'll fix her. They'll show her who the real bosses are.

For a moment, the kids are undecided about what to do. There's not much wind for flying a kite at the moment. Then Anzac says:

— Let's have a game of hockey.

— Haven't got enough sticks, June says.

— Well, we can use some box wood can't we? Anzac answers.

— And I know where a ball is, Daisy says.

The children look at their big brother. He's the one who makes the decisions for them.

— Okay, August grunts. Hockey it is.

The children set about picking teams: August, June and Hope against July, Anzac, Crete and Daisy. They then search for the weapons to play with. Daisy hunts under the house for the hockey ball. Quickly, each team ranges itself against the other, snarling and grunting. Hockey one, hockey two, hockey three and *war*.

Rongo Mahana looks out the window at the children and chuckles.

— Good kids, Teria, he says. Healthy too.

— Too healthy! Teria laughs. What they doing? Playing hockey? Good! Maybe they'll murder each other.

She turns back to Rongo.

— I wonder why Auntie Miro wants to see me? Rongo asks.

— About the hockey tournament here next Easter.

— Pae kare, only three months before it's here.

— Yeah, well Auntie Miro has been pretty sick lately. You saw what she was like at the last committee meeting. Well, there's another meeting next week and I think she wants you to take it over and to take over the arrangements for the tournament, just in case she doesn't last until Easter.

— Is she that sick?

— She's getting old, Rongo.

The words arrow sharply through Rongo's mind. Yes, she is old, Auntie Miro. In her late sixties; maybe she's even hitting seventy now. She could even be older, because nobody knows what her age really is. And it's no use asking her. All she says is:

— How old am I? Old enough. . .

That's all you get from her, plus a broad wink too.

Rongo grins widely. Ever since he can remember, Auntie Miro and Uncle Tama have always organised the Maori hockey tournament for the district. It was they too, who organised all the East Coast and Poverty Bay teams who attended the great national Maori tournaments during the nineteen forties and fifties. That was a time when there was a big following for the sport, and Maori people throughout the country would gather in large numbers at each yearly tournament. They were big huis, those gatherings. Teams would come from Whangarei to the Bluff. By bus, by train, by car they would come. Gathering together. Playing and laughing together.

The tournaments lasted a week. The visitors slept in huge marquees. The bedding was straw, and everyone slept side by side: sleeping together, joking together, and singing together. And on nights when it rained, they huddled close to each other for warmth and to escape the water leaking through the tents. They washed together, they got dressed in front of each other, and there

83

was no embarrassment. Couples made love in those tents while the others pretended to sleep. Some of the cheeky ones though would yell:

— Hey! Is that an earthquake I can feel?

— Yeah, it's an earthquake; might be a volcano erupting too.

— Whatever it is, I wish it would hurry up and get it over with. You can't get any sleep around here!

The hockey was hard and furious during the day; at nights, the partying and dancing was hard and furious too. On the last night, an action song competition was held. Trophies were awarded not only for the hockey but also for the action song competitions.

Then, the national Maori hockey tournaments ended. They were replaced by district tournaments, district teams playing only other teams within their district. Although some of the district tournaments have thrived, the Bay and East Coast tournament has not. Each year, fewer and fewer teams participate; and a Waituhi team struggles on mainly because of Auntie Miro and Uncle Tama. If it wasn't for them, Waituhi's participation in the district tournament would have ended long ago. But Auntie Miro in particular is too stubborn to give in. For a long while, she had even managed a men's and a women's team from the village, both of which had done well in the city hockey competitions each Saturday during winter. Then, the sport of hockey had begun to decline. The village began to field only a women's team. Even that one team became difficult to maintain. Once, a bus driven by Uncle Tama left the village every Saturday for the hockey ground. No more. No more.

The district tournaments are held in different villages each year. This year, it is being held in Waituhi. Financially, it is often run at a loss for the tribal marae concerned. But Auntie Miro doesn't care about that. All she cares about is that Waituhi continues in the tournaments. Even though the sport has almost disappeared from the village, it is not as important now as the meeting together with other district Maori people and renewing the links of tribal marae with tribal marae. The hockey is just an excuse. The meeting together and becoming one district family,

84

even if only for a short time, is the important thing. For there are few times now when the villages and maraes of the district can meet together. The district Maori hockey tournament is one of these few times. If it dies, there is very little left. Seeing the people of the district growing up as strangers to one another is breaking Auntie Miro's heart . . .

And Rongo has seen it breaking, slowly, over the closing years. He has seen his Auntie standing on the sideline of the hockey ground, in tears because some of the people from outlying maraes have not come.

— I better go and see her soon, Rongo tells Teria.

— Yeah, Teria answers. Poor Auntie Miro. You know, Rongo, I don't think she understands that things can't stay the way she likes them all the time. In the old days, the whole whanau would help out with the tournament. You didn't really need money to feed the visiting people. Somebody donated a pig, somebody else a sheep . . . The men took time off to put up the marquees. The women baked the bread . . . Boy! I still remember those nights we spent making paraoa rewana!

— It used to be held in the springtime too, Rongo remembers. There was plenty of kai around then. Plenty of maize. Now it's held in the autumn when crops are poor.

— But the tournament had to be changed to Easter, Teria says. People couldn't come for a week in the spring. If they came, they lost their jobs. That's why they changed the time for Easter holidays.

— Ae, Rongo answers. But even then, they don't come. Can't blame them really. And can't blame people when they don't pitch in together to help out at the tournaments. Money is hard to come by these days. Time is hard to give, too. It's not that people around here are lazy; they're just too busy to help I suppose. People spare what they can, both time and money. It may not be much, but at least it's something.

The two are silent a moment. Then Teria giggles.

— Heck! We're a gloomy pair!

Rongo Mahana grins.

85

I suppose we are, Teria. You never know, having the tournament here this year may just mean the beginning of big things again. You never know, ay! We may be down, but we're not out yet!

He stands up.

— Well! Better go! he says. Thanks for the kai. And tell that brother of mine I might come out and see him next weekend. Okay?

— Haere ra, Rongo, Teria says.

She booms her voice out to her kids.

— Hey! You kids! Come and say goodbye to your Uncle.

The children leave off their hockey game and say goodbye. Then Crete asks:

— Can we come for a ride, Uncle?

— Yes, can we come for a ride to Auntie Miro's place? Hope asks too.

Rongo looks at Teria. She nods.

— Don't bother to bring them back, she says.

The children jump into the car. They wave to Big Mama. Rongo starts the car and backs down the drive. And Teria smiles with relief. She might even be able to have a little moe this afternoon. She walks into the kitchen and . . .

— Hey! The dishes . . .

But the car has gone. Those bloody kids! Heck, they've gotten the best of her again! Boy, they're sure a cunning pack of kids . . .

86

Fifteen

Almost quarter to one. Afternoon already. Half a day gone. What a waste of time, spending it at church. Or is it? Even going to blinkin' church is maybe better than spending the whole day doing nothing in this dump.

Hana Walker stares moodily out the window of the car. Even though she didn't want to go to morning service, at least it filled in time. What is she going to do the rest of the afternoon! Nothing. Plain nothing. Because there's nothing to do in this place.

The car turns into the gateway.

— Open the gate, Hana? Dad smiles.

She gets out of the car and shuffles to the gate. Blinkin' hell! Mud's splashed on her shoes again. When she gets out of here, she'll sure be glad because where she's going, there ain't no mud. There's wide concrete roads where she's going and long tree-lined avenues leading to beautiful houses where wrought iron gates swing automatically open as you approach . . .

— Gidday, Hanaaaa!

Hana looks up. Rongo Mahana's car passing. And one of Teria's kids yelling to her.

She waves uninterestedly at the kids. Huh! She's not having kids in a hurry. She's going to have a good time first. And she's not going to get married early like Teria. And imagine Waka and Ani getting married! She's not getting married to anyone around here, that's for sure. Because if she does, she'll never get away from this dump.

The gate swings open. Hana stands aside as Dad drives the car through. She sees Janey Whatu motioning to her from a window of the Whatu's house. Quickly, Hana nods to Janey, shuts the gate and walks away from the car.

— Hana? Dad calls.

— Won't be long, Dad.

— Where are you going?

— Won't be a minute, Dad.

She runs toward the fence between the Whatu and Baker houses before Dad can ask her any more questions. Always asking questions, that's Dad. That's probably why he's a member of the district Maori Council. He shouldn't ask questions of her; it is too terrible that he makes her lie.

Janey signals that she'll meet Hana down by the trees at the back of her place. Hana climbs through the fence and makes her way there. The back door of the Whatu's house bangs and Janey runs to her friend. Her face is set in a secretive grin. The two girls sit together in the shadows.

— How did you get on this morning? Hana asks. Did you get caught coming in?

— Nah! Janey answers. It was easy as pie.

— See? Hana sniffs. I told you not to worry but you wouldn't believe me, ay! You sure were scared you'd get a hiding!

The two girls giggle together. Then Janey puts her hand down her blouse.

— I got some smokes! she whispers excitedly. They're Mum's but she won't know I pinched them.

— What sort are they?

— Ay? Just smokes, that's all.

— Let's have a look.

Janey shows Hana the handful she's pinched. Hana looks at them closely.

— They're cheap ones, but they'll do.

Janey looks at her friend with respectful admiration. Hana sure knows a lot about smokes and things. And she holds her smoke just like a lady too.

— Well? Hana asks. Don't say you pinched the smokes but forgot to pinch some matches!

— Oh . . . Here, Hana.

The two girls light up. Hana takes a long draw and, eyes closed, slowly leans back against the willow.

— Aaa aah, she sighs.

There is silence for a while. Then Janey asks:

— Heard from Henry yet?

— Henry who?

— Henry! You know, *Henry*!

— Oh, him, Hana says with a look of disgust.

— I just wondered, Janey continues, because your fullas telephone rang and rang while you were at church.

— Well, Hana says coolly, if it was him I would have hung up on him anyway.

— You wouldn't have!

— I would have too. Nobody's going to boss me around or let me down and get away with it. That Henry was always too blinkin' bossy. He expected me to run after him. Not any more. Not this girl! Anyway, there was this other fulla at church and he was making eyes at me. I might take him on.

— No!

— Yes.

— What's he like, Hana?

— Well, at least he's taller than me. Not like Henry. He had on this neat blue coat and he was handsome too.

— Did he talk to you?

— What do you think! And you should have seen that Henrietta Jacobs! She was jealous as anything. This fulla, Dave's his name, he's staying at her house and she's got her eyes on him. Huh! As if he would go for her! Yes, well when we were hanging around church saying hullo to everyone after service had finished, this Dave came over and . . .

— Did he ask you for a date?

89

— Don't rush me! He came up and . . .

A voice calling from far away interrupts Hana. She starts and throws her cigarette away.

— That's blinkin' Mum! she says. I better go, Janey. You better smell my breath first.

— No, you can't smell the smoke. Will I see you later?

— Don't know. I haven't had a sleep yet and I'm feeling tired now. Maybe later on.

— See you, Hana.

Hana slips away. Through the fence. Toward the house. First though, wash her mouth. You never know: Mum just might smell the cigarette smoke. Or worse still, Dad might.

— Where have you been, Hana!

— To see Janey.

Mum nods. Then suddenly, she kisses her daughter on the cheek.

— What was that for, Mum!

— Nothing. Nothing.

— It must have been for *something*, Mum.

— I was just thinking that . . . one day . . . you'll be leaving us . . . leaving home . . .

Hana is startled.

— You're not a baby any longer, Hana, Mum continues. And when I saw that boy at church looking at you I thought . . .

— Gosh, Mum, you're embarrassing!

— I'm not blind, Hana! Mum laughs.

Hana blushes. Hastily she asks:

— Do you want a hand getting lunch ready?

— No. Perhaps you better go and have a sleep for a while before kai?

There is a twinkle in Mum's eyes.

— Mum! Hana gasps.

Mum embraces her.

— As I said before, I'm not blind. But there is something you must promise me: whatever you do that your father might not like, don't let him find out. Don't hurt him, Hana. What he doesn't see won't hurt him. And although people might tell him what you get up to, he won't believe it because he loves you and believes in you. He's a proud man, your father. Too proud, I suppose. Don't hurt his pride. Promise?

— I promise, Mum.

— Good, Hana. Now go and have a lie down. I'll call you when lunch is ready.

— Mum . . .

— Go, Hana.

Hana leaves the kitchen. Dad is sitting in the living room, reading. He smiles at her as she passes along the corridor. She shuts her bedroom door behind her.

No, Mum, I'll try not to hurt Dad. For your sake, Mum. For you . . .

Hepa Walker is feeling very annoyed. He flips the pages of a Sunday newspaper and his annoyance increases, for it seems to be filled with stories and articles dealing with Maori problems or supposed 'problems'. This one, for instance, on page four, with its opening sentence reading:

— *New Zealand cannot sit complacently back and continue to watch its education system turn out a brown proletariat.*

Haven't newspapers got anything else to talk about these days? Why don't they print something about Maori progress for a change! And just look at the heading for this article on page seven:

Maori Crime Rate Due To Pakeha Discrimination In Courts.

With disgust, Hepa throws the newspaper to one side.

Hepa Walker's attitude is not too difficult to understand. Far removed from the supposed slums of Otara in Auckland and Newtown in Wellington, he cannot entirely credit what he reads as truth. Not having experienced overt discrimination, he finds it hard to believe that it does exist. What's more, he is actually embarrassed by it. He is a proud man, unwilling to believe or even to admit that the Maori is inferior or under-privileged. If he does so, then he must see himself in the same terms. And hasn't his own career and present life-style proved the opposite case?

As far as he is concerned the problems are social ones, not racial at all.

Holding this view, Hepa is therefore puzzled by the rise of the young Maori radicals. He does not mind too much when they point out areas where social adjustments are necessary, but he is enraged at the indiscriminate way in which they apportion the blame. You'd think they would know better than to accuse the Pakeha for all their 'problems' or to say that these are due to a 'White racist system'. Always ready to blame somebody for their ills, that's their trouble. But do these brave young warriors try to solve them themselves? No, they're all talk and no action. They can pull things to pieces — even Maori institutions like the Maori Council, the system of Maori wardens, Maori representation in Parliament — but they haven't got anything to replace these with. What do these kids *really* want? Separatism? They're sure causing it with all their moans and menacing talk. They're promoting discrimination, not solving it, and they're causing ill-feeling between Maori and Pakeha and also between Maori and Maori.

Hepa sighs to himself. It wasn't so long ago that a group of these kids had visited the district. They had come to speak on various marae throughout the district on the need for the Maori language to be taught in schools. Their attitude had been aggressive, demanding and belligerent. They had talked about educational non-achievement and cultural deprivation. They had blamed the Pakeha, and Hepa had spoken out against their criticisms.

— We may be different races, he had said, but we are also New Zealanders. We should be building together as one race, but when you talk of blame you separate us.

— Kaumatua, we *are* building for that in our way, had been the answer.

— No, he had said, shaking his head. You are separating us with your talk. And you divide us as well, here on the marae. Yes, we believe like you that Maori should be taught in schools, but we dislike your methods. Think on that.

Hepa closes his eyes, remembering. Then he smiles, faintly.

Children, just children, these 'brave young warriors'. One listens to their talk and is angry until one remembers that they are, after all, just children. But perhaps he is being unfair. Perhaps warrior anger as much as warrior strength and tenacity is needed these days. And even children can lead.

Hepa gets up from his chair. He goes into the kitchen where Dinah is preparing lunch.

— Soon be ready, she smiles.

He kisses her cheek. He starts to say something, then hesitates. Dinah looks at him curiously.

— I was just thinking of our son Frank, Hepa says.

— Yes?

— Oh, just how proud he is making me feel. And Hana, she will make me feel proud too.

Dinah touches him, softly.

— Don't expect too much of her, Hepa.

Hepa laughs loudly.

— Dear, I expect a lot from her . . .

Sixteen

— You ready, Anaru?

— Almost, Dad, Andrew Whatu answers.

Lunch is over. Charlie and Andrew are going down to Rongopai. Andrew is sitting on the steps of the back porch pulling on his gumboots; inside the house, he can hear his father trying to wake Sonny up. Dad sure must be hopeful! Sonny only got back from that party at Sam Walker's a few minutes ago. Every weekend there's a party at Sam's place. He doesn't need a wedding for an excuse. Come to think of it, the parties usually begin on the Thursday and carry on till Monday. No doubt, as soon as Sonny wakes up, he'll going back to Sam's to get haurangi again.

Andrew grins. He looks up and sees Hana Walker smiling at him from her place. Huh! She must have thought he was grinning at *her*. And she's still smiling, too. What a flirt that Hana Walker is. He better watch out: she might be after him.

Shuddering, Andrew turns his head from her. His father comes onto the back porch and sighs:

— I don't know . . . That brother of yours is just going to the pack. Boozing all night and day. But if he thinks he's going to miss out work tomorrow, then he better think again. And that Janey too, she's almost as bad. You know what? Mum actually caught her red-handed with some smokes. Boy, oh boy.

— How long will we be at Rongopai? Andrew asks quickly.

— Let's see: it's half past one now . . . I reckon we should be finished cleaning up by three. Why? There something else you have to do today?

— No. I just wanted to know, that's all.

— Well, the cleaning up inside the meeting house won't take long, Charlie Whatu continues. But I was thinking we might cut down the grass outside. It's getting so high you can hardly see Rongopai. Yeah, so we'll take the scythe and borrow another one for you from Albie Jones. If that brother of yours wasn't so boozed he could've come with us, and the cleaning up wouldn't take so long then. We'll manage though, the two of us. So you wait for me at the gate. I'll get our scythe. Okay?

— Okay, Dad.

Andrew wanders idly round the house to the' front. It isn't too long before Dad joins him, scythe in hand. As they're about to start off down the road to the meeting house, Andrew sees that a sheep has gotten out of one of John Golding's paddocks.

— We better put that sheep back where it belongs, Dad says. Otherwise, John might think another one of those Horis been at his meat again!

He winks at Andrew and sneaks up on the sheep. It baulks from him and runs along the fenceline, away.

— Get him, Anaru! Charlie Whatu yells. Head him off, head him off!

Andrew laughs.

— Huh! What's wrong with you, Dad? Too slow on your feet, ay?

— Never mind about the talk, Dad yells back. Get after that sheep!

And laughing loudly, Andrew heads the sheep off, forcing it to turn back toward Dad who pounces on it. The sheep kicks and struggles beneath him.

— Ride him, Dad! Ride him, cowboy!

— Quit laughing! Charlie yells. What a monster this sheep is! Come and help me lift it back into the paddock.

Andrew approaches his father and the sheep lashes out and

hits him on the leg.

— Ana! Now it's my turn to laugh!

— It wouldn't have happened if you'd been stronger, Andrew moans. You running out of fuel, Dad?

— Running out of fuel am I? Charlie Whatu growls. You just watch this!

He pushes his son away. Then he lifts the sheep above his head and up-ends it into the paddock.

— Well what have you to say to that? Charlie Whatu scoffs, beaming with satisfaction. Not bad for an old man, ay.

— It was just a flash in the pan, Dad.

— Flash in the pan be blowed, Dad snorts. I can still show you a thing or two.

— You want a bet, Dad?

Charlie Whatu is really wild now.

— I don't need to bet, he says. I know what I'm talking about. You want me to show you? Right! I'll race you to Albie Jones' place. I'll fix you!

Andrew laughs again. He picks up the scythe.

— Forget it, Dad, he says. You know I'll beat you, old man.

— Old man?! Charlie Whatu bellows. You've asked for it now, Boy.

He spits on his hands and makes a line on the ground with the heel of his boot.

— Put your feet where your mouth is, he says.

Andrew shrugs his shoulders. He lines up with his father. They get into a crouching start. It seems such a farce to Andrew that he begins to laugh again. And as he's laughing, his father suddenly springs away.

— Hey, Dad! That isn't fair!

All right then! If Dad wants a race, Andrew thinks determinedly, then he's going to get it. And with that thought, he races after his father. Along the road they run, the gravel spraying high behind their heels. Around a bend. And Charlie Whatu is faltering in his stride.

— I'm catching up, Dad! Andrew laughs.

96

And then it seems to Andrew as if his world stops. Slowly it grinds down. Slowly. Slower still. Until his father seems to be running in slow motion, the gravel spraying like crystals from his feet. And Dad's body is leaping and straining in slow agony, his muscles rippling and pushing him forward. And Dad's face is a mask of pain.

The sun seems frozen in an unmoving sky. The world is grinding slower still. And slower. Almost at a halt now.

And Andrew suddenly thinks:

— My father . . . We are only racing for fun . . . and yet your heart is set on winning . . . Why? . . . Why, Dad? . . . Because you are old? . . . Yes . . . Because you are old . . . All your life, you've lived by your strength. Strength alone . . . And you do not want to know that it is going . . . Going fast . . . For once your hands and body and heart slow down there will be no pride left in you . . . Your pride is in your strength . . . Old man . . . Dad . . . Old man . . .

And as he is thinking all this, Andrew feels himself falling back. His father's face sways away ahead. His father's body leaps in front. Slowly he takes the lead, slowly, slowly. And then he turns to look back at his son.

— Ha! Charlie Whatu snorts. Come on, slowcoach!

Andrew comes up to his father. The sweat is pouring from Dad's face and he is bending to get his wind back.

— Well? Charlie Whatu pants.

— Okay, Dad. So you won.

— Am I still an old man?

— No, Dad.

— I showed you a thing or two, didn't I!

— Yes, Dad.

— So aren't you going to say you're sorry you called me an old man?

— Yes, Dad.

— And aren't you . . .

— Oh, stop bragging about it, Dad!

Charlie Whatu laughs and hits his son playfully.

— All right, Son, he says. Come on, let's get that scythe from Albie Jones.

— That's why you won, Dad. Because I was carrying our own scythe!

Charlie Whatu roars with laughter again.

— All the same, he continues, the better man won, ay Son.

There is tenderness in the look that Andrew gives his father.

— Yes, Dad. The better man won . . .

Seventeen

— Maka, can I come in?

— That's not you again, is it Mere? Crikey dick, what do you want this time! Television's starting soon and there's an old movie on with Bette Davis in that I want to see.

— I thought you were going to Miro's this afternoon.

— Crikey dick, I forgot all about that! Oh well, we can play cards while watching the television. You coming too?

— Not me! That Miro Mananui is too much of a card sharp. She cleaned me out at poker last Sunday.

— Yeah, she's a big cheat all right.

— Well, Maka, you want to hear what she says about *you*!

— Has she been talking behind my back again? Whatever she says, it's her who's the cheat. Not me. Anyway, you better help me with the dishes so I can get over to her place before the movie starts.

— Eeee! Maka! I'm not your servant!

— Here's the towel. Just dry up!

— You're mean to me, Maka.

— Crikey dick, stop moaning, won't you? There's not many to do. And while you're at it, you can tell me what's bothering you. Something must be up for you to come over to me. So, what's the gossip?

— Maka, I don't always come here just to gossip!

— So you came here for no reason at all?

— Nothing. Oh, there is one thing though: I saw that Charlie Whatu having a race with his son. He must think he's still a young buck!

— Who won?

— Charlie.

— Aaah! Still a lot of life left in Charlie Whatu! You know, he was sweet on me once, Mere.

— Charlie?

— Yes, him.

— But you're older than him, Maka!

— Only two years. He's fifty-five and I'm . . . never mind.

— You fifty-seven? That's a laugh! Add another ten years and even then you'd be telling lies!

— Just dry those dishes properly, Mere.

— Sorry, Maka. Um . . . And after the race, Charlie and that boy of his went to Albie Jones' place.

— Was Mattie around?

— No, never saw Mattie.

— Poor kid. That father of hers, that Albie, should have given George Karepa a hiding for what he did to her. Never mind. No good bringing up the past.

— Then they went to Rongopai.

— Who?

— Charlie and his boy.

— Oh . . . There! Dishes finished! I told you it wouldn't take long, Mere. There's just time for a cup of tea before I hop off to Miro's place. Hope she won't mind keeping the television on while we play. Come to think of it, I mightn't go over until after the movie.

— But Miro's expecting you, Maka.

— Well, she can just wait her hurry.

— Gosh, Maka, you're brave . . .

Eighteen

August, his brothers and sisters, are playing football at Nanny Miro's place. Uncle Rongo is inside, talking to Nanny. The kids have just had a scrum. The ball bounces out to June. She, Anzac, July and Hope are playing against August, Crete and Daisy.

— Go, June! Anzac yells.

Face down and lips set, June takes off along the fenceline. Daisy tries to tackle her but is knocked aside.

— Bully! Daisy wails. Then she sees August going after June. He'll get her and dump her hard and good job too.

June looks behind. August is catching up. Not far to go to the lemon trees though, her side's goal. She tucks the ball firmly under her arm and tries to run faster. Crete tries to tackle her but she fends him off easily. Huh! This game's only easy.

But Crete has slowed her down. August has caught up, launches himself and barrels her into the ground.

— Let the ball out! Anzac yells. Let it out, June!

Oooo, her legs hurt. Doesn't August know better than to be tough with a woman?

Frantically, June pushes the ball away from her. Anzac snatches it up. But he is hemmed in by Crete and Daisy, though Daisy isn't much of a danger. However, August has gotten up now and is advancing and . . .

Anzac kicks the ball. It arcs high in the air and lands with a loud bang on Nanny Miro's roof. Instantly the window opens. Nanny Miro is there, looking out, angry.

— Hey! You wreckers! she yells. Go and take your fullas football somewhere else!

The window slams down again. The children go into a huddle.

— What'll we do now?

— Better get away from here, anyway.

— Shall we go home then?

— No, Mum might want us to *work*.

— We could fly the kite again. . .

— I know what! Let's go to the Jackson's place, to see Pene. We'll take the football with us. If we play, we'll be even-sided then, four a side.

— Okay then!

The children troop off.

Miro Mananui sighs with relief. She watches with eagle eyes to make sure those kids shut the gate after them. That Teria should take a hand to those kids. Mischief the lot of them.

— I don't know why you want to bring those kids around here, Miro complains to Rongo. They're around here enough as it is.

— But you like kids around your place, Rongo laughs.

— That was when I was younger and could chase after them with a stick, Miro says. These bones are getting old now and those kids are too fast to catch. I like my peace and quiet these days. I'm sick of shouting all the time.

Rongo Mahana looks affectionately at his Auntie. He can't imagine her as a quiet woman. She's always been a harridan. When the village hockey team used to play in the Saturday competition in the city, it was Auntie Miro's voice you heard above all the noise. She had been the coach and her tongue could lash out with withering scorn.

— You call yourself a hockey player, Henrietta? Get after that ball and be quick about it! And you, Wiki Hiroki, what are you standing around for? The goal posts are the only ones supposed to stand still! Hey, Arihia, this isn't a beauty contest so never mind about your hair and just chase that ball ay! Oh, my giddy aunt, if you can't stop that girl, what the heck are you doing on the field! She hit you? Well hit her back then. Are you a mouse or something? Quick now, here's your fullas chance. Hit the ball into the circle, Henrietta. Hurry up, Wiki, after that ball! Never mind about those legs being in the way. Hit the ball. Hit it! *Hit it stupid*! Well, what do you know. You fullas actually got a goal. About time ay? But no time to rest. Back to the start again, girls! And let me see you fullas play some real hockey for a change!

Auntie Miro . . . the girls used to get really wild with her. But that's what she aimed for, because the only way to get good hockey out of them was to get them wild. Once they had their wild up, the girls played terrific hockey. And sometimes they played so well that some of them were picked for the District Rep. team.

But even then, Auntie Miro still kept up her withering scorn. No matter if a girl burst into tears, Auntie Miro kept on and on until the girl got so wild she hit at the ball as if it was Auntie Miro herself. After each game, she would give her praise only grudgingly.

— You fullas were good today, but not good enough. Henrietta, you better start losing some weight. Wiki, it's about time you went for some training runs ay? And as for you, Arihia, the next time I see you patting at your hair instead of swinging at the ball, I'm going to get my scissors and cut your hair all off. Yes, I know you fullas won, but you were lucky that's all. I've seen kids play better hockey than you fullas do.

The hockey. Every Saturday during the season. Those days over now. For there is no village hockey team any longer.

And Auntie Miro? Even though she can still walk, even though she is still on her feet, Rongo can see that she is sick. Old and sick. Her eyes, dull and listless, and only now and then the spark of the old humour and acid tongue. She thinks she's so old, she may not be around at Easter time for the Maori hockey tournament. Teria was right: the old lady wanted Rongo to take over the arrangements about the tournament. They had been discussing it when the football had landed on the roof, disturbing their conversation. The subject is momentarily forgotten.

— How's my mokopuna, Tama? Auntie Miro asks Rongo.

— Last time we heard, he was all right. He was supposed to come back here from Wellington a few weeks ago, but he had to play football. He's getting on well in the football down Wellington.

— That hopeless mokopuna of mine? Miro laughs. He's got style all right, but no kaha! No, he's too much of a gentleman on the field to be any good. He doesn't get wild enough. You and Huia brought him up too soft. You two should have given him to me when he was a kid. I would have made him wild!

With that, Auntie Miro heaves herself up from the couch. She walks out of the room. Rongo, left alone, chuckles to himself. When Tama had been born, Auntie Miro had gone up to the hospital to collect him. But Huia wasn't going to give her son away, no fear. Auntie Miro has always looked upon Tama as one of her own sons all the same. Her youngest son.

— When's Tama coming home then? Miro calls.

— I haven't a clue, Auntie.

— Well you tell him to come around and see me, Miro continues. Last time he was home, he must have forgotten about his Nanny. He must be getting hoha down in Wellington. Too Pakeha, not enough Maori.

— He only had a couple of days off, Rongo says. He had to get back to work in the Post Office ay.

— Aaaah. So he's got a good job then? Some of these no-hopers around here should go down to Wellington instead of sitting on their bums doing nothing, or boozing. Like that lazy niece of yours, Hine, and her hopeless husband, that Jack Ropiho. You know they're staying with me?

— Yes.

— I put them up in the front room. I suppose they're still sleeping. They came back from the wedding with Charlie Whatu early this morning and then went to a party at Sam Walker's place. You know, they wanted to bring their booze here! Not in my house they don't! Jack hasn't got a job. Him and Hine had nowhere to stay. That's why they're staying with me. Boy, people around here think I'm rich.

— Aren't you? Rongo laughs. What about all those shares you have in Maori land?

— Not much these days, Miro calls. Not much at all.

Rongo grins. He hears noises in the kitchen. Puzzled, he calls:

— Auntie, what the heck are you doing in there?

— Making us a kai.

— But I already had a kai!

— Not like this kai! Kanga kopiro.

She comes to the door. In her arms is a big plate of the kai.

— Help yourself, nephew, she says. Tama brought the corn from the stream this morning.

— Where is the old man now?

— Disappeared, Auntie Miro says, her mouth filled with corn. Mmmmm! Don't know what's the matter with me these days; I'm always hungry. I'll have to go on a diet ay, so the men can start whistling at me again. Too fat now and . . . Hey! Can you smell smoke?

— Yes, Rongo answers. But it's only a cigarette.

— What! Miro growls. That damn Jack Ropiho.

She puts her plate down and roars:

—Hey you, Jack Ropiho! If you want to smoke go outside. I'm not having you set fire to my blankets again.

She turns to Rongo.

— Nobody smokes in my house now, she says. Not after that time when this house almost burnt down. All my treasure, all my trophies and your Uncle Tama's whakapapa books, they could have all gone up in smoke. And you know why? Because that damn Jack Ropiho was smoking in bed . . .

Jack Ropiho hears Miro yelling at him. He makes a face and takes another draw on the cigarette.

— Didn't you hear the old lady? Hine snaps.

— You're just as bad as she is, Jack scowls. Moan, moan, moan all the time. Yeah, well she can bloody well wait. I'm not wasting a smoke for that old bag.

— It's her house not yours, Hine says.

— You call this junkyard a house? Jack laughs. I don't know why she wants to worry about this old place. If it burnt down, it wouldn't be worth much anyway.

— That's what you might think, Hine answers. But Nanny Miro thinks different.

— About all this junk? Look at it! Stinking feather cloaks, piupius, those harateke carvings, sports trophies, books . . .

He kicks at a carved wooden wheku.

— Jack, I'm warning you . . . Hine whispers.

She grabs at the cigarette and throws it out the window. Jack jumps up from the bed and grabs at her.

— What you do that for. Ay? Ay?

— Leave me alone, Jack. Leave me alone.

He raises his hand to slap her. And Boy Boy, their son, whimpers in his bed.

— Now look what you've done, Hine says. Go to sleep, Boy Boy, it's all right.

— Well next time don't throw my smoke away, Jack warns.

— I'll throw it out all right, Hine flares. It'd be different if this was our own house.

— You're not going to go on about that again, Jack says.

— Well it's true, isn't it? Yeah, and when are you going to get a job ay? When are we going to have some money of our own for a change? I'm sick of sponging off other people.

— I can't help it if there's no jobs around here. It ain't my fault.

— What do you mean there's no jobs! Hine asks scornfully. You had a good job on Golding's farm until you got the sack.

— He didn't sack me, Jack growls. I quit that job.

— Oh yeah? And I suppose you quit all those other jobs too, ay Jack? You were at the Works and how long did you last there: a week. Then you went out shearing. Okay, so we made some money there, but it's all gone now. So what's next, Jack? What's next?

— Something'll turn up.

— When!

— Oh shut up, Hine. Maybe we'll get out of here and go some-where else to live.

— Huh! I've heard that one before, Hine says. We tried Wellington but you didn't like it down there. So we went down South to Mataura and what happens? You didn't like it there either. We always come back here when we're broke. We may as well face it, Jack: we're going to be stuck here for the rest of our lives.

— Not if I can help it.

— That's the trouble Jack: you can't . . . .

Miro grins at her nephew.

— You like this kanga kopiro?

— By golly, it's good all right, Auntie.

— You want some more?

— I've had enough already.

— You want to take some home with you? I'll put some in a pot. I'll bet Huia would like a feed of this kai, ay. And if that Tama was here, I'd sure like to shovel some down his throat. I don't know what's wrong with that boy. Never likes the Maori kai.

— But he does, Auntie.

— Not the last time I saw him! He was almost sick on the smoked eel. You and Huia brought that boy up too soft. Even his hands are soft. A real soft boy, no kaha in him. If you fullas had given him to me, I'd have fixed him up.

— Not my fault about his hands, Rongo laughed. It was you who bought him that piano.

— Cost me a fortune too, Miro remembers. Never mind. He can still rattle those keys better than anyone on television I reckon. Tell him when you hear from him, that his Nanny's itching to have a sing-song. I like to hear him play that piano.

— Okay, I'll tell him.

Auntie Miro collects the plates and goes back into the kitchen.

— You're not doing the dishes now are you? Rongo sighs.

— Me? Miro answers. Heck no! That's one good thing about being crook. Everybody thinks you're going to keel over at any minute and they won't let you do any work. I reckon I might just stay crook. I'm living like a queen these days!

She comes back to the sitting room.

— But I'm not going to die, she winks. I'm just having those fullas on.

— I know, Auntie, Rongo nods. I know.

Auntie Miro looks at her clock.

— Hey, is that the real time? Three o'clock already? That Maka tiko bum, she was supposed to be around here for our game of cards long before now. Eeee, I bet she stayed home to watch her television. Do you want to watch it too?

— No, Rongo answers. I don't like those old movies.

— Neither do I, Miro says. They remind me about how old I am. And I've had enough people reminding me as it is.

— What's that, Auntie?

— That Uncle of yours, that Arapeta Karepa . . .

— What about him!

— He turned up last weekend to talk to me. He wanted me to swap my shares with him before I die.

— Steady on, Auntie.

— But I told him where he could go, Miro seethes.

— Calm down, Auntie. Calm down now.

— And Tama was so wild with Arapeta, Miro giggles. I haven't seen him so wild for a long time.

She begins to tell Rongo what happened.

Arapeta Karepa is Miro's elder brother. He and Miro were the only children of their parents, aristocrats of the district. Ariki. Miro's grandfather for instance, had been a great chief of the area, a great rangatira. And Arapeta, in his youth, had sought to emulate his grandfather's achievements. His own father had tried to help him in his chosen career as a lawyer and prominent orator on Maori marae throughout the district. Arapeta had not done well in either respect. He lacked the application needed for the former and the common touch required for the latter. However, he had remained a powerful figure in the district and the village by virtue of his lineage. He was a respected, though coolly received, elder of the community. He was too arrogant in his pride.

Miro's parents, in keeping with their status in Maori society, owned substantial property and were major shareholders in three Maori land blocks. Her father, who favoured Arapeta, willed the major portion of the property and shares to his son upon his death. Had it not been for Miro's mother, Arapeta would have retained this majority and Miro would have been left with only a token amount. She had unleashed her long-held of anger to force Arapeta to give his sister enough of the land and shares willed to him so that they would have equal property. Miro's mother had thought her husband wrong in favouring one of his children over the other. She had been a strong-willed woman, a lioness fighting for the rights of her daughter. She had died when Arapeta was twenty-five and Miro was nineteen.

And upon her death, Arapeta had become Miro's guardian with trust over the land and shares owned between them.

Miro had been quite content to let her brother handle her affairs. She had loved him deeply and trusted him implicitly. However, when she had come of age and discovered that Arapeta had sold most of her land to the City Council leaving her with only the shares in the three Maori land blocks, she suffered a crisis of affection. And somewhere inside her she discovered the same tigress spirit that her mother had possessed. She drew on it, using it to assert her independence. She argued bitterly with her brother and took her business affairs out of his hands.

Soon after that, Miro had married her second cousin, Tama Mananui. Arapeta had considered that his sister had married beneath her. He also began to regret his being persuaded by his mother to give Miro the shares his father had willed to him. And he had called on Miro and demanded the return of those shares. Why should the Mananui family benefit from shares belonging to the Karepa family! Another confrontation ensued. Miro, upset, had almost given him what he wanted. Then she remembered what her mother had always believed: always equal sharing, that is the way it has always been.

She had ordered her brother out of her house. Then she had bequeathed her shares to her children. She had wanted to make sure that Arapeta could never get them back. She knew he only wanted them for his own family.

Since then, the shares have remained a source of friction between brother and sister. In recent years, however, it has intensified. Arapeta is getting old. He has come frequently to see his sister. He has given up hope that Miro will return the shares to him; but what he wants still concerns the shares.

The three Maori land blocks in which Miro and her brother are major shareholders, are huge farm stations run by Pakeha managers. Beef-cattle and sheep are raised on them. One is run at a very high profit. The second is not as successful financially, mainly because it contains a big proportion of rugged hill country which cannot hold much stock. The third is definitely run at a loss.

Arapeta wants to consolidate his shares in just one of these estates. For some time now, he has been asking his sister to swap her shares in the first block in return for shares he holds in the two other blocks. He has also been canvassing the smaller share-holders in that block asking if they would sell their shares to him. So far, he's not had much success.

Miro has seen her brother's family become progressively remote from their village cousins and relations. She understands why her brother wants complete control of one block. It is logical in his terms, and in a way understandable, that he would want to form an estate of his own, specifically for his own descendants. But the three land blocks are not for any one family. They are for the complete village family.

The great village family had begun to splinter long before now. Miro does not want to see it splinter further. The land is a way of holding them together. She will never allow anybody, brother or not, to separate the people from the land.

The land belongs to all the people, to all the village people.

It is their pride and livelihood and their heritage for the future. Arapeta has forgotten about the effects of his move on his own cousins and relations. And it is this which Miro despises him for. Arapeta, a rangatira of the village family.

— Don't worry, Auntie, Rongo says. Uncle Arapeta surely won't do anything to harm the family.

— I know my brother too well, Miro shivers. If there's a way, he'll find it. He's clever and although I love him I just don't trust him.

— Auntie, I think you're being hard on him.

— Me, hard on Arapeta? Miro answers. Nephew, he's already called a meeting of the shareholders in the three blocks. And you know I'm scared?

Miro Mananui begins to weep. Rongo puts an arm around her. So strong she is, and yet so fragile.

— Don't you worry, Auntie. Don't you worry.

But Miro still weeps. Then she says:

— I've told that brother of mine that I'll fight him even if it kills me. And I mean that too. Maybe he scares me, but I'm still tougher than him.

— That's the spirit, Auntie.

— Yeah, I'll tell him to put up his dukes. Yeah, put 'em up! And I'll let him have it! I'll fix him.

Rongo Mahana laughs. Then he says:

— You can't blame him really. His family are different from us here. You know, different.

— But that's no reason for him to break up the whole family, Miro growls. He should think about what it will mean to everybody, not just himself. He can take the matter to court if he likes. But if he goes that far, I'm really going to let him have it right between the eyes.

— Uncle won't do that, Rongo says.

— You never know, Miro answers. But if he does, I'm going to say to him: Brother, you've forgotten something. And he'll say: What, Sis? And I'll answer him:

The eldest always looks after the younger ones of the family. Not only his own family, but *all* the family.

Miro Mananui sits there, fierce and proud. In her eyes are flints of anger. For a long time she is silent. Then she begins to shiver as if caught in a cold wind . . .

Jack Ropiho hears Miro weeping.

— I wonder what the tangi is about now, he says moodily.

Hine pretends not to hear him.

— Hell's teeth! Jack explodes. Sometimes I wonder why we ever stay in this dump.

— We stay because we've got nowhere else to go, Hine says.

— It was you who wanted to come here to the old lady's, Jack growls.

— Yeah, and just as well too, Hine says sarcastically. Better to swallow our pride and get some kai to eat.

— Oh shut your mouth, Jack snaps.

Hine sighs. She picks up a magazine and flips through the pages. Jack looks at her and then asks:

— How about seeing if the old lady will give us a loan, ay Hine?

— So you can spend it on booze? Hine laughs. Why don't you do your dirty work yourself.

— She's your relation, Jack says. And she's had her wild up with me ever since I burnt a hole in her bed. It was only a small hole, I don't know what all the fuss was about.

— Jack, you make me sick, Hine says. You're lucky Nanny didn't chuck us out of the house.

Jack is silent for a while. Then he asks again:

— Well? How about it, Hine? Go and ask the old lady.

— Not me! She's already given us enough as it is.

— All right, all right, you don't have to shout. It was only an idea, there's no harm in that is there? Jeez, I can't wait for her to kick the bucket. Maybe she'll throw some of her land shares our way. We'll sure live in style then, ay Hine? We'll be set then. Buy a flash car. A house. Have a good . . .

— Stop it, Jack! Hine screams. She bunches up her magazine

and throws it at him. Alarmed, he goes to hold her. She pushes him away. Resignedly, he closes his eyes.

— Jeez, he moans. How I hate Sundays . . .

Then he hears a horn blast and a voice calling out:

— Jack Ropiho you black bastard!

— Your friends, Hine says cynically. She opens the window. At the gate, a black Ford. Behind the wheel, Sam Walker. Squeezed beside him and in the back seat, some of his mates.

— What you want, Sam!

— We're going down the hotel to get some booze.

— It'll be closed though.

— Not for me, Sam roars. Frank'll let me have a few crates.

— Huh? Hine shouts. I thought your party finished a long time ago.

— That was the last party, Sam answers. The boys and I, we're going to have another party, ay boys!

The car shakes with whistles and beery yells.

— Jack want to come for a ride? Sam continues.

— What do you think! Hine says bitterly. Jack is already tying on his shoes. One look in the mirror and he is off. Out of the window he jumps, and shambles toward the car. There, Sam whispers to him. Jack shakes his head and points at Hine. But Sam pushes him toward her and he comes to stand at the window.

— Well? Hine asks.

— We need some money for the crates, Jack says.

— And? Hine taunts.

— I'm broke . . .

— So?

— Just a few dollars, Hine, Jack says.

Hine slams the window down. She turns her back to it, sits down and closes her ears and eyes so as not to see or hear Jack.

— Hine . . .

Go away, Jack. Go away.

— Hine? Hine!

Jack, go away.

— To hell with you, you fucken bitch, Jack yells. And don't think I'm coming home tonight either. I'll fix you, Hine.

He goes away. Hine hears the car revving up and then a squeal of tires as it roars away. Then she opens her eyes.

So that's that. No use crying. It's never helped anyway. Just a waste of tears. And no use hoping that Jack won't come back. He always does. Perhaps not tonight, but some time or other.

She leans back on the bed. She picks up her magazine again. Maybe later on, she might go and see Mattie. For a few laughs, yeah that's what she'll do.

Then she begins to giggle. Jack, thinking she could give him a few dollars, what a joke. Where did he think she'd get it from! Out of the air?

Miro Mananui explodes with anger.

— That damn Jack Ropiho, she growls. He can't even look after his wife and kid. I should give him the boot from my place.

— Well why don't you? Rongo says. Might do him some good.

— Trouble is it won't do Hine and Boy Boy any good, Miro answers. They have to eat, ay. I wish that Jack Ropiho would hurry up and get a job. Even Hine could work if she wanted to. I don't know, kids these days don't know what hard work is. They're too soft.

Rongo Mahana thinks for a moment.

— Maybe I can give Jack a job.

— Yeah?

— Only for a coupla days, Rongo cautions. Some of my paddocks need discing. I was going to do it myself, but no reason why Jack couldn't do it instead. Tell Jack to phone me tonight. I'll fix it with him.

— Thanks, nephew.

— Come to think of it, Rongo continues, Claude Simpson is looking for some fencers. He's on contract up the Coast for a month. I'll mention Jack to him.

— Do what you can, Miro says.

— Claude might need a cook too.

— Even better! Miro laughs. Get both those kids off their bums! But they really need the money, nephew. They keep borrowing off me. It's about time they stood on their own feet.

Auntie Miro sighs. Then she says:

— Hey! About the hockey tournament.

— Don't worry, Auntie.

— You'll manage it for me?

— Yes, Auntie. Don't know why though, because you're not going to kick the bucket before Easter!

— You never know, Miro murmurs. Still, it's about time someone else took over. I'll call a meeting in two weeks time. You come and get some hints off your Auntie. Boy, you'll need them too. Everyone tries to be boss, but luckily I can still shout the loudest.

— I'll bet you can, Rongo grins.

— There's plenty to learn, Miro continues. Worst is that you have to *tell* the other marae to send teams to the tournament. If you invite them, they won't come. You have to put your foot down and say: come or else. That's when you start shouting. Things are different now. There's not much interest in the tournament these days. Not like the old times.

— All right, Auntie.

— Then there's other arrangements you have to make, nephew. All that financial stuff. I don't know how I've managed; I've never been any good at sums. The marquee to put up, the cooking of the kai to be done, the hall made ready for the action competitions . . .

— Don't worry, Auntie.

— I can't help worrying, Miro says. I tried to get my own big son to do it this year, but he's just hopeless. You will do it, won't you?

— I said I would! Don't you believe me?

— I believe you, Miro nods.

Then her eyes gleam with excitement.

— Hey! You and me together, we should be able to make this next tournament a really good one, ay. Just like the old times,

115

with all those teams parading around the field. It'll do my heart good to see it before I die.

— Don't talk likę that, Rongo whispers.

— But can't you imagine what it will be like? Miro says.

— Yes, Rongo answers. And don't you worry, we *will* make it the biggest and best tournament of all.

Auntie Miro sighs.

— They were good times, she remembers.

— Good times, Auntie . . .

— One last burst, ay?

Rongo winks at her.

— Not the last, Auntie. Not the last . . .

The children have tired of playing football. They sit beside the fence outside Pene's house.

— What'll we do now? July asks.

— Yeah, what? Hope echoes, addressing nobody in particular.

Pene sniffs and idly pulls at some long grass.

— I'd love to have a go flying your fullas kite, he says hesitantly.

— Shall we do that then, gang? August asks.

— Yeah! the kids yell.

— Okay, August says.

Pene gets up. He says:

— I better tell Mum where I'm going. You fullas wait here. Won't be long.

He runs inside. Annie and Kepa Jackson are watching the movie on television. The blinds are drawn; the darkness must just love all this family! Dad is asleep, his mouth wide open ready to catch flies.

— Mum, can I go and play?

— Sssshhh, Mum growls. She is watching Bette Davis saying goodbye to the man she loves. Both Bette Davis and Mum are crying. Yeeecch! Thank goodness the movie is almost finished. Words come onto the screen, it goes blank, and Mum lets out a long wail.

— What's wrong, Mum? Pene asks. Didn't you like the picture?

— Course I liked it, Annie answers. What do you think I'm crying for!

Puzzled, Pene shrugs his shoulders. There's lots of things about grown-ups that are really funny. He asks his mother:

— Can I go with August and them to fly their kite?

Annie Jackson looks at her watch. Almost quarter to four. She nods her head.

— Thank you, Mum, Pene says. We're going up the hill where the graveyard is. Good wind up there.

— Well, as long as you don't go into the graveyard, Annie cautions. But if you do, you wash your hands when you come out. Don't forget ay. Always wash your hands after you've been into a sacred place.

— Can I take Nanny with me?

— No! Mum snaps. That Nanny of yours is flat out having a moe. You must have made him walk miles!

— Is he all right? Pene asks alarmed.

— Yeah, but you be careful with him next time.

— All right, Mum, Pene nods. Can I go now?

— You can go. But don't be too long. Soon be tea-time.

Pene kisses his mother. He goes out of the room but before joining the other kids, decides to see Nanny Paora. The old man is in bed, asleep.

— Wish you could come with me, Pene whispers. Have a good moe, Nanny . . .

Then he runs out of the house.

— About time! Crete says.

— What took you so long! asks July.

— Mum was watching a kissing film on the television, Pene explains.

The kids screw up their faces. Then they walk down the road, past Nanny Miro's place, around the bend until they are almost home. There, they go into a huddle and decide that August sneak home and get the kite while the rest wait for him at the bend. If they all go home, Mum might make them stay and do the dishes, the lazy thing.

So August gets into the ditch beside the road and begins to snake his way toward the house. Then he flashes under the fence and sidles round the back. As he creeps past Mum's window, he hears her snoring. Asleep, as usual. She sure loves her sleep! And she is still snoring when he leaves the house, kite in hand.

The kids troop up the hill, piping happy laughter toward the graveyard . . .

— What are those kids up to now! Miro says suspiciously. She can see them from the window, like tiny ants against the sky.

She points them out to Rongo.

— I just know they're up to mischief, she continues.

— Stop your worry, Auntie, Rongo laughs. Looks like a kite they've got. See? They've launched it now. It's a beauty, too.

Miro sniffs distrustfully.

— It might be beautiful, but those kids have probably loaded it with rocks. Yeah, and they'll fly it over this way and let me have it!

— Oh Auntie . . .

— I know those kids, Miro growls. Mischief the lot of them.

Rongo Mahana laughs out loud. Then he says:

— Pae kare, look at the time! Four o'clock already and I still have to dig some spuds up. I better get a move on.

Miro nods. Then she exclaims:

— Hey, nephew, can you put a bet in for me at the T.A.B. tomorrow? On that horse, Gadabout? I had a dream last night and in it I was a young girl and I saw all my old boyfriends again. There they all were, standing in a line, asking me for a dance. So it must be Gadabout, the horse which will win tomorrow.

— Might be, Rongo laughs. But there's another horse, called Dancer, running tomorrow.

— And I was dancing, Miro frowns. Now you've gotten me confused, nephew.

— Tell you what, Rongo answers. I'll put a few dollars on both horses. If one comes in, we share the winnings. Fair enough?

— Fair enough.

Miro sighs as she gets up.

— Well, nephew, if you have to go you better go. And you will see about getting Jack a job ay. And when Tama writes, you let me know how he's getting on in Wellington? Hey! You sure you have to go now? I'm dying for a game of cards. That Maka tiko bum was supposed to play me this afternoon.

— I can't stay, Auntie, Rongo answers.

He hugs her closely. She puts her arms around his neck.

— Don't be sad, Auntie.

— I'm always sad when people leave me . . .

She sees him to the door. One last embrace, and then he goes to his car. He starts the motor and turns the car on to the road. And as he leaves Auntie Miro's house, he catches a glimpse of an old woman climbing over a fence.

— What took you so long, Maka tiko bum! Miro yells.

— Don't you shout at me, Miro Mananui!

— Were you too scared to play cards with me, ay? Miro taunts, arms akimbo.

— I am not either!

— Well, come on in, you're not too late. What shall we play today then? Euchre? Two-handed Five Hundred? Or . . . Strip Jack Poker!

— Eeee, Miro, you rude thing.

Miro chuckles to herself.

— I'll fix you, Maka, she says. I'll fix you good, Maka tiko bum . . .

Nineteen

Andrew Whatu hears a shout and sees Rongo Mahana waving from a car speeding past. He waves back and rests awhile from his scything. Hard work this, and his back sure feels sore. But there is a deep sense of satisfaction in working with the land, a pleasurable feeling of achievement.

He turns to watch his father rhythmically bending to the work of scything. After long apprenticeship on the land, Dad works with a freedom and fluidity of movement beautiful to see. At his own pace he works, each action measured to that pace. Time does not control him; he does not seem aware of time. He has lived his life at his own pace. Although this may slow down as he grows older, he will continue to live at the pace demanded by his body. Not straining, not urging it to do more than it can. For it doesn't really matter how long a task may take; only that it is done.

— Hey Dad, Andrew calls. You said we'd be finished by three but it's after four now.

Charlie Whatu grins as he leans on his scythe. He takes his hat off and wipes at his brow.

— So what's another hour here or there? he says.

— I don't care what you do with your time, Andrew answers. I care about what I do with my time though.

— You think this is a waste of time? Charlie asks.

— No . . . Andrew answers. But I've other work to do, Dad.

I can't work to Maori time like you do. There's a Pakeha world which is my world, Dad. Gosh, if the whole world was full of Maoris it would be chaotic! People would make appointments for one hour and arrive the next. Trains, boats, planes, nothing would run to schedule!

Andrew pauses, grasping the enormity of his idea. Dad just laughs:

— Don't worry about the world, Son. Let it go the way it wants to.

— I wish I could, Dad, Andrew sighs.

His father smiles at him.

— So you want to get home, ay? he says. No time for talking then. We'll finish off the scything and get it done quick.

Father and son bend to the work again.

Together, they have accomplished a lot this day. Not only have they almost finished scything the long grass, but they've also cleaned up the inside of Rongopai, the meeting house. Some of the people of the village, they used to be ashamed of Rongopai once. Imagine it! Ashamed of their own meeting house! Now though, it's a different story. Ever since that man from a city art gallery declared Rongopai a historic monument, the village people have begun to see the meeting house in a new light. At the time though, they had been astonished at that man's judgement:

— This old meeting house historic? This old thing a monument? Heck, it's falling to pieces and it hasn't even got any carvings in it!

The absence of carvings was precisely why Rongopai was unique. It was a painted house, one of a very few left in the country. Of them all, Rongopai was the most beautiful.

The art gallery man had wanted to dismantle Rongopai in sections, transport it to Auckland, and reconstruct it there. But the people of the village said:

— No, although we have been embarrassed by our house, it must remain here. And even though some of us have felt ashamed of Rongopai, it is ours. We will restore it ourselves and perhaps it will forgive us.

Restoration work was begun. Pita Mahana travelled south to get raupo for the damaged interior of the house. Charlie Whatu and some of the local boys rebuilt part of the roof. The grime of long years of neglect was swabbed off the paintings by some of the village women. There is still a lot to be done, but a start has been made.

And Rongopai is beginning to breathe again. With each new breath it takes, its people are gradually reviving their deep Maori spirit. As the meeting house beats out loud its heart, so will the village blood renew itself. So long stagnant, now stirring. Replenishing traditions, becoming the focal point of all village life. The marae; the meeting place.

Is all this too much to hope for? Perhaps. Perhaps . . .

> *Karanga tia ra!*
> *Karanga tia ra!*
> *Pohiri tia ra,*
> *Nga iwi o te motu.*
> *Haere mai ra, haere mai,*
> *Ki huinga ropu,*
> *E runga o Rongopai.*
> *Haere mai ra, haere mai!*
>
> *We call you!*
> *We call you here!*
> *Assemble here,*
> *All the people.*
> *Come, come,*
> *To the celebrations*
> *Here at Rongopai.*
> *Welcome! Welcome!*

Yes, perhaps again the big meetings. Perhaps again the orators meeting here and the action song competitions. The karanga, the singing of the women. The haka, the rousing roar of the men. The tap tap tapping of the pois too. The liveliness and the love for life. The aroha.

A renaissance of all these things and of Maori art, Maoritanga. And all that which has been lost in the last generations regained. Perhaps. Perhaps.

But it may be too late for any revival. The heart may have been silent for too long already. The family has changed too much perhaps, changed by the European way of life. And yet he, Andrew, hopes for renewal of Maori values.

The meeting house was built for Te Kooti before the turn of the century. It was not carved in the elaborate manner of other meeting houses in the country; instead, it was painted with bright and swirling colours.

Wind, rain, sleet, sun, have all left their mark on the paintings on the porch of Rongopai. The wood is cracked and splintered and much of the paintwork has peeled. The colours are faded on the maihi, the boards extending like arms from the koruru which forms the apex of the roof. Spiders have spun webs inside the porch, weaving them across the kowhaiwhai designs.

The meeting house has been standing arms outstretched for over eighty years now in this fashion.

It is a large meeting house, Rongopai. Although its exterior is drab, the interior still retains the magical and strange beauty and whimsical spirit with which it was painted those long years ago. The paintings, still intact, seem infused with their own illumination which even the darkness of the house or the years cannot dim.

It is like entering a strange surrealist world. The panels are tall trees, elaborately painted in greens, blues and reds. They extend along both walls like a pathway into an illuminated forest. Some of the panels are painted with traditional Maori designs in curling reds, blacks and whites; others with sinuous twining plants like vines curling to the roof. Fantastic birds flit through the forest. People climb about the branches, and glittering creatures of Maori mythology twine among the rafters.

The trees take root in the dirt floor of Rongopai. Clustered at their bases are scenes of life known by the young men who painted the meeting house. A man stands with piupiu skirt and taniko band around his head; but in his hair he wears not the traditional royal huia feather but a Scotch thistle. A painted woman, dressed in a gown with a hint of a Victorian bustle, holds a rose to her lips.

Two men spar in a boxing match, stilted figures which seem to move, sway and bend toward each other. Delicately daubed horses lift their hooves in a timeless race. Savage figures brandishing taiaha and mere reach out from the darkness. Strange animals peer from behind the painted foliage.

The paintings are a blend of the Maori and the Pakeha worlds. They illustrate a new world of two races joining. Perhaps the young men intended to show how the Maori world was changing. Whatever the intention, for Andrew Whatu Rongopai symbolises the twilight years of the Maori. As it had been foretold, so it had come to pass: the shadow behind the tattooed face, the pale stranger, had gradually emerged and begun to alter an old way of life.

When Rongopai had been completed the elders of the village came to view the work. They were shocked with what they saw. They closed the doors on Rongopai and prophesied that Te Kooti would never enter there. The house remained tapu for many years. Only recently was the tapu removed. And now, Rongopai is emerging from the darkness.

— Hey, Boy! Dad calls. Too much of the dreaming and not enough of the scything!

Andrew pulls a face at his father.

It has been many years since the last hui was held here. It had been a good time, a large gathering of a family which had not met together since their first scattering by the four winds.

If the heart of Rongopai beats loud enough, the family will gather again. Let there not only be Pakeha culture to grow up in; let there be Maori culture too. And, Andrew prays, let the people meet often before being scattered to the winds again.

He looks up and sees the painted eaves of Rongopai holding up the sky. High above it a kite is dancing in the wayward current.

He sweeps the ground with his scythe . . .

Twenty

Far above, the kite; far below, the village.

Tossed by the wind, the kite soars high. The expanse of earth beneath it enlarges and the village becomes a small cluster of houses encircled by green farmland. Even further away, the mountain ranges are darkening as the sun goes down. Shadows mark the valleys, arrows of green pattern the ridges still lit by the sun. A car traverses one of those ridges, winding homeward on a twisting road.

Ani has her head on Waka's shoulder. She reaches up and pulls a wisp of sheep's wool from his hair. He would kiss her, but the kids will see. Trust Mum to bring them along today! This day is the first he and Ani have worked together. He was the press-man at Maera Station; Ani helped Mum with the fleeces. It wasn't too bad. Different somehow with Ani there. No boredom, no hardship yet.

In front, Miriama and Pita Mahana are silent, not really listening to what Rawiri Mahana is saying. They are both tired. Pita's face is strained with the fatigue of the shearing. Miriama's hands are beginning to ache. One would think that after a while you would get used to the pain. But why does it still hurt?

Pita misjudges his speed and the car swerves at a corner. Alarmed, Miriama nudges him and he smiles at her. She relaxes.

If only she could go to bed when she gets home. Trouble is the kids will have to be washed and their clothes gotten ready for school tomorrow. Then she'll have to get tea ready and before you know it, it'll be after eleven before she finally gets into bed. Early start at Mairangi tomorrow too. Jack must have been joking to think he could cut out the sheep in one day. Getting old. Feeling her years, yes. She listens to Rawiri's talk, but does not really hear what he is saying.

Rawiri. He doesn't want to think of tomorrow. He starts his new job at Golding's in the morning. As a labourer, always a labourer. Too many kids to support, that's the trouble. He and Teria, they've too many mouths to feed. Old man Golding, he's not paying much either. But there's no room for pride when you need the money.

Higher still the kite soars. Beyond the farmland is the city, encircled by the sea. Roads converge upon it like threads of cotton. They bend through the suburbs into the downtown area.

In one of the suburbs is a small trim house with a large lawn and bordering gardens. A man and woman are sitting down to dinner. The woman is Rose Johnson, foster-daughter of Nanny Paora, and the man is her husband David.

— I was thinking of visiting Dad tonight, Rose says.
— He's your father, David answers.
— You don't mind do you? Rose asks anxiously. I haven't seen him for some time now.
— Of course not, dear. Do you want me to come with you?
— If you wish to; but I'll be all right.
— Against Annie? David asks, incredulous.
— I've a right to see Dad, Rose bursts. After what Doctor Park told me about his condition, I feel rather worried. Annie shouldn't have taken him from the hospital. And as for my putting him in a home, I wasn't doing that to get rid of him! Couldn't Annie see that? I wanted him to receive proper medical attention. I was doing it for Dad, not for myself.

David sighs.

— Dear, we've been through all this before, he says. You had the opportunity to return your father to the hospital. Yet, you let him stay in the village.

Rose is thoughtful with despair.

— Because . . . because . . . Oh, David, I thought that Annie could, just possibly, be right about Dad. That being in a hospital would not be as good for him as recuperating in his own village, among the people who mattered most to him. That if there was no hope of his getting better, then he should live his remaining days in the place where he'd been born. And then, I saw what my actions must look like from Annie's point of view. I didn't like that, David. And it was so unfair.

— Dear, don't get upset, David whispers.

— I can't help it, David. It's just that my people value their old ones so highly that they feel disgust for anyone who would do that to their father. They hate me because I would do that not only to my father but to their kaumatua. But I'm not putting Dad away! Can't they understand that?

— Ring Annie, dear. Tell her we're coming out to see the old fellow.

— They've never liked me, Rose murmurs. Never. They think of me as a Pakeha not as a Maori. They think I've changed but I know, inside, that I haven't. It's their attitude to me that's changed. Ever since I married you, David.

— Dear . . .

Rose smiles wanly.

— I'll give that sister of mine a ring. I'm not so strong; I do want you to come with me. Isn't that silly! Being afraid to return to my own people. They make me feel so much like a stranger. Like a stranger.

The kite swoops back to earth. The world constricts, becomes smaller. Then a gust of wind flings the kite toward the hills. It brings into focus a village far away, similar to Waituhi.

Here, a number of shops are clustered around a petrol station.

The station has been busy today. And right now, a car is standing at the petrol pump. George Karepa and his bride, Alice. Coming to see his Auntie in Waituhi before travelling to Wellington.

— How much petrol, mate?
— As much as she'll take. Yeah, and check the oil too, ay?
The garage attendant nods. He smiles at Alice and she grins back. Known her since she was a toddler, Alice. Married yesterday. Husband seems a rough type. Alice could've done better. None of his business though.

There is a No Smoking sign near the petrol pump. George flips a smoke from his cigarette pack and lights it.

— Let's just piss off to Wellington ay, he says to Alice. Never mind about seeing Auntie.
— But she's expecting us, George.
— Yeah, well we're already late setting off.
Alice presses his arm. George moans:
— She'll just talk, talk, talk, and we'll never get away from her.
— You're scared of going back, aren't you George, Alice says.
— Me? Huh!
— You are, and I know why, Alice continues. But do you think I care about your past? Everybody makes mistakes George, and I don't . . .
— Shut up, Alice.
— You don't have to yell at me.
— Well just mind your own fucken business ay?
— George . . . I didn't mean to . . .
The garage attendant returns. He frowns when he sees George smoking. Can't he read?
— That'll be two dollars fifty, mate.
George hands him the money. The attendant checks it. He sees Alice looking strained and says to George:
— You've got a good girl there, mate. I hope you'll both be very happy.
— Yeah, George answers. He guns the motor and the car squeals away.

— You didn't have to be rude, Alice says.

— Just shut up won't you?

Ahead is the road leading to Waituhi. The car turns on to it.

— And so we're going there, are we? Alice asks.

George does not answer her. Tight-lipped, he stares ahead at the road. Behind the car, a cloud of dust billows and slowly disperses across the paddocks.

Slowly the kite falls back to earth. Below is the village. The houses still look small from this height and the people even smaller. In the distance, Rongo Mahana is lifting the last sack of potatoes into the boot of his car. Over by the meeting house, two people are bending scythes to the long grass. A light suddenly snaps on in one of the houses and Miro Mananui is glimpsed closing a window. In another room, Hine Ropiho is lying on a bed reading. Her husband Jack stumbles out of Sam Walker's place to vomit on the grass.

The old homestead where Pene and Nanny Paora have been today is darkening. Annie Jackson is watering some plants in her back vegetable patch with a hose; she does not hear the telephone ringing in the house and Kepa can't be bothered answering it. Loud rock music blares from the window of Hana Walker's room. Mattie Jones is washing her hair at an outside tub. At Charlie Whatu's place dinner is ready. The kai is getting cold.

The kite, caught in the middle of the four winds, becomes motionless. It seems suspended almost above the meeting house, the centre of the village. Then slowly it begins to turn. Each turning brings brief glimpses of village life and village people.

The kite turns, the kite turns. And as it turns, the darkness lowers.

Andrew Whatu throws down his scythe.

— Dad! he calls. It's five o'clock already and I've had enough. If you want to stay here all night that's your worry. I'm going home right now.

Charlie Whatu pretends to look surprised.

129

— Why didn't you tell me before it was so late, he says. You're the one with the watch. Not my fault that we're working after five is it!

— My fault? Andrew gasps. He picks up his scythe and advances on his father. Dad laughs and edges away.

— Come back here you coward, Andrew says. Face me like a man!

He throws away his scythe and runs after his father. They tussle and box each other. Then Charlie Whatu says:

— All right, all right, I give in! I'm too tired to fight you. Yeah, you wait till I'm too tuckered out before you attack ay. Cunning all right. Did you learn that out of your books, Son!

Andrew laughs and launches himself upon his father again. Charlie yells and pushes him away.

— Enough, Son, he says. Don't fight your old Dad. Keep some strength to fight off your mother. She'll be wild with us for coming home so late. We go home now.

They pick up their scythes and walk to the gate. Then Charlie Whatu says:

— Hey, have we locked the meeting house?

Andrew shrugs. Dad gives him a key.

— You're the fast runner, Dad winks. Go and check the door for us ay?

Running back toward the meeting house. The maihi loom higher above him, the head of an arrow pointing at the sky. Stepping on to the porch. No, the door isn't locked. Strangely silent seems the meeting house in the twilight.

— Hurry up, Son!

Andrew pulls the door shut. The sound is like a sharp report which repeats itself across the village. Like many doors slamming *shut*, shut, shut, shut . . . Echoing, echoing away. And as he turns the key, Andrew whispers to himself:

— A meeting house, it should never be locked.

He turns and walks swiftly to where his father is waiting.

Hine Ropiho puts Boy Boy down and looks over the sill of

130

Mattie Jones' window. Mattie is drying her hair and watching Kara swinging two long pois in her hands. Mattie laughs as Kara gets her pois twisted.

You feeling better now, Mattie? Hine says.

Mattie starts and her face closes like a mask.

— So it's you, Hine.

— I thought I'd come around, Hine explains. Jack's gone to Sam Walker's and I was getting bored sitting at home.

— That party still going?

— Yeah, they've started up again. You feel like going along later? Mattie grimaces and tosses her hair.

— I've had enough for one day, she whispers hoarsely. Enough for a lifetime . . .

She is still and silent for a moment. Then she says:

— Well come on in then, Hine.

Hine moves from the window and Mattie hears her going round the back of the house. Suddenly, Hine swears. Then she comes hobbling into the room with Boy Boy.

— What happened to you! Mattie giggles.

— A scythe at the back door, Hine moans. I could have gotten killed! And don't you dare laugh at me, Mattie Jones!

— Charlie Whatu must have left it there, Mattie tells her. And I'm not laughing, Hine.

— You are so too, Hine answers.

— Well wasn't my fault was it? Mattie says. Go blame Charlie and that son of his. They were working today, cutting the grass at Rongopai. Some people never give up.

Mattie makes room for Hine on the bed.

— Hop on, she says. Don't think I'm getting up just for you. Hey! You can show Kara how to do the long poi ay?

— Can you, Auntie Hine? Kara asks.

— Course I can, Hine answers. Here, give them to me and watch carefully. I'm terrific at the long poi.

— Show-off! Mattie says.

Hine gets the pois into motion. They look like the blurred wings of a butterfly and Kara screams, entranced.

— See? Hine scoffs. Nothing to it!

She gives the pois back to Kara.

— Go and practise in the other room, Mattie says.

— Yeah, Hine continues. And show your mother just how easy it is.

She begins to laugh and then suddenly realises what she has said.

— Mattie, I'm sorry . . .

Mattie looks away. She sees a car passing, and her heart leaps. *George. Don't leave me. Don't.*

She springs from the bed and runs to call from the window. Then she remembers. George. Married now. No use calling for he will never answer. No use. No use.

Mattie grips the window sill. She arches her head and closes her eyes and lips against the pain. Then slowly she sighs:

— Oh, Hine . . .

— Enough, Mattie, Hine soothes.

— I . . . I . . .

— You're better rid of him, Mattie. He was no good for you. Plenty more fish in the sea, Mattie. Plenty.

Mattie begins to weep. One would think that she would be exhausted of tears now. But they still come. Spilling from between her closed eyes.

— Kia kaha, Mattie. Be strong, girl.

Hine puts her arms around her friend. Suddenly, Mattie shrugs them away and screams:

— *Damn George Karepa.*

She strides to the dressing table and pulls open a drawer.

— That party at Sam's, let's go.

— Mattie . . .

— I want to go. I want to go.

Mattie pulls a comb savagely through her hair. Her face becomes cruel. Her eyes narrow, her lips become bitter.

— Go to hell, George Karepa. Go to hell.

Annie Jackson rests from her work in the garden. Kepa has

come to help her. It's getting late. Where's that damn kid, that Pene, gotten to!

Curiously, she watches the shadows against the curtains of the window next door. George Karepa, talking with his Auntie. Too scared to call on Annie and Kepa. Yeah, he's slunk back here like a dog with his tail between his legs. If that George is bad to Alice then pae kare, he'd better watch out for himself.

Not her worry, Annie shrugs. Though George sure is lucky getting a good girl like Alice. She might even make him into a new man. You never know.

The telephone rings in the house. Kepa is nowhere to be seen; he's probably gone to answer it. But the phone keeps ringing. Puzzled, Annie looks for Kepa again, and sees him returning from the woodshed. Quickly she runs inside. She picks up the receiver and hears the call clicking off.

— Hullo? Hullo!

Annie puts the phone on its cradle. Wonder who that was? Never mind. If it's important they'll ring again.

She turns to go outside again, then decides to look in on Nanny Paora. The old man, still asleep. E koro, poor old one. Be waking soon, be wanting some kai, And that Pene too.

How come that boy isn't home yet. It's already late. When he comes in, he's getting a boot up the behind.

— Wish Nanny Paora was here to see the kite, Pene sighs.

His heart thrills as the kite dances in the sky. The light from the falling sun glows in his eyes. Around him, the other children dance like flickering shadows.

The kite is at the limit of the string's length, yet it tugs and pulls as if it wants to go higher. And Pene's heart, it seems to want to go with the kite. To soar and swoop across the hills. To look down upon this green land, the paddocks where sheep and cattle graze and on the village too.

The lights are coming on. The houses are twinkling like fireflies in the dusk.

— Nanny Paora, wish you were here . . .

He cannot take his eyes from the kite as it flies above the hill. Nor can the other children. They do not see a car stopping to let off their father.

— Thanks for giving us a hand today, Pita Mahana tells Rawiri.

— Don't thank me, just pay me, Rawiri laughs.

Pita grins. He starts the car.

— Soon be home, Miriama, he says.

— The sooner the better, she answers.

Already the kids are asleep. And Waka and Ani, they seem to be having a moe too. Everyone's tired. She is tired. Even a kite, dancing on a length of string cannot bring a smile to her lips.

Rongo Mahana looks at his watch. Pae kare, six o'clock already. Better get home otherwise Huia will rip into him. She really gets angry whenever he stays out too late. It's always been the same, even when they lived out here. Every night, she would yell from the verandah:

— Rongo Mahana! Come home! Come home!

But that was long ago. No, not too long ago really. Two years perhaps? Two years too long. Trust that Huia to want to move back to the city. After all the moving around they had come back to the village and started to put down roots. Then she had wanted to start moving again.

— For the kids, Rongo. So that they can get a good education.

Rongo looks across the farm. The hills, quiet now. The shadows falling. The land sighing for his return for he is the blood of the land.

— Soon, Friend, Rongo whispers.

He smiles as he remembers how good it had been to live here. He, Huia, Tama his eldest, Ripeka, Mere, Wiki and the two younger ones.

And he chuckles as he remembers Huia's impatience with city life, how crowded in she feels. Won't be long before she will feel the land calling her back. Perhaps even Tama may want to return too. From Wellington.

The wind blows cool. It is heavy with the promise of rain.

134

Rongo shivers. He may be too old to take up farming again. No . . . if he can run from one goal line to the other like he did last Saturday, then it proves he's still got a lot of kaha left in him. He sure showed those young fullas how to play football! Yes, and he'll show them again next week too. Can't keep old Rongo down.

Feeling good, Rongo executes a few snappy steps before jumping into his car. Slowly, he eases it along the track toward the road. One of these days he'll have to put some gravel down. One of these days.

He stops the car at the gate and opens it. He drives the car through and then gets out to shut the gate. He sees his Auntie Miro sitting with her mate, Maka, playing cards. Sounds like they're having their usual argument again. Those two, both cheats!

And a soft look steals over his face.

— Don't you worry about the tournament, Auntie, he promises. Don't you worry. We're not done with yet.

From her window, Hana Walker sees Rongo Mahana leaving the village.

— One of these days, I'm going to leave and I'm never coming back, she whispers to herself.

Then she sees another car turning out of the village. George Karepa and Alice. Going to Wellington. Must be a fantastic life down there. All those parties, always something going on. She might even meet someone just like George. Wow, that'd be something.

There seems an emptiness in her life just waiting to be lit up by bright city lights. There seems an aching silence which cries out for loud music and loud laughter.

Hana draws her knees up to her body and holds them tightly as if trying to fill the emptiness she feels.

— One of these days, she says. Please, one of these days soon.

— So he's gone now.

Mattie Jones stands at the doorway of Sam Walker's place. The air is cool. The night is dark. And George Karepa's car, gone. Stabbing through the darkness.

Fighting back the tears. What the hell. He was a no good bastard anyway.

She turns back to the party. Everyone laughing. Everyone drinking. Everyone happy.

— Oh God, Mattie screams.

Silence. Then Sam comes and puts his arms around her.

— Never mind, Mattie. Never mind.

— Get away, Sam.

— You can marry me, if you want, Sam smiles.

— You? You, you black bastard?

Sam laughs.

— That's what I like to hear, he says. Makes me feel good to hear your compliments.

Everyone laughs with him. Mattie puts her head on his shoulder.

— Make me happy, Sam. Make me happy.

Sam picks up a guitar. Softly, he sings:

> — *I wonder if I should go*
> *or should I stay?*
> *It's been so long since you*
> *went away . . .*
> *I'll have the last waltz with you,*
> *two lonely hearts together,*
> *I fell in love with you,*
> *the last waltz will last*
> *forever . . .*

The others join in the song. And Mattie remembers her days with George. The days when her heart soared; the days when her heart was lonely.

And she seems to be running after a car fast disappearing in the night. She cries out a name and the car stops. George is waiting for her. She runs into his arms and he whispers her name and tells her not to cry.

The tears fall. The tears will always fall.

Annie Jackson shuts the window against the noise of the party. Then she goes to the telephone and dials Teria Mahana's number.

— Teria? It's me, Annie, here.

— I was just about to ring you, Teria answers.

— Look, is Pene over your place?

— No. And I suppose my kids aren't over with you?

— Not here, Teria.

— Just wait when they get home! Teria growls. It's almost half past six and looks like rain coming. I'm taking a stick to them all.

— Yeah, well if you see Pene, you tell him there's a stick waiting for him too.

— Okay. See you.

— Hooray, Teria.

Annie goes to the back door. No sign of Pene. He knows better than to stay out at this hour. Just wait till she gets him.

Rose puts the telephone on its receiver.

— David, the line's busy. I can't get through to Annie.

— And you still want to go out there?

— I've tried to ring her twice before, Rose says.

David turns off the television.

— Get your coat, dear, he says. It looks like it may rain.

— You'll come with me, David?

— Of course, dear. I'm not letting you face your sister alone.

Above the kite; far below the village.

It is very dark now. Suddenly, the kite begins to be tugged earthward. From the outer·perimeter of the village it is pulled back toward a hill where children stand. Over lighted houses. Over the meeting house, Rongopai. Back toward the hill and lower in the sky.

A woman runs from a party, seeking a shadowed place. Two huias quarrel over a game of cards. An old man stares vacantly at the ceiling above him.

Lower and lower the kite descends. Across the graveyard and finally to the ground and at the feet of children. They whisper to one another. Then they separate. Six go one way, one goes the other.

The boy is like a small animal darting in and out of the moonlight. Along the road he runs, over a fence he jumps, and up the steps to his house. He opens the back door and his mother's angry voice greets him.

It is seven o'clock. Far away, a car is leaving a suburb of the city. The headlights search out the night. It is a half hour drive to the village . . .

Twenty-one

Pene is sitting at the table, having his kai alone. He feels very unhappy.

When he'd gotten home, Mum had given him a hiding. It had hurt and he'd cried. And Nanny Paora, his eyes had watered a little too. Nanny always cried when Pene cried. They were mates.

— I'm all right, Nanny.

— Poor . . . mokopuna . . .

— Oh, you're good to me Nanny.

— Mokopuna . . . crying . . .

Yes, Mum had really been wild with Pene. After his hiding, she'd hustled him into the bathroom.

— Look at you! she'd growled. Your clothes dirty, your feet dirty. Damn kid, I don't know what's the matter with you. Next time, you just come home early or I'll take the broom to you.

The water had been cold and Pene hadn't wanted to stay in the bath too long. But he scrubbed himself as clean as he could and by the time he had finished, he was shivering. Mum had come to inspect him and then told him to get into his pyjamas.

— Poor . . . mokopuna . . . Nanny Paora had said again.

And the old man had stroked Pene's head and made soft reassuring noises.

Then Mum had called:

— Pene! You ready for your kai now?

— I don't want any, Mum.

— Pae kare, Mum had growled. I made it for you and you better eat it, boy.

So Pene had seated himself at the table and Mum had dished his kai out.

— If it's cold it's your own fault, Pene Jackson, Mum had said. Kai won't be waiting for you next time.

— Yes, Mum, Pene had sniffed. He'd begun eating and Mum had gone to watch television with Dad and Nanny Paora, shutting the door behind her.

Now Pene has finished his kai. He still feels unhappy, but he hasn't cried too much. It hasn't been much fun having kai alone though. He didn't mean to stay out late.

— I've finished, Mum! he calls.

— All of it?

— Yes, Mum.

—Well? Do your dishes then.

Lips trembling, Pene takes his dishes to the sink. He runs water into the basin. In the other room Kepa says:

— Don't you think you're being a bit hard on the boy?

— No, Kepa. That boy has got to learn who's boss around here. We worry about where he is; he has to learn that. And Dad, Paora, you just stay right there in your chair. Pene can do the dishes by himself. He doesn't need your help.

— Mokopuna . . . sad . . .

— No, Dad. Mokopuna *bad*, very bad.

Pene's eyes smart with tears. He begins washing the dishes. Out the window he catches a glimpse of his brothers, Mana and Kepa Junior, hopping over the fence and going to the party at Sam Walker's place. They never get hidings from Mum. . .

Towel in hand, Pene dries the dishes. He puts them away in the kitchen cupboard. Then everything is done. To be on the safe side though, he wipes the table down and sets the chairs neatly around it.

— I've cleaned up my dishes, Mum, he yells.

— Well come here then, Mum calls back.

Pene walks toward the sitting room. He hesitates at the door. Looks like a good programme on television.

— Can I watch? he whispers. Please, Mum?

— No, Annie answers firmly. You've been very naughty and anyway, school tomorrow. Go to bed now.

Pene kisses his father and Nanny Paora goodnight. Then he flings his arms around Annie.

— I'm sorry, Mum . . .

— Go to bed, Annie says.

— I didn't mean to . . .

— Go to bed! Annie says again.

Pene brushes at his eyes and goes to the doorway. He hesitates and asks:

— Can I sleep with Nanny tonight, Mum?

— Just go to bed, Pene, Mum snaps.

Pene runs down the passage and shuts the door behind him. Tearfully, he gets into bed.

After a while, he hears Mum leading Nanny Paora to bed too. She talks to the old man for some minutes. Then there is silence for a moment. And a moment later, a soft tapping at his door.

— Go away, Nanny, Pene whispers.

— Mokopuna crying . . . like the sky crying . . .

— Go away, Nanny. Go away.

The soft click of Nanny's door closing. Silence.

Annie Jackson sighs with relief. She settles down to watching television again. Although the sound is turned up loud, she can hear the laughter of the party at Sam's place. Be good to go to a party . . .

Kepa nudges her.

— You were sure mean to those two, he says.

— Pene and Dad? Annie answers. Somebody around here has to be strict with them.

— All right, all right, Kepa grunts. Don't get on your high horse, Annie.

Silence falls between them. Annie Jackson starts to fidget. This is a boring programme on television. She feels like a few laughs, not a documentary. She gets up and turns the set off.

— Huh? Kepa sighs. What's gotten into you now!

— It was a stink programme, Annie says.

— Nothing much else to do tonight, Kepa answers. Switch it back on.

— Oh, let's do something different for a change, Annie says restlessly. Let's go over to Sam's.

— Ay? Kepa asks, startled. Doesn't sound like you to want to go partying up large on a Sunday. What about the old man?

— He'll be all right. Well? Are you coming or staying!

Kepa gets up and puts on his boots. Annie covers her head with a scarf. All set now. First though, see how Pene and Dad are.

— You asleep, boy?

Pene pretends not to hear. So Annie closes his door. Better leave the passage light on, just in case Pene or Dad want to go to the lav.

— Shake it up, Annie! Kepa calls.

She goes out the back door. Together, she and Kepa walk to Sam Walker's place. Across the grass they go, toward the yellow lights glistening in the rain.

— Shouldn't you fullas be in bed? Sam laughs.

Annie pushes him to one side and shakes herself.

— Wet out there, she mutters.

Sam cuddles her in a bear hug. He says:

— Have a beer, it'll warm you up.

Annie takes off her scarf. Through the haze of cigarette smoke she sees Mattie Jones and Hine Ropiho, sitting near a heater. She makes for them, and puts her feet close to the warmth.

— Getting cold outside, she says to Mattie.

— Cold, always cold, Mattie answers vaguely. Always cold . . .

A lot of people have come to Sam's place. It doesn't take long to smell the beer around here. One sniff and they come. To drink, to laugh, to talk the night away, and to sing:

I have a band of men

And all they do is play for me,
They come from miles around,
Just to play a melody.
Beneath the stars
My ten guitars . . .

It's not unusual, partying on a Sunday. Nothing much else to do in this village. From payday Thursday to work on Monday, there is always a party somewhere. And if you get too boozed to make work, not to worry. Plenty jobs around, surely. If not, what the heck, something will turn up sometime.

Oh oh dance, dance, dance
To my ten guitars . . .

Familiar village faces. The same old party atmosphere. This party no different really from those many in the past, those many still to come. Just the usual, with the usual crowd. Nothing changes much.

And laughter when someone stumbles out the door to vomit on the grass. Jack Ropiho this time, emptying his guts so he can fill them again with more booze.

All the regulars here. And Mattie Jones, heavy-lidded and fatigued with loneliness and desperation.

— Snap out of it, Annie tells her. No use pining after George Karepa now.

— Mind your own fucken business, Mattie answers.

— All right, Mattie . . .

— That's the trouble with this place, Mattie continues. Nobody minds their own business around here.

— I was only trying to help, Annie says.

— Yeah, well I don't want it; I can look after myself.

— Suit yourself, Annie shrugs.

She watches as Mattie downs her beer in one long swallow. The foam trickles from the corners of her mouth.

— That's the girl! Sam laughs.

— Some more . . . Mattie yells.

143

She sways drunkenly, holding out her glass. Someone starts to sing teasingly:

> *Look what you done, what you done George Karepa*
> *Look what you done, what you done George Karepa*
> *Look what you done to Mattie's heart . . .*

And Mattie begins to sob brokenly.

> *You made a date and you said maybe,*
> *Then you run away with another baby,*
> *Oh look what you done to Mattie!*
> *She's got a lonely, lonely, lonely,*
> *Lonely heart . . .*

And Mattie grips her glass and throws it blindly. It smashes against the wall above Sonny Whatu.

— Stupid bitch, he yells.

But everyone else just laughs. And Sam Walker says:

— You sure like breaking my glasses, ay Mattie?

— Wrap up, Sam, Annie Jackson interrupts. You fullas should know better than to tease Mattie.

— Can't she take a joke? Sonny complains.

With a cry, Mattie makes for the door and slams it after her. Hine sighs:

— That damn Mattie . . .

And goes out to comfort her.

The party settles again. Sonny takes up the guitar.

> *Black pearl,*
> *Precious little girl,*
> *Let me put you up where you belong . . .*

Suddenly, as he is singing, there is shouting outside.

— Annie!

Quickly, Annie Jackson puts down her glass. She opens the door and the light falls upon Pene, standing there in the rain. He tells her what has happened, and she yells to Kepa to come with her.

— What's up? he asks.

— We're needed at home, she says grimly.

Kepa looks toward the house. Funny, all the lights are on. A car is in the driveway.

Pene is already half way home, running quickly through the grass.

Annie puts on her scarf again.

— Hurry up, Kepa, she yells.

Together, they follow quickly in the footsteps of their son. There is a distant roar of thunder, muted and hollow. An increase of wind, whipping at the grass. It slaps against two shadows swiftly making their way homeward. . .

Twenty-two

When Mum had called to see if he was still awake, Pene had
pretended not to hear her. She'd closed the door behind her, there'd
been some soft sounds he had not been able to identify, and then
the tapping of Mum's footsteps along the corridor. The back door
slamming. Then Mum and Dad talking as they passed under his
window. A snatch of conversation.

Pene had sneaked a look out the window. Darkness and rain.
Two people walking swiftly toward Sam's place.

For a moment longer, Pene had waited. Then quickly, he'd
pushed back the blankets and tiptoed into Nanny Paora's
room.

— You awake, Nanny?

— Like the sky crying . . . mokopuna crying . . .

Nanny's fingers had reached through the darkness to flutter
on Pene's face. Tracing his profile, caressing his cheeks.

Then suddenly, Nanny had started coughing, a low wheezing
cough, arching out from deep inside his body.

— You all right, Nanny? Pene had asked, alarmed.

He'd held his Nanny close to him. The spasm had passed.

— Aah . . . Aah . . . Aah . . .

— Nanny? You better now?

— Aah . . . Aah . . .

It was then that Pene had heard people approaching the house.

146

Mum and Dad? If they found him still up, Mum might get angry again.

A knock at the door.

Pene hurried quickly back to his own bed.

Another knock. Then a slight grating sound.

— Annie? Kepa? Is anyone at home?

Pene strained to hear the strangers.

— Someone must be in, a voice said.

Two people coming down the corridor. Stopping and opening Nanny Paora's door. A faint cry:

— He's here, David! Alone in the house . . .

Pene ran to the door. Auntie Rose and Uncle David. And Auntie Rose sitting on Nanny's bed, hugging the old man.

— I've been so worried, Dad. So worried about you.

Pene had approached Nanny's bedside.

— Hullo, Uncle David had smiled. Where are your parents?

— They've gone out.

— Gone out? Auntie Rose had yelled. Just where have they gone to?

— Sam Walker's place.

Auntie Rose had closed her eyes and her body had trembled. Her lips had set with determination, and she'd turned to Nanny.

— Dad, she'd whispered, I'm taking you home with me. I'm not leaving you alone in this house.

— Nanny isn't alone, Pene had answered. I look after him, I'm good at looking after Nanny.

— How can you possibly do that! Auntie had said. Just look at this room. Filthy. Disgustingly filthy. And can't you see how cold your Nanny is in this room?

— Dear, it's not the boy's fault, Uncle David had interrupted.

Auntie Rose had become quiet. Then she'd begun looking for some clothes for Nanny.

— What you doing? Pene had asked, alarmed. Nanny Paora, he's all right here, he's not cold. You ask him, Auntie Rose. You're not cold, are you Nanny? You're not . . .

Auntie Rose had gently pushed Pene away.

147

— Come on, Dad. Put your feet on the floor, Hold up your arms so I can dress you.

Pene had been near to tears.

— Nanny doesn't want to go away from here, Auntie. Truly he doesn't. Nanny loves it here, ay Nanny.

— That's enough, Son, Uncle David had said firmly.

And Nanny Paora had smiled:

— Mokopuna . . . like the sky . . .

Pene had rushed at his Uncle, fists bunched.

— You just leave Nanny alone, he'd yelled.

Uncle David had picked him up and forced him out the door.

— Nanny? Nanny! Pene had sobbed.

For a second he hadn't known what to do. Then he'd yelled through the closed door:

— Mum will stop you. You just wait and see. You just wait . . .

Rose and David heard the young boy running from the house.

— David . . .

He'd smiled at her and pressed her arm.

— Darling, you have to face up to Annie sometime.

Wanly, she'd looked up at him. Then she'd turned back to dressing father.

The door explodes open and Annie Jackson storms into the house. Her face is wet with the rain, her eyes grim. She strides into the sitting room where Rose and David are waiting, sitting with Dad between them on the sofa. Annie pauses at the door.

— Get out of my house, she whispers.

Rose puts her arms around Dad.

— Get out before I throw you out, Annie yells.

Annie advances and Rose cries:

— Annie, please . . .

And Annie laughs loudly.

— Please Annie, she mocks. Please Annie, Annie please, please Annie . . .

— You left him here alone, Rose says.

— And so?

— He needs proper attention, Annie. I'm taking him home with me. Try to understand.

— Understand? Annie sneers.

— He's coming home with me, Rose says levelly.

— Not over my dead body! Annie snaps.

David tries to intervene.

— Look here, Annie . . .

— You keep out of this, Annie says to him. This is none of your business.

There is silence for a moment. At the door, Pene and his father appear. Pene runs to his mother:

— You won't let them take Nanny, will you Mum?

— And why shouldn't I? Rose bursts. I've a right to look after Dad.

And Annie laughs again.

— You, his daughter? You, Rosie? Just what sort of daughter are you then? What you going to do with the old man, ay? Just tell me that.

— He needs medical attention, Rose pleads. Anyone could tell, just by looking at him, that he should be in hospital. You shouldn't have taken him from there, Annie.

Rose makes to get the old man to stand. Annie's eyes glitter dangerously.

— You try to take him out of this house and you'll be dead before you touch the door.

— Then I'll call the police, Rose answers.

— You may be married to a Pakeha, Annie says, but you're still not Pakeha enough to do that to me.

— Annie . . .

— No, Rose, Annie answers firmly. Dad is staying right here with me and that's that.

Rose sighs and closes her eyes. She puts an arm round her father.

— Oh, Annie, you were always too strong for me. Always. And you and all the people around here, you're all the same. Thinking you're right. Has it never occurred to you that you may be wrong?

Even once? That I could be right?

— Dad stays here. With me.

— But has it, Annie? Rose persists. What do you give Dad out here, just what?

— You don't need to be told, Annie answers. We give him love which is much more than you've ever showed him. I'm not letting him go, Rosie. I'm not letting you put him into a home.

Rose begins to weep.

— Oh God, Annie, what sort of monster do you think I am? Do you really think I would put Dad away?

— You tried once before, Rosie.

— Oh yes, Rose giggles hysterically. It was called a home wasn't it, that hospital. And of course I was going to keep him locked in there. And you saw bars on the window, didn't you Annie. And it looked like a prison, didn't it Annie. So you put two and two together and . . .

— You better go, Rosie.

— I'm not going without Dad! Rose screams.

— Then I'll drag you out myself. Your fine airs may work outside, but not here, Rosie.

Rose stands, trembling. She yells:

— Listen to me, Annie. Don't talk, just listen to me for a change. If I thought Dad was recuperating better here in the village I'd leave him with you. But he isn't getting better. Can't you see that? He needs a doctor and nurse to look after him. Are you any of those? Annie, you think I'm sending Dad to a home. You're wrong, Annie, so wrong. I want him back in hospital. And after they've done what they can for him, then you can have him back. I love him as much as you do, Annie. Forget that you hate me, just this once. I'm doing this for Dad. For him, Annie.

Rose puts her hands to her face, covering her tears. And in the silence, all that is heard is the sound of her weeping and the rain tapping gently on the roof. Tapping insistently at Annie's memory.

Rose and Annie, two girls brought up by Nanny Paora and

150

Nanny Harata. Not really sisters; Paora and Harata not their real parents. Yes, and Rose was right. She, Annie, had always been jealous of her. Rose, so pretty and delicate. The favoured one it had seemed to Annie. The one with charm and grace. Educated at Queen Victoria Boarding School. Majoring in Chemistry at Otago University. Travelling to Europe. Marrying a Pakeha. Knowing everything, having everything.

When had it begun, this hatred of Rosie? When had it started, this distrust of everything Rosie did? But the most important question: when should the hatred stop and the trusting begin . . .

Annie looks hard at her father. She sits down in a chair.

— Oh stop crying Rose, she sighs.

Outside, darkness and rain. Wind beginning to sigh and wan moonlight shining.

— We better talk, Annie continues. Pene, take Nanny to his room.

— No, Mum, Pene cries. I won't let Nanny go away.

— Do as you're told you damn kid, Annie yells.

Pene trembles. He leads Nanny Paora from the sitting room. At the door he says:

— No, Mum . . .

But she does not hear.

— We talk now, Rosie.

The clock ticks away the time. The sounds of the party at Sam Walker's place ebb through the wind and rain. Inside the Jackson house, two sisters and their husbands effect an uneasy reconciliation and discuss the matter of their father, the kaumatua of the village. Five minutes pass, then ten, then fifteen. The time ticks onward to half past eight.

— It's settled then, Annie Jackson sighs.

— Settled, Rose echoes.

— You want a cup of tea?

Rose nods. Annie says to Kepa:

— Better see if the old man and Pene are all right.

Kepa goes down the corridor. Annie bustles in the kitchen. Rose smiles into David's eyes.

Then Kepa returns. There is a strange look about him.

— The two boys all right? Annie asks.

Kepa does not answer.

— What's wrong! Annie says alarmed.

— Pene and Dad, Kepa answers. They've gone.

The moon disappears behind a dark cloud . . .

Twenty-three

Come Nanny, quick Nanny. Hold tightly to me. We must get away, far far away. Come Nanny, hurry Nanny. You will always be with me and I will never let you leave me. Never.

Pita Mahana is watching television. The telephone rings and he nudges Waka to answer it. Groaning, Waka lets go of Ani.

— Hullo? Who is it? Oh, gidday, Kepa. What? You want Dad? Hang on.

Waka returns to the sitting room. He says grumpily:

— I knew it was for you, Dad.

Pita sighs as he gets up. Aue, his back is really sore.

— Gidday, Kepa.

— Pita, you seen Pene and the old man?

— No. What's up?

— That Pene's run away. With the old man.

— Ay?

— We been hunting for him, me, Annie, that hoha Rosie and her husband. Annie's getting worried. It's getting late, almost nine now.

— Boy, you should have rung earlier. Nanny Paora out there in that rain?

— Yeah, that's why we're getting worried.

— I better come and help you.

— Could you? The sooner we find the old man the better.

— Don't you worry, Kepa.

Pita puts the receiver down. He goes into the bedroom where Miriama is reading.

— I'm going out, he says.

— Not again, Miriama groans. Phone calls in the morning and phone calls at night, don't people know we have to sleep some time?

Pita soothes her and then tells her what has happened. Quickly she gets out of bed.

— I'm coming with you, she says.

— No, you better stay in bed, rest that arm of yours.

— Nothing wrong with my arm! Miriama snaps.

— You just stay in bed, woman!

— And you just keep quiet, Pita. I'm coming and that's that. Who do you think is the boss around here!

They get dressed. They tell Waka to come with them. Then hurriedly, they rush into the night.

Quick Nanny, come Nanny. We must get off the road now. If we stay on the road, we might be seen. Here Nanny, I will help you over the drain. Can you climb over this fence, Nanny? Oh, you must, you must. Here, here is a place where the wire is slack. I will hold the wire apart while you climb through. Quick Nanny, hurry.

— Stop the car! Rose shouts.

David slams on the brakes.

— Over there, David, shine the headlights over there by that fence.

The electric whine of the windscreen wipers flicking aside the rain. A cone of light directed upon a paddock waving darkly with maize.

— I thought I saw something, Rose says. I must have been mistaken. Oh, David, this is all my fault.

Rose bites her lips against the tears threatening.

Tremulously she whispers:

— Drive on, David. Drive on . . .

The headlights sweep away from the paddock. The car slowly continues along the road.

Hana Walker sees torches moving in the paddock beside the house. Every now and then, they converge before separating again. To and fro the lights move.

— Some people are sure mad around here, she sighs.

She flips over a page of a magazine she is reading. She hears the sound of calling outside. The quality of the sound alarms her, so she puts on her brunch coat and goes to see Dad.

— What is it, Hana?

— Dad, something funny's happening outside.

Her father goes to the window, then quickly walks out onto the verandah.

— Hoi! Who's there!

— It's us! a voice yells back.

— Us who! What the heck you fullas doing in the rain?

Dad goes off to see what's happening. Mum comes to stand with Hana, peering into the darkness.

— Looks like Pita Mahana, Mum says.

Dad and Pita talk together. Then Dad returns. His face is grim.

— Get dressed Hana, he says, and put on a raincoat. Mum, you get that big lamp of mine ay?

— What's wrong, Dad?

— Nanny Paora's missing. Him and Pene. Hurry, girl!

Quickly, Hana runs to her room. She kicks off her slippers and searches in her drawer for a thick jumper. She hears Dad phoning someone, telling Mum to get his medical kit just in case, organising things.

Dad, on the Maori Council.

And all of a sudden, she feels so proud of him.

Nanny Paora is missing. The village people are quickly gathering in groups to find him.

155

*We're safe now, Nanny. The car has gone. But we cannot stay here.
Where shall we go, Nanny? Where shall we go? Come, Nanny, we
cannot rest here. When we are really safe, then we can rest. Lean on
me, Nanny. You're so heavy. So heavy.*

Andrew Whatu hears footsteps approaching the house. Suddenly, there is a staccato rapping on the door. Hana Walker is
standing there, a frightened look in her eyes.

— Dad sent me over, she says. Nanny Paora and Pene . . .

While she is explaining, Charlie Whatu comes from the kitchen.
He says to Andrew:

— Get the torches, Son.

— Where are they?

— Use your eyes and find them, just find them.

Andrew nudges past his sister Janey. She asks:

— What you doing all dressed up, Hana?

— I'm going to a dance, Hana jokes. Yeah, to find Nanny Paora
and Pene.

—Then I'm coming too, Janey says.

— And have you getting lost too? Not likely.

— Too bad! Janey answers. Won't take me long to get dressed.
We'll team up. We'll be mates ay. Where shall we start first?

Hana looks into the darkness, into the rain.

— Everywhere, she says. Everywhere, and anywhere.

Annie Jackson rushes to the door.

— Kepa? Is that you, Kepa? You found Dad?

Kepa shakes his head.

— Damn that Pene, Annie says viciously. It wouldn't have
been so bad if he'd gone off alone. But the night is cold and Dad . . .

— Turi turi, Kepa interrupts. We'll find them. Pita, Miriama
and Waka, they're all looking. Hana and her dad, Charlie and his
kids too. Don't you worry.

— Don't worry? Annie yells. I'm out of my head with the worry.

— We'll find them.

— You tried the old homestead? You tried the meeting house?

156

— Not yet.

— Well get out there then, Annie screams. What the hell are you doing standing here?

— Don't get hysterical about it, Annie. There's so many other places to search.

— Look, I'm coming with you, Annie says determinedly.

Kepa grabs her roughly.

— You just stay here, Annie. Just in case they come back.

Annie struggles in Kepa's arms. Then she begins to sob brokenly.

— Just wait till I lay my hands on that Pene. He's going to get the hiding of his life.

Charlie Whatu stalks along the road and down the path to Sam Walker's place. He picks up a wooden slab and hurls it at the tin shed. The sound mocks the thunder.

— What you want to do that for! Sam says. My ears are ringing with the noise.

He stands in the doorway, sheltering from the rain. Charlie says angrily:

— Yeah, and your ears will ring some more if you don't put your boots on quick. Boozing, that's all you think about.

— Easy, easy, Sam protests. What's gotten into you!

— We need a search party, Charlie answers. You and your drunk mates are it! We're looking for our kaumatua, Paora.

Charlie explains what has happened, and Sam turns to shout:

— Party's over, all boozers out.

— With all this beer still to drink? Sonny Whatu moans. Might be over for you Sam, but not for . . .

He sees Dad standing there. He is suddenly ashamed. But Charlie simply whispers:

— Come on, Son. There's work to do.

Sonny and Charlie walk into the rain. There is a moment's silence in the shed. Then Joe says:

— Well? What we waiting for? Let's go! I feel like a night stroll.

The party begins to break up. Hine Ropiho shakes Jack, but he shrugs her away. Blow him then. He can just stay here, the bastard. Rotten as always, rotten with the booze. But she's not going out there alone. Too dark out there. So she shakes Mattie awake.

— Come on, Mattie.

— Where to? Mattie answers drunkenly. Where we going?

— To your place first, then we're going hunting.

— At this time of night? Mattie asks, trying to push Hine away. You're crazy, Hine. I'm staying right here. Warm here. Warm.

— Oh no you don't, Hine snaps.

She makes Mattie stand.

— I can't walk . . . Mattie says helplessly.

— You got legs, stupid, Hine answers grumpily. You can walk all right.

She drags Mattie protestingly outside and down the road. People are swaying in the rain, still drunk from the beer.

— God, this road sure ain't as straight as it was last time.

— Yeah, even the ditch is crooked.

— What ditch?

— This ditch.

— What the heck you doing down there!

— It got in my way . . .

Hine sighs to herself. None of this crowd will be of any use finding Paora. They can't even see straight.

Hush, Nanny. Can you hear, Nanny? People are coming. Lie still, lie quiet. Don't make a noise. Don't move. The maize stalks crackle when you move. So don't move. Don't talk. If we are quiet, they won't hear us. They'll never hear us.

Mattie screams and pulls away from beneath the cold tap.

— No you don't, Hine says firmly.

She forces Mattie beneath again.

— What you doing, Hine! Mattie yells. Her hair hangs in thick ropes about her shoulders.

— Well, Hine replies simply, if the rain won't sober you up, maybe this will.

Finally, she lets Mattie go. Heck, she's still under the weather. Too bad, she'll just have to manage, boozed as she is. Too dark out there, and Hine isn't going looking for Paora without a mate.

The outside light suddenly switches on and Mattie's father looks out to say:

— What the hell's going on! Albie Jones asks.

— Trying to get Mattie sober that's what, Hine answers grumpily. I'm not carrying her around the paddocks.

— Ay? You fullas mad or something?

Hine tells him about Paora and Pene. Albie Jones sighs and thinks how soft and warm his bed is ... Then he shrugs his shoulders and starts pulling on his boots. He wasn't feeling very sleepy anyway.

— What's going on out there? Maka says.

— Stop trying your tricks, Miro Mananui snaps at her. I know you, Maka tiko bum. Just because I'm by the window, you pretend to look out of it but instead you're sneaking a look at my cards, ay.

— Not, Miro! Look for yourself. There's drunkards rolling all over the place.

— I know your tricks, Maka. Just play cards!

— This ain't a trick, Smarty, Maka says in a huff.

She tries to concentrate on her hand, but the scene outside is too distracting.

— I must have the d.ts., she murmurs.

— Stop cheating, Miro snaps.

— You're the only cheat around here, Maka answers.

She looks out the window again. Looks like a hunchback out there. No, it's Hine Ropiho carrying Mattie Jones. Now Hine's leaning Mattie against a bush.

A knock at the door.

— Paora and Pene, they're missing, Hine says.

— See, Maka glares at Miro. I told you something funny was going on.

— And something even worse will happen if you don't finish this hand, Miro growls.

Another visitor enters. Mere, wearing a scarf, holding a candle in her hand.

— Bit late for church isn't it? Miro says sarcastically.

Mere takes no notice of her. She looks at Maka.

— Well, you coming Maka?

— Where?

— I thought we'd take a walk over to the meeting house. Old Paora's bound to make for it.

— The kehuas will get you, Miro chuckles.

— You can't frighten me, Miro Mananui, Mere sniffs. Come on, Maka.

Maka gathers up her purse. Miro sighs and looks ruefully at her cards. What a waste of her three aces.

— Hang on a minute, she says finally. I'm coming with you fullas. Don't think you can get away from me so easily, Maka! After we've found Paora, then we finish our game. I'll fix you, Maka tiko bum! You cheat!

Teria Mahana rushes to the phone. The last time it rang her kids told the caller that he had dialled the jail. The time before that, June had picked up the receiver, screamed loudly, then calmly put the receiver down again. Those kids, too smart, that was their trouble.

— Hullo?

— Teria? It's me, Annie. Teria aue . . .

Alarmed, Teria hears Annie Jackson sobbing distantly. She whispers to Annie, telling her hush.

— And I'm here all by myself, Annie says. I don't like being alone, but Kepa says I better stay here just in case Pene and Dad come back. I'm so scared, Teria.

— Don't you worry, Teria answers. I'll be right over.

Quickly she picks up her flax kit and puts on a coat. She kicks Rawiri awake and tells him to come with her. Then she goes into the living room where her kids are watching television. She switches the set off.

— Mum no . . . they moan.

— Quiet the lot of you! Teria booms. You fullas like playing detectives, ay. Well, here's your chance to put your play into practice. Pene and Nanny Paora, they have to be found. You kids know these hills better than anyone. And your Nanny is a very sick man. So your mission is to find them both, Pene and your Nanny. And I'll skin you all alive if you come home empty-handed!

The children scatter. Teria grins. Then, before leaving the house, she picks up the phone and dials a city number.

Rongo Mahana listens grimly as Teria tells him what has happened in the village.

— I'll be right out, he says. See you in half an hour.

He rings off. Then he calls to Huia:

— I'm going out to the village, dear.

— Don't you dear me! Huia snaps. She's still angry that Rongo didn't get home earlier than he did. That husband of hers, he doesn't know where his home is!

— Yeah, well . . . Rongo murmurs.

— What you going out there for! Huia asks. Too late to go picking spuds.

— Our kaumatua is missing, Rongo answers.

Instantly, Huia is putting on her shoes and pulling the windows shut.

— Don't just stand there, she says to Rongo. The car won't drive itself out of the garage!

Rongo runs from the house. The night dark and cold. The rain falling heavily now.

Quick, Nanny. Behind this tree. Someone's coming up the track. It's Dad, Nanny. He knows we're going to the old homestead. What shall we do now, Nanny? Where shall we go now? To the meeting house? To Rongopai? But people may search there, too. Oh, Nanny, I wish I knew what to do, where to go. But no matter what happens, we'll always be together, ay Nanny. Always.

No one sleeps in the village this night. Torches spear the dark. The hands of the clock tick another hour past. And the Sky Father weeps, sending his tears to rush and swirl amid the hollows and along the contours of Papatuanuku, the Earth Mother. Within the dark rift between Earth and Sky there is little shelter from the grief of the parents. The lightning is the Father's rage, the thunder is his anguished cry of helplessness. Too long have Rangi and Papa been apart. Too long has Rangi fought to clasp the earth again.

Between them, shadows call and search in deadly seriousness.

— What now? David asks.
— Down the road again, Rose whispers.
— Dear . . . David says helplessly.
— One more time, David. Please, just once more.

— Any luck, Pita?
— Not yet. Me and Miriama looked into Rongopai and then in the Hall. Nothing. And you?
— Golding's farm. Nothing.

— Kepa, you sure you looked everywhere in the old homestead?
— I keep telling you I did, Annie.
— Well, try again damn you. Try again, for me.

— Come on, Janey. What's wrong now!
— I'm so tired, Hana. And I'm sick of walking over all these hills. Anybody'd think I was a horse or something.
— I knew I shouldn't have let you come with me, Janey Whatu. I'm never letting you come with me again.

— Hoi, Charlie! Seen anything?
— No, Tama.
— Wish the rain would stop or the moon would come out. Trust Paora to pick a night like this!
— Yeah, that old man, when he does something he sure does it well.

— You reckon we ought to try down the river?
— No, Charlie. Not yet.

— If you don't stand up straight, Mattie Jones, I'm going to leave you here.
— Well why don't you! I didn't want to come in the first place.
— All right, I'll go then.
— Good riddance.
— The same to you doubled.
— Well? Off you go then, Hine!
— Mattie . . .
— Oh, what now Hine Ropiho!
— I think we're lost, Mattie.

— Where to now, Rongo?
— We'll try the creek, Huia. You feeling all right?
— Course I'm not. And if I'd known we'd be tramping over our own farm again, and at this time of night, I wouldn't have believed it. I'd have stayed at home.
— No you wouldn't, Huia. I know you.
— Yes, Rongo, I suppose you do.

— August, where are you?
— Over here, June.
— Over where?
— Just follow my voice, Stupid.
— Boy, I sure am glad I found you, August.
— Where are the others?
— We're all here, August.
— Good, because it's too dark to see anything and we better stick together.
— I'm sleepy, August.
— Never mind, Hope. Soon, we'll find Pene and Nanny. Then we can go home. Then, Hope.

— Wait for me, Miro.

— Huh? You tired already, Maka!

— My legs just ain't what they used to be, Miro.

— What do you mean aren't? They never were any good even when you were young.

— Oh, wrap up, Miro Mananui. Miro? You coughing again? Miro!

— I'm all right, Maka. Don't you worry about me. Just worry about Paora. Instead of talking, let's get to the walking.

— Once more, David. Once more down the road.

— Never mind about the rain, Andrew. Be strong, boy.

— Come on, Janey. One more hill.

— We'll try the river now, Pita.

— Look, Mattie, I'll give you a good hiding if you don't stand straight.

— Let's rest for a while, Rongo. Just a while.

— Don't worry about my cough, Maka. Just worry about Paora.

— Kepa, you sure you tried everywhere? Kepa, hold me close. I try to stop the tears but . . .

— August, I thought I saw something!

— Where, June?

— Over there . . .

— No, you must have seen the meeting house.

— But August, it looked as if it moved . . .

Twenty-four

— Cold, mokopuna . . . makariri . . .

The tin cookhouse near Rongopai. Dark. Rain-glistening drops falling through the makeshift tin to darken the earth floor with stains. Between the boards shuttering the window the wind echoes hollowly. The musty smell of decaying wooden table and trestles. The rusted hooks above the kitchen hearth squeaking softly. Charred stumps of wood beneath them. To one side, a shattered pot.

The sharp banging of loose tin clattering in the whistling wind.

— Cold, mokopuna . . .

In this place is where they have found shelter, Pene and his old nanny. And Pene has covered the old man with some sacking in the cookhouse. But the rough hemp does not afford much warmth for Nanny and Pene is worried about him.

— You really got soaked, ay Nanny, Pene whispers.

— Ae, mokopuna . . .

— Oh, Nanny.

Pene hugs his grandfather close to him. The old man feels very small and very bony. His hands and face are like ice. Anxiously, Pene presses himself against the old man, trying to warm him with his own young warmth. But all he feels is the cold from Nanny Paora seeping through to him, and fingers of ice clutching at his heart.

— Nanny . . . Pene sobs.

The last hour has seemed a whirlwind of panic. Of helping Nanny through endless paddocks of tall slapping maize, across roadside ditches, over barbed fences, and along the mud-slipping contours of the hills. Running, always running. Stopping only occasionally to rest, before running again.

And all the time the rain steadily falling, gradually worsening. And everywhere, torches trying to break through the fabric of the night.

— Mokopuna . . .

— I'm all right now, Nanny. See? No more tears fall from my eyes.

They'd first tried to make for the old homestead. They'd almost been discovered. At each turning, there had seemed to be torch-light. Between the torchlight there had been a narrowing shaft of darkness arrowing toward Rongopai where the apex stabbed at the sky. There had been nowhere else to run.

They had almost made it to Rongopai. There had been just a few more steps to the door. And then had come the voices:

— Pene . . .

    Paora . . .

All night the voices have haunted the boy. Over the thundering rain they have called. They have said that Nanny is ill, Nanny is sick, Nanny needs warmth.

— It's hopeless, ay Nanny, Pene says. I wanted to take you somewhere, but we have come nowhere.

A quivering of old lips. Eyes glistening. And a vein-wrinkled hand reaching out to calm a young boy.

Then suddenly, a gasp of pain and battling for breath.

— Aaaa . . . Aaaa . . .

— Nanny? Nanny!

He grips the old man roughly, forcing him to breathe. When the attack has passed, he cradles his Nanny in his arms.

— We go home, Nanny. We must go home.

And you and I, Nanny, there will never be any dreamtime for

us. They will take you away from me and I will never see you again.

And Nanny, I had forgotten you don't only belong to me. You belong to all of us. You are very old, Nanny, our father, our kaumatua.

I am sorry, Nanny. I am so sorry.

Calmly and with great gentleness, Pene kisses his grandfather. He helps the old man to his feet.

— Lean on me, Nanny. We go home, now.

Together they approach the door. Pene struggles to open it. The rain stings his face.

— Come, Nanny.

Slowly they step into the rain. The village alight with stars trickling in the dark. Voices calling with the wind.

And suddenly, Pene feels Nanny trying to wrench away from him.

— Nanny?

Voices calling.

— Nanny?

Voices calling across the years, fusing past with present. And the old man turning to face Rongopai.

— Nanny, where you going? Pene yells.

The old man's face is agleam with light. A shaft of light from the porch of Rongopai.

— No, Nanny, I won't let you go, Pene says fiercely.

The old man does not hear. He walks slowly toward the porch, where shadows wait, where people sing.

— Don't listen to them, Nanny, Pene cries. Let me take you home. There's nobody here, Nanny. And that is only the wind calling.

His tears mingle with the rain, for there seems to be some strange strength in the old man which cannot be restrained. No matter how hard Pene tries to hold him back, Nanny is stronger.

— Oh Nanny, don't go away from me . . .

Voices calling, shadows beckoning, another world opening its arms to welcome the old man.

Desperately, Pene throws his arms around his grandfather. His hold wavers, his feet slip, and as the old man pulls him along with him, the ruts made by Pene's feet deepen and lengthen

Then suddenly, other voices calling:

— Pene!

— Over here, Dad! Over here!

Torchlight swings back and forth across Rongopai. It dazzles Pene's eyes.

— Come quickly, Dad, Pene yells.

He panics. He lets go of his grandfather and runs to his father. They embrace in the rain.

— Stop him, Dad, Pene screams. Stop him.

Dad looks puzzled.

— Can't you see, Dad? Can't you see the shadows? Can't you hear them calling?

There are no shadows. There is no calling. There are only he and Pene, and an old man standing before Rongopai. Three steps to the porch.

Nanny Paora takes the first step.

— Dad, stop him!

His father does not move toward Nanny. Through rain and falling tears Nanny is walking away. And only Pene can see the village as it once was. Only Pene can understand where Nanny is going.

To a village of small wooden houses where people are still family together. To a meeting house which is not decaying or falling, but which still holds up the sky. To a community hall which rings with family gatherings and is not yet deserted. To the warmth of the village hearth before the flame had begun to grow cold.

To the family, the village family, waiting for Nanny Paora. To family aroha, but more than that, village aroha. Family together, before the great family began to splinter apart.

— Let me go, Dad, Pene screams. Let me go.

He leaps from his father's arms. He runs toward Nanny Paora, away from the cold of his world toward the warmth of Nanny's world. The shadows sing, the shadows beckon.

168

— Nanny, wait for me.

Running fast across a distance which seems to lengthen and lengthen further. Hands outstretched.

The second step.

And a boy cries:

— Take me with you, Nanny.

The old man turns. One last look back. One sad, lingering look . . .

I cannot always stay with you, mokopuna.

Don't go, Nanny.

I cannot always be with you, mokopuna.

Then take me with you, Nanny.

You must let me go, mokopuna.

No, Nanny.

Try to understand, mokopuna. Try not to be afraid when I turn from you.

Don't, Nanny. Don't turn from me, Nanny.

Haere ra, mokopuna.

Nanny, without you my world will be darkness.

Then you must make the light come again, mokopuna.

How, Nanny? How?

You will find a way. My own light grows dim, must fade. Your world finds little need for it.

We do need you, Nanny.

Kia mau ki o tatou Maoritanga, mokopuna. That is your way. When I am gone, you will find it.

Nanny . . .

Haere ra, mokopuna. It is better that I go. For too long I have lingered here. Haere ra.

And Pene screams again.

— No, Nanny. Take me with you, Nanny.

The rain roars, the rain falls . . .

Twenty-five

— So it's over, Mere.

— Yes, Maka.

— And the boy, is he all right now?

— Pene? Ae.

— So what happened, Mere? What happened?

— Something strange, Maka. Even Kepa doesn't really know what it was. Only that his son was screaming at him and pointing toward Rongopai at shadows which Kepa could not see.

— Ah . . .

— Kepa thinks the boy was delirious, ay.

— Or perhaps . . .

— Yes, Maka?

— Nothing, Mere.

— Anyway, they're both home now, Pene and the old man. At least they were when I left. But just as I was leaving the ambulance came. Paora's probably on his way to hospital now.

— What a night it's been.

— Oh, you should have been there, Maka. Everybody else was there. Crowding into the house to see if the old man was all right. Then the doctor came. I was the last one to leave. Yes, and I suppose I better get off home now.

— You sure your clothes are dry enough, Mere?

— Yes. And thanks for the tea.

— I'm sorry I didn't have any sugar. And the old man, old Paora?

— Who knows? He's in a coma. I reckon if he comes out of it he'll live. If he doesn't . . .

— Course he will! But even if he doesn't, well, he is an old man ay. We can't keep hold of our kaumatua forever. Still, we'll have Rongo Mahana and Andrew Whatu, even Pene himself and some others who will carry on.

— What on earth are you mumbling about, Maka!

— Nothing. Perhaps everything.

— Sounds like you're porangi, Maka.

— Maybe I am. Ah, Mere, it was good to see everyone uniting to find the old man, wasn't it! For a while, we were a family, just like the old times, ay.

— Yes, just like that, Maka. But I better get going now. See you tomorrow.

— See you, Maka. Pae kare, this rain, this night . . .

It is half past eleven.

Along the road which passes through the village, a woman is hurrying swiftly home. And as she passes each house, the lights wink out. Slowly. One after the other.

— Goodnight, Pita.

— Sleep well, Miriama. Plenty work tomorrow.

— Ae, always work. Always work to do.

— Hush, Pene.

— I'm sorry, Mum. I didn't want Nanny to be taken from me.

— Go to sleep now, Son. Dad and I will stay with you until you sleep.

— I want Nanny, Mum. I want Nanny Paora.

— We can't have Nanny all our lives, Pene.

— Hana? Turn off your light now.

— Okay, Dad. And Dad, gosh you were . . . I mean, I felt so proud, Dad.

— Goodnight, Hana.

Dad, I shall try not to hurt you. But one day I will go away from you. Perhaps to Wellington. And Dad, then I might hurt you. One day. One day.

— Watch the road, Rongo!
— Who's the driver, Huia! You or me?
— You, but I'm the boss. I don't know, we always keep coming back to the village.
— I think it wants us to come back, Huia.
— I suppose it does; I suppose we will.

— Put out the fire, Andrew.
— All right. And Dad, we'll go to Rongopai next Sunday ay. To clean it up some more.
— Yes, Son. We'll rope in some more people to help us. Come on, now. School tomorrow.

— If that Maka tiko bum thinks she's getting out of this game of cards, she's got another think coming. And if that Arapeta, that brother of mine, thinks I'm not going to fight him about our land then he's got a big surprise ahead of him.

— Jack Ropiho? How come you're always so drunk!
— Lemme sleep, Hine. Lemme sleep.
— No! Get undressed first.
— Hine, tomorrow you ask Miro for a loan, ay? You ask her.
— Do your dirty work yourself, Jack Ropiho.

— You kids in bed yet? August? July?
— Yes, Mum!
— Are you fullas asleep?
— Yes, Mum!

— That you, Auntie Mattie?
— Yes, Kara.
— Where you carrying me, Auntie?
— You come and sleep with me tonight. You come and make

me warm. Your Auntie, she's cold this night. She's cold and very lonely.

— I'll keep you warm, Auntie Mattie. Don't you be lonely, don't you be cold. And don't you cry, Auntie.

A woman hurrying swiftly home. She opens a gate and then steps into her house, away from the rain. Only a sprinkling of lights remain shining in the village.

Far away, two cars point toward the city. One turns into the drive of a house in the suburbs. The other follows after an ambulance speeding to the hospital.

Back in the village, only three lights are shining now. Look into one window and you will see Annie and Kepa Jackson watching over their son Pene. At the second is Mattie Jones, tears spilling between the fingers covering her face. And at the third, Mere is getting ready for bed after having walked from Maka's place. She switches off the light.

Only two lights remain. Then one light. Then it too winks out and the village is left in darkness.

High above the village the clouds break apart and the moon floods the earth with its pale light. So wan. So calm And in that light, the village seems serene, as if nothing could destroy or even possibly disturb its calm. Yet there are undercurrents, ebbing back and forth like the tides are compelled to do by this moon in this sky. What of tomorrow? No matter: the tangata whenua are still here, still in this place.

The moon brings peace to the land and peace to the people of the land. Rangitane, the Sky Father, ceases his struggle to clasp the Earth Mother, Papatuanuku. His tears diminish, he ceases to sigh. Papatuanuku folds the village and her children into her warmth, the warmth of Mother Earth. No matter if they love her or not, they are still her children and she will love them and protect them until, until . . .

The village sleeps.

Rongopai, the painted meeting house, still holds up the sky.